To Barbara

Of Honest Fame

M. M. Bennetts

Dragon International Independent Arts
www.diiarts.com

This novel is entirely a work of fiction. The names, characters, and incidents portrayed in it are the work of the author's imagination. Any resemblance to actual persons, living or dead, events or localities is entirely coincidental.

Portrait of Edward Impey (1785-1850), c. 1800 (oil on canvas) by Sir Thomas Lawrence. Private Collection. Photo © Bonhams, London, UK/The Bridgeman Art Library. Used with permission.

Langley & Belch's New Map of London (1812)
© The British Library Board. Maps 3480. (88.)

This first hardback edition published in the United Kingdom in 2010
by Dragon International Independent Arts

ISBN 978-1-907386-24-4

Dragon International Independent Arts
Suite 133, 80 High Street
Winchester, Hampshire SO23 9AT, UK
books@diiarts.com
www.diiarts.com

Printed and bound in the UK by the MPG Books Group,
Bodmin and King's Lynn

To the uncounted lost

Auch die keinen Frieden kannten,
Aber Mut und Stärke sandten
Über leichenvolles Feld
In die halbentschlafene Welt:
Alle die von hinnen schieden,
Alle Seelen ruh'n in Frieden!

Johann Georg Jacobi
(1740-1814)

Those too who knew no peace,
But still offered courage and strength
On the corpse-strewn field
In a world half-asleep:
May all who have parted hence,
May all souls rest in peace!

By the same author

May 1812

Of Honest Fame

"The drying up a single tear has more
Of honest fame than shedding seas of gore."

From Canto the Eighth, *Don Juan*
George Gordon, Lord Byron

Prologue

"Planta!"

"Oh cock." Planta rolled his dark eyes toward the office's narrow ceiling and sighed. Already it had been a long day and it was not yet gone midday. And *he* had been in this mood since early morning.

Planta laid down the stack of papers he had been sorting and made to rise from his desk.

"Planta!" The voice again bellowed through the open doorway.

"My lord?" Planta came to stand at the door of the Foreign Secretary's inner sanctum and produced what he hoped was a willing smile.

"Oh, there you are…Tell me, Planta, did I not recall several of my agents in from the field earlier in the month?"

It was a rhetorical question and Planta knew *he* knew the answer. "Yes, my lord."

"Then where the blazes are they?" the Foreign Secretary barked.

Planta shifted his weight from one foot to the other and kept the smile in place. It was looking tired. He did not attempt an explanation. *He* wasn't in listening mood. "Not here, my lord."

"Well, get them here!"

"Yes, my lord. Right away." An impossible task. And if not impossible, then certainly improbable—given that at least two of the individuals in question were in France and proving most elusive. Which was, of course, what they were meant to be. Elusive, that is. And in France. Indeed, it was that very art of elusion, in France, which made them so…useful. Invaluable even. A point which he, Planta, would not be mentioning. At least not today. "Will there be anything else, my lord?"

"No! Yes. Do those fools not understand the meaning of an order?"

Planta considered the painting upon the opposite wall, listing sidledywry to the left. "It would seem not, my lord…Though it may be that they have got caught up in the bad weather in the Channel, my lord," he temporised. "Will there be anything else?"

Chapter I

1

The decaying walls of the garret room were blotched and mottled—green, brown, ochre and grey—with the damp and grease, soil and soot of half a century. But the boy lying on the bare straw mattress did not notice. Nor would he have cared if he had. Sprawled upon the worm-riddled bed like some jug-bitten spider, he gazed idly up at a crack in the dingy plaster. Like a river and its tributaries, it ran, raw and gaping, up one wall before breaking into smaller cracks which rent the ceiling plaster to reveal, here and there, the rotting roof struts above.

Another crack spanned the breadth of the low ceiling and it was this that the boy regarded with some degree of interest: the jagged path it carved through the ceiling, the blistering edges of damp plaster that would drift or fall to the floor in powdery clots when next it rained—perhaps to scatter with it the bodies of long dead insects or spiders or mice.

Early summer in Paris: the air hung hot, still and rank over a city of beggars, women, children, old men and cripples.

Just weeks ago—and for many months—it had been a city of bustle and prowess and pomp, a city of military spectacle, as regiments from all over the Empire assembled in their bright glory. The Illyrian infantry regiments, the Chevau-Légers, and the multitudes of cavalry—the cuirasseurs with their helmets and breastplates gleaming in the weak sunlight, lancers in crimson and blue, hussars in braid and bearskin, the dragoons in helmets and uniforms of every colour—hundreds upon hundreds of men—tall, moustachioed and grand, warriors and heroes to a man, they, and their sleek matched horses, drawn from every corner of the continent, all parading in their splendid coveted honour.

Daily, every street and alleyway had been clogged with the drays and wagons of the commissariats, jammed with baggage wagons and cannon and strings of snorting horses and camp followers; while the city's notaries, oblivious to the cheering crowds, the choruses of 'Vive l'Empereur', worked frantically and without ceasing, writing and copying the wills of so many thousands. And among that constant throng he had passed—unnoticed and unseen—just another young male in a city of men. And he had come and gone freely, an unknown, unobserved, no one among the press.

But now it was quiet. The soldiers were gone. The tents and horses and mules and grooms, the kitchen, cellar and forges were gone too, all following their beloved Emperor to the East. To Berlin and beyond. Pour l'Empire. Pour la gloire. Into the deathtrap that lay beyond Prussia.

Frowning suddenly, the boy rolled off the bed. And standing, stretching, calculating, he stared at the body on the straw mattress opposite. The boy, Brioche he'd been called, had been dead since morning. Kicked and beaten and dead. His thin ribs crushed by a guardsman's boot. Dead because of his resemblance to another plain-faced boy.

"Poxy cullion," the boy murmured, though not in anger.

He'd spent his anger years earlier, when the brutality of heroes and guardsmen was new to him. Now…well, now, it was all detail work. Then, he would have sought personal vengeance on the great bastard who'd done this. Now he just made them look like fools. Fools, every one.

He went to the window to peer through one grimy pane. The watcher was still below, his dust-coloured clothes blending with the limestone and shadows of the house opposite, rendering him almost invisible. But not invisible enough.

"Cock…" the boy muttered.

Then, his lips pressed tight into an uncompromising line, he returned to his bedside and drew a rapier-pointed knife from out the back of his stained breeches. Gripping the mattress at one end, he slit it open; the blade sliced easily through the rotting fabric and straw.

He replaced the knife in his waistband and reached into the mattress to remove handfuls of the matted straw, arranging them in neat clumps atop the mattress until they appeared almost as a series of interconnected ant-heaps.

He crossed to the body. And squatting beside it, smoothed the dead boy's lank hair from off his forehead and sketched the sign of the cross in the air over him. Brioche, the baker's son, left to starve in the streets of Paris after the army had taken his father to bake bread for Napoleon's generals. Poor bruised Brioche.

He took hold of the mattress to drag it and the battered child upon it to his own gutted bed. And grunted with exertion. Brioche, dead, weighed more than ever he had in life.

Silently, he hauled the unstiffening body onto the bed, onto the spread straw, then slit apart the second mattress to strew its contents over the body. Then, gathering up a handful of tallow candle stubs he'd collected, he placed them, one by one, nestling them amongst the straw.

His task finished, he crossed to the opposite side of the room and crouched down against one wall to wait. To doze and patiently to wait. To wait until midnight, when the sky was blackest and all that was left of Paris was asleep. Or better still, drunk.

He closed his eyes, resting his head against the wall with its coating of mould and grime. Just a few hours to wait until he lit the funeral pyre. Then, once the flames took hold of the tallow and lamp oil and straw, an escape through the blackened skylight above the landing and out over the rooftops, out to the Porte St. Denis.

It would take them days to discover that the charred remains were not his, if ever they did discover it. And by then, it would be too late. By morning he would be out of the city; in three days he would be beyond their grasp.

He rose and went to the window to watch as their sentry gulped down the contents of a bottle. The boy checked the battered watch in his pocket. Nearly seven. Five more hours then. The sentry belched and ogled a young woman—a prostitute in a stained gown and tatty bonnet—as she strolled past him.

2

It was the barrenest strip of beach in all of Brittany. Fiske did not like it. He liked a beach with plenty of cover. Or even better, a deep cleft of an inlet in which to land—like at Biville in the old days. Anything but this expanse of sand and pebble as broad as it was long, stretching out for miles below a headland where half the French army could be lying on their bellies waiting to blow his head off, and him none the wiser.

He sniffed hard, clearing his head. Sand and small shells crushed and crunched underfoot. Grimacing, he gave his dinghy a last backward glance. It was still there—the only vessel of any kind as far as the eye could see. The storm that finished the Frenchies at Trafalgar six years earlier had also paid a call here, emptying the beach of its sand and smashing the local fishing fleet. Once, a long time since, the beach had been a favourite haven of wreckers, and the Bretons—a superstitious folk at the best of times—regarded the storm that ravaged their coast as those drowned sailors' revenge. And mayhap they were right. So though the sea had returned the sand, the beach was believed to be haunted, and now only smugglers used it. Smugglers, or intelligence men.

It was not a good night for landing in France. The wind had been whipping down off the Channel all day, amassing enough cloud to give old Noah a nasty fright. Fiske reckoned he had an hour, a little more, a little less, before the storm broke in earnest. He didn't fancy rowing back to the Cutter in driving rain.

He came to the edge of the beach. The path to the headland lay ahead, a straggling ribbon of packed earth between borders of cleavers and quitch grass. He checked, listening. Nothing. Nothing but the thundering of the waves and the keening of the wind over the deserted landscape, and in the farthest distance, the creak and bang of an unlatcheted shutter. He walked on, his collar turned up against the wind, shoulders hunched against the rising gale.

He was nearly upon the house before he could make it out—the lichen covered stone walls, the boarded-up windows, the rag stuffed through the hole in the one remaining pane of glass. Burrs caught at his stockings as he hurried up the garden path. The wood door was rotting on its hinges. The cottage looked deserted, dead. Fiske raised his fist and banged on the door.

There was no answer.

"The pox take you, Dupont," Fiske swore. It would be just like him to be off whoring when he was wanted. "Idle cock."

He banged again. Hard.

Nothing. Nothing but the wind and the silence indoors.

"I shall kill him if he's away, sodomitical bastard…" Fiske promised himself. He hammered on the door, then turned to scan the garden for any sign of life, any furtive movement, anything. Nothing. Nothing but the howl and roar of the wind. He turned, beating on the door till it rattled.

"Qui est là?"

Fiske caught his breath and gave the door a final pounding.

"Eh bien, soyez patient! Je viens, je viens."

Fiske stashed his hands in his pockets and waited.

Through the one green-stained window came a glimmering of weak light. The door rattled as inside the bar was removed and the bolt shot back. A moment later, it swung open.

"Est-ce que vous faites du miel pour les abeilles?" Fiske said sharply.

The man standing within the distorting halo of the tallow candle was not one Fiske recognised. The sheen of sweaty grime covered his face. His hair hung, thick and dark, in greasy strings over his forehead, ears and neck. The ragged jersey and torn canvas trousers he wore were the same as countless poor fishermen or deserters on either side of the Channel. His feet were bare and dirty.

"Est-ce que vous faites du miel pour les abeilles?" Fiske repeated.

The fisherman eyed Fiske warily, then spat. "Mais non. Moi, je préfère chasser au nom des lions." His breath was foul.

"Good God, it is you, Dupont! I couldn't tell." Fiske lowered his voice. “Castlereagh’s recalling you on the instant. He wants you. Now.”

Narrowing his eyes, the man paused, perhaps in surprise, then stepped back and jerked his head for Fiske to enter. “It’ll take me a few minutes. Viens.”

Fiske shut and barred the door behind him.

“Anyone see you?”

“No. Not that I could tell. Anyone with a grain of sense is indoors with their windows shuttered an’ barred,” Fiske grumbled.

Dupont snorted. “Aye.”

Fiske followed him into the cottage’s main room and sat cautiously upon a broken-backed chair. Beneath him the ground was sticky with wine that had spilt and dried. Against one wall was a wooden bedstead with nothing upon it but a fouled mattress and a blanket, a single moth-eaten blanket liberally spattered and stained with wine, or blood. A dark layer of dust and ash coated everything. From behind the wooden sideboard, he heard the scrambling and scratching of mice. “Did anyone ever tell you, you live like a pig, Dupont?”

“It discourages unwelcome visitors,” Dupont retorted. He knelt down beside the unswept hearth and slid the point of a gutting knife along the edge of the ashy hearthstone. Carefully, he prised it up, lifted it out and propped it against the grate. “Does old Nosey know that I’m off?”

Fiske shrugged. “How would I know? They don’t tell me anything.” He hesitated. “But…I’ve heard that the boy has gone missing.”

Dupont gave him a hard, angry look. “The boy?”

Fiske shrugged again. He knew, as he said, nothing.

From out of the earthen cavity, Dupont drew a brace of military pistols, a sheaf of papers, a leather purse, and a polished brass spyglass.

“’Struth now, that’s a bonny piece,” Fiske murmured.

“What, this?” Dupont held up the spyglass. “It does the job.” He slid the stone back into its niche and brushed a handful of ashes over it. “I’ll follow you out to the Cutter in my own boat, then cut it loose. If they find the wreckage, they’ll blame the storm.” He dumped his few belongings on the table, then slid his feet into a pair of water-stained shoes. “Take the things on the table, will you, Fiske?”

"Yes, all right." Fiske thrust the purse and papers into his pockets and the pistols into the waist of his breeches. "There's nothing else? After all this time?"

"No," Dupont said shortly.

Fiske had heard different.

Dupont shook his head, his expression hard and empty, and snuffed the candle. "Shall we go?" He followed Fiske out of the cottage, slamming the door behind him.

3

Three days of solid rain—an unrelenting torrent of water it had been—had left the roads grey and thick with a deep heavy layer of mud. It coated the carriage wheels, sucking at the horses' hooves and splattering the carriage and the horses' flanks with great gobs of brown muck.

Dunphail had come into this sodden corner of south Kent at the rumour of a mill between…'Struth, did it matter? He had been unable to find a decent bed any nearer than Rye. Then the authorities and the rain had arrived. Simultaneously. As if by prearranged signal.

Word that the mill was cancelled had been slow to reach him. By the time it had, the rain had started. So he'd waited. Filling in the time with endless games of patience in a close private parlour when he couldn't find a partner for a hand of piquet. And waited. Avoiding the amorous overtures of a serving wench who fancied herself, and floating his insides on a sea of local ale. And waited.

When the clouds had finally broken this morning, he'd needed no more encouragement than that. He ordered his horses hitched to the carriage and drove out of the inn yard and over the pebbled surface of Mermaid Street less than half an hour later. But even now, mounting billows of silver and black cloud blanketed the sky, the wind had sharpened, and he was still driving at this snail's pace over country lanes, between ditches full of rainwater turning brackish, the horses stumbling in the rutted and churned up clay and mud, no more than half the way back to London.

"God's balls! Not another bloody market crowd!"

Dunphail's groom, More, the short and solid individual who sat beside him on the front seat, squinted into the distance at the gathering of people—peasants and farmers they looked to him—blocking the road ahead, and cast a wary eye at his master.

"Aye. It does look tha' way, dun't it? I'll blow the yard o' tin, shall I?" he said evenly and reached for the long copper horn which rested at his feet. Three short blasts ought to clear the road.

Dunphail reined in gently, squeezing upon the reins as one squeezes a sea sponge in the bath, slowing the horses to a quieter pace. "Aye."

Sucking in his breath, More put the horn to his pursed lips and produced three honking blasts that blared out like an elephant's trumpet in a water fight.

"Sod you for a devil, More. Are you tryin' to deafen me?"

At the sound of the horn, those at the edge of the crowd had turned. Seeing the approaching carriage and its team of blood horses, they reached for their friends or children to hurry them to the side of the road.

But the knot of those at the core of the crowd did not turn, their attentions fixed as they yelped shouts of encouragement or grunted their approval. At something. A dogfight perhaps?

"Daft Southron clots." Dunphail's speech lost its veneer of Englishness easily. "Blow it again, More." Gently, he slowed the horses to a plodding walk. They grew nervy in a crowd.

Again, More blew the horn. Three short blasts that barked through the chilling afternoon air.

Now the crowd did part, some to either side of the road, leaving at the centre of the lane the spectacle that had drawn them in the first instance: a towering brute of a man with long curling hair, beating, with repeated blows to the face and head, a boy.

The man raised his hand and brought it down, backhanded and hard across the lad's cheek, knocking his head back. Blood spattered from the boy's mouth onto his chin. It spilled from his nose over his cheeks and down his throat, staining the fabric of his shirt. The man tightened his grip on the boy's jacket, raised his fist for a blow to the jaw and landed it.

"God's balls," Dunphail swore. He halted the carriage.

The boy's head snapped back and he staggered. A cut below his eye was bleeding freely.

"Sweet Christ," More grunted, his eyes widening. "That were a nasty blow."

The man cuffed the boy's ear. Twice. Three times. The ear flushed crimson.

The man slapped the boy twice more, then drew his fist back and smacked the other side of his face. The boy's cheeks burned red.

Dunphail's jaw clenched, unclenched. For there was something peculiar here. Puzzling. Something about the way the boy was receiving the blows. Passively it was. Almost practised, you might say. Like a staged fight. His face was bloodied, but…'suredly, so many blows should have wrought more damage. Odd. The boy's hands remained unresisting, unopposing at his side. Very odd. "What's that, More?" Dunphail shook his head to clear it. He prized a good mill more highly than most. But this? He stood up. "You! I say, you there!" His Englishness was back.

A few of the local people, their eyes growing cautious, backed away from the brawling couple, backed away from the perch phaeton and the matched dun geldings. For with the unwanted arrival of 'Quality', the atmosphere had changed. A mother took her small son's hand and dragged him protesting off toward a whitewashed cottage.

"I say, you there! Stop! Stop beating upon the lad!"

The bully grabbed a handful of the boy's hair, yanked his head backward, then slammed his knuckles against the boy's jaw.

"D'you not hear? I said, stop!"

The man threw Dunphail a look of contempt and raised his fist again.

"I say, stop!" Dunphail roared.

With a provocative, sly smile and sneering sideways glance, playing to his audience, the bully pulled his arm back another inch in preparation for a face-shattering blow.

The villagers glanced warily from the gentleman in his well-cut clothes and his gentry-voice to the man in his leather waistcoat, and back again.

The man loosed his blow.

Frowning, his whip hand held high, Dunphail snapped it. Hard. The full length of plaited leather whistled through the air. The thong coiled about the bully's wrist, jerking it back and high over his head. He screeched with pain, or anger. The horses shifted and sidled.

"I said, stop thrashing the lad," Dunphail enunciated, yanking on the whip handle.

The villagers edged farther away.

"Who's the lad?" Dunphail demanded, dragging the whip upward, hauling the bully's arm up into an unnatural position. "And, what is it he's done? Who owns him then? Does no one claim him?" He raked the crowd with a look. "And who might you be, laddie?" He directed his last question to the big man, now struggling to free himself.

The man let out a ferocious stream of obscenities and oaths, startling those nearest him. An ex-soldier then. Or a navy man, a pressed man.

"Fetch the lad, More," Dunphail ordered.

"What? Milor'?"

"Sod it, I said, 'bring the lad'. Sweet Christ, is everyone gone deaf?" A bright red flush stained Dunphail's cheeks. "No one claims him. 'Struth, if we don't take him, yon billy'll do more than just sort him. An' I've no wish to add that to my conscience. At least, not today."

More shot Dunphail a queer look. Since when did he have a conscience? It was nobbut a common lad. A thief from the look of him. Mud-stained and bloodied.

"Right, then." More hopped down from the phaeton's high step and stamped across to the boy. The onlookers stepped back, out of his path.

More nodded briskly to the lad. "The laird says you're to come awa' wi' us." His accent was a curious blend of the London stables and alehouses he frequented and his native Highland district.

"I'll teach you to mess with John Brown!" the big man snarled.

More eyed him with marked disfavour. "Don' get niffy wi' me, son," he barked, neatly slamming his knee into Brown's groin. As he doubled over, gasping, More brought both fists up hard, smashing Brown's jaw upward just as Dunphail tugged on the whip. "I can 'ave the scrote off a stallion like 'e quicker than ye can spit," he snapped. "Now mind yoursel'."

The boy had not moved.

"Did ye not hear? What are ye, deaf? Th'laird says you're to come wi' us the now, so get on wi' ye." He gestured toward the waiting carriage and the horses which had begun to fidget and snort. Sweet Christ! Daft Southron buggers, gormless to a man.

The boy considered More with his one unbruised eye. Blood was smeared across his cheeks and chin. His bottom lip was split and swelling. "Yes. All right." He swallowed raggedly. Blood oozed from a cut in his top lip and flowed from his nose. His temple and cheekbone were bruised to a stippled scarlet. "Thank you." For all that his words were slurred, he spoke like a gently reared child.

Graceful, proud, like a trained athlete or an unvanquished prize-fighter, he walked past the man who would have beaten his face in, away from the gawping crowd, his narrow shoulders squared and his head held erect.

A young widow in black disengaged herself from her neighbours and hurried to catch up with him. "Here. Take it." She thrust a crumpled handkerchief into his hand, then rushed back to the safe anonymity of the crowd without ever having looked directly at his bleeding face.

The boy remained still for a moment. He drew a deep shuddering breath, blinked, then began to daub, gingerly and ineffectually, at his nose and mouth. Behind him, the villagers murmured and nodded amongst themselves. Small children stared with round eyes.

At the corner of the carriage, the boy halted to train his unflinching and impassive gaze upon his rescuer, to measure him, even. An outsider he was. An alien and a stranger. A Scot. As unlike himself as could be. A well-heeled Scot, with a handsome Scots face, the forehead high and smooth, the nose thin with an aquiline cast. The mouth was thin too, with a slight fullness at the centre of the bottom lip; his hair the colour of old, age-tempered red oak beside his fair skin; and his eyes, beneath flyaway brows, were an inky grey. A tall man too, and well-knit, broad through the shoulders, his legs and arms in good proportion to his torso, wearing well-cut 'Quality' clothes. He would know him anywhere now.

Dunphail affected not to notice, sparing the boy only a cursory glance. Dark matted hair, a battered face, a black eye, probably or possibly of twelve or thirteen years, wearing nondescript clothes that had seen better days. He was too thin, probably lousy, and unquestionably stank. Dunphail looked away. "More, release my whip."

Like the others, More had been watching the lad—considering the fluid, effortless gait, the unnerving absence of tears. "Oh aye."

More surveyed John Brown's acne-scarred face without enthusiasm—it was contorting unpleasantly, the muscles working in his jaw. "Bring your arm down slow-like, laddie, an' I'll undo the lash. But don't go messin wi' me or I'll finish wha' I started. D'ye ken? Aye… Good." Deftly he unknotted and unwound the whip from about Brown's wrist and hand.

The instant he was freed, Brown jerked away from the groom. Shoving past the still-curious villagers, he ducked between two cottages and out of sight. None spoke to nor stopped him.

More shrugged and returned to the phaeton, patting the horses on their rumps as he passed. "Good lads." The boy had not moved.

"Can ye no' manage? Right then, I'll gie ye a hand," More said, stepping up onto the front wheel and extending a hand to the lad to haul him up.

Dunphail drew in the length of his whip and shortened the reins in his fingers. "See to his face, More."

More surveyed the mosaic of bruises, blood and skin thrashed raw, and scowled. "You'll pardon my askin', milor', but wi' what?"

Dunphail slapped the reins. "Walk on." The geldings stepped into action throwing the boy against the seat back. "Use what's left in the flask."

The carriage bowled through the centre of the village. Then, before its few thatched cottages, blacksmith's and alehouse were behind them, Dunphail snapped the whip over the leader's head, and the horses quickened their pace to a measured trot.

"What is your name, child?" Dunphail asked. It was a demand, not a question.

More rummaged in his coat pocket for the flask.

"Boy, sir." He spoke as through a mouthful of pebbles.

"Show th'laird the proper respect," More growled. "He's the

Marquis o' Dunphail. Dunphail of Abriachan. An' don't ye forget it."

"Your Christian name?" Dunphail clarified, never looking from the road.

The boy hesitated. Despite all appearance of impassivity, to speak, to move at all, cost him dear. "Boy, my lord."

"That's it? Boy?"

"Queer name for a lad," More grunted, soaking a handkerchief in brandy from an etched and polished silver hip flask.

"Yes, my lord."

"And your surname, Boy?"

"Tirrell. Boy Tirrell, my lord." He said it flatly.

"Here, now. Look this way, will ye?" More said, gentle as he patted and dabbed at the scraped flesh beneath the boy's eyes. The lad winced, his spine straightening instinctively.

"Trust me, it's painin' me twice as much knowin' it's fine French brandy I'm washin' your face with," More grumbled.

The boy might have smiled but his eyes were stinging and his mouth had grown immobile. "Ow!" he yelped through clenched teeth.

"Aye, that's cut deep." More daubed at the split lip again. "How're your teeth? Loose, are they?"

The rain-flattened countryside, all miry fields and drooping foxgloves, went past unnoticed.

"No. Not really," Boy answered. His jaw was stiffening with the bruising. "They'll mend."

More busied himself with wiping the crusting blood from off the boy's chin and throat. "You're familiar wi' this sort o' thing, then?"

The boy paused. "It happens," he said simply.

More gave a nod. "Aye. It will do."

A patchwork of small scabs was forming across his bruised cheekbones. The side of his jaw was darkening—crimson to violet. His left eye had swollen shut and the bruises about it bled into one another like paint on an old, muddied palette.

More tossed the bloodied handkerchief at his feet. "That's the best I can do for ye, laddie. A bit o' raw steak would help wi' the eye, but as for the rest, it'll just take time."

"Yes. Thank you."

Though they drove through the occasional squall of rain, drenching, and cold as snow, Dunphail neither slackened the pace nor stopped. More folded his arms across his chest and waited, a dour expression marking his craggy face whenever he glanced at the boy beside him. Eventually the pasturelands and hop fields gave place to the orchards and neat country houses of Greenwich, the roads widened, and the traffic grew heavier and noisier with drovers and goose-girls with their herds and flocks, with horsemen, with hackney and post carriages, private vehicles and drays.

The boy volunteered nothing until they reached the wastelands—the rubble fields and dust heaps and collections of miserable huts that formed the outskirts of the metropolis. There, through his teeth, he thanked Dunphail for his timely rescue and having brought him to Town, and requested that he might be set down at Westminster Bridge, if that was convenient. He spoke like a gentry child, his speech unmarked by local accent, nothing like a common lad. Dunphail acquiesced. More bristled and waited.

But by then they had become caught up in the lock—the disorderly mass of carriages of every description, to be found at every approach to the city, all blocking, manoeuvring and obstructing one another as far in every direction as one could see, their drivers muttering oaths or swearing loudly or silently cursing—which was the approach to Westminster Bridge. And somewhere amongst this crush of humanity and horses and vehicles, the boy slipped from the carriage seat and into the crowd, there to be seen one moment, then gone the next, vanishing facilely into a flock of tradesmen and children.

At length, his face set like an undertaker's, Dunphail brought his horses and carriage to a halt before an imposing red brick house on Mount Street—the house he had shared with his cousin, Hardy, until just recently. With three floors and an attic, it was too large for a single gentleman. And he would have preferred Bath stone. Or granite.

"There was something very odd about that lad, milor'," More commented.

Dunphail ignored him. "Stable them down well, More." He knotted the reins about the whip stand. The Englishness had returned to his speech.

More climbed down from his seat and went to the horses' heads. "Did ye not notice?" He rubbed the leader's chin. "Good lad.

"He didna cry. Nor cry out! Did ye notice that? There's no' a man alive wha hae ta'en sich a beating wi'out a tear. An' his hands. There wasnae a scratch on 'em. D'ye see? He'd no tried to defend himsel'. Not at a'!"

Dunphail surveyed the sky. The clouds were thick and heavy. More rain. He reached into his pocket for his snuffbox. Then, blandly: "No." He sniffed. "And he took the punches. Prepared for them, and accepted them, so that he received the least amount of hurt from each—coached by an expert fight-master, I should have said. Any other child would have been unconscious. Or dead. But there was nothing broken, was there? Not even his nose so far as one could tell. Or do I mistake?" he questioned. Then as More confirmed it with a shake of his head, he shrugged. "'Struth, it was a rare performance."

"Aye! Does that no' bother ye?" More demanded.

"No, More. 'Struth, why should it? It's nothing to do with me. He was a smuggler's brat. Or a thief. In all likelihood, both. Born to be hanged, I dare say. All of which don't concern me in the slightest."

"Then why'd ye stop it?"

Dunphail favoured the groom with a rare piercing glare. His nostrils flared slightly. "Because I happen to dislike murder." He paused. "No. 'Struth, I don't give a gunner's damn. However, I should very much dislike bein' made an accessory to it. Now, stop standin' about an' stable the lads, will you?" He strode round the phaeton and up his two front steps. "Christ, why do I put up with him?"

"You put up wi' me," More retorted, "on account of I'm the only man south o' the Tay wha can handle your poxy sow-tempered cattle!"

Dunphail took a pinch of snuff. Od's life, he detested Town life these days. He shrugged. No. He just needed to go wenching later. "Aye. That'll be it, then."

Chapter II

1

The broad leaves of the plane trees cast few shadows on the neoclassical limestone and brick houses which lined the three sides of Berkeley Square. It was too early in the day for shadows—dawn is a time of purple shade and unorchestrated bird-song but few shadows. The boy dodged behind the equestrian statue of King George at the centre of the Square. Then broke into a run across the closely scythed grass. Neither the solitary horseman in front of No. 11 nor the two tradesmen in leather aprons, exchanging gossip outside Gunter's at No. 7, spared him more than a glance, despite the hour.

London was a city full of boys. Apprentice boys, street boys, climbing boys, grocers' boys, errand and thieving boys, all running over the clay and gravel streets and closes; haunting the alleys in the slums of Whitechapel or nipping between the well-kept mansions of St. James's; darting between carriages, wagons and individual riders in the Strand, in Piccadilly, in the mews, on London Bridge or Blackfriars or the new bridge at Westminster.

Boy liked London for that. No one ever noticed him. In London, he was just one more boy in an endless procession of plain-faced, poorly clothed children. Though today, well…well, today it was nothing short of a miracle that he hadn't been marked. The swelling about his eye had gone down but the skin was the colour of ripening plums, and the bruising along his jaw and temple was visible still, though now fading to a softening green.

"...poxy sodomite," he murmured, cursing from habit.

He rounded the corner onto Hay Hill. On either side of the street, the vast stableyards behind high wooden walls were quiet yet. The rows of sash windows in the two four-storeyed houses—Palladian mansions they were really, new-built, stark and proud whatever the hour—those were still darkened, their heavy curtains still drawn against the night and light as he jogged past. It was just as he liked it: silent, no one about, and nothing to distract him—at least, or especially, when his face was as conspicuous as at present.

He slowed to an unhurried walk. For even Dover Street was deserted, its building sites and half-constructed townhouses silent, still, except for a solitary brown and black calico cat swishing her tail as she stalked her breakfast amongst the rubble and broken bricks that lay in piles everywhere.

At the entrance to a garden off Burlington Gardens, he paused, cautious again. And like a hawk, he scanned the windows of the buildings opposite, the nearby rooftops, the street in either direction. Nothing. And no one. To be sure, it was *precisely* as he liked it.

Still glancing about, he strolled into the garden. Ignoring the trimmed hedges and the neatly ordered beds of box and mid-summer flowers, he made his way to a plain door at the rear of a white stone and red brick building—blood and bandages they called this kind of fancywork, appropriately enough. With a final check of the surrounding garden and overlooking buildings, he inserted a small key into the keyhole and turned it. The lock was well-oiled. With equal care he withdrew the key. He opened the door and slid inside. Then, silently, unobtrusively, closed it behind him.

Inside was as dark as ink, black as a mine shaft. He waited for his eyes to adjust. Then, without so much as the clicking of the latch, he relocked the door and returned the key to his pocket.

His old leather shoes made no sound on the worn carpet. Tracing his fingertips along the wall beside him, he walked down the hall. At the foot of a darkened stairwell, he took hold of the wooden handrail and started up the steps. The rail was slick with polished wax.

The rooms occupied by this branch of the Foreign Office were a slipshod affair in his opinion. Hastily transformed dining and bedrooms was what they were. With few exceptions, they looked it too.

He stopped at the second landing and wary, alert to any sound or even breath, headed down the dark hall to the small office that was no better than a miserly dressing room with a desk and chair replacing the wardrobe and mirror. The key was kept above the frame of a portrait of a young naval officer which hung near the door. Boy retrieved it from its hiding place, opened the door, then replaced it.

From somewhere nearby, he heard a long muffled creak, and froze. Was it a bed, groaning under the weight of its occupant? Or a floorboard? His hand on the doorknob, he remained still, straining to hear. Nothing. It was, then, a bed. He leaned back and searched the gloom in either direction for slits of light appearing above or beneath any of the doors which opened onto the hallway. Nothing. No light. Not even the whisper of an intake of breath.

Slowly, gently, Boy turned the handle, opened the door and slipped within.

The narrow office—desk, chairs, bookcase—was awash with pale light which filtered through the half-drawn curtains. Boy closed the door and remained leaning against it, listening, gauging the silence.

Lithe and graceful as an unsought deer, he crossed to the door of the adjoining office and found it unlocked.

Like the outer office, this room too was suffused with the grey light of early morning. It muted the stark edges of the classical frieze and the white pilasters which adorned the sea-green walls. It softened the outlines of the many chairs and the two library tables under piles of maps, both rolled and flattened.

Leaving the door open, he returned to the desk to test each of its several drawers. All locked.

"They would be," he said under his breath and reached into his jacket sleeve for a wire pick. And bending close to the desk, he inserted the crooked end of the wire into the small keyhole and slowly rotated it. The latch clicked. He smiled his satisfaction, then replaced the pick in his sleeve, slid open the first of the drawers and removed the top sheaf of papers.

"Hunh…" He scanned the top sheet. "Hunh? They've recalled Shuster. Good Lord." He sat down heavily and continued to read.

2

Like everything else in the small house on Curzon Street, the blue damask curtains in the dining room had seen better days. Bare-patched, the fabric eaten away by generations of ravenous moths, and stained, they were firmly shut against the morning sun. And were likely to remain so. Both the Shusters had hangovers.

Harry, in a creased shirt and worn buckskins, was a sorry sight. Awake and sober, he may have been a well-looking young man with kindly blue eyes and brown hair, but cropsick, and lacking both interest and vanity, he knew himself only as a pale imitation of his elder brother, Georgie. He was slumped in a carver at one end of the table with his eyes closed and a pained expression marking his face, his long legs in soiled and scuffed riding boots stretched out like a fence railing between table and sideboard. Before him, a plate of eggs and grilled kidneys had long since grown cold.

The elder by four years, Captain Sir George Shuster concealed the effects of his carousing rather better. Minus only the blue coat that would change the colour of his eyes from their natural light green to blue, he was cleanly shaven, and dressed in proper civilian morning attire, buckskins and a buff waistcoat. His starched cravat had been knotted with military precision. His dark hair, though still damp from the bath, was neatly brushed. Perhaps his head was harder. More likely it was just experience, but only the extreme pallor of his fair skin betrayed the true state of affairs.

"God's garters, you look like death, Harry," he observed eventually, without concern and without looking up. A continued morose silence was his brother's only response. George closed his eyes and sat, head in hand, for a long while. Then, without interest, he at last began to sort through the post on the table before him, turning one and then another over, like cards in an idle and unwinnable game of patience. He lifted the final one, regarding it with detachment. The handwriting on it was all too familiar. He eyed it with the natural suspicion of one whose eyes were on the verge of feeling something extremely unpleasant, like hot daggers or molten needles, then flexed his jaw and stiffened it. "It didn't take her long, did it?" he remarked to no one and shrugged.

He had been back in England for less than a fortnight, yet stale drunk as he was this morning, he was still distinctly alive to the exquisite pleasures of being clean and louse-free: of having slept between clean sheets, of having clean water in which to bathe, of cakes of scented soap and freshly laundered shirts and starched cravats. And equally conscious of all that he had left behind. And it was as if, each morning, a veil of cleanliness washed over him, rinsing away the hellish residue of the past months. And, he recognised too, both with his head and, even more, in his gut, that here and now in this house, here he could afford to be drunk and foolish in the evening, or stale drunk and silent in the morning. Here, he might at any hour allow his guard down and none would gainsay his indiscretion. Nor perish because of it. He paused, just to breathe. In, and out.

He turned over the letter and broke open the seal with his knife, scattering shards of blue wax over the white tablecloth. "Oh cock, it needed only this," he said indifferently and sat back in his chair, absently gazing into space, before resuming the struggle of deciphering the scrawled and blotted script which covered several pages—none of which were numbered.

Harry opened his eyes to peer at his brother. "Did you say something?"

"No," Georgie murmured, scanning for the gist among the jumble of words and blots and crossings. "Never mind…A letter from our mother."

"You did say something," Harry mumbled. "Is that coffee still hot?" Gingerly, he hoisted his lanky frame upright in the chair. "What's the letter?"

Georgie shook his head dismissively. "Have an apple, Harry."

"It ain't from Mama, is it?" Harry asked, squinting, looking ill, and ignoring his brother's offer of fruit. The mere thought made his stomach churn. He yawned, leaned on the table to steady himself, and with great care slouched down again.

"Yes," Georgie said finally, frowning as he attempted to match the words at the bottom and top of each page in an effort to determine which page led to which. And upon the rising tide of distant nausea and tired disdain, unable to discover any logic, he shook his head, and tossed the whole of it aside.

"'Struth, it didn't take her long," Harry said to himself. Then: "What is it now?"

"Oh, the same…The same…I dare say it always is…" Four years away, and all spent in the company of men, had lessened or even destroyed any tolerance for her frequent maternal strictures—though clearly she had little notion of this alteration to his character or her ability to influence it.

Harry gave a desultory grunt for answer. He scowled, winced, then massaged his forehead. "What's she got to reproach you with? 'Struth, you've only been back in the country a sennight," he protested mildly. "You've not had the time to do more than sleep. And visit your tailor." With visible effort he rose from his seat to reach for the coffeepot. "'Slife, you're a great war hero, ain't you?"

Georgie shrugged, and tried again to make sense of the final page. "That would appear to have escaped her notice." He did not look up to see the withering expression his brother wore. He smiled mockingly. "It's always the same…my infamous neglect of the family fortunes…" He lifted a page to turn it over. And turned to the second sheet, scanning it. "And then there's your extravagant idleness…which I have signally failed to check…and which it would appear causes her no end of agitation by day and night…" He turned over to the last page, eyeing it with distaste. "And, yes, here we are, this is good too: Theresa shall require a more generous dowry…" he finished carelessly and prodded an apple core with his knife.

"What?" Harry boggled at last, and poured the dregs from the coffeepot into his cup. "I say, you might have left some for me." He sat back down with a thud. And mumbled: "No dowry is goin' to sweeten the taste of that evil nostrum…"

"What was that?" Georgie said.

"Theresa." Harry scrunched up his face, then tenderly rubbed his forehead as if he expected to find that a crack had opened up between his eyebrows. "You ain't seen her in four years."

Georgie raked his fingers through his hair, disarranging it. "No…Horrible, is she?"

"Fat." Harry sipped at his coffee. "Gad, this is vile."

"Do shut up about the coffee, will you?" Georgie said affably, still perusing the letter.

"Ugly, if you want the truth," explained Harry, returning to the subject of their sister, his eyes closed. "Has spots, you know. I wouldn't have her."

"Oh. She might improve…"

"Not her," Harry said with finality. And belched.

"Oh…Now do listen to this. You'll like this." George peered at the page through rheumy eyes—at least they felt rheumy. "'Your reputation as a here and thereian has given me cause for great consternation over the years, though my dear cousin Fitch has…always assured me that such excesses must spring from your frequent association with the dissolute and rakish company which forms the main of the officers' mess…would no doubt lessen as you gained your maturity…'"

"What?" Harry set down his cup with a rattle and started out of his chair. The sudden movement was too much. He put a hand to his head. "Ow!" he complained.

"No, wait," George stalled with a gentle laugh. "There's more."

"'Struth, someone's been very busy on your behalf," Harry murmured, sinking back into his chair. He narrowed his eyes. "You ain't a here and thereian, though. Never was, no matter what *she* may say. Anyway, you was with the army in Spain."

"Thank you for the vote of confidence…" Frowning, George reread the page and gave a half-hearted chuckle. "And apparently—according to her—it's more than time that I should be setting up my nursery…"

"What?" Harry choked, swilling down the last of his coffee, and sputtered. "Ow!" he winced. He clapped his hands down hard on the top of his head. "Ow! You? She must be off her head. What would you do with a parcel of brats? Or a wife? Christ, it makes my head hurt!"

Eventually, his coughing and soft laughter subsiding, Harry squeezed his eyes shut against the pounding in his head and said suspiciously: "This is about the debts, ain't it? I never outrun the constable, Georgie, you know I don't! I may be idle, but I'm never extravagant. Well, hardly ever."

"It ain't you and you know it." Georgie stabbed the apple core again, this time splitting it open. Two brown seeds shot onto the carefully mended tablecloth.

"It's Mama, ain't it?" Harry said, looking decidedly green. "Hell's bells, I think I'm going to be sick! You could sell this place," he suggested, glancing about the dining room and noting, for the first time, the peeling ceiling paint and soot stains above the empty fireplace. "We could take bachelor's quarters," he managed, swallowing hard.

"I can't. It's mortgaged to the hilt. Like everything else."

Harry subsided, glowering, into his seat. The remembrance of his family's indebtedness had a sudden sobering effect on him. "Castlehouse?" he asked after an interval.

"Castlehouse too."

Tactfully, Harry paused.

"But we'll manage," Georgie said, shrugging again. "There's my prize money, which should cover both our needs…And…" he hesitated. "And my current services do not go unrewarded…I promise you, I'll bring us about."

The nausea subsiding, Harry crossed his arms over his eyes, stretched back in his chair and yawned. At last he said in a thin voice, "Tell you what I say, I say ignore her. I shall go down to Castlehouse and take on the job of estate agent. What d'you say to that?"

"You're still nazy, Harry, if you think that. God's garters, you can't even do your sums…" Georgie said, laughing. He stood up and reached for his coat. "'Struth, you're right. What would I do with a parcel of brats? Christ in heaven! In any event, I fancy I'm only here for a few weeks at most. And I 'suredly have no idea when I shall be next posted. Nor where. Or do you suppose she was thinking on some Spanish señorita when she mentioned marriage?" he asked, an imp of a smile lurking in his eyes.

Managing a laugh, Harry rolled his eyes. "I'd love to see her face..." He frowned. Thinking *was* an effort. He laid his head down on the table and resting his cheek upon the table linen, stilled the rising bile with a series of deep breaths. And speaking half into the cloth he said thickly, "But I shall tell you this, George, whatever you do, before you do take some silly chit to wife, you'd better make damned sure that you can bear the sight of her across the breakfast table."

Uncertain that he had heard correctly, Georgie looked up from shrugging his coat on and adjusting its lapels. "I beg your pardon?"

Without moving, Harry looked up at his brother and managed a half-smile. "Well, upon my life, a sour face at breakfast would ruin your whole day if you wasn't careful...So just make bloody certain that her face at the breakfast table ain't goin' to have you castin' up your accounts. That's all I mean to say," he explained.

Georgie gave a crack of laughter, and put his hands to his temples, as if to hold his face in place. "Sod it, my head! What in Christ's name was we drinking last night?"

"Blue ruin. Champagne. And rum punch," came the unequivocal response.

"Ye gods and little fishes!" Left-handed, the captain snatched an apple and pitched it at his brother. "Have an apple, Harry. It'll cure what ails you."

Unflinching, Harry reached out to catch the apple, saying softly: "Do you miss it?"

Georgie hesitated. Did he miss it? The twenty hours a day spent in the saddle, racing both day and night through the wilds and mountains of Spain to bring the latest intelligence to headquarters? His former companions, both alive and dead? The constant devilish danger? The lives he could not save? Being shot at? Aurélie Des Champs? 'Struth, miss it? Always. "No," he said evenly. "Not much. Except, to be sure, for the damned typhus fever. That I shall always miss."

Chapter III

1

To be employed in the Foreign Office, one needed to be two things: exceptionally hard-working and exceedingly well-mannered. Which made a kind of sense when one considered that the Foreign Secretary, Lord Castlereagh, kept his staff reduced to the barest minimum, while at the same time cultivating for them a reputation for dilettantism, inefficiency and indolence. Though nothing could be further from the truth, reflected Planta, as he passed by the portrait of a young naval officer on his way to his small office on the first floor. He supposed such a reputation did have its uses in this war of wits with the French…and the Whigs. But just what they were…

He reached into his pocket for his ring of keys, then fumbled in the hall's dim half-light for the key that unlocked this particular door. He found the key, and with an unavoidable amount of jingling, unlocked the door and opened it wide.

"Oh hang." He had neglected to shut the curtains before he'd left yesterday evening. That made it twice this week. He glanced at the small gold carriage clock he kept upon the mantel. Just half past nine. Very good. His lordship would be arriving at about half-ten. Planta dropped the keys onto his desk and set his locked leather satchel beside them before crossing to the window to draw the curtains fully back and throw up the sash. The meeting with the Captain had been set for half-eleven which gave them plenty of time...The maps needed to be reordered and hung. Lord Myddelton was due in after lunch to translate the report from di Borgo—who was probably wanting more money. Sir Charles Flint had requested an hour after that, and would also be in want of funds no doubt, and Mr. Cooke would see his lordship after dinner about...The double doors to the inner office stood open.

"Oh cock," murmured Planta under his breath. It would be just like his lordship to come here directly from his early morning walk—dawn walk described it better. Or dawn hobble with his gout so bad. "Indolence and inefficiency, my hat!"

He went to the door. "My lord, I..."

Seated at the farthest library table, papers strewn across the surface before him and on the Turkish carpet behind him, his head and thin shoulders silhouetted by the sunlight streaming through the open window, was a boy, furiously scribbling.

"I'm back, Planta." Boy dipped his quill into the open inkstand before him.

"Oh, it's you." Planta hesitated, then said, "He was expecting you days ago, you know! And he was livid when you didn't turn up. How long have you been here?"

"He's never livid," Boy returned evenly, without raising his head or pausing in his writing.

"Well, he was then. How did you get in? Oh, I'd forgot, you were told about the hidden key. And we've been hearing every sort of rumour about...Od's my life, what happened to your face?"

Boy laid down the quill and turned to look directly at Planta so that he saw the full extent of the bruising.

"God's teeth!" Planta enunciated softly.

"I walked into a wall," Boy said, picking up the quill again to dip it into the ink. "I shall need more ink presently, Planta."

"A wall, you say? You walked into a wall?" Planta repeated, nodding his head in a doubtful manner. "Well, I suppose you know best." He turned and went back into the outer office, calling out, "I presume that's a full report you're writing for him."

"Yes, Planta. It is."

"No wall ever did that," Planta remarked to himself. "I'll lay any odds you like, but no wall ever did that.

"He's not going to be happy about your face, you know," he called to the next room. "He was wanting to send you to Nottingham."

"Nottingham? What's in Nottingham? Or should I say who?"

"I'm sure I don't know. Something to do with those riots they've been having up there since last year, I should imagine. He wanted someone invisible." Planta sat down behind his desk and took up his keyring. "I dare say you've picked all the locks."

There was no answer.

Planta leaned close and studied the keyhole for any new scratches on the metal, then inserted his key. The drawer was still locked. "I don't believe it," he murmured. "That dressing down he got the last time must have done some good." He opened the drawer and lifted out the top sheaf of papers. They were just as he'd left them, the black ribbon around them just as he'd tied it.

Boy listened to Planta in the next room, searching for any sign of a forced entry, any irregularities among the contents of his desk, and smiled to himself. He wouldn't find any because there weren't any to find. He had seen to that. Made certain of it. "Silly cock," he whispered, but without malice. No one caught Boy Tirrell twice. No one. He frowned and laid aside the quill to reread his last paragraph.

Joseph Planta had been Lord Castlereagh's private secretary for years now. Not yet five and twenty, he was a tallish young man with curling brown hair—a young man of remarkable ability, efficiency and discretion, a meticulously-kept person with a faint air of suppressed disapproval. Boy knew Planta disapproved of him—he could smell it like some tangible thing—and rather assumed he disapproved of the whole intelligence business. (Didn't everyone, even while they enjoyed the fruits of it?) Not that Planta ever voiced this or any other opinion. He also, Boy knew, possessed more confidential information about the war, both Houses of Parliament, foreign trade and exploration and every body involved in any or all of these activities, than any other man in the kingdom, with the sole exception of the Foreign Secretary—or perhaps Sir Charles Flint.

"Did you say you needed more ink?" Planta asked from the

doorway.

"I beg your pardon? Oh. Oh yes. Yes, I did."

Planta advanced into the room carrying a freshly-filled standish, but stopped some feet short of the table where Boy was seated. "One hesitates to ask, but is this sea of papers entirely necessary?" He nodded toward the paper-strewn floor. "Or might some of them be gathered up? Or even placed in some semblance of order? Perhaps you would care to attend to it before his lordship arrives?" He handed the ink to Boy and departed.

Boy was on his knees sorting through his morning's work when Lord Castlereagh arrived, singing Ahle's *Liebster Jesu.* He could hear the stately lilt of the sacred melody, though not its English words, from the next room, announcing as plainly as a calling card the presence of the Foreign Secretary.

He rose to his feet as Lord Castlereagh limped through the door, his carriage now marred by the gout which forced him to favour his right leg.

Boy bowed deeply. "My lord." *He* was the reason anyone engaged in this line of work. With one or two exceptions, there wasn't a man who wouldn't go to the gallows for his lordship, or to hell and back, if that was what was needed.

Lord Castlereagh made his halting way into the room. At forty-three, Robert Stewart, Viscount Castlereagh was a handsome man with greying hair, piercing dark eyes and an aquiline nose above a shapely mouth. But it was not, nor had it ever been his personal grace and beauty which made his friends adore him and his adversaries respect him. It was the quality of his temperament: his clear judgment, his common sense, his calm courage in the face of uncommon crises, his self-command and political realism, his patience and conciliatory demeanour toward those of differing opinions, his unfailingly affable and amiable manners. "My dear child, you have returned to us at last." The honourable members of the House of Commons of which he was now Leader had another word for him—they called him a gentleman. His coat was of his favourite plum colour. "...You must pardon my limp. The gout has been particularly troublesome of late."

Boy straightened. "My lord."

"Great heavens, child, your face!" In spite of the pain such action must cost him, the Foreign Secretary hurried across the room to place gentle hands, 'cellist's hands—on Boy's vivid cheeks. "'Fore God, what has happened to you? Who did this to you? Are you much hurt? My dear Boy, this is dreadful, quite dreadful!"

"It was in Kent, sir. I had never seen him before."

"In Kent, you say? Kent? I don't like that." Gently he shifted Boy's face toward the light, minutely examining the bruises and scabs that marked his cheeks, eyelids and jaw. Quietly, he said, "This is dreadful, Boy. Quite dreadful. Here…" He gestured toward one Moroccan covered chair. "You must sit down and tell me.

"Joseph!" he called, using the voice he normally reserved for his replies to the rowdiest Whig backbenchers. "Joseph! Oh, you're here. Some brandy for Tirrell, here, if you please. And if you would be so kind as to fetch me the ottoman…"

"Right away, my lord." Planta brought a low jacquard-covered ottoman from the corner.

Cautiously balancing his weight on one leg and lifting his gamy foot just off the ground, Lord Castlereagh settled himself in his chair. Planta slid the ottoman into place beneath his lordship's gouty foot.

"Ah, that is very much better. Thank you. And now the brandy?" The Foreign Secretary focused his shrewd dark eyes on Boy's face and leaned his head against his left hand. Sunlight glinted on the gold ring he wore on his small finger. "Now tell me…"

Boy had always found his lordship a good listener—a careful, intelligent, insightful listener. Without emotion, he related his story: the endless parades of troops in Paris, Brioche's death, his precipitous but premeditated departure from Paris, his trek through a northern France now depleted of men, livestock and grain, the bangster awaiting him. He omitted little.

When he had finished, Castlereagh sat silent, pondering, his eyes still narrowed upon Boy's paint-box face. Then he shifted in his chair and all at once seemed to take in the stack of papers on the nearby table. "And this is a full report?"

"Yes, my lord. A full report for the past five months."

"Documents?"

"From the War Office mostly," Boy said, with the glimmer of a grin. "Some commissary lists for the new campaign. Though the French are still calling it the 'Polish campaign', I have information that they mean to press on into Russia, if you please. Lists of promotions. Artillery lists. Provender lists. Orders for horses from Holland. And letters. I'm afraid there wasn't as much to be had on the Peninsula…Bonaparte seems to have lost interest in that…" he fretted.

The Foreign Minister laughed. "'Struth, child, you are an amazement to us all. I suppose they're all accurate." His eyes narrowed shrewdly.

"Word for word, sir. As ever."

Lord Castlereagh smiled. "But how did you come by them?"

"Upon my life, sir, they're that short of footmen in Paris these days they've even taken to hiring girls to do the heavy work…And one of the night watch has a fondness for good wine," he said earnestly. "It's a pity, sir, that such a connoisseur should be forced to spend his evenings guarding a draughty and ancient library full of musty old papers when he should be donating his knowledge and expertise to the city's vintners and publicans. Do you not agree, sir?"

Lord Castlereagh closed his eyes. "Upon my word, I shall not even contemplate the lengths to which you will go to acquire such precious information for us."

Then: "You are positive your bangster broke no bones?"

"It's as I told you, my lord, it was getting to be a close run thing, but then this Marquis of Dunphail called a halt to it and his groom patched me up. But he hadn't touched anything but my face! Which was odd. I can only believe he meant to disfigure me before I stuck my spoon in the wall."

"It very much sounds to me as though he meant to stick it in for you…But what *I* cannot fathom is Dunphail's interference." Lord Castlereagh sighed and leaned his head back against the chair's wing. "That simply don't square. It will bear watching. This does make things awkward though…I had wanted to send you to Nottingham…"

"Mr. Planta mentioned something about that…" Boy murmured. "I can still go. My face will be healed in a matter of days, my lord. I can assure you, it will."

"No. No, I need someone there now. Great God in Heaven, I needed someone there three months ago! It will have to be Shuster or Jesuadon. As for you, I must confess to being most concerned, Boy. You were nowhere to be found for weeks on end. Not that I am criticising. It is a very good thing, most times, but we did rather wish to locate you. Then Fiske heard some fishermen—I suppose he meant smugglers—he generally does, though he thinks to spare me—saying you'd gone missing. And then you turn up in Kent, too close to North Cray for comfort, getting the devil beaten out of you—which may be of some significance. Who knows?

"Something is amiss. They've smoked you. Or someone has. I do wish we knew a great deal more of this Savary! How I long for that old devil Fouché. One always knew where one stood when he was in charge. But this fellow, Savary..."

Boy stiffened. "They call him *le séide* in Paris, sir...the fanatic..." he explained softly. "Napoleon's fanatic. They do say he will do anything for him. Anything." He blinked. "There's even a joke making the rounds about it, you know. *'Si l'Empereur lui disait de vous tuer, il vous prendrait tendrement la main et vous dirait: je suis au désespoir de vous envoyer dans l'autre monde, l'Empereur le veut ainsi...'*" Boy smiled cheekily. "If the Emperor told him to kill you, he would take you tenderly by the hand and say to you, I am in despair to send you to the next world, but the Emperor wants it so."

"Great God, that is what they say of him? 'Fore heaven, I would not wish for such a thing to be said of me!" exclaimed the Foreign Minister. "I shall want to know everything you know about him, Boy. Everything! Who works for him, who spies for him, who is now under arrest, or missing; I need to know his friends, his enemies...everything."

"Yes, sir. I understand, sir—friends, family, mistresses, enemies, cousins, who they're following, who they're spying on and why...I shall begin this afternoon."

"Is Talleyrand in danger?" Castlereagh questioned sharply.

Boy shrugged. "When ain't he?"

Castlereagh smiled, his expression warming. "True." Then: "But I cannot and will not agree to any more of these bloody risks of which you are so fond, Boy. Not with a madman like that in charge! You must lie low, as I see it, and I mean low—here in London—until this blows over. And there must be no more of your pranks. D'you hear me, Boy? No more pranks!" Lord Castlereagh lowered his voice in emphasis, his habitual calm in no way ruffled by the gruesome details of Boy's recitation.

"If you mean getting those documents, there was no risk attached. I tell you, sir, Paris is emptied of men. And the fire, sir, the fire was not a prank neither."

"'Struth, child, you nearly burnt down half the rue Caulaincourt! And if there are no men in Paris, how is it that your friend Brioche managed to meet his death beneath the heel of a guardsman's boot?"

"I got out, didn't I?"

"Yes, but that is not the point. Boy, this time, you must do as I say.

"Was that a knock I heard?" He leaned his head forward so that he might see the door. "Come. Shuster, is that you?"

Cognizant of the incongruity of his shabby, not quite ragged clothes with the measured luxury of his surroundings, Boy squirmed in his seat. Though why it should suddenly bother him, he could not say. Until a fortnight since, Shuster had lived in utter squalor. True, his own room in Paris, before he'd burned it down that was, had been vermin-infested. But the appalling filth of that hovel of Shuster's…he drew a deep breath, and clutching the glass in his ink-blotched right hand, he finished his brandy.

The door swung wide and Georgie Shuster looked in. "My lord?"

"Yes, Captain, come in, do. I will not rise to greet you though." He waved a hand at his slightly swollen foot still resting on the ottoman.

Shuster smiled blithely. "No, my lord. Your gout still troubling you, is it, sir?" he asked cheerfully as he ambled into the room, his hands thrust deep into his pockets and his hat, a high-crowned bevor, pushed back on his head, school-boy fashion. He strolled first to the open window and peered out. There was no watcher opposite. Not in the street below. Not in the windows opposite. "I tell you, sir, the silly Frogs are getting sloppy. Slackers." He turned from the window.

"Hallo! Bloody hell, Tirrell, what's happened to you?" Georgie removed his hat and tossed it onto the nearest table, then leaned toward Boy and lifted his chin delicately, surveying both sides of his face. "Nice. Very nice." He scrutinised the bruising along Boy's temple.

The boy bore the examination impassively. "I might ask the same of you. Lud, I'd not known you knew what a cake of soap looked like. Let alone how to use it. I walked into a wall. What do you think happened?"

Georgie snorted. "A wall, eh? 'Struth, no wall ever did that, Boy! What did he look like, this wall of yours? A smuggler you got on the wrong side of, was he?"

"What did you say he looked like, Boy?" Lord Castlereagh asked. "Tall, wasn't it? With tightly curled hair and acne or pox scars? He called himself…"

With his forefinger beneath Boy's chin, Georgie turned his face from one side to the other, observing the various shades of discolouration thoughtfully.

"John Brown," Boy said quietly.

"John Brown?" Georgie queried. "What? He called himself John Brown? He was no John Brown. He was an amateur. A novice. A Captain Hackum." Georgie pronounced. "It must be a coincidence. No professional ever did this." He peered again at Boy's cheek and ear through narrowed eyes. "How did you take the punches? Prepare for them, did you?"

"Coincidence?" Lord Castlereagh demanded. "Coincidence? I do not believe in coincidence. There is no such thing as coincidence!"

"But, sir, it cannot have been one of Savary's lads," Georgie protested, turning to face him. "'Struth, they'd never have made such a botch job of it. Look at him! If it had been one of Savary's henchmen, he'd not be here! It would have been a swift dagger to the heart or a garrotte…They're fond of the garrotte, Savary's lads. You ask anyone." He looked again at the bruising about the boy's ears. "But this, this is the work of a bangster-to-let. Tirrell is bruised…yes, badly bruised. But nothing is broken! Which don't figure at all. Boy took the punches, as he and I and countless others would know to do, but the cove who did this—he clearly didn't know the trick of it. And he gave his name. Never, not for all the game pie in England would I tell anyone my name. And certainly not when I was busying myself with beating his stupid face in!" Georgie grabbed a straight chair and swung it round so that he might sit backward upon it, his face away from the noonday sun which now flooded the room through the three tall sash-windows, making a patchwork of light upon the multi-coloured Turkey carpet. He shook his head, puzzling over the anomalies.

His nostrils flaring, Castlereagh said, "Well, you are the expert." Then: "But I don't believe in coincidence," he restated. "There is no such thing."

Georgie fell silent and pensively bit at his bottom lip. "Well…if it ain't coincidence…then it's someone who wants us to believe he's one of Savary's men."

"Yes…" agreed Castlereagh. "But who?"

Georgie shook his head. "I don't know, sir. Flint might be the one for that. Or Jesuadon. I've not been back for long enough to know my way about the London stews…"

"Yes, of course. And I need you to go up to Nottingham in any event."

"Nottingham?"

"That's what *I* said," Boy murmured.

"Yes, Nottingham. You do realise, the pair of you, that things do happen in places other than France and Spain, do you not? I wish to know the identity of this General Ludd, the fellow behind all these riots we've had up there, and there's no getting anything out of the Home Office. Or Bow Street. I need to know if he is another of Savary's John Browns. There are far too many similarities to those little 'revolutions' the Frogs have staged all over Europe, do you see? It bears all the hallmarks of Naples. And I find it hard to credit that there is no connexion. Upon my life, I do wish for the old days when Fouché was in our pay…"

"And how am I supposed to…"

"'Struth, Georgie," Boy exclaimed. "All it will take is a slow crawl through the inns and public houses…'Suredly you can manage that!"

"And after that," Lord Castlereagh continued imperturbably. "I shall want you to go to Edinburgh Castle. They have a prisoner there who appears to know a bit too much about us and I shall want you to speak to him."

Boy stood, a shuttered look coming into his eyes and his habitual graceful composure inexplicably ebbing from him. "If it's all the same to you, my lord, I shall take my leave now." He paused, searching for some plausible excuse for his withdrawal. And found none. Bowing, he said quietly, "I'm no good when Shuster starts in with his stories of interrogation."

Georgie threw him an odd, confused look.

Castlereagh nodded. "Yes, yes, of course.

"Have Planta supply you with funds. And stay in London. When the bruising fades, we'll see…"

"Not Spain, sir! Not Spain in high summer. I don't even speak the language! Let me go back to Paris. They'll never get at me again. They'll never even get near me. I swear it!"

Georgie snorted in derision and rested his chin on the chair's high back.

"Boy," the Foreign Minister said quietly, quelling his protests. "You speak the language very well. But we shall see…And I am not asking you. I am ordering you. I shall want to talk to you again after I've had an opportunity to study your report and these documents, yes? And you shall be back later this afternoon to begin the work we discussed, yes? Good…I shall expect you then.

"Now, Shuster, tell me this. How well acquainted are you with Dunphail?"

Chapter IV

1

White's Club had been dispensing companionship and coffee for over a century. Nowadays, it was the most popular gentlemen's club in London, its premises on St. James's Street both stately and sumptuous. But it had begun as a simple arrangement. In modest surroundings. A coffeehouse it had been. Nothing more. Its proprietor stocking the day's and week's newspapers for his patrons to read while they drank his wares. A comfortable cosy place it had been then. Pepys had drunk his coffee here. Or was it chocolate? Castlereagh couldn't recall.

The dining room was still called the Coffeeroom, but a Morning Room and a Gaming Room, among other amenities, had been added for the members.

Still. Still, it was the one place in this part of the city where a man might converse with another, one not belonging to his particular set of friends perhaps, without arousing comment. Or even idle curiosity. Castlereagh liked it for that. Indeed, it suited him admirably.

The Morning Room was thin of patrons. Difficult to be out and about by eleven when one went to bed at four. The wing chairs in the bow window which faced onto St. James's Street were empty, save one. In it, Lord Alvanley sat, his chin sunk in the folds of his great starched cravat, his eyes closed, his breathing deep and regular, and his waistcoat buttons straining against the rise and fall of his ample girth. It was too early for Mr. Brummell to have even finished his daily bath.

Castlereagh limped across the room—the tapping of his walking stick silenced in the heavy carpet—to sit in a corner wing chair. A waiter brought him his coffee and silently placed it on the table at his elbow. Three old gentlemen, men of his father's generation in kneebreeches and full coats, sat at a table nearby, arguing in scratchy voices about the effect of the French war on their harvests, their purses, their roofs. Two smartly dressed Corinthians, their boots highly polished, their clothes reeking of horse, passed through the Morning room and nodded to him on their way to the Coffeeroom and their breakfast. One was Myddelton's friend, Pemberton. Friend too to Dunphail, wasn't he?

A horsefly drifted through the open sash window, buzzing loudly. It lumbered on the air like a dropsical cat, before alighting on Alvanley's sleeve. Alvanley slumbered on. The fly crawled an inch or two, then flew off, finding by chance or mistake the open window and its escape.

Castlereagh sipped at his coffee.

Alvanley stirred and settled.

Outside, sparrows hopped and chirruped, pecking at bits of warm manure in the street. A pair of newly-shod horses clattered past.

Castlereagh leaned his head against the chairback to look down his eagle's beak of a nose and ponder his gout-ridden foot. It was not improving. And hurt like the very devil.

He closed his eyes. In a voice barely above a whisper, he began to hum the 'cello's melody from the latest Haydn string quartet, marking the time on the chair arm. The second movement—marked Adagio. Which was lovely. Truly, remarkably lovely. With that lovely dip…just there. Dear Haydn, such a composer he had been. What an incalculable loss his death had been. (Damn Bonaparte. Damn all Frenchmen.) Castlereagh paused, rubbing his thumb over the hard, ridged fingertips of his right hand, and opened his eyes to inspect them. His callouses. Heavens, they'd grown soft. It would be painful to play for anything above an half hour with them grown so soft. Really, he needed to practise more. He closed his eyes and sighed. The perennial question, when?

Thos Jesuadon was a dissolute. There wasn't a tavern, publican, bawd, harlot or gaming hell in all London that he didn't know. Or didn't know him. At half-ten in the morning, the toes of his evening pumps were scuffed, their sides streaked with a dusty layer of mud. His stockings and black evening breeches were likewise grey-flecked with dirt. His cravat hung loose, lank and soiled about his neck. His fair skin was unshaven, and his hair lay in tangled curls on his collar. His eyes were bloodshot. A half-drunk bottle of claret dangled from his left hand, while in his right, he cradled a much-used glass.

Uninvited, he came and sat down beside Castlereagh. He hiccoughed softly and set his bottle and glass on the table. An only child, his father would have disowned him years ago, had not he first suffered an apoplexy and died. His mother refused to speak to him or to mention his name. It was said he had squandered his inheritance at the tables, but no one knew for certain, nor did his few close acquaintances think it likely. For he was an expert card player and punctilious in matters of play and pay. However, only an aunt, too far removed from Town to know the gossip, still acknowledged him. Jesuadon poured himself a glassful of wine and drank it down. An acrid scent of cheap perfume hung about his person, a lingering trace of his previous evening's amusement.

Castlereagh smiled genially. "A very fine morning. The fog appears to have lifted for the present. Young Bretherton says he's being followed," he murmured by way of a greeting. He nodded politely to the old gentlemen who were now rising from their seats.

Jesuadon stared at his empty glass, then refilled it. "Henry Bretherton? Our Henry?" He hiccoughed. Henry Bretherton was a clown and a coxcomb. A vain, silly peacock of a coxcomb. He was also adept at appearing far stupider than he really was. He was a master at it. He'd been doing it all his life. Jesuadon didn't like him.

"The very same." Castlereagh hummed a few bars of *Liebster Jesu.*

Jesuadon took a gulp of claret.

Alvanley muttered in his sleep, smacked his lips, then began to snore.

"He fears he has been sniffed out." Castlereagh signalled to a passing waiter to remove his empty coffee cup.

Jesuadon belched. "Who could possibly suspect Henry Bretherton of anything other than pinching the chambermaid?" He closed his eyes, almost, it seemed, dozing off.

"Precisely the reason that I am concerned," Castlereagh said mildly. "He is too good a courier to risk. And as you say, who would suspect him?"

"I don't believe it," Jesuadon stated, opening his eyes and slouching back in his chair to stare blindly out of the window. A soft haze filtered the sunlight. He gave a sudden start. "I don't believe it. Infant Tirrell, perhaps. But not young Bretherton."

Castlereagh drew a deep breath. "To be sure, Tirrell is also being followed."

"Now that don't surprise me," Jesuadon said, pouring the remains of the claret into his glass. "The damned Frogs are obviously stupid, but no one can be that stupid."

"He was caught and nearly beaten to death. In Kent it was—near North Cray, so I've doubled the watch there. The bangster in question said his name was John Brown, which both Shuster and Tirrell assure me must be coincidence. But I do not believe in coincidence. So I want you to look into it. Look into both situations. Tirrell is at the lodgings in the Almonry, I suspect. Or did he say Seven Dials, this time?"

Jesuadon studied the wine clinging to the rim of his glass, then drank it. He wiped his mouth on his shirt cuff. "That beating must have been a fake. My word on it. 'Struth, I can't see anyone laying hands on Tirrell." He looked directly at the Foreign Secretary for the first time since he had sat down. "He's an eel, that lad."

Castlereagh leaned his head against the chair's padded wing and said patiently, "I give you my word, Tirrell's beating was not a fake. My only wish is that it had been. 'Pon my soul, the child is lucky to be alive and in one piece. His eyes had been blackened to the colour of my coat. As had his jaw. It is all fading now, thankfully, and there appears to be little permanent harm. But I must tell you, even so, Shuster did express the opinion that it was not the work of a professional."

"I'faith, he would know." Jesuadon hiccoughed. "Right then. I shall see to it."

"Thank you. I expect Tirrell will be leaving for the Continent by the end of next week, so look in on him soon, will you?"

Castlereagh ran his thumb back and forth over his callouses, hesitating. He folded and unfolded his hands, then brought them to rest on the chair's arms. "Now tell me, what do you know about Dunphail?"

"Dunphail?" The question surprised him. Slouching back in his chair, Jesuadon pressed the heels of his hands to his eyes. Then, removing his hands, he turned to stare bleakly, blearily, out of the open window. "Nothing. The usual. What everyone knows. He's a friend of Myddelton and Pemberton, ain't he? Was at school with 'em. He's Ned Hardy's cousin. And he spends most evenings in the schools of Venus on King Street."

"Ah…That, I had not known. Anything else?" Castlereagh focused his shrewd eyes on Jesuadon's tired ones. An unusual colour, Jesuadon's eyes. Amber and green. But perhaps not atypical in one of his fair colouring with such pale skin and faded red-gold hair.

Jesuadon shook his head. "No. He plays a fine hand of piquet. And a better partner at whist you'll not find. Did you want something arranged?"

"No. Oh no," Castlereagh assured him. "I simply wish to know."

"Why? What's he done?"

"It was he who rescued Tirrell from that nearly fatal beating."

Jesuadon lowered his chin into his cravat, suppressing another burp. "'Swounds, that don't sound like Dunphail. Did he know who it was he'd rescued? It wasn't all a feint, was it? No?" Jesuadon rose slowly to his feet, his expression in that brief instant sharp, alert, considering, and quite at odds with his appearance and reputation. "I shall see what I can find." He slipped his hands into his coat pockets. And without looking again at the Foreign Secretary, he strolled away.

Castlereagh closed his eyes and pressed his fingertips together beneath his chin.

Alvanley sputtered, shifted his head slightly, and sighing, slept on.

2

Like a musician setting out to practise his scales before he begins the real work of the day—deliberately, routinely, absently—Jesuadon set off to find the boy by strolling eastward up the Strand, in the opposite direction from the Devil's Acre. He loitered for a bit in Covent Garden, wandering amongst the single-storey timber lock-ups and wooden stalls of the fruit and veg men and the flower sellers, who were all shouting and hawking their wares to the crowds, while he enjoyed, though not with any particular interest, the promenading of young prostitutes there. And laughing off the blandishments and playful caresses of a pair who wished to rouse his passions or pick his pockets or both, he bought a ripened peach. Then, he ambled northwards towards the Rookery, to idle in the passageways and lanes there, all the while swigging from his ubiquitous claret bottle, before taking a hackney carriage in the direction of Clare Market, where he remained, drinking, propping up a mouldering hovel at the entrance to a court known as Dark Entry—while anyone ill-advised enough to follow him would have long given up for boredom.

Eventually, he made his way toward Drury Lane and from thence took a hackney carriage down the length of the Thames toward Westminster Abbey and the notorious Devil's Acre. Castlereagh might quaintly refer to it as the Almonry, but any creature who had had the misfortune to walk the cess-soaked alleys and streets of this stinking slum with its whores, thieves and debtors, beneath the grim and blackened ruins of old houses which leaned precariously or were shored up by great blackened timbers, knew it for what it was. Still, it was better than the Mint.

Jesuadon slipped down a side alley and lounged near a doorway, then made his way up a back staircase to the top floor where he found not the eel of a boy with his bruise-blotched face, but a pair of whores, or perhaps a young prostitute and her bawd, new to Town and eager or anxious to make the acquaintance of this (to their eyes) well-dressed toff, to turn his unlikely appearance to their benefit.

As through a drunken haze, Jesuadon swept them both into his arms, bestowing upon them each smacking kisses and convincingly mismanaged and hopeless fumblings. And then suddenly, stopped, saying, "Sorry, my lovelies. Not today. My profoundest apologies. Another time…" Before bowing his way foolishly from the room as if he were about to spew his guts. Which he did, beside the doorway to the alley. And set forth again. This time in the direction of St. Martin-in-the-Fields and the slums thereabouts.

Adam Sparrowhawk was a tall lean man with a ruddy open countenance and a thatch of black hair who ran a public house of almost respectable character near Charing Cross. That is to say, he ran a tavern and city inn where the male gentry could come in safety and openly carouse with their inferiors, and the girls were clean. Under the guise of being too preoccupied with his flourishing business and the running of things—the delivery of casks and kegs, of fowl and vegetable, the supervision of his kitchen, the maintaining of order and a modicum of decency—Sparrowhawk appeared to remember little, few faces and fewer names. And remembered everything. Jesuadon fancied he might have preferred to have joined the army. But the Foreign Office and Sir Charles Flint had had other more pressing employment for him, or better pay, and so he remained where he was, the proprietor of the rambling public house near the centre of all comings and goings, arrivals and departures, Charing Cross.

And it was there that Jesuadon finally ran the boy to ground. In a single room under the eaves of Sparrowhawk's bustling premises, at the end of a warren of halls and false doorways, the sole access to which was via a private staircase that rose up from a small door beside the kitchen's vast roasting hearth. Only those known personally and well to Sparrowhawk were even aware of its existence.

And having helped himself to two bottles as he passed through the kitchen, Jesuadon paused just outside the final rear false door, knocked twice, and let himself into the long low room, the far end of which was dominated by a large unmade four poster bed with the curtains half drawn. But the boy was not, as Jesuadon had expected him to be, lolling upon the bed, or asleep, or even reading. Instead he was seated at a small table finishing his dinner, the last of a meat pie. The smell of the gravy and grease hung rich and redolent upon the air. He looked up without alarm. "What do you want?"

Jesuadon paused on the threshold, looking and looking at the damaged face—the eyes were now unswollen, but across his cheekbones like two great scabs the skin was stained a vivid plum red, which faded into temples mottled purple and yellow and brown. Likewise his jaw. Jesuadon winced and screwed up his mouth. "I've spent half the day looking for you…" he complained, coming to sit at the small table. "The Guvnor said you was down the Devil's Acre." He set the bottles down on the table and uncorked the nearest.

"I didn't like the company," the boy said, sniffing hard. "You stink of cheap whores, so you can't have been searching the whole time." Pointedly, he got up and stalked across to the open dormer to perch upon the sill, propping his feet against the window jamb as he looked out upon the street below where an onset of rain was causing the pedestrians to hurry or put up umbrellas against the downpour. "If you ain't careful, you'll end up poxed, you know. With your brains shrinking and your bits falling off…"

Silently, Jesuadon eyed him. And undeterred by the apparent rancour, ignoring it even, he picked up the three books on the table to read their titles. Then setting them aside, he helped himself to the heel end of a small roundel of dark bread, and began to mop, meticulously and slowly, the remaining gravy from off the dish, and to eat it. Finishing at last, he licked the residue from off each of his fingertips. "So, how bad is it really?"

The boy said nothing, but continued to look away.

"Was he following you?"

The subject of the question was never in doubt. "He cannot have been," the boy snapped with a startling bitterness. "I would have noticed."

Jesuadon pressed on: "But he caught you…"

Tirrell said nothing but stared straight ahead at the wall. For despite that appearance of insouciance in the face of such danger which he had presented to Lord Castlereagh, to Planta and to Shuster, he had been left profoundly shaken, and his customary detachment had been seeping away day by day, displaced by a fear or even anguish that had little to do with his physical hurts.

Jesuadon regarded him. A caught spy was a dead spy. They both knew it. Patiently he waited, drinking steadily. Had the boy been killed he would have been searched. 'Struth, it didn't bear thinking on. "Look, you pea-brained whelp, I need you to tell me what happened, so stop buggering me about an' tell me!"

The boy slanted him a truculent glance. "No! Why should I?" he said. "I've already told the Guvnor..."

"I know what you told Castlereagh," said Jesuadon starkly, patient again. "You told him what you thought he could bear to hear. 'Struth, you protected him as we all do. But I need to know what happened. Was you followed?"

The boy sat mute for a long time, sat in brooding anger all the while the light faded and afternoon bled into evening. Sat taciturn, still and unyielding, as Jesuadon finished one bottle and started on the second. Then, giving way, he shook his head. "No," he answered positively. "No, Savary's men had been out watching for about a fortnight in Paris. But then, once I was out on the rooftops, there was no one."

"And there was no one following you across the Channel?"

"No. The crossing was too rough."

Calmly Jesuadon regarded the claret bottle in his hand. "Can you be certain?"

"Yes."

"So...if he did not follow you from France, where did you pick him up?"

His head hanging, again, the boy slowly shook it. "Dashed if I know." He shrugged. "It must have been somewhere past Winchelsea." He rubbed his hair with the effort of thinking, exhaled loudly, then left the window and went to lay flat on the bed.

Jesuadon watched him. "So...what happened?"

Boy sighed. "It's as I told the Guvnor. I was passing through this hamlet, cottages on either side of the road, nothing more, and he lurched into me, quite deliberately I would have said, and said, 'Hey, what do you think you're about...' Or something like that. And then he cuffed me hard, about the ear. Just like that. I give you my word, Thos, he came out of nowhere."

Jesuadon sat silent, a scowl on his face, digesting this. He took a long swig from the bottle. "And then?"

"And then he nearly beat my head in..." The boy's jaw tightened with remembered fear and planning and exploding pain. "I did not resist. Of course. There would have been no point. All I could think was that if I did as Shuster had taught me, and prepared for those blows, that somehow I would come out alive. So I just kept saying to myself, Wait for it, prepare, take it. I just kept Georgie's voice in my head as if he was there beside me, telling me what to do..." For an instant, the boy covered his eyes with his hand, propping his head up.

Tactfully Jesuadon waited. "You did right..." He took a last swig from his bottle and found it treacherously empty. He belched, wiping his mouth on his sleeve. "So what did he look like?"

"What can it matter?" Boy said, once again inexplicably angered.

Jesuadon gave him a hard raking glance, a surprisingly steely and clear-eyed look that sat ill with his debauched demeanour. "What are you hiding, you infernal brat?"

"What?" the boy cried. "What have I to hide? Nothing! I hide nothing. I have nothing to hide! I don't remember."

"Red hell an' bloody death, you pestilential child! From the bruising along your temple, it's a dashed miracle he didn't crush your poxy skull," Jesuadon shouted. "That he failed to do so is nothing short of a marvel! For he certainly intended it. And the Guvnor wants to know why. And he has set me the not insubstantial task of finding this bangster. So, tell me what he looked like before I choke it out of you, you infernal nocky-boy!"

Mutinous, breathing hard through pinched nostrils, the boy stared hard at him. "Scélérat," he mouthed upon an emission of breath.

Steadfast, Jesuadon remained as he was, did not give way. Then, he peered into the bottom of the first bottle as if unaware of the boy's rage, and softening his approach, sighed and repeated, "The Guvnor has set *me* the insignificant task of finding him, d'you see? And if I am to do so to his lordship's satisfaction, I shall need to know who or what I am looking for." He looked up again and now smiled amicably through the shadows. "So...what did he look like?"

The boy shrugged and did not reply. Then, he closed his eyes. And setting aside the anger that gnawed at him, and the hateful scourge of vulnerability, at last used the talent for which he was justly renowned, the talent which made him such an asset, which bound him head and hand to the Foreign Office, the talent to recall and remember every detail, of faces once seen, of documents once read, of music once played. And with a bleakness he could not contain, he began bitterly: "It all happened so fast, I didn't stop to take him in. But he was tall. Very tall and big. Deep-chested and broad, with these massive forearms—like one of Cribb's bruisers. And ugly." He gave an unexpected angry laugh. "Truly ugly." He paused, considering, then began again: "Beetle-browed with dark eyes and a low forehead. His cheeks was pox-scarred too. An infernal cribbage-face he was, if you want the truth. He must have been in the ring at some point. But…his nose…'Fore God, that must have been broken at least half a dozen times." He looked up in recollection.

"He sounds a picture," Jesuadon murmured gently. "A rare and choice specimen for the phiz-mongers…"

Boy gave a reluctant chuckle. "Aye." And continued, more easily now: "He had brown hair. In tightly matted curls. And quite long. But I'm not convinced he was a Navy man, for he had no tattoos. Or none that I saw. But he could have been army."

"Scarred, was he?"

"No…Yes," the boy corrected himself. "There…" He ran his middle finger over his left brow and down his temple.

Jesuadon narrowed his eyes. "Sabre or bayonet?"

"Sabre," the boy replied instantly. "Or knife."

Jesuadon folded his lips together, storing this detail along with the others, like grain against the coming winter. "Excellent."

The boy lay back against the unmade bed, reflecting, reviewing it all, moment by moment, blow by blow, again in his mind. As he had been doing since it happened. Then, suddenly alert, he sat up, blinking. "French. He was French," he pronounced definitely.

Jesuadon leaned forward. "Can you be certain? How do you know?"

The boy shook his head frantically. "I don't know," he exclaimed. "His smell? But I would swear to it. I know it. He was French."

Jesuadon rubbed his face and his hair and his temple. "Christ, Castlereagh is going to have Flint's head for this," he said baldly and without mercy. "And his bawbles, if he ain't careful." He blew out a breath of air. "Anything else?"

"He did say his name was John Brown."

"Ha!" Jesuadon exclaimed harshly. "Coincidence!"

Boy shook his head. "Castlereagh don't believe in coincidence. He said so himself…" He plucked at the coverlet. "What will you do when you find him?"

"What do you think?"

"He's mine," the boy said shortly.

"Not if Castlereagh gets to him first, he ain't. You'll be lucky to spit on his coffin…"

Aggrieved again, the boy rolled onto his side, turning his back upon Jesuadon.

Jesuadon yawned, rubbed his eyes. "So tell me about Dunphail? A bit of luck then?"

No answer.

"You can get off your damned high ropes, Tirrell, and tell me about Dunphail," he said wearily.

"There is nothing to tell! I had never seen him before."

Jesuadon rolled his eyes. "But you'd recognise him anywhere now, I'll reckon."

"Well, yes, of course I would," the boy admitted.

"And you don't think he knew your bully-boy or anything of that nature? It wasn't a set up, was it?" And correctly interpreting the fury of the disdainful glare, and not needing the stinging response, Jesuadon said, "All right, all right." He stood and stretched. "I'm going…" Then: "The Guvnor says you're off to the Continent as soon as your face is healed."

The boy sat up. "That's right. Holland. And then Austria."

Jesuadon nodded. "How was it in Paris?"

Boy shrugged. "Empty. No one but a few lowly government officials and dogsbodies left. And the whores. Everyone else is gone. The building sites are all deserted. It's a wasteland."

Patiently, consideringly, Jesuadon regarded him still. Then: "'Pon my life, not many would have survived, you know. But you did. You did well, Boy. You did well." He belched.

"Sod it all, tell you what, come out with me tonight," Jesuadon offered. "'Struth, it's more than time you lost that precious virginity of yours, lad…My word as a gentleman as was. It'll do you a world of good…best thing for you."

Chapter V

1

It may have been the Year of Our Lord 1812, but neither such civilised and civilising refinements as dominated the newly built West End of London, nor such standards of dress and cleanliness as Mr. Brummell had initiated, had penetrated here in the Rookery, the notorious enclave of the indigent or criminal Irish. Though to be sure, Thos Jesuadon had never feared to walk here. With his red-gold hair, he might have been taken for one of their own.

The Black Swan was a low alehouse, but it was not the meanest in the parish of St. Giles. Dark, despite the long light of the June evening, the air was thick and stale with a fug of tobacco smoke and too many unwashed bodies—worse with the heat and humidity of early summer—its panelled walls and uneven ceiling blackened with layers of tallow and soot.

Jesuadon, now dressed in a creased, stained coat, shouldered his way through the roomful of drinkers—whose bumpers of ale and many bottles of blue ruin covered the surface of every table—toward the bar, and came to stand beside one who looked a thorough-going rogue in a brown coat. Expecting to wait, Jesuadon propped an elbow on the bar.

The large man beside him shifted uneasily as if he disliked the proximity of strangers to his person, and continued to stare straight ahead, before shifting the whole of his attention upon his tankard of ale and the gin bottle beside it. He might have been a fence, a pickpocket, a thief, an occasional worker, or turned his hand to all of these in his time. But nothing about him was memorable, nothing except perhaps his lashless eyes.

Jesuadon slid a coin across the counter to the innkeeper, a corney-faced man of uncertain temper. Without speaking, the innkeeper put a bottle of equally uncertain claret on the counter before him, then brought up a glass from below the counter which he placed beside it. The transaction complete, the innkeeper moved further down the bar to bargle with an acquaintance.

Jesuadon uncorked the bottle and ignored the glass. "Yes?" he said crisply.

The lashless eyes blinked. And in a voice barely audible above the rascally, boisterous merriment and hubbub, he said, "As to the Scottish gentleman, there is nothing.

"I cannot say what the Guvnor's after, but there is nothing on him. No great expenditure. No sudden increase in the ready. He passes every evening the same. The theatre. The better end of King Street. His club. He ain't badly dipped. And he rarely plays except at his club and then only with his particular friends.

"He appears to have taken a fancy to a little seamstress, I believe she is. Or a milliner. And I expect he will succeed in that. He has a great deal of address, from what I've seen. But I hardly think that merits a watch, if you don't mind my saying so. Why is he interested?"

Jesuadon shrugged, almost imperceptibly. "No idea. He did something…unusual."

"Well, he's got no foreign connections that I could find. If that's what he wants to know."

"Damn. Anything else?" Jesuadon shook his head. Another dead end, then.

"No. I have made enquiries. But no one has seen the individual you describe. Though I agree with the boy. He sounds army or navy to me—with that hair. But the foreign community has had no additions. No additions and no losses. Not in Soho. Not in the districts. They're just the same as ever. And the dockside yielded nothing neither. I'll send a lad down to the Mint though, on the morrow, just to be certain. But I don't see your man going unnoticed there, do you?"

Jesuadon shrugged again. "I suppose it's possible. But I doubt it." He closed his eyes against the frustration. Castlereagh would be far from pleased. Sniffing hard, he reached into his coat pocket, fumbled for a moment and withdrew his hand. A twist of paper fell from his pocket. He reached to pick it up from the filthy floor. "Yours, I believe," he said with a nod.

"Why thank'ee, sir," the lashless man said distinctly. "Very kind, indeed. 'Tis a welcome thing to meet with an honest man. Thank'ee, indeed." He drank down his ale thirstily, then ordered another.

2

In Spain he had slept on his horse in weather like this, Georgie remembered. With his great cloak wrapped about him just as it was now, tucked about the saddle and under the stirrups. They all had. But even so, he was wet through—soaked to his smallclothes. He had been this hour and more. His back ached where the surgeon's knife had been none so clever after Talavera. And the reins were slippery and sliding through his fingers. And still, overhead, the massing tiers of dismal blue-black cloud burgeoned and mounted and swirled. Then, with a thunderous roar, it came, the raindrops, hard and sudden, pelting his cheeks, beating down upon the horse's neck and nose, clattering on the ground and in the standing water, stinging and hard as hailstones. There were songs about riding home to one's sweetheart in soakers like this, but he didn't know them. Not in English, anyway. And he'd forgot how it rained like this at midsummer in England. In Spain, this kind of rain was a pleasure generally reserved for the month of May.

Nottingham had been an infernal waste of time. After spending days on end hunched over pints of local ale, listening to the local tradesmen, yammering on in their thick regional dialect which was none too soft on the ear, he had discovered what? Like others before him, he had heard a fair old bit of inflammatory bilge about the rights of men to work their looms by hand without the introduction of soulless machinery. And he had little doubt that there were or had been French agents in the area. But he couldn't prove it. He could discover no name, beyond rumour of some mythical general called Ludd. Nor had he any doubt that the Government had been right to call out the militias to stem the tide of rioting, for the damned French were always at it. 'Struth, it was all of a piece. And these were damnably unsettled times. Still, he had no names and could prove nothing. The locals had long since grown suspicious of strangers. And the weavers and mechanicals spouting their pernicious Frenchie ideals were in their cups, but sober or sluiced, would barely have known one end of a pike from the other. As for organising a plot? Ha! They hadn't the stomach for it. Nor the rage. Nor the taste for blood. Not like the damnèd godless Frogs.

And now Edinburgh. Where he was meant to interrogate some idle cock of a French prisoner of war who appeared to know too much. Which was probably nothing more than a few lucky guesses, a fevered imagination, and bloody boasting, designed to gain him preferential treatment from the other desperate scum incarcerated there.

The dank city lanes were empty of few but himself. For who would have business they would not postpone in such weather? From out an open window, he heard a fiddler beginning to practise or play, a thin ribbon of music promising warmth and an evening's pleasure for some. 'Struth, he wished for a woman here, with fair hair and fairer skin, to share his dinner and then his bed.

Ahead, the great walled fortress of the Castle rose up from out the sheer grey rock-face of the Mound. And above, the ceiling of well-charged cloud continued to pour forth its wares, the granite sky reflected in the water-stained stone-face of the fortress walls and the buildings within their protecting, their slate roofs shining dark with the wet. Grey upon grey, dark upon dark, and all built so long ago that it might have risen from the volcanic spine of rock rather than having been raised there, stone by stone, by the sweat and will of man. And all he could think was thank Christ he'd not been sent to reconnoitre for a siege engine. For you'd not take it. Not with mining, not with cannon. You might starve them out. But there was no other way in than up through the old mediæval town, the High Street to the Lawnmarket to the Castle

Approach, with tall houses lining the street. Six storeys tall, even seven, they were. But, by God, a defending army might house a whole regiment in one of those, ready to blast you to hell and beyond…

The bay hunter he'd picked up in York, after his own horse had pulled up lame, had spooked at every shrub and clump of heather since they'd crossed the Tweed—and at every cow pat, the rangy beggar. Whoever said that fleas were the only creatures capable of jumping sideways hadn't met with this pisser. But now, with pale stone houses on either side of him, all muted to a monochrome of mud by the constant downpours, and the wind and rain beating against him, he had settled, and had lowered his head to plod slowly on up the hill onto the Castle's Lower Ward.

They passed under the 16-pounders of the vast stark bulge of the Half Moon Battery and into the Middle Ward through the great stone Portcullis Gate, the guardsmen saluting as Georgie rode past, although they could see only the outline of his officer's bicorne under its oilskin cover.

Straightening in the saddle, stiffening his back, Georgie squeezed gently on the greasy wet reins to halt. The rain appeared to have ceased for the moment. But within the expanse of the Middle Ward and the castle fortifications, all was still grey.

Grey above, beneath, within and without. The leaden sky and perpetual rain had transmuted all the pale limestone buildings to a grim charcoal; and the soot from the coal fires had stained the walls too as it trickled over the stone-faces and pointing. Here and there, stones in the outer wall had been blackened by the wet and stood out against the constant grey, as did the great blackened cannon—another sixteen pounder—which pointed out over Nor'loch. The few soldiers on duty, their red coats covered by heavy oilskin cloaks, heads down and shoulders hunched, hurried from place to place, avoiding the deeper puddles. And overhead in the skyful of billowing grey, a single red kite was taking advantage of the break in the squall to circle and soar, searching for a meal before the next cloudburst, his feathered chestnut chest visible below and bright against the white of his underwing.

Georgie sat for a moment, water still trickling from his temples and sideburns, then swung his leg over the saddle to dismount. "Good lad…" He patted the bay's rain-soaked neck. "Good lad." 'Struth, he could do with a bath…and a sweetheart.

But from the moment a servant came to lead his horse away, and he had stood to salute Colonel Fitzroy, the garrison's jowly commanding officer, he found himself swept along on a tide of civilities. First, he must be made welcome, must be shown to a private chamber—and yes, to be sure, a hot bath provided right away—he must be invited to the Officers' Mess for a formal dinner, as guest of honour no less; he must be feted, must be toasted and have his health drunk, must be celebrated by this collection of parade ground soldiers, few of them with any experience of the world beyond this small provincial posting. (Indeed, their eager questioning and barracks' humour showed them to have little sense of life on campaign or their country being at war at all.) And then, but naturally, he must speak to them of the Great Man, his lordship, the Duke of Wellington.

He kept a tight smile in place as Colonel Fitzroy poured them each another glass of cognac. For now, with an alertness which sat at odds with an evening's drinking, Georgie had begun to fancy that the Colonel was procrastinating. Or prevaricating. Or a bit of both. Which made no sense. Particularly after all the cognac.

The Colonel raised his glass. "To the Duke of Wellington, our brave Commander in Chief." A large man, he was possessed of a booming mellifluous voice.

"The Duke," Georgie repeated. And drank down his nth glassful. Deliberately he set the glass upon the table. They had moved from the Officers' Mess to the Colonel's private quarters—a neat panelled chamber with a window looking out on the Middle Ward.

"Another?" offered the Colonel, reaching for the bottle.

Georgie shook his head, gathering his few remaining unfuddled wits as well as he might. "I thank you, no, Colonel. I should be making for my bed." He paused to focus. "Colonel, we have, ehm, not referred to it, but…if you will permit me, might I enquire if this is a convenient moment in which to discuss the purpose of my visit here? For I feel sure that Horse Guards will have written to you of my business in coming."

He had dressed for the evening in the full glory of his A.D.C.'s scarlet uniform with blue facings and gold epaulets upon both shoulders.

"Yes, yes. To be sure, so they did," the Colonel replied, his bluff after-dinner glow not at all dispelled. "Though there was no need, you know. No need whatsoever, I give you my word. To be sure, I replied to their letter not a sennight past to tell them just that very thing."

Georgie favoured the Colonel with a swift glance, his pleasant cognac haze dissipating, then veiled his surprise as his mind fumbled with the word, 'what?' For the Colonel had had the notice of his coming from Horse Guards—and who was so unwise as to say 'no' to Horse Guards? Confounded and disbelieving, with the utmost mildness, Georgie said, "Forgive me, sir, might I be so bold as to enquire as to the reason?"

"Well, there was no dashed point to it, d'you see? No need," the Colonel said, still altogether amiable. "It's as I wrote them in the report. The fellow they wished for you to question escaped, do you see? And met with an accident." He shrugged. "He died, I'm obliged to say. And there's an end to it. Your journey has been wasted."

He wasn't prevaricating. Or procrastinating. Stunned into sobriety, and watching Fitzroy's mouth closely, Georgie could see that. Could see that there was no glistening of nervous sweat upon his upper lip. Curiously he regarded him, the career officer whom the fellows at Horse Guards kept at home to kick his heels—without a doubt they had their reasons—though he had assumed it must be lack of connexions. And clearing his mind, now wary, and alert to every nuance of speech, every expression which sat upon the Colonel's overhanging forehead, every quiver of his florid countenance, with a deceptive courtesy, Georgie said, "I beg your pardon, sir?"

Fitzroy did not notice. "Upon my word, it was a damnable cock-up, I make no bones about that," he confided. "And so I told them. I'd gone off for a few days to pay a visit to a cousin. And returned to find the very devil of a commotion, with Le Brun gone. Escaped—no one knew how—and all hell to pay. That's the problem with these infernal Frenchies. Too clever by half and not an ounce of honour in them, damn them." He waggled his head in disgust over the whole race.

Staring blindly ahead, Georgie sat, remained, as he had been, apparently at his ease, while his mind struggled with a dozen conflicting emotions. Chiefest among them that Castlereagh would have a fit of apoplexy when he heard this. Oh cock! He gave his head a minute shake to clear it. Wellington would have demanded the resignation of Fitzroy's commission. Or a court martial. In his inner breast pocket, he could feel the folded and sealed papers that were his orders, signed by the Foreign Secretary. The orders that said he took his orders directly from the Foreign Secretary, and the Commander in Chief of the Army, and as such was Fitzroy's superior officer. And keeping his face an affable blank, Georgie, the interrogator upon whom Wellington relied, pulled himself ruthlessly and hastily together to prompt gently: "And had no one any idea of his plans or destination? The other prisoners, perhaps?"

As one who knew himself to have done his duty and made a damned fine fist of it, Colonel Fitzroy bestowed a warm but condescending smile upon the junior officer. "Well, to be sure, Captain, his cell mates was not inclined to speak at first, but I soon had them talking. And it came about that he had bribed and threatened the fellows with beatings…"

Upon the word 'beatings' Georgie stilled. Remained perfectly and utterly still, while the Colonel gabbled on: "…so that they covered for his whereabouts that evening. And then, he picked the lock and made his escape in the ordure wagon. And I regret to say, it was only discovered in the morning. A full search of the Castle was conducted, I can assure you. But he had gone."

"He escaped in the night wagon?" Georgie repeated, diverted. Great God, they should have been able to follow his scent for miles.

"No, no." The Colonel countered. "No, I fancy he made his escape by hanging onto the undercarriage, don't you see? For to be sure, 'tis the one wagon the men would not have searched…"

What? Sweet Christ! Georgie's mind reeled with the slackness, the appalling stupidity of the whole business here. Nor indeed could the Colonel say for certain that that was what had happened. "I see," said Georgie. And he did. All too clearly. "And when did all of this occur?" he asked, now with friendly interest, subduing and subsuming his anger, deflecting his rage, while his mind scrambled for the links between what he already knew, what he had been looking for and what might have occurred here…if only he could get to the truth.

The Colonel did not detect his guest's increased sobriety, nor did he realise that he had mistook his man. He frowned as he considered Georgie's question. "Oh, well, I dare say it's getting on for a month now," he said, nodding thoughtfully. "Yes, that will be it. For I was at my cousin's at the beginning of the month of June. To be sure, so I was." Then, surprisingly, his tone brightened. "But, do you know, it ain't quite the cock-up it sounds. Upon my word, so it was not. A day or so later, do you see, he was found, on the coast. Dead. With his face beaten in. It seems the damnable traitor had tried to make free with some fisherman's wife, and I don't doubt the fellow had taken exception to it."

Dead, with his face beaten in, Georgie's mind echoed. With his face beaten in. It meant nothing. Georgie drew a long breath and remained apparently unmoved and untroubled. "And where would that have been?" he probed.

"Oh, along the coast, to the east, near Dunbar, it was." The Colonel, believing himself to be in the company of an uncritical listener, continued to confide: "We've not spoken to the fisherman yet…I make no doubt but that he's in hiding because he killed his man. But we'll soon discover his whereabouts, you have my word. He shan't escape me…"

Georgie paused, narrowing his eyes, cloaking the evidence of his growing fury. For there were too many coincidences here. And his lordship did not like coincidences—he said he did not believe in them. "Out of curiosity, Colonel, did the escaped prisoner, did he perchance speak English?"

"Yes, oh yes," Fitzroy nodded, and assured him cheerfully. "We try to ensure they all speak English. It makes our job easier, don't you see?"

Castlereagh would suffer an apoplexy for this.

Still, and barely breathing, still, and wholly self-possessed, Georgie said quietly: "And remind me, the prisoner's name?"

"Le Brun, Captain. Jean le Brun, he was called."

Georgie nodded. Le Brun? Brown. Jean le Brun. John Brown. The nom de guerre of all French agents working in England. Red hell and bloody death! What the fuck of a confounding devil was this? But it couldn't be. Could Colonel Fitzroy be the complete cretin he appeared?

And Jean le Brun was dead. He had to be. With his face beaten in. Like Boy. Almost like Boy. 'Sdeath, was this some new deadly tactic that Savary's men were adopting?

Like a man scrambling up a crumbling rockface, his mind clutching for fixed handholds, within himself, Georgie quelled the clamour of emotion to silently digest the implications. And drew another deep breath. At last, patiently and entirely unflustered, he murmured, "Forgive me..." he shook his head, smiling as if the pleasant cognac haze still encircled his brain. "Too much of your excellent cognac, sir—where up the coast did you say he was he found?"

"Oh, not far, Captain. Not far at all. An hour's ride, no more."

"And the fisherman's wife. Who spoke to her?"

The Colonel appeared startled. "Why, no one, Captain," he declared in some surprise. "Od's death, she was a fisherman's wife!" he exclaimed. "To be sure, my men enquired in the village and that's what they was told. But upon my word, after such an ordeal I cannot believe she was in a fit state to talk to anyone. Though one can never tell with such creatures as fishwives—I make no doubt that such rough treatment is all she's used to. Perhaps 'twas she who beat his face in, eh?" he joked.

Georgie managed a quizzical smile. He had observed many who had suffered the bouts of French savagery. During his years in Spain. And France. He blinked away the memories. "I see. Thank you, Colonel. Upon my word, you have been helpfulness itself." He paused, then added with an express air of apology, "But...if I might, in the morning, I should be most grateful for a guide to take me to the place where the body was found. And I shall hope to speak to the fisherman's wife as well. If she has recovered from her ordeal. For she may be able to give me a description of her attacker." He'd speak to the woman and then he'd know for certain.

The Colonel nodded conspiratorially, and winked. "Oh yes, oh yes," he agreed. "To be sure, they'll want a witness, I fancy, and everything confirmed all right and tight, in Horse Guards, won't they? It's always the same. Very right and proper, I call it though. Very right and proper, to be sure. Shall we have a last glass? What do you say?"

Chapter VI

1

Overnight, the rain had stopped, leaving the countryside around the city fresh and green and lush—as unlike the barren plateaus and mountains of Castille or the storm-battered coast of Brittany as could be. Puffs of slow cloud idled their way across a blue sky, while high over Calton Hill, a pair of red kite circled, weaving patterns in the air. And scattered over the hillside which dropped down from the Castle fortress—now bleached to a pale gold by the bright morning light—foxgloves, wild pink and tall, were bending and bowing in the sharp breeze.

They made their way out of the city at a smart trot—leaving behind the bustle and hum of hawkers and tradesmen and military drill, into the rolling farmlands to the south and east, Georgie and Fletcher, the awkward and silent young man whom Colonel Fitzroy had provided to act as guide and escort—to canter along the grassy verges and narrow by-ways between fields of rippling grain, bordered by the dry stone walls, which broke in two the constant winds that buffeted crop and cattle alike. They passed through Haddington with its churches and fine houses. And continuing east, Georgie paused to ask Fletcher about an ancient ruined fort they saw atop a low summit. Fletcher regarded the ruin in question, then shook his head. "I am sorry, sir, I do not know…"

At last they came to Dunbar—quaint, small and prosperous with a well-kept kirk and graveyard, a Market street lined with neat stone houses, stark and fine with shining brass knockers, and elegant draperies in their windows. And walking through the busy lanes, their horses' hooves clattering on the grey cobbles, every now and again, the Captain would slow to touch his hat to the finer young ladies they saw.

"Ladies…" he said, stopping to admire a pair, a very pretty brunette and her friend, whose hair beneath her bonnet was the colour of ripening apricots.

Fletcher watched wide-eyed, overcome with shyness in the face of such practised gallantry. Remaining behind the Captain, he waited, blushing, while the brown-haired girl acknowledged the Captain's salute with an inclination of her head and the other favoured them both with a cool look before, arm-in-arm, they crossed the narrow street and went their way.

"That was Miss Hall of Dunglass," Fletcher volunteered in a tone bordering on the craven. "Daughter of Sir James."

"Which is?" Georgie remarked absently, watching the pair of them, lost in his own thoughts and contemplations.

Fletcher risked a nervous look at the grand officer sitting on the fine bay hunter beside him. He swallowed and cleared his throat. "The brown-haired young lady, sir."

"And her companion?" Georgie asked, his gaze fixed upon the crowd into which they had vanished.

Fletcher shook his head. "Dunno, sir."

Georgie turned to him, a distracted, pleasantly lop-sided smile upon his face. "Never mind, Fletcher," he said, his thoughts clearly still wherever they had been. "Shall we press on?"

The cottages and houses nearer to the harbour and sea front were not so fine as those farther inland. Fletcher led the way through narrow wynds to a maze of low cottages and dismal huts a little way along the coast, where weeds grew, where what had once been windows were boarded over, and shutters hung askew, and children played unattended in the dirt among the dwellings and remains of upturned, beached dinghies.

Fletcher halted and dismounted. "This is it, sir."

Georgie gave the cottage a long, measuring look, observed the salt-stained, peeling whitewash, the sagging roof, and the grimy windowpanes, then dismounted and handed his reins to Fletcher. "Guard the door, Fletcher."

It was not an order Fletcher had been expecting. "Yes, sir."

Georgie drew a deep breath. "Admit no one."

"No, sir," he said, now standing to attention at the door, the reins of both horses still in his hand. The horses began to tear and graze at the long grass nearest the doorway.

Breathing in deeply again, Georgie knocked upon the half-open door, then ducked his head to avoid the lintel and entered the darkened croft. Inside it was as he fancied it must be. Indeed, it was as he himself had lived until recently—the one room divided by a ragged curtain on a line, the whole almost as dark as a cave, the pervasive smell of damp earth, the few furnishings unwashed and rough.

Upon his entrance, the creature on a mattress raised above the dirt floor upon a rickety structure of boards and crates, and covered by a thin quilt with fraying edges, struggled to sit upright. Standing beside her, a woman with a weather-hardened face and grizzled hair pulled from her face into a bun, regarded him with such hatred. "Wha'ur ye come here?" she hissed. Then, without waiting for an answer, continued to rant and spit, saying a great deal more which Georgie imagined was to his discredit, though he understood little.

He waited until she had finished, said all she had to say, then bowed, and narrowing his eyes, said soberly, "I am Captain Shuster. I understand you feel most keenly that my presence in this house is an offence, that as a soldier I am a disgrace to my family, and as a man, I am a disgrace to my King and my country. You may well be right, though I trust it is not so. However, I believe this lady, Mrs. Ramsey…" he gestured toward the cowering creature in the bed whom he could barely see. "…Was most cruelly set upon by an escaped prisoner of war. I further believe that she has also suffered the loss of her husband, possibly at the hand of the escaped prisoner, and it is my duty to find the truth of the matter. Is she well enough to speak to me?"

The fishwife put her head to one side and considered the grave eyes of the soldier with the fancy gold braiding all over the chest of his scarlet uniform and his gold epaulets and the plumed bicorne he held under his arm. She had never seen a so fine a uniform. Nor been addressed with such courtesy by one so grand. He was as unlike the soldiers who had been here before as finnan haddie from cow's milk. "Aye," she said finally, and wiping her hands on her soiled apron, left the bedside.

Georgie remained standing until she had left the cottage. Then, he set his hat on the seat of a broken backed chair, and taking a stool from beside the table, came and sat beside the bed.

"I am Captain Shuster…"

Maggie Ramsey was not a young woman, but not older than forty years, he believed, though life had been neither kind nor easy for her.

"Aye," she said softly, regarding him as he regarded her broken face—the chilblains upon her cheekbones, the mosaic of shattered capillaries just beneath the surface of the skin about her eyes, the disfiguring swelling of her nose and mouth—though she could detect no hint of disgust or mockery in his solemn gaze.

"May I?" he said at last, placing a finger beneath her chin so that he might turn her face toward the light.

She allowed him, allowed and endured his long scrutiny. And said softly, "I cannae see fra oot that eye nae mair. He blinded me," she whispered ashamedly.

Georgie, steadily regarding the still healing eye, its cornea displaced by a harsh blow, and a pale cataract forming on the surface, said, "Yes, I can see that he did." And still, he pondered and studied her mashed face. Then, settling back on the stool, very gently, he took her hand. "Will you tell me what happened?"

"He broke ma face too," she said, whimpering as a child, the tears only now beginning to trickle from the corners of her blind and seeing eyes.

"Yes," Georgie agreed. And gingerly touched the place, the lumpen spot where her jawbone was still mending. "Yes. He broke your jaw. Just here. Does it pain you still?"

"Not sae mich…" she murmured, bemused by his empathy, wholly disarmed by his prosaic tenderness.

"Will you tell me?" he repeated solemnly.

She was still for a time, then said, "'Twere a day like ony ither..." Her fingers smoothed the shredding edge of the quilt where the patched fabrics had faded to grey and the worn threads no longer held. "I was doon upon the shore, waitin' for the boats tae come in when I saw this man coming toward me. He was very tall. An' big. I didnae pay him ony heed, I was watchin' for the boats..."

"What did he look like, this man?" Georgie interrupted.

"Big, like I said. Very tall. An' wi' a great tangle o' hair, all in curls like a lass's. Brown, it waur..." She paused then, her mouth and chin buckling. Then her grip on Georgie's hand tightening, she told how he had grabbed her as though she were a whore, which she was not. Told how he roared and ripped at her clothes as she fought him and threw her to the ground and slapped her and hit her. Told how she had screamed and screamed. How she tried to get away but he caught at her clothes and gave her such a beating and then he had begun to...

She faltered, unable to continue. And cowering, closed her eyes, and shook her head from side to side as the tears ran down her homely face.

"He raped you," Georgie said softly, steadily.

She drew a long shuddering breath. And awash with tears, she regarded him fearfully. But there had been no condemnation in that voice or in his words. Nor disgust at her degradation. And searching, neither could she see condemnation in his face, only experience and a great terrible sadness. She wiped at the tears and sniffed hard. "Aye," she confessed, nodding. "Aye, he did. I begged him tae stop, but he took nae notice. I dinna ken how mony times he did it...Ma heid, I couldnae see some o' the time. An' some o' the time, it went black...but he just went on an' on. He never stoppit. I didnae ken a body could hurt sae mich. I was all over bluid. I couldnae fight him," she wept. "An' I just lay there while he kept on a' me."

Georgie nodded. "Yes," he murmured. It had been the same in the villages and hamlets of Portugal and Spain, he thought dully. Wherever the French soldiers had been, it was always, always the same.

"I thocht I was aboot tae dei, but then, I heard a voice I kend callin' for me. It was ma husband, comin' tae look for me, wantin' his keill. He shouted, an' come doon the hill, but the man was up an' upon him. He beat ma puir man like he did me. I couldnae move. I couldnae even lift ma heid. An' then I saw he had a knife. I tried tae call oot. But it was too late. He stabbed him. Stabbed him tae death. He killt him, just like that. Then he got up an' come at me agin. He was covered a' over in ma husband's bluid. An' mine. Then he gave a kind of a laugh an' he gie'd me a kick. An' then he went off. Just like that."

Stilly, Georgie sat and stared straight on. "Yes…" he nodded, blinking. She did not know, could not tell the measure of his rage. He clamped his jaw hard against it. "And then?"

"I just lay there, waitin' for deith. Prayin' for it. I was beggin' for it. But it wouldnae come for me…" Her voice broke.

"It was dark when they cam lookin' for me. An' then they found us. It was days afore I woke. They'd had the doctor tae see me. He said it was a miracle I was alive at a'."

"Yes, it is," Georgie concurred.

She drew a sobbing breath. "Who was he? Why'd he do sich a thing?"

"The name he uses is John Brown. Or Jean le Brun. Though what his real name is, I cannot say."

"He blinded me. An' murthered ma husband. An' broke ma face."

"Yes," Georgie said, still as soft as snowfall. "I know…"

Then, certain of the answer: "Can you recall, when he was beating you, did he hit you anywhere but your head? No? I see."

He held her hand while her tears abated. And felt where in her hand bones had been broken and were now mending. Then, finally, he said, "Thank you for telling me…" He bowed his head, then took her cold hand in both of his. "I cannot bring back your husband. Nor can I erase what was done to you. But upon my life, I give you my word, I will catch him. I swear to you, I shall catch him…

And again soft, he said, "Have you family or friends close at hand to look after you?"

She nodded tearfully.

He held her hand for a while longer, then stood. And reaching into an inner pocket drew forth a purse. "I cannot give you back all that you have lost. Would that I had that power. But this…" He hesitated as he contemplated the knitted metal purse which held a collection of sovereigns and guineas. "This should pay for the doctor and some blankets… and pay for your care and keep for some time to come," he said, laying it on the bed close by her hand.

She turned her face to regard him closely and at length with her one good eye. "Thank ye, sir," she whispered. "God bless ye for your kindness."

"I shall take my leave of you now…" he said, and bowed as formally as if she were a duchess. Then, he replaced the stool by the table and retrieved his hat. And with a final look at the sad battered woman, he ducked his head and came out into the yellow afternoon sun.

"Come, Fletcher," Georgie said, blinking at the light as he took the reins from the young soldier to lead his reluctant horse away from the collection of huts and hovels, and the small crowd of fishwives and children huddling silent and watchful, just out of sight.

Fletcher said nothing until they were mounted and away from the fishermen's enclave. Then he asked earnestly: "Sir? Sir? Will she live, sir?"

Georgie hesitated, gazing out at the sea and the raucous drifts of herring gulls searching and scavenging among the waves. The skin was tight across his cheekbones. "I shouldn't think so" he said evenly. "It's difficult to say. I do not know the extent of her internal injuries. But I fancy that as soon as she is able, she will fill her pockets with stones and walk into the sea."

Fletcher looked upon the officer whom only that morning he had thought haughty, arrogant, pampered even, and nodded. "Yes, sir."

Georgie blew out a breath as if to clear his lungs and head. "Come, Fletcher. Take me back to Edinburgh. I have dispatches to write. And then I must return to London." And gave a lop-sided smile from which the many ghosts had not been banished.

Chapter VII

1

The hard rain that overnight had flattened the countryside round about and kept all Londoners indoors—thieves, prostitutes, and rich men alike—had flushed the gutters and ditches and lanes clean of muck, leaving only the odd small pile of cabbage leaves, straw and soil. From his perch on a broken wall, a small boy—a stunted London street Arab he was, a human squirrel even, shoeless, coatless and grimy—scanned the lane in both directions.

You could find all sorts in the gutters after a storm like that…you could never tell…all it took was a careful eye. Because folk was ever so careless. You could find the odd shilling. Or pennies and silk handkerchiefs—all it took was a trained eye. If you was really lucky, you might find a drunk still asleep, his pockets not yet rifled. Which, slipping and clambering down from the wall, was what he thought that great green lump up at the entrance to Dark Mews was. It looked like that—the body of the man face down in a ditch, a puddle of rainwater and slurry at his back. From around the corner of an evil blackened building, the boy cast a suspicious eye about. He didn't like witnesses. Not that there was many such about at this time of the morning, even here so near to Charing Cross. Still, it paid to keep a wary eye. You never knew when some Runner-man was like to be passing by on his way home.

He crept along the broken wall toward the sleeping drunk. As he neared, his anticipation leapt and grew. He could feel his wealth increasing, which was a fine feeling, for that green coat was cut from good cloth. If he could have that off him, that'd be more than a week's gin, that would. And still drunk as a lordling the cove was, not moving a muscle. He'd have that coat off him for sure.

Alert and wily, he crept toward the drunk and gave him a swift, sly nudge—for certainty—with his toe. He barely moved. Or didn't move. Hard to say. Still sly, he poked at him again. The same. The very same. Very drunk then. Blue ruin and a soft head, the child scoffed. Silly bugger. Daft toff. He bent low over him, ready to slip his fingers into his breast pocket, to turn him slightly over—better for searching out hidden trinkets. And saw his face.

Choked on a shock wave of breath, the word erupted out of him. "Cor!"

For the cove wasn't drunk. He was dead. With his face beaten into a misshapen, mottled pudding of caked blood and darker bruises. Blood had dried beneath the swollen slits that were once his eyes and beneath his nose and ear. It had trickled and spilled and stained the fine lace and linen of his collar and cravat. And had dried into dark mats in his hair and crusted over the blue bruising and blood clots at his temple.

The boy stared, still and impassive. Then, carefully, he lowered the man back onto his face in the gutter. And with a darting glance in each direction took to his heels. For he knew of a cove what had an interest in doings like this. Most times, he was found down in the Rookery. He paid well too. If only he got to him first.

2

"So, it's definitely him then, is it?" the lashless man murmured without raising his eyes from the ground, as Jesuadon finally emerged from the grim passageway of Dark Mews.

Jesuadon stood, regarding the scene before him with a jaundiced eye—the early drinkers, the shabberoon pick-pockets, the scroungers and rogues, the bustling red-faced women. For he was in an evil temper—stale drunk and dishevelled, his black coat half on, his cravat loose about his neck and his shirt and waistcoat only partially buttoned. He'd been dragged out of bed to rush down here at this infernal hour of the morning. No, it hadn't been his own bed he'd been dragged from. It was the bed of a pretty little seamstress who lived off Clare Market. And given this latest turn of events, that was probably a wise thing. He looked with loathing upon faces and folly in the scene before him and did not give way to the stream of oaths that lay ready on his brain and tongue.

"Yes." And it bore every indication that it had been the work of Boy's John Brown. No blows to anywhere but about the head. And he'd searched him too—but not found what he was carrying. That pocket Jesuadon had emptied himself. And of course, no one had seen or heard anything. 'Struth, Bretherton had been a fool and a clown, but fool or no, no one deserved a death like that. "Yes, it's definitely him."

And looking neither right nor left, Jesuadon pushed his way through those nearest him, those on their way to market or their day's employment, to stride down the muddy street toward St. Martin's Lane.

Still apparently studying the ground, the lashless man blinked, and shifted his weight from one foot to the other and back again and considered. It was a right mess this was and no mistake. He waited until Jesuadon was nearly out of sight. Then, shrugging as if he'd been too long still, he made his way down the lane to follow. At a discreet distance. To St. Martin's Lane and down the great length of it to the Strand, slowly and cautiously, losing himself in every available throng or crowd. For Jesuadon did not like being shadowed. He was most particular about that. Doggedly, he stayed well behind, not catching up with him until Jesuadon was in the private chambers he used under the eaves of Sparrowhawk's premises, standing at the washstand, splashing water on his face.

The lashless man entered the room quietly. And seeing through the doorway the pale skin of Jesuadon's half-naked back, he prudently took a seat in the parlour and prepared to wait. Jesuadon, catching a glimpse of that ashy reflection in the shaving mirror, did not acknowledge it. Silently, the water dripping from his chin and hair, he rubbed at his face and eyes, and then stood, hands on hips, staring into space, lost in terrible contemplation of this morning's events. And their potential consequences. Finally he turned, stripping off his remaining clothes, to step into a tub of steaming water behind a corner screen.

The man listened while Jesuadon splashed and scrubbed—he was taking a deal of trouble over this washing of his—and patiently observed the patterns of light cast by the sun through the worn dimity curtains upon the bare floor. At length Jesuadon emerged from his bath, water pooling on the floorboards, unaware or uncaring that he was observed, to dry himself and then to shave, meticulously removing the stubble of three days' growth of that red gold beard. And finally, stopped, and laying aside the straight razor, eyed himself in the mirror, mercilessly studying his own reflection in the spotted looking glass.

Without knocking, the lanky figure of Adam Sparrowhawk entered the small chamber, walked past the lashless man and into the next room. "Did you want me?" he spoke in a low voice.

"My hair. You'll need to trim my hair…Do it!" Jesuadon said in reply.

Wordless and vacant-eyed, Sparrowhawk drew a small scissors from an apron pocket and began to comb and snip, comb and snip, comb and snip, the locks of marmalade hair falling unheeded to the floor, there to catch the light.

The lashless man heaved a quiet sigh. And only when Jesuadon emerged some half an hour later, dressed as befitted a gentleman, point-device, all neat and polished and trim, his dark coat brushed, his boots well-polished and his cravat as fine a piece of starched severity as ever there was, only then did he stand, hat in hand, and look upon Jesuadon's fine fair face. His eyes were glittering and angry. Wet almost, with tears of outrage.

The lashless man blinked in surprise.

"I'll leave you now…" Sparrowhawk said and ducked from the room.

"Was it our man then?" the lashless man ventured.

Jesuadon flexed his jaw. He wished he were drunk. He stared off into the light. And said harshly: "What you mean is, Barnet, was it the same man who beat Tirrell and tried to kill him? Yes. Though I doubt there were any witnesses this time. He will not make that mistake a second time, I think."

The lashless man lowered his gaze and plucked at the tattered rim of his low-crowned hat. He considered. "Had he been searched?"

The drunken, dissolute manner had vanished. Jesuadon gave a single nod. "To be sure, his pockets had been cleaned out. But the back panel in his coat lining was still intact."

"Anything important taken then?"

Jesuadon shrugged and shook his head. "I don't know. I've no way of knowing what he was wont to carry about with him. I took the packet he had on him." He clamped his teeth together. "What about the guttersnipe who found him? That street Arab?"

"He said not. I shall kill him if he's lied and he knows it."

Jesuadon gave a nod. "Good." Then, unexpectedly: "You did right to come for me."

The lashless man nodded slowly. Then screwed up his face. "But why all the washing?" For that didn't figure. Jesuadon had seen death before. Plenty of times. They both had.

Jesuadon's expression hardened, his mouth tightened, and his eyes were suddenly again ablaze and fierce. For a brief odd instant, Barnet feared a beating.

"I am about to go before the Guvnor to explain how it is that his orders was disregarded and a deranged French crasher is still at liberty," Jesuadon said, biting off the words. "I am about to go before him to explain that his favourite courier, Henry Bretherton, whom I had always thought a damnable fool, was telling the truth. He was being followed. And now he is dead—beaten to a swollen blackened blancmange, just like the Boy. Because of our negligence, yours and mine. I shall also have the doubtful pleasure of telling him that I have given orders for the Bretherton's body to be dumped far from where it was found—which he will not like—so that there can be no questions from his family and no Runners prying into the matter neither." The muscles in his jaw continued to tick and flex. "And I have the not inconsiderable task of explaining that somewhere and somehow there is a leak in this damned system. That, before God, there is an inside man somewhere giving the orders, and this damned John Brown knows precisely who he's looking for!" He swallowed, and gentled his voice. "And I did believe a bath was the least I could do.

"And now, if you value the rather fine wages I pay you, you had better go and find the murdering bastard who did this. Because if you do not, I do assure you, I will not answer for the consequences..."

3

From the darkened hallway outside the Foreign Secretary's offices, Georgie could hear the commotion inside, the voices raised in anger, the shouting. Apparently Lord Castlereagh's renowned affability and cool temper had deserted him. For the moment. And someone, poor devil, was having his ears chewed off. Georgie stood before the young naval officer's portrait, ordering his thoughts, composing himself. Then straight away opened the door to Planta's office and went in.

It was empty. Planta wasn't there. And the doors to the inner office were firmly shut. Georgie closed the outer door behind himself and waited.

He heard the voice rising yet further—the words indecipherable. And swore under his breath in anticipation. Then heard the hard sharp thwack of something hitting the wall. And instinctively recoiled. And drawing himself to his full height, tugged hard at the waist of his uniform jacket and fingered the top edge of his black cravat.

The inner doors opened. Planta emerged, a hastily adopted blank expression on his thin face, streaks of black ink splashed across his cheek and upon the white folds of linen at his throat.

"And change that shirt and cravat before someone sees you!" the Foreign Secretary bellowed furiously.

His nostrils pinched, his back against the doors he held shut behind him, Planta permitted himself a single sniff. Then, feeling some explanation or even warning was requisite, he confessed, "His lordship has been voicing his concerns. About the boy."

Georgie regarded the stained cravat, the smeared ink across the secretary's unusually haggard face. "Ah. Yes. So I perceive."

His mouth tightening still further, the concern present in his tired eyes, Planta said, "Is he safe, do you think?"

Georgie did not pretend to misunderstand. "I don't know."

"No," Planta agreed. "I see." He nodded. "Thank you."

He reopened the doors and made a small bow. "His lordship will see you now, sir." And to the Foreign Secretary: "Captain Shuster to see you, my lord."

"Ah, Shuster…" Lord Castlereagh looked up with a cordial smile, although he did not rise from his chair at the large desk in the centre of the room. His tone was most pleasant. "Do come in. I shall not rise…the gout, you know…the gout…" The desk was covered, as ever, with stacks of papers and rolls of maps.

"My lord." Georgie executed a formal bow. He glanced at the floor. An inkpot lay on its side by the carpet's near edge. A spattering of ink still dripped from the skirting board.

Silently, Planta shut the doors behind him.

Lord Castlereagh blew his nose. "Do you know, I have had a most remarkable letter…just in the past few days it arrived…" He rummaged among the papers upon the desk. "Now where has it got to?…" He started in on another pile and eventually withdrew a large creased sheet of foolscap. "Ah, here we are." He peered at it. "Yes. Yes, this is it. And I, ah, I should like to read you some of it, if I may…to gauge your opinion of the contents, don't you know…Now, where was it…" He scanned the page, turned it over and back again. "Ah yes, here we are…

"Do listen to this, will you?" And in his pleasant baritone began: "*…When we arrived, the place was absolutely deserted. Almost all the houses had been pillaged and their furniture smashed to pieces and thrown in the mud; part of the town was on fire, a frenzied soldiery had forced every door and window, breaking down everything that stood before them and destroying more than they consumed…The churches had all been stripped, and the streets were encumbered with the dead and the dying. Husbands had seen their wives raped, fathers their daughters, sons their aged mothers…*" Suddenly, Lord Castlereagh looked up, his eagle's beak of a nose stark, his dark eyes questioning. "Does any of this ring familiar, Captain?" he said.

Standing fully at attention, sickened and sickening, Georgie stared straight ahead gazing at nothing. And swallowed. "Yes, my lord."

"Does it indeed? There is more, you know…" Castlereagh promised, still dangerously genial. "*...As we proceeded we found a more horrible spectacle awaited us, for another four men had been strung up with the difference that they had not only been hung, but nailed through their chests to the trees on which they had lost their lives...*"

Rocked by a sudden stabbing rage, Georgie clenched his jaw against the sharp edge of revulsion welling up in his stomach, his thoughts now overrun with the litany of hellishness being related with such frightening, calculated ease.

"It is the same in every village through which we pass. Burning and ravaged houses, peasants with their throats slit and their eyes gouged out while the few survivors appear as skeletons risen from the tomb."

Narrowing his gaze, Georgie squared his shoulders against the blistering onslaught: These were the horrific facts of this damnable war, that it was fought not between armies of men, but waged by French savages to the barbaric destruction of all, of anything that stood in their path.

"Everywhere, violated women lay bleeding and dying in the charred remains of houses and children with their bones sticking through their skin clung to the bodies of their dead parents, everything that had possessed life lay quivering in the last agony of slaughter and awful vengeance."

None were spared. When he had been with scouting parties in Spain, they had not even been permitted to bury the dead, in case the French were still in the area. A muscle beneath Georgie's eye began spasmodically to tick.

"And that, Captain? Is that anything you recognise?" Castlereagh rasped, raking him with a withering glare.

He stood so stiff he shook. Tears had gathered in his eyes. He knew the scene. He knew all of the scenes. Knew them too well. They tore at him, haunted him, asleep and awake, him, and every other soldier of his acquaintance. Though he rarely wept, he could never become inured. He blinked. And strove to regain his detachment, that detachment upon which his sanity and the lives of his men had depended. Only once had it failed him. It would not happen again. "Yes, my lord." He fixed his unfocused gaze on a point above the Foreign Secretary's head.

"Do I need to continue, Shuster?"

Unbowed, all equanimity shattered, he did not hesitate. "No, my lord."

"And where would you imagine this letter was sent from, Captain?"

"To be sure, it might be anywhere, my lord," Georgie replied promptly. "Anywhere the French army has been, my lord. It might be Portugal or Spain. It might be Italy. I dare say it might even be Prussia or Poland, now that they're headed that way, sir. It is what they do, my lord."

"Yes, Captain Shuster," the Foreign Secretary barked, now rising to his feet to lean heavily on the desk. "It is what they do!" he raged. "They maim and mutilate and rape and murder. In every country they visit, it is what they do.

"And now, now that fiend Savary is sending his agents here—to commit these hellish abominations here! On our own soil! Savary and his infernal minions have brought this war of utter destruction to us!" He quaked with the force of his fury and dread. "And thanks to that feckless waster, Jesuadon, I have not been able to halt it. That woman in Dunbar was raped and beaten and her husband killed because that mumping devil Fitzroy let a French prisoner escape and did nothing! And when he was meant to be searching the city for him, that slubberdegullion Jesuadon did nothing but loll about in doss houses drinking his way to perdition!" he roared, picking up the nearest thing to hand, a book, and hurling it.

It thumped hard against Georgie's shoulder and fell to the ground. "Yes, sir," he agreed, standing taut and tall and unmoved.

Castlereagh sank back down in his chair to shield his eyes with his hand. "Henry Bretherton is dead, you know. Killed. By that damnable rogue, John Brown." He drew a deep shuddering breath and sighed.

"Yes, my lord," Georgie replied, his voice dropping in sadness. "I had heard."

"He was a good lad, Henry was. From a good family. I know Jesuadon thought little enough of him, but I rated him very highly. He never let me down," the Foreign Secretary said, his anguish plain.

"No, sir."

"What he must have suffered, the dear boy…" Castlereagh murmured in dismay, his anger now apparently finished. "Upon my life, I shall never forgive myself."

But the wigging was not finished, not by a long chalk. "Where is he now though, eh? Where is this infernal assassin who is hunting down my men and killing them as lambs to the slaughter? Where is he?" Castlereagh roared.

"I do not know, my lord," Georgie answered dully.

"Jesuadon tells me now that there must be a leak, you know. That this appalling attack on Bretherton was committed by the same man who gave Boy such a basting. The monster who attacked your woman up in Dunbar…"

"Yes, my lord. Her description of him does fit that of Boy's."

He sat, the Foreign Secretary, his chin in his hand, contemplating the letter before him. And a profound distress still gnawing at him: "They take turns raping the women, did you know? Whole detachments of them, I'm told. As many as twenty or thirty French soldiers take it in turns severally. They tell me they drag them into the town squares to rape them there, in front of everyone, did you know that? Yes, of course, you did. Forgive me, Captain, it is a damnable thing," he said bleakly.

"Yes sir." And his face like ice, Georgie continued: "And when they've finished with them, they shoot them. Or bayonet them. Though frequently, they just leave them there to die. Those who can still walk generally drag themselves off to take their own lives.

"It's habitual, sir. The French have been at it for so long that they do not regard it. I have spoken to survivors of the Vendée. That's where it all started. But that was only the beginning. I believe the atrocities were worst in Egypt though—from all accounts."

"Were they?" Castlereagh whispered, and looked up suddenly to gaze upon the tanned face of the soldier before him, held still and blank as that of a painted stone effigy. "Worse than these?" He gestured helpless and horrified at the page before him. "Upon my life, it is all so unthinkable!" he exclaimed, his voice breaking, undone by the enormity of the French terror. "Dear God in Heaven, how do we stop this infernal Corsican madman and his hellish armies?"

Soberly, Georgie regarded the Foreign Secretary, witnessed the full flush of the futility and rage and despair sinking him. "The only way to stop it is to stop Bonaparte. But we will stop it, my lord. You are stopping it, as God is my witness. You and Lord Wellington. For indeed, every soldier of theirs we kill is fifty or more lives saved, a score of women and children protected, another village left standing instead of burnt and pillaged and razed."

Lord Castlereagh appeared to consider Georgie's words. "It may be so," he said at last. He rubbed the bridge of his nose with one finger. "I have told Jesuadon I want this John Brown brought in alive. When he is, I shall want you to question him. And I want that leak found too. I don't care who it is. I want him stopped. Now!"

"Yes, my lord."

"Thank you, Captain."

Georgie waited. The interview was over. Pulling himself again to his full height, bemused and ready to be drunk, Georgie made his obedience. "My lord."

Chapter VIII

1

Jesuadon did not like Whitechapel and generally avoided it. He did not like the smell of the place. With its scores of slaughterhouses and the stench of death and offal, even a plentiful supply of rogues and whores and drunkards held little appeal. But he had come here nonetheless. And with his well-trimmed hair and the sweat washed from him, he was as conspicuous as a clear day in May—or would have been had the raucous company of The Grape been sober. They were not. And had not been for several hours.

Jesuadon acquired a bumper of ale and a bottle of Hollands from the tapster, and seeing there were no empty tables at which to drink in solitary rumination, found a vacant seat in the depth of the inglenook, at a table occupied by a man wearing a blood-stained butcher's apron beneath his brown coat. A lashless man with a bald pate.

Barnet grunted and spat.

Jesuadon poured himself a glass of gin and drank it down. And sat, blinking rapidly, as the spirit burnt its way down his throat and his eyes filled with water.

"I have a sense you ain't going to like this," the lashless man said, though his tone hinted that he cared little, one way or the other.

Jesuadon slanted him a damning look. "What?"

"It's about that John Brown what's been causing all the trouble."

"What?" Jesuadon repeated.

"It appears he shipped out early that morning."

"What?" It was an emission of breath, no more.

"Aye," Barnet confirmed with equal parts of detachment and disgust. "He went straight from basting young Bretherton down to the docks at St. Katharine's, the crafty sod. And shipped out on a small boat. A privateer, by the description—with a fair old number of flags ready for hoisting." He gnawed at the inside of his cheek. He could sense the rage beginning to pulse through Jesuadon at his elbow: he was breathing ever so deliberately as if he was keeping himself in careful check.

Barnet rubbed his face with grimy hands, and drank the foam off his ale. "There's more..."

Jesuadon poured himself another glassful and tossed it off. "Yes?"

Barnet watched from the corner of his eye while Jesuadon's features settled into the familiar grim emptiness. And waited, sipping at his ale, while Jesuadon pushed away a young prostitute who'd come to smooth her hand upon his thigh.

"He was bound for Holland."

He waited, silent, while Jesuadon digested this.

Jesuadon dragged at his cravat, untying it, then continued to tug at it until the ends lay crumpled and dishevelled upon his chest. He sat up to hunch over the bumper and gave a soft belch. "He's gone after the boy…" he concluded. It had been inevitable.

"Aye," Barnet agreed.

Jesuadon drank off the contents of the bumper. "We're all dead men."

Barnet sniffed and wiped his nose with the back of his hand. "I don't see that," he protested, rather louder than he intended. He hushed. "Tirrell's got a fortnight's head start on him. He could be anywhere by now."

"I shall have to tell his lordship."

Barnet's expression grew cagey. "I'm damned if I would," he retorted. "If it happens and Brown catches him, he'll know soon enough. No cause to borrow trouble that I can see."

"We are all dead men," Jesuadon repeated, now with certainty, staring blankly ahead. He drank down a third glassful of Hollands.

"And the leak?" Barnet murmured into his tankard.

"You're meant to be finding out, you plaguey lobcock. Or had you forgot that?" grunted Jesuadon. There was a sourness about him this evening.

Barnet darted him a sideways glance. "It could be a Whig..." he suggested.

"How in the blazes could it be a Whig?" Jesuadon snapped, turning on him, a surge of emotion animating his bleary eyes. "Flint has this business sewn up tight as a tailor."

Unimpressed, Barnet shrugged again. "Someone who has rooms near Planta's little office? Which ain't, if I may say so, quite so discreet as the Guvnor thinks it is. All it would take is a fortnight of watching. Anyone could do it. That street Arab what found Bretherton could do it."

"And did he?" Jesuadon snapped.

"No."

Making no comment, thinking perhaps, Jesuadon looked out upon the drunken company at the surrounding tables and grimaced. At a centre table, the young prostitute was now perched upon someone's knee. Which someone, amidst the laughter of his companions, started to sing the chorus of *Barnacle Bill*: "I've just got paid and I want to…" His companions joined in: "Get laid…I'm Barnacle Bill, the sailor." It was as musical as a choking goose. The crowd roared with laughter.

Barnet smoothed his hand over his head, front to back, front to back. "But what I don't see is…" He paused, considering his half-drunk ale. "That attack on Tirrell. There's something that don't square. The boy burned the place in Paris to a cinder, didn't he? So the Frenchies must think he's dead. Ain't that right?"

"Yes. Unless they've suddenly acquired supernatural powers." Then, in the act of pouring himself a final tot of blue ruin, Jesuadon stopped. Stopped, still holding the bottle mid-pour. And finally, deliberately set the bottle on the table. "Oh cock."

Barnet waited for elucidation.

"Oh cock," Jesuadon breathed. "You're right." He let out a sigh, but sat straighter nonetheless. "Oh Christ."

Barnet watched, studying the flushed faces of those about them, and waited.

Jesuadon gazed out, blinking as if just awakened. "We've been…I've been looking at this from the scut end. Piss." He sat still a moment longer. "Brown didn't follow him here. Brown was already in place. He had been for months," he pronounced. "And he probably ain't the only one." He took a last mouthful of ale and allowed it to dwell in his mouth before swallowing. "Boy set fire to the house, leaving that other boy's body to be found and mistaken for his. So Savary's lads think him dead. But that don't matter. Because Brown ain't taking his orders from Paris, he's taking them from someone here." He bit at his bottom lip. "Brown knew who he was looking for. He passed through London on his way down to Kent. Piss! First the boy and then Bretherton."

Jesuadon leaned forward again, resting his elbow on the table and rubbed his forehead and eye with the palm of his hand. "This has been in place for months," he declared. "And whoever is giving the orders hasn't heard from France recently neither…'Struth, what a damned cully I've been." He drank down his final tot. And again his eyes filled with water. He blinked it away. "We're all dead men."

Barnet signalled to the barman his need for a refill. "What do you want me to do?"

"What?" Jesuadon said absently, still biting at his lip. And shook his head. "'Struth! Set a watch on Planta's office, will you? See if anything turns up."

Barnet hesitated. "We'll need to do more than that, won't we?" he countered.

"Yes. A great deal more. We need to find him. The spymaster here. For whoever he is also knows that contrary to what Paris may believe, Tirrell is alive. And that sodomitical shuffler, Brown, has gone after him." He exhaled slowly. "Oh, sod it."

And lowering his head over his tankard, all the while Barnet watched the jostling crowded room. Jesuadon leaned his head against the settle back, his face set, his eyes narrowed in thought. The barman brought two tankards and placed them on the table. Barnet counted out the pennies and slapped them into the barman's hand.

They both waited until he was well away from their table before beginning again.

Jesuadon narrowed his gaze still further. "So, he's in London, our leak is," he murmured. "Has to be. Because Bretherton was never used outside of London. He's here," he repeated. "Red hell and bloody death," he swore, but almost to himself. Then, he drew a deep breath and exhaled it. "Od's teeth, I am fed up with this…" He coughed and spat. "So…What do you reckon we're looking for then?"

The lashless man cleared his throat, then belched. "Money," he said, nodding. "I'd say we was looking for money. It always comes down to that, dunnit? I should follow the money. And that right fast. For if they know who Tirrell is, then who's to say which of us is next on the list."

Jesuadon rolled his eyes. "Money?" he mocked. "That's your best guess, is it? Money? And if we can't find the money to follow?"

Barnet shrugged again and sighed. And said without rancour: "Then there's no cure for it. We're *all* dead men."

Chapter IX

1

The age of highwaymen was long since over. Indeed, the great gibbets on Hounslow Heath had been cut down these seven years past. Tom Ladyman could remember his father telling him of it when he was still a lad and calling it 'a sad day'. For this was a new century, a new era of peace and order and law, and the age of highwaymen and their reckless deeds of murder and mad gallantry belonged to the old century. Like powdered perukes and jewel-encrusted high heels. Now, if such a thing existed at all, it was only in the fevered imaginations of lady novelists, or maggotty poets with no experience of life beyond their opium-induced phantasies.

But Tom Ladyman was bored.

And tired. Tired of the rain which had fallen unchecked for the past fortnight, turning the New Forest into a pestiferous quagmire and putting a halt to most things including the proper dealings of free-trading. Which was not, in spite of what some people—inlanders mostly—might think, anything other than a sound business proposition for the exchange of goods between willing partners, designed to secure the present and future prosperity and well-being of all concerned. Especially in these days of war and blockades and shortages and suchlike. To be sure, it was a rational man's answer to that Corsican tyrant's damnable attempts to strangle good English trade. It made sense. Perfect rational sense. But who would put to sea in an open boat exposing all that precious tax-free cargo in these conditions? No one was that daft. Well, perhaps, those desperate pissers up in Westphalia. They'd put to sea in any weather, but who was counting them?

Yet until the weather cleared the Warnes had no work for him. Lovey had said there'd not be another shipment until the paths dried out some. Which left a fellow with nothing to do but sit and drink. Which was pleasant, fine even, for a day or two. But a fortnight? A fortnight of naught to do but drink, reread last month's newspaper, and kick at the smoking logs in the hearth! A man was like to go mad with nothing to do but that. And it was high summer.

Ladyman leaned back in the settle and groaned. And drumming his fingers on the table, reviewed it all again. A lark on the High Toby was not such a rum idea. For what could go wrong? Black Ben had stamina and speed, no one would expect it, and at least it would be doing something. It was a less than an hour's ride to the London road. Then, a fast gallop, the sweet music of pistol shots ringing past the ear, a little jingle in the pockets—he wasn't anticipating anything much—a bit of loose change, that was all, and then off. A perfect cure for boredom. And mayhap on the morrow it would clear some.

Ladyman scratched his head for a moment, regarding the cottage wall, whitewashed and bare, deciding. 'Struth, he'd go mad if he stayed here another minute. He got up. What could go wrong? And, dammit-all, he would look quite dashing with a muffler up about his chin and a domino over his eyes. To be sure, it would make up for what he lacked in height. A pity he hadn't any lace at his cuffs.

2

Lady Wilmot placed her hand firmly over her mouth and did not cry out. Did not sob or even sigh. Although that day and that hour—that moment which she had dreaded more than anything she could yet remember—had come upon her, she made no sound against it. Instead she faced the cracking red leather of the coach's faded interior, the tarnished and blackened brass buttons of the padded door, the fading curtains at the window, and held her hand over her mouth, biting her lips together. And otherwise remained as she had schooled herself to be—placid, docile, serene.

Indeed, she marvelled at her own outward composure. For she had not known that one could feel such detachment in the face of debasing cruelty or vindictive abuse. But, after five years, that was all that was left her.

She risked a glance at the plump and pristine prim-faced creature sitting across from her, staring resolutely out of the opposite window—though with the cloud at dusk there was little to see. Her lady's maid. To be sure, there would be no consolation from that quarter. None. For she was his creature—the lady's maid he had foisted upon her, to bring her into fashion, he had said. How curious. And what a very odd notion of fashion.

Five years past, when she had married Sir Robert, she had been intelligent and determined and love-struck. She had wed him willingly and happily, swayed by his compliments and wry attentiveness into believing that he appreciated her wit and pretty face. But Sir Robert had married her for her family's money. For her, for her mind, her gentility, her family, he had nothing but scorn and derision.

Although, indeed, at the outset, he had not been openly unkind. Only confident in his superior understanding of all things intellectual and fashionable. Which she had believed, at the time, only proper in a gentleman of his rank and abilities. Then too she had believed that babies would come and she would have everything to make her the happiest of women—a fine house, a fine husband and fine children.

But soon had begun the sly and private remarks which undermined her confidence, the streams of small talk which had no purpose other than to emphasise her inferiority, and his disregard for her every effort to please him, to keep household—indeed, her inadequacy in every respect of fashion and figure. And the greater her efforts to please him, the greater his disdain. Within another year, what demeaning comments he had made in private, these too began to be made in public, so that her mortified and mortifying tears were no longer a secret shared between herself and her pillow.

And day upon day of these blighting, slighting, idle remarks, which so often he punctuated with a cheerful little half-laugh, left their staining mark, and the bright expectant young lady she had been faded into a silent wretched cowering creature, a wife too frightened to speak even of household or estate matters and so risk another humiliating set-down, a woman apologetic for her very existence. And, when, despite his frequent use of her, she failed to conceive and her distress over her lack of a child had grown into perennial despondency, he used her more and more ill.

Then last year, during one of his frequent sojourns in Town, had begun his friendship with that poet—that brooding, hard-drinking, sneering, debauching, violent poet. Or perhaps Sir Robert had known him previously. Many called him a genius. She did not. And when he was praised in public, she held her tongue. For with that friendship, Sir Robert's contempt and cruelty toward her had become yet more marked and painful.

The coach rattled slowly on toward London, splashing through the many puddles, slowing often for the slippery mud. The days and nights of rain had left the roads rutted, heavy and slow.

And tonight, tonight if he did as he had threatened, if he gave her to his friends as he said he would? Mocking her tears and revulsion, he had laughed that he had lost a wager and she was the forfeit. It was commonplace, dashing even, in fashionable circles, he said. She drew a deep breath, of despair and resolve—what kind of man does such a thing? Still, as her monthly flow had waned, she had decided what she would do. If indeed he carried out this final act of her degradation. Tonight, she would leave the house by the servants' entrance, hail a hackney carriage to Westminster Bridge, never to return. Though of a certainty, there was no heaven for suicides. She knew that. And she would be buried in a pauper's grave. And the shame brought upon her family would be great, so very great. In all likelihood, they would not speak her name again. She folded her lips together, contemplating her inevitable disgrace and damnation. Then, quietly, so quietly that her maid did not notice, she slid her hand into her lap, and plaiting her fingers together, began fervently to pray. For courage. For pity. For forgiveness.

3

Across the moon, the covering of fog was as a muslin scrim, diffusing and blurring though not obscuring the bright round light, while across the black surface of the open road and bordering fields, the mist lay, lightly rolling like distant laughter. In the darker shadow of a plane tree, Ladyman sat, easy and quiet, sitting as he had been for nearly an hour, astride his large black gelding, his presence hidden from the main road by an overgrown hawthorn bush, all covered in white and fragrant flower.

Tom Ladyman was a patient man.

Five years in the company of free-traders had taught him that. How to wait, silent, still and easy. And to wait, relaxed and unstirring in the saddle. To wait and to listen. To listen to each sound—the hooting of owls as they swooped and flew and perched in their hunting. To listen to the snapping of twigs in the undergrowth, to the silence and the grunting of badgers on the prowl, to the feeble rustlings of nestlings or hedgehogs moving through the dense foliage of the forest. And still to sit quiet. And even the black knew to remain still, not even to peck at a leaf or twig for extra fodder while he waited.

Then, at last, he heard it. The rumbling, clattering, clip-clop noises he had been waiting for. Those sweet welcoming sounds—the grating and rolling of coach wheels, the even pace of horses trotting—a slow measured trot, it was. He smiled to himself. And gave Ben's neck a pat. 'Struth, this? This was going to be a doddle.

Leaning forward, he edged just out of the shadow to gain a better look. Free-traders learn to see far and fine in the dark. The carriage lanterns were bobbling unevenly in the dark, but still he could make out the silhouette against the dampening sky. He looked hard. A lone driver. With neither guard nor outriders. Could his luck be so far in? Od's bodkin. And as it neared, he saw that the carriage itself appeared well enough, smallish, and not in the latest style—possibly the coach and pair of an oldster with money aplenty but no fashion's fool. And the pair pulling it were steady and slow, reliable you might say, with great cobby hooves. And still no outriders. Not even one. Ladyman craned to listen.

No. No extra hoof beats. None. Damme, this was bantling's play.

Buoyed up, his breath quickening with excitement, Ladyman sat up the straighter, adjusted the domino over his eyes and pressed his hat firmly down, then checked the poppers at his waist and in his saddle holsters. And gathering in his reins, he gave a swift hard squeeze to the horse's sides.

"At 'em!" From statue-still to a swift canter in two strides. And rushing forward, he raised the pistol and fired off a shot.

The carriage horses—with their great powerful necks and large feathered hooves—unused to excitement or to the thunder of a pistol shot, staggered and skittered for a few strides, then stumbled forward, tripping over their own feet. And then, just as suddenly, halted in confusion as the coachman hauled in on the reins, pitching the inside passengers first sideways then forward onto the coach-floor with an unmistakeable thump.

Tom, coming to a stand beside the leader, replaced the pistol in its holster and pulled out the other, and aiming it at the driver pronounced those grand-sounding words he'd been practising since he'd first hatched the plan for this famous bit of sport: "Stand and deliver!" Od's teeth, it sounded fine.

The response was not what he expected.

The old coachman glared at him, jutting out his grizzled chin. "Well, ye'll have nothing from me, for I've not been paid, I tell ye," he shouted.

Tom blinked in surprise.

A passenger was struggling—with much bumping and scraping—to let down the near coach window. After a moment, it thudded open.

"What is it?" said a frightened female voice. Young, she sounded.

Wriggling his chin clear of the muffler, Ladyman pronounced again, only more clearly this time, and he fancied with more authority: "Stand and deliver!"

"What?" It was the merest whisper.

"I've not been paid, I tell ye," the coachman grumbled again, and curiously, turned his face away from Tom and the proceedings, as if to say it was nothing to him what was enacted.

Suddenly, the carriage door was thrust open. And without anyone to let down the step for her, a young woman stumbled and fell from the carriage, holding on to the door handle to keep her from landing into the road. She was panting with fear. She paused, hesitating as if to steel her will. Then, with a long frightened look into the depths of the carriage interior, she ran forward. And clasping at Ladyman's boot, she laid her cheek against the stirrup.

"Please, sir…please, I have nothing. No jewels, nothing. I am sorry…" she apologised.

Confounded, Tom stared.

She glanced up at him. Tom Ladyman had never seen the face of such distress before, though it was a pretty face—dark-eyed and sweet—with a frame of dark hair.

"But please, sir, I beg of you. Please…" she continued in that urgent whisper. "Please, whatever it is you want, I shall give it to you. Only… Only, please, will you take me with you? Please, sir," she pleaded. Her voice throbbed with fear and desperation.

Bewildered, Tom blinked. "What?" he croaked.

"Please, sir, I beg of you. I shall do anything you ask. Anything at all. Just take me with you. Please, sir, anything…" she begged, cringing and darting a look back at the carriage. "I shall do anything. Only do not, I beg you, make me get back in that coach. Please…"

"Madam! Lady Wilmot!" came a sharp belligerent voice.

Tom looked back to the carriage. So the sweet-faced creature was titled, was she?

The young Lady Wilmot froze. And there was fear in her eyes.

"Lady Wilmot, pray, return to the carriage at once!"

A middle-aged, hoddy doddy lady's maid, more arse than body, was struggling to alight. She came down hard, but on both feet, in the mud. Tom heard her tsking in vexation. "I do not know who you think you are, you good-for-nothing ruffian, but I shall have the law on you, you mark my word!" she snapped. "Madam! Return here to me upon this instant," she demanded.

Tom glanced warily from the one to the other. There was something wrong here. And he didn't like it. And he much disliked the maid.

"Please, sir, do not make me…" Lady Wilmot whispered to him.

"Please. She is taking me to London…My husband, he beats me. And…and uses me most ill. Please, sir, take me with you.

"He says…he says he has lost a wager and that I…I am the forfeit. He says means to…he means to…" Lady Wilmot stopped, trembling, unable to complete the sentence. "I swear to you, it is true…"

The abigail shook our her skirt and arranged her cloak ostentatiously about her. "Enough of this, madam! Come away from that filthy creature." The expression on her ugly face was plain, her mouth pursed up prim and tight as a cat's arse. "Madam, you will leave that disgusting rogue's side this instant. For I give you fair warning—I shall tell Sir Robert of this."

And much put out by her mistress's patent refusal, she hoicked up her skirt to stomp across the mud-rutted road. "Do not imagine for an instant that I shall not."

"Please, I beg of you, do not listen to her," Lady Wilmot persisted, tightening her hold on Ladyman's mud-crusted boot, her words quickening with dread. "Please…She is his creature. He is a terrible man. I believe he has even worked for the French. He…"

"…And as for you, you country put, I find it abhorrent that such a low creature was not transported years ago," sneered the abigail. "Or hanged. For 'tis all you're good for, to be sure. And you may be sure…"

But Ladyman had had enough. He aimed the pistol at the maid. "Shut your gob or I'll blow your face off!" he barked. "'Struth, 'tis a lumping hellcat…"

The woman glared at him and stumped forward. "You shall do no such thing, you damnable wretch, for I shall have the law upon you, you filth, you Sir Reverence, you…"

Od's balls, what was wrong with the woman? Without considering, swiftly, rashly, he dismounted, thrusting the reins into Lady Wilmot's hand. "Hold 'im!" he snapped.

"I tell you, you are not fit to black my master's boot or…"

Furious, he stormed forward, raised the pistol butt and brought it down hard across the abigail's screwed up face. "Shut up."

She shrieked. And clutching her face, collapsed to the ground.

Tom strode back to the black. Holy saints and angels, this was all wrong! A frigging disaster, this. And like any sensible man, which he knew himself to be, upon discovering that the situation was not as he'd intended—a bit of screaming, some histrionics and there's an end to it—he'd been poised to do the sensible thing, and scarper. But then the lady had said that remarkable thing about her husband…and, well perhaps, if that were true, if that indeed were true…then perhaps something might be rescued from this bloody farce of a hold-up. Nor could he be unmoved by the real distress in that sweet voice. Hell's bells and buckets of blood!

Angrily, he took hold of the reins and a handful of mane, and fitting his foot back into the stirrup, hauled himself back into the saddle. Then leaned down, extending his hand. "Take hold of my arm," he ordered, and hauling the frightened woman up, he caught hold of her as she settled into place at the front before him.

"But I 'ent been paid!" the coachman grumbled.

Tom stared at him. "That, my good man, is not my problem!"

"But I 'ent been paid," the coachman repeated testily.

"You can take the sour-face maid!" Tom barked.

"Nay," the coachman protested. "I'll not have 'er. 'E pays 'er. 'E don' pay me…for all I drives 'is 'orses!" he said righteously. "An' I 'ent been paid!"

"Sweet holy Christ!" Tom muttered, struggling and fumbling to find a loose coin in his waistcoat pocket. His fingers closed over a half-crown. Pulling it free, he tossed it at the coachman, who for all his age caught it with a deft hand.

The coachman regarded it with suspicion. "I thank 'ee, sir. I'll not forget your kindness. Ye may count on tha'."

"Ha!" Tom exclaimed, wheeling the great black sideways, before plunging down a murky path and disappearing into the dark thickets of the Forest.

Chapter X

1

It was the same conversation as ever. Held in those same low voices of murmurs and grunts and mumbled monosyllables, and all barely audible above the din. Though it was not the same doss house. Though it might have been the same, for in every respect of low stained ceiling and blackened walls, cheap drink, cheap harlots and drunken revelry, it varied little. All except the name—this was The King's Head—was a replication of every other. And today Barnet's balding head was looking sunburned and pink, and the stench of so many unwashed bodies in close proximity was possibly worse, on account of the humid weather. For once, Barnet had left his blood-stained butcher's apron at home. Or perhaps he had left that occupation for another less sanguinary business. Jesuadon did not ask.

Jesuadon had not been drinking steadily all day. Which had done nothing to improve his temper. For it had been nearly a week since their last meeting. A week of no news. A week of nothing. Of no one knowing anything. Of nothing but idle absent shrugs and blank incomprehension. And silence. A week while the fools on the streets did little but pass the time slavering and speculating over the Prince Regent and his fat trull of a wife—as if such things mattered—apathetic to the deaths in their midst, the death stalking all of Europe, all of them blind—blind, drunken and dull. "Yes, what?"

The lashless man wiped a hand over his rounded belly and stared passively into the thin froth of his ale. "…Reckon you won't like this," he murmured, then raised the tankard and drank, holding the ale in his cheeks, tasting the wetness, the bitterness.

"What?" Jesuadon said it on an exhalation of breath.

Barnet swallowed down his mouthful. "He was down the Mint, our John Brown."

"And you missed him," Jesuadon concluded tightly.

Barnet had feared a worse reception. Much worse. He inhaled with relief. "Yes," he admitted.

"When?"

"The day I told you we'd not found him, but then I'd not yet sent a lad down the Mint," he said without hesitation.

"Splendid. That will make the Guvnor rejoice. I can hardly wait to break the happy news," Jesuadon said sourly.

Barnet waited, ignoring the outburst and the tuneless singing from the far corner, waited and drank. Waited while Jesuadon tossed off a glass of wine and refilled and drank another. "There's more," he said at last.

Jesuadon darted a glance at the mouldering ceiling. "Go on, then. Delight me," he invited, his eyes gaining a dangerous glittering menace.

Barnet remained unmoved, unthreatened. "It is my belief that he may well have passed through London before that as well. On his way to Kent. To meet up with the boy."

"What? When? Where was he?" Jesuadon snapped.

Still, Barnet remained unflustered. "Just beyond the city limits. In one of those shanty villages outside the city proper, it was. A rag-taggle hugger-mugger sort of place, nothing but a collection of sheds and hovels on a few acres of waste ground, it is. Low. Very low. Most of the folk there being itinerant or criminal in one way or another. I doubt if you'd know it. Tomlin's New Town, they call it."

"I know it." Jesuadon rubbed his eyes and yawned. "And what did he there?" he asked, perhaps already knowing the answer.

The lashless man sniffed his contempt. "Tried to rape a female."

Jesuadon's expression toughened. "And why did we not hear of this?"

Barnet shrugged dismissively. "I dunno. But it seems some of her neighbours heard the set-to and came to her aid. After which, our John Brown, if it was him, wisely loped off." He said it succinctly, then drank his ale.

"Was it him?"

"I reckon so." Barnet shrugged. "Though from what I could gather, her rescuers was more than to happy to give our Mr. Brown an ample tasting of his own medicine. Which may, I fancy, account for that measure of reluctance in their coming forward with this information. Howsoever, I believe I have made it clear that there must be no such reluctance in the future." Then without apology, he continued: "Then again, until the good Captain came back from Edinburgh, we wasn't spreading our net wide enough and was looking in the wrong places, to my way of thinking. It will not happen again," he said without compromise.

"Right," Jesuadon concluded. Apathy, apathy. It would spell the death of them all. "Anything else? Do we know where else he might have gone? His contacts? No? Find out."

Barnet nodded and drank down the last of his ale, holding it for a long moment in his mouth before swallowing, then motioned to the tapster for another. He slid a coin across the bar-surface, then leaning heavily on the bar, regarded the head of foam on his refilled tankard with affection. And then, soft, sweetly even, he murmured, "Tom Ladyman's brung you a parcel."

Jesuadon, in the act of downing a glass of porter, narrowed his gaze in surprise. "What?"

"Tom Ladyman's gone and brung you a parcel," Barnet repeated. And there was a thread of humour in his quiet voice.

His voice now higher: "I beg your pardon?" Jesuadon gaped. This was too much. "What in the devil is Tom Ladyman doing this far north?" he ground out. "He's meant to be down in Hampshire, the plaguey sauce box!"

His companion slanted him a glance, the first of the evening. "'Tis a very special parcel," he averred, giving a quick nod of approval. And again that thread of humour. "'Tis waiting for you at Sparrowhawk's, from what I hear."

Jesuadon's temper snapped, that edge of temper which had been threatening all day to break out, now wholly erupting. "What the devil is all this buggeration about parcels, you fecking poxy quire?"

The lashless man, who had been savouring his information, treasuring it, enjoying it as a sweetmeat in Lent, smiled, showing his decaying teeth. "'Tis a lady," he said, with a swift appreciative wink.

Jesuadon looked at him hard, fury mounting. "What in the name of all that's holy would Tom Ladyman bring me a woman for?" he barked.

The repellent, confident smile grew. "Well, now, it would appear he grew tired of waiting for the weather to clear, what with Warne being none so keen to take shipments in the rain, as I understand it. On account of the paths through the Forest being so mired and all. So he's took to the High Toby…and as chance would have it, he's brung you a lady," Barnet said airily. And added: "Perhaps he knows more o' your habits than me…"

Jesuadon nearly screeched: "Taken to the High Toby? What?" In sudden rage, Jesuadon caught at his hair. "Tom Ladyman is a hell-born babe and a cursed idiot, and the devil may fly away with him! Od's my life, it is bad enough having old Charlie Flint sending the Revenue Officers off in every direction to keep that fool from harm. But now he's meant to interfere with Bow Street's business as well, is he, to protect that bloody young lobcock? I shall damned well kill him for this!"

Jesuadon sniffed hard as if he had a cold coming on, and narrowed his eyes to peer angrily at Barnet. "You, sir, are a fuckster, sir," he ground out, and turning on his heel, left.

The lashless man ran a cool soothing hand over his sunburnt head, and smiled appreciatively at his newly-filled tankard. "There now. I did enjoy that, you know," he murmured, crooned even, to nobody.

2

Adam Sparrowhawk was in the kitchen of his vast premises, unloading and inspecting baskets of vegetables when Jesuadon came stomping in. He heard him enter and did not look up.

"Adam," Jesuadon said, with a nod of greeting. "I understand Tom Ladyman's been in…" he added warily.

"Aye." The nod was almost imperceptible. "The parcel's upstairs." Sparrowhawk gestured toward the backstairs. "Stowed in the safe room for you." The sound of his voice rumbled and echoed its way up from the well of his deep chest.

Jesuadon exhaled his exasperation, but said nothing. And started for the door beside the great hearth. The next time he saw Ladyman he would give him such a rating. Or sack the rollicking bugger.

"'Tis locked," Sparrowhawk growled.

Jesuadon turned to glare at him. "It's locked?"

Sparrowhawk gave a nod as he returned to counting cabbages.

Jesuadon hesitated. "You wouldn't happen to know why he brought me this particular parcel, would you?"

Sparrowhawk favoured him with a long silent measuring and yet curiously blank stare, then said, "He said you'd want to know."

Jesuadon stopped at the door to watch him, and to wait for whatever else he might add. It was generally worth the wait when or if Sparrowhawk spoke. Though he did so most infrequently. "What would I want to know? Did he tell you that?"

"That he did not say," Sparrowhawk pronounced in his laconic way and reached for another large basket—this filled with leeks. And without looking up, he added: "I don't know. Reckon he had his reasons. But he was dead certain you'd want her," he finished, dumping the leeks out upon the long scrubbed table to count them as he had the cabbages.

Jesuadon waited in case there was more. There wasn't. Nor did Sparrowhawk look up again. Od's balls, why did he engage in this pestilential business? And shaking his head, he ducked his head under the low lintel and began the weary trudge up the four flights of stairs, to the safe room under the eaves.

3

She heard the key in the lock before he entered. And stood beside the bed to face him. Whoever he was. And as the door opened, she had begun, catching her bottom lip between her teeth, trembling, to unfasten the buttons and pins at the bodice of her gown. For the moment of payment had come. The moment she had been dreading as she had lain curled up in a tight ball on the bed at night. Or as she had sat, silent and empty and dazed, during the past two days. Sat, and remained sitting, wholly disconnected from life as she had known it and unable to think beyond the moment, unable to still her quaking or dispel the fear that gnawed at her insides. It was that moment which would begin and end her shame. And she told herself repeatedly that she could bear it. Whatever it was. However he might use her.

She had done the unthinkable and run away from her husband and master. She was dead to her family now. Worse than dead. Disgraced and fallen. Without hope of redemption. And if she did not please him, this man, would he turn as violent as Sir Robert? But at least…at least, she told herself—unable to banish the terror that at any moment she might be turned onto the street and she did not know what she would do then—he would be a stranger to her and to her shame, and she knew that she must find some solace in that. And she hardly looked up as he entered the room—she could not bear to—but with clumsy stupid fingers, unhooked the buttons.

Thos Jesuadon stood in the doorway and peered in stunned disbelief at the young woman.

Dark hair and darker eyes. Pretty, with a neat figure. Wearing a well-cut gown, with her hands and face clean and her face unpainted. A lady.

But why in hell's name was she undressing? Christ Almighty, had Tom Ladyman turned bawd?

Incredulous, he almost gaped. For she was shaking so she could barely stand as, biting her bottom lip in fear, she fumbled with the ribbon at the neck of her chemise, and unloosing it, let it fall open to reveal the top half of one breast.

Clearing his throat, Jesuadon found his voice. "What the devil…?" he choked.

Upon her breast and across her chest lay a dappling of bruises, both fading and fresh.

She froze. Then looked up. And saw him clearly for the first time.

He was tall and fair and he was a gentleman, and he looked tired or cropsick or brittle. Her dark eyes filled with tears. She shook her head. "What?" she whispered. And swallowed painfully. And despite her fear and wretchedness, read the utter lack of comprehension in his pale face. Like a dashing of cold water. "Is this…Is this not what I am here for? What you…"

"No!" he declared, regarding her still with that look of astonishment.

"Oh," she gasped. Instinctively, she reached to cover her breast with her hand, to hide her nakedness and shame. Beyond that, she could not think.

"No," he repeated.

And blinking with surprise, Jesuadon turned his face aside and withdrew through the half-opened door. "I shall, ehm…return presently…once you have had a chance, um, to put yourself to rights." He closed the door firmly behind him. What the blazes was all this?

She was dressed again when he returned, a tray in hand, upon it a teapot, a jug of milk, a pot of sugar lumps and two mismatched cups and their saucers. He regarded her uncertainly, then set it upon the small table. "I thought you would prefer it to a tankard of ale," he said, studying her reaction.

Wholly lost—for if he did not want her for that, why was she here?—she folded her lips together and nodded fearfully. "Thank you," she whispered, confirming his initial impression of her.

Undone and confused, she remained cowering near the corner of the chamber. The books, Boy's books, his clothes and all his things had been removed. The window was shut, despite the heat of the day and evening and the stuffiness of the attic room.

Jesuadon glanced at her. It seemed she was too frightened even to move. He poured out a cup of tea. "Milk?"

She nodded. "Oh," she breathed. "Oh, yes, thank you," she said, still in a whisper.

He brought her the cup, which she took, as he had anticipated she would, with a tentative smile, like a lady. He made no attempt to touch her, even accidentally.

"Have you eaten?" he asked.

"Oh." She nodded again. "Yes. They have brought me food, very good food, every day." She was regaining her voice, though still it was pitched quite low, and soft, and throughout she retained that troubled and hesitant manner.

"Good." He went to the window and opened it against the heat.

"They warned me against going near the window," she ventured.

"Did they?" Jesuadon said, not caring. He drew a deep breath of the fresher evening air, then returned to the table to pour himself a cup of tea. He waited for her to sit, which she did eventually, perching on the edge of the bed, and then he, himself, sat down at the table, crossing his legs. And waited. 'Slife, this was going to be a long evening.

"Perhaps you might begin by telling me your name?" he said finally.

She regarded him—again fearfully. And blinking rapidly several times, she said brokenly, "But are you not…going to…"

"What? Force you? Rape you?" Jesuadon shook his head and smiled gently. "No," he said succinctly. He threw back his head for a long moment, then said with an unaccustomed amiability: "I take no unwilling women to my bed…so you may be easy on that head. To be sure, I never saw the attraction in it."

"Oh," she murmured, nodding almost to herself, as if she truly hadn't known.

Jesuadon tried again. "Come, you were going to tell me your name," he said as easily as he could.

"Oh." She almost smiled. "Marianne Wilmot," she said nodding as she was wont to do—for reassurance perhaps. "Lady Wilmot," she admitted with diffidence. "Wife…to Sir Robert." The trembling had returned.

"More tea?" he enquired, watching her, deliberately breaking in on her troubled thoughts. There was intelligence in those lost dark eyes.

"I beg your pardon? Oh. Oh, yes. Thank you."

Patiently, his every action full of courtesy, Jesuadon poured her more tea. And waited. Biding his time.

The breeze through the open window had begun to clear the room of its closeness, the sounds of the street below providing a constant but not unwelcome background of the grinding clamour of the city, punctuated by friendly laughter or rambling jollification.

Jesuadon paused, pondering how he might gain her confidence. What did she know? And did she know she knew it—whatever it was? Probably not. "Perhaps you might tell me, if you would care to, how you came to be here, ma'am?"

She drew a quick breath, darting a sober glance at his face. She lowered her gaze to contemplate her mismatched empty tea cup. And drew another breath, almost a sob. She blinked rapidly. And wetted her bottom lip as she considered how to begin the tale of her fall. "I was on my way to London with my maid," she began in that low hesitant voice. "My husband had sent for me…to join him," she said, risking another anxious glance at Jesuadon. "I did not wish to come."

"And why was that?" Jesuadon asked, calmed by her fear.

She swallowed, choosing her words. "Sir Robert…" She stopped. "Sir Robert is…a great gambler, I believe. And…" she paused again, hesitating, contemplating her tightly folded hands.

Jesuadon watched her carefully. "And?" he encouraged.

The shell of her composure deserting her, her gaze remained fixed on her hands. "He had said that he recently lost a wager. It would have been for a great sum, I do believe. But upon this occasion, the stakes had not been money. I do not know what it is he would have gained had he won." She held her lip between her teeth for a moment.

"But as it was, he lost. And I was to be…" She looked up at him, the expression upon her face once again lost and her eyes once again filling with tears. "I was to be the forfeit." She wiped at her eye and cheek with the back of her hand. "To be used…as…"

"I understand," Jesuadon cut in, sparing her the shame of articulating her planned fate.

He regarded her not unkindly. Hers was a common enough tale, that of a plausible gamester marrying for money, and when the money is finished, wagering for other more exciting stakes. 'Struth, it had been all the rage among Devonshire's circle set some ten years ago—probably still was over amongst the Melbourne set. Though the ladies in question were hardly the virtuous little country wives Marianne Wilmot appeared to be. Jesuadon narrowed his gaze. But why on earth would Ladyman think this of any interest?

"Oh," she whispered. "Yes." She wiped ineffectually at the tears and at her nose. Then surprisingly put up her chin. "I had told myself I could endure even that. But when it came to it, I found that I could not. So…so when…Mr. Ladyman held up our coach, I took my chance, do you see…"

Still and furious, Jesuadon sat. Ladyman had told her his name. He had told her his name. Od's balls, the secure network had unravelled, was unravelling as he sat here. Small wonder the Frenchies were dropping them like sleeping cats on a doorstep.

"…I climbed down from the carriage and ran to him and begged him to take me with him. I did not concern myself with what he would do to me. I did not care if he beat me or set me to scrub floors. As long as I did not have to…For Sir Robert meant to…He meant to…" she said in a rush, desperate for him to understand.

He did. She saw it in his eyes.

"Yes," he said softly. "And then, what happened?"

"Oh." She shook herself, willing herself to recover. "Well, my maid…well, she too got out of the carriage. And when she saw him, she began to speak to Mr. Ladyman in the most offensive of terms. And me. She demanded that I should come back to the carriage. But I…I did not. I would not," she clarified. "And then when she began again to speak so to Mr. Ladyman, calling him such things as I had never heard, he got down from his horse and he hit her."

"What?" Jesuadon exclaimed, thrown off balance. "He hit her?"

"Oh yes," Lady Wilmot nodded several times in approbation. "Yes. And I liked him the better for it," she affirmed.

"I see," Jesuadon said in wonder. "And then what?" he asked, faintly, for he had now begun truly to question where this might lead. What had Ladyman been thinking? Or was he just fuddled?

"Oh. Oh, he returned to his horse and once he had remounted, I begged him again to take me with him. I told him what my husband meant to do with me. I would have said anything at that instant. Betrayed any confidence to gain my release. So I told him that I believed Sir Robert has worked for the French…"

Jesuadon caught his breath and remained perfectly still. And said nothing. Barnet would have felt the quiver of interest run through him. She did not notice.

"Perhaps I should not have said it. Perhaps it was a confidence too far. But I do not care," she said defiantly. "For it was then he took pity on me, and it was at that moment that he reached down to hand me up. And so we rode off," she finished.

"...Leaving your maid and the coach behind," Jesuadon said patiently, gazing out of the window, pondering the slow fall of dusk, the noise of the city, the sounds of horses clippety-clopping on the packed clay and gravel streets, the sounds of laughter as those who worked only in the evenings came out to ply their trade, while his mind spun with questions and conclusions and repercussions and plans of investigation.

She nodded. "Yes. I do not recall much of the ride after that. Except that it was long and I was surprised to find that he had brought me here."

And returning his attention to her: "And the bruising upon your breast?" Jesuadon asked quietly. "Was that Ladyman's doing too?"

"What?" she gasped, glancing fearfully down at her carefully refastened bodice. "Oh...Oh, no! No." She shook her head. "No, Mr. Ladyman was ever kind to me," she insisted. "He took no liberties, not any. I do assure you. Upon my honour!"

"I see," Jesuadon said. And again, he did.

There was a knock at the door. Jesuadon rose and went to open it. It was Molly, Sparrowhawk's armful of a common-law wife, handing him another tray, laden as before with teapot and cups and saucers. He took the tray from her and waited while she shut the door behind him.

And only as he busied himself with pouring the new-brewing tea through the strainer into another set of mismatched cups and saucers, did he ask, almost incidentally: "It seems curious that you should mention that your husband works for the French. Whatever would give you such an idea as that? For surely, such a course would be quite dangerous, do you not think?" he probed.

She may have been frightened—to be sure, she had been abused and made desperate with guilt—but Lady Wilmot had long given up any illusions she might have cherished about the man she called 'husband'.

She looked at Jesuadon quite seriously, then hesitated, for despite her fear and that nagging conviction of her moral fall, no one had yelled at her or berated her or disparaged her for two whole days together. And it seemed she was not, at least not immediately, in danger of being thrown in the street to beg or to sell herself. "It was very late one night, some months ago…" she began, accepting another cup from him. "Thank you…And Sir Robert had been up late drinking with friends. I had gone upstairs sometime earlier, for their company was not for me. But I was bleeding, so I came downstairs to the kitchen…"

"I beg your pardon?" Jesuadon stopped her, suddenly for all his disinterest disgusted. "He beat you when he had guests in the house?"

"What? Oh! Oh no," she shook her head, surprised into almost smiling. "No, it was not like that. It was…" she stalled, unable to explain the indelicacy.

"Ah," said Jesuadon, inexplicably more comfortable with this unspoken explanation.

She nodded. "And when I was returning to bed, I heard him say that it did not matter how much he lost, for he could always get the money from the Frenchies. That the Frenchies would pay him for anything he would tell them."

Jesuadon sat calm as calm, his eyes clear as polished amber. "He said that? How very curious. Preposterous, even," he said with deceptive disparagement.

She nodded. "Yes."

"But were those his exact words?" he questioned, his tone still blasé and uncommitting.

She nodded again. "Yes. Yes, I do believe they were." She paused, then finally, calm, decided against whatever it was she had thought to say, and instead drank her tea.

Jesuadon sat quietly for a while, staring out the window at the deepening sky. At last, he rose. "It is growing late, Ma'am. I shall leave you now. Is there anything you require?"

She gave him an odd look. Then, her lips trembling: "Oh." She blinked as if amazed by his kindness. "Some fresh linen would be very welcome, I thank you," she admitted.

"I shall see to it," he said, still regarding her with that peculiar clear-eyed manner.

She blushed a very bright pink.

He stopped at the door. "I shall return tomorrow or the next day…I am Jesuadon, by the bye. I have a passing acquaintance with Sir Robert. But he shall never learn of you from me. You have my word on it."

"Th-thank you," she stammered. Then clear-eyed, she said softly, "Mr. Jesuadon…sir…what will you do with me?" Her hands were laid one over the other below her chest, like a Renaissance Madonna's.

Regarding her soberly, Jesuadon had no answer. "I do not know," he admitted. To return her to her husband would endanger Ladyman. "I take it that you have no children?"

"No." An expression of loss and regret crossed her face. She shook her head. "No."

"Ah," he nodded. Then: "You will be safe here for the present."

She nodded and did not attempt a smile.

Bowing, Jesuadon left her, locking the door behind him. Then, thoughtfully and slowly he made his way down the stairs to the kitchen, where he found Molly—not serving tables or in the bar as she frequently was at this hour—but red-cheeked and perspiring with the heat, her arms and hands covered with flour and small gobbets of raw dough as she rolled the pastry for her meat pies. Jesuadon came to stand beside her and placed two guineas on the floured table at her hand. "When you go out in the morning, could you look into the purchase of some fresh linen?"

She stopped rolling the circle of dough on the table, and gave him a friendly, knowing glance. "Anything else?" she said, slipping the coins into her apron pocket.

"I fancy she might welcome a change of clothes as well. Something more suitable for the warm weather, perhaps. Though not conspicuous."

She gave a heartfelt sigh and shook her head. "I'll see to it, my lamb," she nodded and did not look up from the lump of dough and floured rolling pin again.

But she said it to no one, for already Jesuadon had slipped from the kitchen into the cooling dusk, and begun to walk, uncharacteristically fast, across the innyard and out toward The King's Head in Seven Dials.

Chapter XI

1

"Wilmot?" the lashless man repeated scornfully. "You're cocking about, ain't you?"

"Yes. No!" Jesuadon exclaimed.

Barnet had not been at The King's Head when Jesuadon returned there. Nor had he been gracing any of the other gin houses of doubtful regal affiliation in Clare Market or the Rookery. As Jesuadon had learned as he had scoured the dimly lit streets and alleys, asking news of every crossing sweep and loiterer in his pay. For the better part of the night, he sought the lashless Barnet, striding from parish to parish, doss house to doss house, always on foot across thoroughfares crowded with carriages and hackney coaches, frequently breaking into a run over the course of the night—indeed, every time he thought he caught a glimpse of Barnet and his balding pate and chuffy face with its lashless all-seeing eyes in the distorting gyrating shadow of a linkboy's torch, or passing beneath the insubstantial halo of a street lamp, or through the square patches of light thrown on the streets by windows and doors opened wide to the evening cool. But never, not in the throngs of drunken labourers nor among the young bucks out for an evening's carouse, nor idling amongst the city's prostitutes now drunk and leaning half-dressed in doorways, had he discovered him. He had been nowhere. Only now, at last, the night far spent, and the city's grinding roar lessening to a predawn hum, had he run him to ground here in this quiet corner just off St. Martin's churchyard, in Mrs. Meadows' Chop Shop, a step away from Porridge Island, here, as he sat with his back to the wall, finishing the last of an eel pie and sluicing it down with a tankard of small beer.

The other tables about him were empty—their stools and chairs stacked atop them, awaiting the final sweeping of the plank wood floor. The few remaining lit candles were barely more than fitfully flickering stubs in the wall sconces which dispensed little light. And only Mrs. Meadows herself, fussing in her kitchen, tidying, arranging the remaining cuts of meat, and preparing for the morrow's business, remained.

Aching with weariness and in want of sleep, but wanting the quarry more, much more, Jesuadon, who had spent the hours of his search considering this new information and what it might or might not signify, rubbed his eyes. "I want a watch set on his house. And I want him shadowed at all times, night or day, is that clear?"

Barnet nodded, and laying down his fork and knife, wiped his mouth with the back of his hand. "Wilmot…" he repeated derisively. "Wilmot. Where does he live? Mayfair? Stephen's Hotel or some such? Right. I shall get a crossing sweep on the front door in the morning…" His broad frame filled much of the wooden settle upon which he sat.

"No. Do it now."

"Right," Barnet agreed, undismayed by the urgency in Jesuadon's manner or the fact that he would not be seeing his bed for another hour at least. "But Wilmot?" he questioned again. "You ain't cocking about? We are talking about the same chappie, ain't we? Smallish, dark eyes, crimped dark hair, dandified?"

"Makes a very great deal of his cravat and pleated shirt ruffle, yes. The very same."

Barnet grimaced, and regarding the low ceiling, kept his thoughts to himself. Or believed that he did. He passed his hand over the smooth skin of his bald patch. "Anything else?"

"I don't know," Jesuadon admitted warily. His elbows resting on the table, he pressed at his eyes with the heels of his hands, pondering, wondering, questioning. "But upon my word, it's all a bit peculiar…" he began.

"What is?" Barnet growled.

Sitting up straighter, Jesuadon screwed up his face. "Well, to be sure, there ought to have been a hue and cry raised, do not you think? His wife has been missing for how many days now, and nothing's been said. Or not that I have heard. 'Struth, I should have expected there to have been a hue and cry raised after Tom's little escapade, but I've not heard of it. Have you? Which seems 'odd', don't it?"

"Well, I shall tell you what," Barnet began, speaking plainly for once. "Odd or no, we don't want Bow Street poking their nose round. Nor the river police neither."

"No. We don't. I'll speak to Flint, ask him to have a word..." Jesuadon paused, still considering. "But here's another oddity, when Ladyman took her..." he said, tracing the wood's markings on the table top with one finger. "He left the maid screaming in the road, having hit her."

"Didn't like her much then, did he?" Barnet commented drily.

Jesuadon did not smile, though his eyes gleamed. "So what happened to her? And to the coachman?"

"The coachman? Oh, I can answer that," Barnet said with sudden and unexpected good cheer. "Tom paid him off before he took her."

"What?" The word was choked out. It was one surprise too many.

"Well..." Barnet still chuckled. " He said the coachman had been complaining that he'd not been paid, so before he left, Tom tossed him a half-crown."

Jesuadon clasped his head between his hands. "I don't believe this."

"Well, it's the truth," Barnet declared.

"And the maid?"

Barnet shrugged. "That I cannot say."

"Can't or won't?" Jesuadon snapped. "Find out!"

Barnet puffed out his cheeks, unhappy with the order. "It'll mean a trip down there."

"I don't give a whore's arse."

"Right," Barnet sighed, and finished his beer. Then with no small regret peered into the bottom of the tankard. Thoughtfully he paused. "So, do you think it's our man this time?"

"I don't know," Jesuadon admitted, shaking his head, and rising from the table to begin his slow walk home. "Od's life, I wish I did know. Castlereagh will be asking me that before long, too. But I do not yet have the answer."

"Do you mean to keep her then?" Barnet asked wisely.

"For the moment," Jesuadon said. "For the moment, I believe I must." He paused, then added pleasantly. "I rather think Wilmot plays in Byron's company most evenings…"

Barnet rolled his eyes. "Gad, you don't suspect *him*, do you?"

Jesuadon shrugged and almost smiled. "No," he said, banishing some comforting thought. "'Sdeath, I wish I might. But no. I ain't saying he don't need the ready, but where would he find the time? He's far too busy poking that poxy little cock of his into anything that moves to have a spare moment for treason, wouldn't you think?"

"I hadn't heard he was that particular," Barnet jeered. "About them still moving, that is."

Jesuadon gave a whisper of sardonic laughter. "'Struth, nor had I. But I dare say we should keep an eye out, just in case." He made to leave.

"And where are you off to then?" Barnet said, suddenly testy. He had been anticipating company for the dawn's work.

"I?" Jesuadon said, raising an eyebrow in query at the implied disrespect. "I am off home to bed. My own bed," he crooned. "For on the morrow, I shall want to begin following that infernal money trail you're so deuced keen on. And I shall want a clear head for that."

Barnet regarded him, a certain grim excitement sparkling in his eye, before producing a slow reluctant grin. "'Afore God, and from the bottom of my soul, I do pity him…"

2

Jesuadon did not see Lady Wilmot again until five days later.

She was seated near the window in her room under the eaves. Away from the window, but still near enough to be in its light fall. A pile of folded linen or bedding lay on the floor beside her. She sat, her dark head bent slightly over her work, carefully sewing.

She looked up at the sound of the door opening though, her needle poised mid-stitch, smiling even before she saw who it was. She was not expecting him, though her eyes warmed at the sight of her visitor. "Oh. Oh, Mr. Jesuadon. I did not look to see you." There was a brightness to her this morning though she was still very pale. She made to lay aside the cloth upon her lap.

"No, do not get up." He held up a hand up to halt her.

"Oh." She resumed her seat while Jesuadon bowed slightly.

She gestured at the pile of linen beside her. "Molly has said that I may stay here for as long as I like…to do the mending," she said, smiling.

"Has she?" Jesuadon blinked in surprise. It did not sound such a great bargain to him.

"Oh. Oh, yes. I had asked her if there was any way in which I might be of service—for she has been so very kind to me…"

He saw that she was now dressed in serviceable and plain—though still fine enough—muslin. (Molly had done well.) Her hair was simply plaited and coiled at the back of her head, though tendrils had escaped to curl about her face. A dressing table with a mirror had been added to the room's furnishings. How had such a girl come to marry a Sir Robert Wilmot? For she was damn'd pretty, so she was. Fine of face and neat of figure.

"…And she said that she could always use help with the mending." Lady Wilmot again gestured at the pile beside her. "There is so very much of it in an establishment of this size, do you see? So I am very pleasantly employed." And he could see that she was.

"But come, do sit down. Have you news?" she asked, her expression clouding over.

Barnet had said they had begun looking for her. Though he had said it with a laugh. For, for the moment they could find no trace. Wilmot himself had gone to see the coachman, who staunchly denied ever having set forth on the journey, maintained that he had not even put the horses to the carriage for the journey, and that he had not been paid. And his equally irascible wife had corroborated.

The maid had been found wandering, muddied and hysterical, in the Forest sometime during the next day, but her rantings were put down to the onset of brain fever.

A couple of Wilmot's hirelings had tried questioning those in the public houses roundabout, but the locals were Gentlemen of the smuggling fraternity to a man, so they had seen and heard nothing and had nothing to say on the matter except that highwaymen hadn't pursued their business in the Forest for these ten years.

And only the maid said different. And she was a woman.

Yet there was no question but that Lady Wilmot had vanished.

A reedy-looking individual had begun asking after her in some of the lower end rooming houses in Southampton, and then Portsmouth, Barnet had mocked. Still, it wouldn't be amiss to keep an eye out. As yet, her family hadn't been informed...But at some point, it would become an embarrassment for Wilmot. The authorities might even suspect him of murder. Which would be good news for them. A man like Wilmot under pressure was bound to get careless.

"May I?" Jesuadon gestured to the chair, then at her nod, sat down. He regarded her thoughtfully. "Little of note. Nothing that need concern you. Though it would appear that Sir Robert has at last begun looking for you," he said gently, noting her brief intake of breath. And instantly wished to sooth her fear. "In, er, Southampton and Portsmouth, I'm told."

"Portsmouth?" she marvelled, her dark eyes growing round. "Whatever would I do in Portsmouth, sir?"

Jesuadon had no answer. "Perhaps Sir Robert believes you have friends among the naval fraternity? Or amongst their wives?" he suggested.

Now it was her turn to look bewildered. "But he must know that I do not!"

Which startled Jesuadon into exclaiming, "Sir Robert seems to know very little of you at all, ma'am. If you'll forgive me for saying so." He should not have said it.

An odd expression crossed her face. "Oh. But of course," she said, making little of his impertinence at having made such a personal observation. Though to be sure he had seen her undressed...She brushed aside the thought and willed herself not to blush. "No, you are quite right," she continued, beginning to stitch again. "Sir Robert does not know me at all."

Jesuadon continued to observe her. "He will never find you here, you may trust me to see to that." He waited while she recovered some measure of her equanimity, then: "Can you tell me, ma'am, does Sir Robert cheat at cards?"

She dropped her sewing into her lap, and appeared perplexed, though perhaps it was only at the lack of preamble to his question. "Oh. Oh, no. No, I do not believe…" She broke off. "I do not think so. I do not know," she admitted finally. Then: "But, could anyone cheat at cards and still lose so much?" she exclaimed.

Jesuadon paused, pondering her candour. "No. I should not imagine so, now that you say it." He had played against him just the once, to strike up the acquaintance he must now pursue. Deliberately and skilfully, he had lost. Not too much, but enough. "And dice?"

She shook her head. "I am sorry, I do not know." She folded her lips together for an instant and peered at the stitching she had done. "But… but I believe he does not much favour dice," she said at last.

"No," he nodded, giving a rare smile.

And Lady Wilmot saw that his teeth were very straight and very white, which was odd in one who drank so heavily—there was a corked bottle tucked into the outer pocket of his coat. Nor was he as florid as one would have believed he ought to have been.

"This becomes a trifle delicate, ma'am…" Jesuadon began. "Can you make me a list of all those of Sir Robert's friends who were wont to visit you in Hampshire? And those you noted in London as well? And if you was to write down anything of the relationships, whether they was friends from boyhood, or recent acquaintances…"

Lady Wilmot gazed at him levelly. "Oh. Yes. Yes, of course I will do so." And as before, she knew a great deal more than she believed she knew, for Sir Robert had always enjoyed bragging of his town amusements and acquaintances, dwelling upon such things to emphasise her inadequacies and his own social triumphs. "Right away."

Jesuadon rose. He had accomplished his business there. "Then I shall leave you now." He returned the chair to its place at the small table.

This time, she did lay aside her stitching, and rose to curtsy to him.

"…And return, if I may, on the morrow…for that list." He bowed, taking his correct leave of her: "Lady Wilmot." And quitting the room, he carefully and quietly locked the door behind him.

Chapter XII

1

Boy had been running for days. For weeks. For miles. Running under the merciless glare of the midsummer sun. Running east. Running through the waves of heat that rose from the parched flatlands of northern Germany and Prussia.

He had first come ashore near Hohenkirchen, in a small inlet amongst the shallows and dunes just west of the Danish coast. Landed there along with so many bales of smuggled cotton and sacks of sugar and coffee and God knew what else. And since that night when he, his face blacked with lamp soot, had been rowed ashore in the shadows of a cloud-covered midnight from the smuggler's vessel, anchored and bobbing beyond the sandbanks that were the hazard of the north German coast, since then, he, the least precious of the landed goods, had been running.

Avoiding France as he had been ordered.

Running. For his king and his country. Listening, watching. Gathering intelligence and information for his lordship. In the muted grey twilight before dawn, or long into the dusk-drenched half-lit summer evenings, to escape the midday heat and the watchful eyes of French agents. Passing the hottest hours of the day in barns or abandoned outbuildings asleep, to appear cautious and tousled near dusk, to take up his journey once more.

Past the acres of fields stripped bare of their crops, through a countryside depleted of men and livestock and fodder and grain. Across a sea of mud, the roads churned to impassable cart tracks, wet, clogged and rutted, and six inches deep in clag, worse than ploughed fields. And these the best of the notoriously bad German roads, they were.

He kept to the verges where he could, and sought out the trails through the ancient towering woods, unchanged since Roman times, making his way through the resonating stillness and the infrequently pierced gloom, running soft upon the forest floors of oak leaf mould and fallen pine needles.

Running. Zigzagging across the abandoned countryside, past the smoke-blackened houses and empty, eerie gothic churches which sat deserted and silent, discarded like the playthings of some long-dead giant. Dodging the few travellers and fewer carriages by diving into ditches or behind the low walls and hedges to wait, still and alert, for minutes or longer. To wait until the roads were quiet once more. And only then to emerge, and wary, to begin again.

Nor were there many who would have spoken to him. Not now. Not in the villages, nor in the markets. For the Germans were a notoriously silent people. And that silence had grown to a fermenting, echoing, cavernous thing as French taxes and reparation payments and the numbers of French agents and troops quartered upon them had mounted, crushing the once prosperous merchants and manufacturers and guildsmen beneath their leaden weight. And everywhere there was suspicion.

It had been near Hamburg, weeks earlier, that he'd learned that Napoleon and his vast pox-riddled army had left Dresden on the 29th May on their way to Thorn and Danzig and farther east than that even.

And so he followed in their wake, running across the bleak Silesian plains where the bleaching blinding sun burnt down as savage as the nights were cold. Across this land now wholly defiled and barren, stripped and ravaged like the few poor souls who had once eked their living from this hostile thin ground. For wherever the French army had marched, they had scythed down the unripened corn and the barley. And what they had not stolen for their horses, they had wrecked, riding hell for leather through the green crops, trampling it all to dust, their pillage leaving raw gashes in the forbidding landscape. The poor thatch from the peasants' huts, they had taken to feed their horses too, while their few wood fences had fed their cooking fires.

There were corpses though, both of horses, bloated with colic, and of men. Score upon score of them—stretched out or contracted, robbed and half-naked and rotting in the blazing summer sun and shimmering heat—all those distinguished young men he'd seen parading through the streets of Paris only months ago. All dead upon this battlefield without a battle, all along the roads and in the waysides. And it was the same on every road he travelled.

There were magpies too, feeding on the dead. And overhead, flocks of jackdaws and carrion crow. And black kites circling. And flies, everywhere flies. And packs of wolves by night.

And mile by mile, the aching desolation increased, as did the fearful sense that he had strayed into some madman's deranged vision of hell, while the rain quietly pattered on the sodden ground and in the puddles and splashed his face.

He had been here in the destitute flatlands of eastern Prussia before. Backward and empty and silent it had been then. Drought-stricken, with its grass brown and brittle, its fields of corn all straggling and bent and dwarfed, while the women pulled ploughs steered by their waiflike children. And the only music was the weeping melancholy of lone Jewish fiddlers playing late into night. But it had not been like this. This despairing wreckage of a land, shorn of all vegetation, the hamlets of mud-huts or tiny wooden cottages all reduced to piles of rubble and cold ash. As if some vast plague of human locusts had swept through, consuming everything in its path, so that nothing remained. No towns or houses or churches or children. Nothing but the litter of this foul army of devourers, their abandoned drays and gun wagons, shakos and booty—clothes and valuables and trinkets strewn as flotsam in the wake of a wreck—and the thousands of corpses, all slain not by some human enemy, but by the flux and disease. And only the flocks of pale storks overhead recalled the place it once had been.

And so he ran, now avoiding even the primeval pine forests. Those lush deep green places of raucous, natural quiet and rare shafts of too bright light. For these were now the haunts of the many bands of refugees and vagabonds. Home too to the marauders and deserters from Napoleon's Grande Armée, who nightly went forth to rape and pillage and rob.

And so he continued. Across Europe's lattice-work of crossroads which were the burying grounds for suicides—the countless and uncounted women and girls who had been violated unto death by this army of men who raped and murdered as easily as breathing. Though there were none left to bury them now. At the crossroads or elsewhere. Like their tormentors, they lay where they had fallen, their torn, bloodied clothes the only testament to their tortured ends.

And still running. Across these plains of devastation, where the pall of ruination and death hung over the land like a heavy fog. Through the squalls of rain that soaked the French army through their light summer uniforms, causing the unfixed dyes to stain their skin, these soaked him too—though he was better suited to drying out or taking shelter than they. For nowhere, nowhere on these sandy, hostile flatlands was there shelter large enough for an army of half a million men or more, plus their women and children.

Ahead, beneath the sullen sky lay another of the too many nameless sacked and abandoned villages. Now no more than a collection of unconnected walls and a lone church tower, it appeared from the distance.

Slowing, like a reconnoitring soldier, he searched for movement, for sign of the living, to the left and to the right, to the foreground and beyond. And saw, as he had so many times and forsaken places before, nothing. No trace or indication of deserters or the cowering dispossessed. No movement. Nothing. Overhead, a single black kite hovered and held, scanning the earth for a likely meal, and seeing what the boy saw, the utter stillness and desolation of the place, mounted upon a wave of air and departed.

Keeping low to the ground, his feet making no sound upon the crumbling earth as he ran, Boy came to rest against the remains of a low wall. For evening was approaching and he'd not eaten since morning.

And perhaps somewhere within the hamlet's empty walls, he might find food, or at least shelter for the night. And if there was no food to be had, well enough—a day's run ahead, in the far distance, lay Kozno with its landmark white and red baroque cathedral spires.

He no longer feared recognition. 'Struth, who was there to know him now? Or to own him? For he was as tanned as a gypsy child, caked in mud and splatter, streaked with the sweat and grime of weeks on the run, and dressed in the tatters of his trade. 'Struth, if ever he had been clean as a gentry child, it was a thing of the distant past.

He rubbed his face. And listening still to the relentless silence, broken only by the harsh cawing of the jackdaws, and alert to any movement, scanning, scouring for any furtive sign, he slowed to pick his way through the heaped rubble of the dilapidated cottages to the church tower. And there, near what had once been the church door but was now a gaping hole leading to a roofless and pillaged tumbledown wreck of three walls and no altar, near where in the small graveyard the gravestones had been smashed and the graves desecrated, he paused to draw breath, and stooped down to write with his finger in the dust of the ground, to trace the sign of the secret society which was his safety and succour.

Resting his cheek against his knee, he drew a deep breath. And then another. And waited. For nothing. But listened to the aching resonating stillness. The sound of desolation. And reflected upon his isolation. And the sound of death. The death of a country.

And waiting until his breath had grown quiet as a stone…he heard a sound.

And stopped. Froze.

A rustling.

Wholly still and unbreathing, he waited, keeping his eyes fastened on the ground and the secret symbol. Waited for a second sounding. Then slowly allowed his hand to creep along his waist the hilt of his knife. And closed his fingers around the smooth horn of the handle. Ready to draw. Readier to throw.

It was a rasping intake of breath.

"Junge?" it whispered.

His name. In German. Not Polish. Or it might just be a guess and not his name at all. But there was no one here who knew him, so it was a trap. He listened, straining, his hand tightening on his knife, preparing.

"Junge?" It was louder this time, though still tremulous. And again the wheezing, painful, rasping breath.

He squinted into the distant shadows, recalling. Remembering. Tracing the sound and pronunciation through his past. He knew the voice. Knew it well. It belonged in Westphalia. In a small village near… He raised his eyes from the ground, tensed, and glancing everywhere. "Pater?" he ventured. He must be here as a hostage. And slowly, Boy rose to his feet, alert, and readied his grip on the knife.

"Mein Junge! Is it you?" came the soft unhappy cry.

"Pater?" Boy repeated, still tentative, his every pore open to every movement, every change in light or sound.

A priest, elderly and infirm, wearing a tattered, rusty black cassock with a badly frayed hem, his large nose drooping and angry with chilblains, came creeping and shuffling from out the doorway of the ruined church. And beginning to snuffle and to weep, he cried, "Mein Sohn! Mein geliebter Junge!"

Boy hesitated, glancing about. But saw no one else. "Pater." Extending his arms, he went forward to embrace the old priest. "Pater, was ist Ihnen zugestoßen?" And hugged him close. "Was ist hier geschehen? Die französiche Soldaten? The French? Have they harmed you?"

"Nein, nein…"

Boy laid his cheek against the old man's grizzled face, holding him close as he wept. And repeated gently, "Pater, was ist Ihnen zugestoßen? What are you doing here? Why are you not at home?"

Shuddering, the priest wiped a hand across his nose and face and released himself from the comfort of Boy's close embrace. "It is you," he wept. And the tears spilled down his thin sagging jowls. "It is you." He patted the boy's cheek, an incongruous gesture. "Mein Sohn. Mein geliebter Junge!" And unable to still his tears, he shook his head from side to side in his relief and disbelief.

"Ja. Ich bin es wahrhaftig!"

"Ach, ach...It is a miracle that you have come here." Clinging to Boy as to the hope of life, he continued to shake his head sadly from side to side, while the boy held him close. And only eventually, did he allow himself to be led back through the doorway of the ruined church from whence he had come, which for all its dilapidation was still his place of refuge. "Ach..." He did not mop away his tears. "Ach, mein Sohn. It was in May, I came out of Westphalia to see a cousin who had been long sick. So how long ago it is, I do not know. He died the evening I arrived, so I remained to oversee the funeral and the disbursement of his will. But by then, by then, the French soldiers were everywhere." And still within the circle of the boy's arm, and still weeping, he led the way to sit upon a broad stone which had been pulled from a wall and now lay sideways. "You have never seen so many men, Junge. I tried to go back, to return home, but by then it was no longer safe." His face crumpled, though he did not cry again, but sank down wearily. "They were everywhere. As far as the eye could see on any road, they were there. Pillaging. Marauding. Begging. For already, do you see, already they were starving."

The boy narrowed his eyes. "Was bedeutet das? They ran out of food, do you say?"

"Ja. Ja," the priest insisted. "Already they had run out of food and supplies. And fodder. Ja, they had not even drink. And without even to drink, they went mad. They all of them went mad." He sat silent for a moment, recalling the horror of so many wild and raving creatures, men reduced to the behaviour of rabid dogs.

"They starved?" Boy repeated for confirmation. "All of those soldiers, they starved?" he questioned again, unable to comprehend it. For he had seen the commissary lists in Paris...

"Ja, so war es. They starved."

The boy blinked and was silent. "Christ have mercy."

"I have never seen so many men." The priest shook his head from side to side in awful regret. "And all of them sick, dying of the flux...They were boys though, you know. Nothing but boys. All just children. Many of them no older than you.

"And then they came into Prussia. They had expected to live off the land. Their officers did not know there had been the drought last year and that there was no harvest."

Boy looked out, away from the devastated village, beyond, seeing in his mind's eye the strewn ditches and corpse-clogged roads, and now, only now, beginning to understand.

"They did not know that spring had come so late and that planting had been late and there would be no grain." He looked pathetically upon the boy's face. "They found me one day, hiding, praying in the church. I thought it was the end. But it was a party of Italians. They had been hunting for acorns to eat—for that was all there was. But when they saw me, that I was a priest, they begged me to come and hear the confessions of their dying countrymen. So I came. I could not refuse..." He fell silent again.

Then: "It is worse across the river though."

"You have been across the river Nieman, into Russia?" Boy said softly, sharpening.

"Nun ja. They begged me to come. What could I do? Die französichen Soldaten, the French, they spat upon my robes, but the Italians, they begged me and kept me hidden at night. So I came.

"We crossed at the end of June. They had brought these vast bridges with them. Pontoon bridges they called them. It took days for all of them to cross over into Vilna. But then the rains came. And in four days of those storms, I think they must have lost half the army..."

"What?" Boy mouthed, the breath knocked out of him. "What? Half the army?" It was too incomprehensibly ruinous. "What happened?" he asked, recoiling. For this was worse than even he had seen. And he could not comprehend it. Whom must he tell? And how quickly could he tell them?

"They drowned," the priest said firmly.

Boy shook his head to clear it. "What do you mean, Father, they drowned? In the river Nieman?"

"Nein! In the roads!" he insisted. "The roads, the rains came and washed away the roads and turned them into bogs, and the men and their horses, they sank into the mire and they were drowned. And at night, the water, it froze. And the men, they froze to death, there in the open."

"Oh, mein Gott!"

"Ja!" exclaimed the priest, straightening and suddenly alert. "So war es. Und Napoleon, Napoleon, he did nothing! He knew nothing. They drowned, these boys. And froze to death. And the horses, they were screaming as they drowned, and he did nothing. He was there in Vilna and he did nothing. It was ruination. Chaos! It went on for days! Whole regiments, they perish, so."

"Mein Gott," Boy repeated. "Mein Gott…How many died there, do you think?" he groped, struggling with the scale of the losses.

The priest shrugged helplessly. "I heard some say ten thousand horses. And another, forty thousand horses. I do not know the truth of these sayings. The hospitals I visited, they were filled to bursting. The dead, they filled the streets. They were digging the trenches outside the city walls and just throwing the dead in. I came away then. I could not bear it in that charnel house, that Hell, God forgive me…" And then, he began to weep, overcome.

"Nein, weine nicht…don't cry…" Boy murmured, gathering the elderly priest once more into his arms, to comfort him like a child. "Nein. Weine nicht…" he crooned, holding back his own tears. For it was too much to comprehend. Even for him, even after all he had seen. There and elsewhere. "Shhh…shhhh…"

And all at once, he sensed that they were not alone.

Straightening, he stiffened, although the old man in his grief seemed not to notice. And he looked about him, again searching the area for any movement near the piles of rubble, any evidence of that stirring which is a body drawing breath. And raising his head slightly, listened for any sound that was not the weeping priest. Everywhere. Behind or near every tumbling of carved stone. Or lurking in every darkened corner. And could see nothing. No person, no glint of a blade or a rifle's barrel. None of it.

"Shhh…"

And then, there in a far corner of the ruined church, he saw it. A slight fluttering of something. A movement.

But no, there it was again. That corner of fabric that might have been the fabric of a sleeve, or skirt. Alive, or dead.

And keeping one arm still about the priest, Boy again slid his free hand along his waistband slowly, to take hold of his knife. And waited. Watching without appearing to watch that darkened corner of the ruined building. Watched, tightening his grip on the hilt, as finally a child, a small dirty barefooted child of indeterminate sex, with ragged hair in a ragged nightgown, edged forward from its hiding place.

Boy kept his grip firm on the knife and did nothing. Waited. Regarding the child with wary disbelieving eyes. For where were the parents? Or siblings?

But the child did nothing. Nothing but stand, hardly breathing, staring and gazing at Boy and the old priest, a strangely blank expression in its round eyes.

Boy bent to whisper in the old man's ear. "Pater Wilhelm, there is a child…"

"What?" The priest shook himself free, struggling with his disordered emotions. "What?" He looked up. And saw. And coming to his feet, he shuffled toward the child.

Was this another trap? Following suit, Boy rose and coldly positioned himself. It was easier to throw a knife, standing. Easier to get the arc right through the air.

The priest came to child, and took its hand to draw it forward. "Come, mein Schatz. Come, Liebling."

The child did not resist, but came slowly to stand before Boy, docile and unquestioning.

"When I returned, I found her here. Among the ruins, when I returned from across the river."

And as she neared, Boy saw that it was neither innocence nor trust that kept her gaze so clear, but trauma, and loss, the expression of a child's mind which had seen too much violence and death and could no longer record any event or person but was now hollow. And might always remain so. "Who is she?"

"I don't know." Pater Wilhelm shrugged, looking helplessly at Boy. "I do not know if she was a child of this village or from an outlying farm. Nor if she is French and was accompanying her family or her father and became separated from them. I can discover nothing. She does not speak, nor cry, nor respond to any language that I know. So what am I to do?

What must I do? I am a priest. I know nothing of children. Nothing of small girls."

He was meant to go on across the Nieman. He was meant to send his intelligence on to London and to St. Petersburg. And to Vienna. He should leave them and cross the Nieman. For he had meant to intercept as many reports from Napoleon as he could before they reached Paris—intercept, read, memorise, and return to their couriers. He was meant to send regular reports. They depended on him. They all depended on him. Di Borgo and Castlereagh, all of them. And if he did not, if he did not… "You must take her, Pater. Take her south. Into Bohemia. To Prague. You will be safe there. You will both be safe there."

The old man's eyelids fluttered with uncertainty. His face crumpled. He too had seen too much for any body. "But how will I accomplish such a journey, Junge? There is no food to be had. Not anywhere. You have seen the countryside. There is nothing. And I am an old man, I cannot carry a child all the way to Bohemia or Bavaria…" he protested, suddenly querulously angry.

"No," Boy said quietly. "No, I shall come with you as far as I can. I'll find us a donkey. I have money. You shall be safe with me, both of you. I shall take you." And setting his face, he thought of England. Of Jesuadon. And his lordship. Of Flint. They would not be so pleased with him when they heard of this. If they ever did. It would all depend upon what he could learn in the south…He looked kindly at the priest, then bent to scoop up the broken soul of a child into his arms. "Come." He had left his mark in the sand. If the brethren were out looking for him, they'd find it and know. "Have you food for tonight, or must we journey on to find some?"

Chapter XIII

1

The Macao Club was an Englishman's dream of Oriental Splendour, a sumptuous melding of opium-induced Kubla Khan and Far Eastern Grandeur as conceived by one who had never travelled beyond Calais—with diaphanous draperies tented over the main rooms and the walls painted with lively scenes of various Oriental pleasures being enjoyed by ladies and gentlemen of Eastern aspect. Though curiously, all were gowned and garbed in the latest London fashions. The club's location had been wisely chosen too, located as it was on Lower Bury Street, just a convenient stroll from the demi-mondaines' residences on King's Terrace and the gentlemen's clubs found on St. James's Street, and it fell, in respectability, somewhere between the two. Strictly speaking, it was a gaming hell, a magnet for those gamesters whose one true pleasure in life was the winning and losing of vast sums of money they frequently did not possess. However, on the sofas beneath the billowing silk curtains other delights of the evening might, at least, be initiated by gentlemen and their companions of the fairer sex.

Yet for all his known habits, Jesuadon had never ventured there and knew the place only by reputation. That, however, was about to change. And upon leaving Lady Wilmot's chamber, he had returned to his own set of rooms to prepare for the first of many evenings he would spend there—which he had begun by going to bed. To sleep.

Upon waking, he had taken a bottle of good champagne from Sparrowhawk's cellar, and uncorking it, emptied the contents into his steaming bath. Later, dried, with his nails pared and buffed, he dressed as meticulously as if he were dining in company with Brummell himself—heavily starched white cravat, starched ruffles, black coat, pale waistcoat of silk twill, and buff breeches. Passing through the kitchen on his way out, he stopped to help himself to a kidney pie, and then drank a pitcher full of milk, before availing himself of two bottles of his favourite claret.

He arrived in Lower Bury Street just as the debauched poet and his friends were chatting up the Macao's bruiser of a porter, and he, warmly welcomed by Wilmot, who was already drunk, joined their party. It was just gone midnight.

Inside, he found the place much as he had expected: the usual unhealthy mix of titles with cool heads who played for high stakes but could afford their losses, seasoned gamesters, intemperate hangers-on, febrile young bloods and high-class whores, all playing, wagering and drinking at tables beneath garish, billowing draperies of parrot green, salmon pink and acid turquoise, surrounded by the outlandish murals which would appear quite at home in the Brighton Pavilion. And regarding it with a discerning eye, surveying the crowded tables full of genial idiots carousing and sporting their blunt, and the ill-concealed gropings of those who'd brought their mistresses along, now that he considered it, everything about it was exactly like the Gaud of Gauds, the Brighton Monstrosity. All that was lacking was Prinny, dressed for the occasion like a misfit cross between an Indian Panjandrum and a Scottish Noble or some such. 'Struth, no wonder he had avoided it before now.

And taking in the names of those he observed, he seated himself beside Wilmot at the faro table and set himself to bet foolishly against the bank and to lose as much money as he might without arousing suspicion. And to watch: All those coming. All those going. The hardened gamesters, the demi-mondaines and their amours, the impressionable anxious overloud young men, the proprietor, the poet and his friends, the waiters. All of them. Who greeted whom. Who sat with whom. Who talked. Who appeared a fixture. Who was there on sufferance. Who lost.

Who won. Every last one of them.

Wilmot seemed to be fairly well-known and on familiar terms with nearly everyone. Which did nothing to narrow the field.

By two, Jesuadon had lost nearly two thousand pounds—a paltry sum by comparison with the others at the table—and appeared to have drunk several bottles of claret. Though Wilmot, still lounging and garrulous at his side, and wagering upon the cards without any care for what had been previously discarded, had lost and drunk more. Much more. And with the bank still winning against all, Jesuadon pushed back from the table, declaring that he reckoned he'd be off home.

"No, no, m'dear Jesuadon, you must not go yet," Wilmot protested loudly. "'Ssure you, 'ssure you, m'dear fellow, the night's still young—a mere babe at that!" he proclaimed. And laughing uproariously at his own wordplay, added: "A suckling, a veritable suckling, no more!"

Jesuadon shook himself as if gathering his wits. He checked his watch. "Is it so?" He gave a demi-bow. "Well, then, m'good man, if you will do me the honour, p'raps a hand of piquet then…" he slurred.

"What's that? Oh, piquet. Yes, 'ssuredly, damned fine idea. Damned fine…" Wilmot said, leering at a buxom young brunette—well-dressed and well-jewelled—seated between two young bloods, and flirtatiously, teasingly, bestowing her kisses on each in his turn. "Cannot afford to play against the bank when m'luck's this out…ha ha. A pest'lential whore, lady luck…Not like that fuckish bit of jam over yonder, what?" With effort, he hauled himself upright, and rose unsteadily from his chair to lead the way—tripping over another chair to a chorus of catcalls from his particular friends—to a small table for two. And snapped his fingers for the waiter to bring them a fresh deck.

By three though, Jesuadon reckoned he had won enough for one evening. Just enough. Certainly he'd had a sufficiency of Wilmot's company for one evening. Others too had begun to rise from the tables. And Wilmot, sensing that the luck had perversely but irrevocably turned against him for the present, was growing bored, peevish even. And seeing the debauched poet with his arm about a woman, he winked at Jesuadon and declared that they must no longer sit about, but should go out and see what other amusements might be had.

Still agreeable, Jesuadon accompanied him to the door, weaving as he walked, thus assuring that the porter would remember him again, and went out into the night air.

It had just come on to rain. Behind them, Byron had disentangled himself from the demi-rep to join them in the street. And Wilmot, guffawing at some offhand quip of the poet's, proposed that they go in search of a night watchman to box. "Famous sport," he pronounced, mashing the words only slightly. "For Byron's very handy with his fives, don't you know? Fights like the professionals…never fails to tap his man's claret, do 'ssure you, Jesuadon," he boasted.

Delightedly, drunkenly, Jesuadon agreed with the plan. But then, amidst his enthusiasm, he began to cough, and clutched at the Macao Club's iron newel post for support. But it was not enough to keep him upright. For the more he coughed, the more he wobbled and doubled over, and appeared to be sickening. Until at last, the porter intervened, and abjuring Wilmot and Byron to have a care of the cleanliness of his front steps—much to their amusement—he summoned a hackney from down the street. And hauling Jesuadon up, he dumped him on the hackney seat, and slammed the doors upon him.

"Stephen's Hotel…" Jesuadon muttered in a strangled voice, giving direction.

But as they had turned the second corner from Lower Bury Street, Jesuadon straightened, and called a halt to the jarvey. And climbing smartly down from the carriage, stepped directly into the arms of the lashless Barnet.

"Follow them," he snapped, sharp-eyed and wholly sober. "They're on Lower Bury still."

2

The following morning was a fine one. The winds from the south had swept away the hot, humid air under which the city had been sweltering, replacing it with a breeze straight off the sea, and outside the window, the sky was remarkably clear—for London. Jesuadon, sitting slouched in a chair away from the light of White's bay window, appeared cropsick or perhaps still corned. He was neither. Nor was he still dressed for the evening—the previous evening—in stained white stockings, soiled evening pumps and a crumpled, dirty cravat. But habitual eyes will see what habit predicts, and those passing through the Morning Room would have said, had they been asked, that, to be sure, though he appeared almost gentlemanly in appearance upon this occasion, it was plain that Jesuadon was as drunk and disgraceful as ever. Such opinions bothered him not at all. Not today.

Lord Castlereagh came in just before noon. And waving away the attendance of the porter, he stopped to gaze about him as if in relief at his surroundings. And then, still with that expression of contentment, with a slight bow and an intent gaze upon him, he took the seat nearest Jesuadon.

Jesuadon seemed not to be impressed, but looked away after a moment, then down upon his still clean and polished nails. He drew a deep breath and exhaled slowly. "I have begun the game," he said softly.

The Foreign Secretary permitted himself no smile, but clasped his hands together and held them tight against his mouth. "Did you? Excellent. And all went well?" Only the alertness of expression in his dark eyes betrayed his approbation.

Jesuadon gave a little sniff. "Yes. He played faro most of the evening. But then I persuaded him to try his luck at piquet. I even let him win a little."

"Did you? How very considerate. And then?" The sweet tone belied the shrewdness and sharpness of the question.

"He lost. Moderately. Most moderately. 'Pon my word, I would not wish him to fancy himself outplayed," he relayed affably. "But he paid up almost instantly. Sent his man 'round here this morning with a draft on his bank."

"Did he? This morning, eh?" the Foreign Secretary queried. "Hmn. How very interesting. And prompt, too," he remarked.

"Yes."

"Anything else?" Still that same genial, gentle tone.

"Not to speak of." Jesuadon sounded bored, or aggrieved. "I have made a list of everyone who was there last night, as well as those he spoke to—his particular friends, shall we call them—which I shall give Barnet. It's not much, but it's a start, I dare say…Oh, and *she* is providing me with a list of his friends. Those who have visited their home in Hampshire. And those she can recall of his London acquaintances."

"Is she, now?" the tone lowered and deepened with interest. "That will be useful. Very useful. I confess I shall look forward to reading that. As will Flint, I make no doubt. Anything else? Did he mention her?"

"No," Jesuadon said firmly, disapprovingly even. "But I shall tell you this, I don't like the company he keeps," he grumbled. And for a moment, the Foreign Secretary fancied he saw true anger in those amber eyes. Though to those who believed what they thought they saw, such a statement must appear incongruous.

"Ah. Do you not?" the Foreign Secretary soothed. Jesuadon was looking fatigued, he thought. He narrowed his eyes. "Shall you want assistance? No, not for the moment? All right, then. Have it your own way. Still…" And then, his expression hardening, he said in a voice which varied considerably from the amiable expression on his handsome face: "Bring me proof."

Jesuadon sniffed hard. And flexed his jaw, grinding his teeth together. "I will," he stated unequivocally. "…tiresome little fuckster," he ground out. And rose to depart.

Lord Castlereagh took no offence at the obscenity, but courteously nodded his farewell, and did not stand to follow him out. Instead, he settled further into the corner of the wing chair in the empty Morning room, and choosing a newspaper from the table beside him, idly leafed through it—frowning over the latest casualty reports from the Peninsula, and the equally unedifying and scurrilous commentary about the Prince Regent's finances. And only after he had finished that and laid the paper aside, did he rise and make his way from the club.

3

The weakling light of a watery afternoon sun was slanting through the office window. It painted a diffuse patchwork on the worn Turkey carpet and washed the narrow room with a grey gloom. Still. Still, at least the rain had stopped. For the present.

"Tell me, Planta, have we heard anything from young Tirrell?"

Planta winced, and looking up at nothing in particular, thought but did not give it voice: *Oh cock*. "No, my lord," he answered plainly.

Lord Castlereagh glanced up sharply as his private secretary came to stand in the open doorway of the inner office. "Not anything? No word, nothing?"

"No, my lord," Planta repeated, as if in confession. Though why he should feel guilt or the need of atonement over that infernal brat's disappearances and misdemeanours he hardly knew.

"Nothing, you say? He has been gone for how long? We should have heard! Something!"

"Yes, my lord. I did hear that he got safely away, and without further incident. But I feel sure I told you that," he rehearsed patiently. For his lordship was plotting. Planta knew he was plotting. Planning. You could hear it in his voice, read it on his face. It was always the same. He'd grow all sharpish and fretful and shrewd and demand to know where everyone was.

"Yes, yes. But, 'struth, he has been gone for well over a month! And he ought to have sent word. I have told him that. Over and over again. But he does not listen. Get someone onto it, will you? Check with someone down at Burley, will you? See what they may have heard. For I shall want to know the moment there is any news. Is that clear?"

"Yes, my lord. Clear as glass, my lord. Will that be all?"

The smile was genuine, if distracted, as the Foreign Secretary looked up momentarily from the letter he was writing, his snappish words of only the last moment now forgot. "Yes, thank you, Joseph, yes…when Captain Shuster shows his face, send him in directly, will you?"

It was nearly an hour later when Captain Shuster stuck his head around the door. Planta looked up from a pile of reports. And seeing only Planta and no evidence of his lordship, Georgie slipped through the gap to insert himself into the room. He closed the door gently behind him, instantly filling the small room with his tall, taut presence. And gestured toward the inner office with his head. "Is he in?"

Planta nodded. "And expecting you," he mouthed significantly. For

Planta liked Captain Shuster. Liked him very much. And respected him. The captain was not in uniform today, but he still carried himself like a military man, like the cream of the officers' mess in fact. Which of course was precisely what he was. Though one knew that he hadn't always been so…so point-device. Then he too gestured toward the doorway of the inner office. "You're to go straight in."

Georgie's quicksilver smile flashed in sympathy. "Ah," he murmured, his pale eyes lighting. "Like that, is it?" And drawing a deep breath, sobering, he pulled himself to his full height—readying himself for inspection. And hoped it was enough. Determined that it must be enough. For today he meant to ask for permission to return to the Peninsula and to his regiment.

"Shuster, is that you come in?" came the stentorian voice.

Georgie lifted his chin in acknowledgement of Planta's shared forewarning. Then he straightened still further, and presented himself at the open doorway to make his obedience. "My lord."

The inner office was, like the outer, caught in that melancholy shadowless world—neither bright nor dark—of the tepid gloom of a sunless summer's afternoon. His lordship was at his desk which was covered in the paraphernalia of his position. A heap of rolled maps stood precariously beside piles of beribboned reports, while at the centre of the eruption of paperwork, he was engaged in his prolific letter-writing. At his elbow was a stack of letters already written and sealed.

"Come in, Shuster, do come in…shut the doors behind you, will you? Don't mind me, I shan't be a moment…" His lordship did not look up, but continued writing. He came to the bottom of the page, stopped, reread some portion of what he had written, paused again, then signed his name and sanded the page.

Georgie did as he was bid.

Castlereagh did not wait, but started in directly, even as he was shaking away the sand and folding the page in quarters: "And how have you found things at Horse Guards?"

Having closed the doors, Georgie leant his weight against them and waited while his lordship sealed the missive shut. Then, guardedly: "As you would expect, my lord. They have little or no idea of what it is like on the ground in Spain…No notion of what a difference the men's pay or rations arriving on time can mean to a regiment. I do believe that they, most of them, are muddling along with the best will in the world, but they cannot conceive that their indecisiveness or lack of diligence may mean the difference between life and death to the regiments out there." He shrugged. It was what he had expected to find. Heaven knew he'd heard Wellington ranting on the subject often enough. But certainly it was no reason to keep him kicking his heels over here. 'Struth, it appeared to him as another make-shift job to keep him tied here. It had served no genuine purpose. Or none that he could see.

"Ah yes…yes, I see."

Georgie shrewdly suspected that he did.

"Anything else?"

"No, my lord, not to speak of."

"You detected no weak points in their intelligence?"

Georgie left his place at the doorway and came forward. "'Slife, I didn't say that, sir. But nothing that looked remotely suspicious or untoward. Or if there is something, you shall want someone on the inside, someone they know and trust, to sniff it out. Not someone like me, whom they all suspect of being a spy for Wellington and his commissariat—that is, when they wasn't reminding me that I ain't in Spain now, and here there are procedures to be followed…"

"Ah yes," Lord Castlereagh frowned. "A most unfortunate attitude, that. But one, I fear, we shall never successfully eradicate. It's envy, of course. But I dare not say it." He rubbed his chin as he unrolled then contemplated one of the maps before him, and then compared it to another. "Planta! Planta! Oh, there you are! Have we some burgundy? Can you fetch that…And take away this stack of letters and see that they are sent off within the hour, will you? Good. Excellent. Thank you." He extended the handful to Planta, then pulled forward a small map of the coast of northern Germany. He peered at it disconsolately.

Georgie paused. Drew breath. Now was his moment. "But as you are no doubt aware, my lord," he began. "I have just returned from a few days in Bath…" Where he had gone to see his mother and sister after an absence of six years. The last time he had seen her, Theresa had still been in the schoolroom. And to be sure, at first, all had seemed well or pleasant enough. But soon enough, his mother's endless prattling, with the endless stories of Theresa this and Theresa that, and her friends, her *many* friends—all of them inconsequential and remarkable only for their vapidness—and her *many* conquests and all their doings, had begun to dominate every meal, every conversation. Which had then been interspersed with the now familiar sly remarks. The same as in her infrequent unwelcome letters. Till at last had begun the litany of complaints he'd been waiting for from the off: *his* abandonment of the family, *his* preference for his military career over the proper care of his mother and sister, *his* unwillingness to marry as she dictated which must surely bring about his ruination of the family fortune and reputation. God's garters, you'd have thought he'd taken to the High Toby to hear her. While, to be sure, in public, her demeanour had been fawning—a show of sugared almond sweetness. Yet that had only served to make her private railings even more vexatious. And 'fore God, at one and twenty, his still unmarried sister was bidding to become her very image.

All unknowing, Lord Castlereagh regarded him warmly, with certain fond expectation. "Ah yes, so you have. Were they not delighted at the very sight of you!" he exclaimed heartily. "They must be exceeding proud! And all went well, I make no doubt."

No. No, on the whole, it been an unremitting disaster. A disaster brought to a close by the accusation of his unkindness to his sister in the face of her constant love and care for him. To which he had unwisely retorted, 'You mistake, madam! Thanks to the vicious slander you have spoonfed her all these years, she has no more care for me than I have for her…' After which, he had stormed out. And returned to London—riding much of the way through the harsh downpours. Then he had passed the next day with his man of business, arranging his affairs so that he might return to Spain at the earliest opportunity (for there'd be no going back to Bath) and Harry take on the day to day running of Castlehouse. To Spain, where, please God, he might do what he was best at—shooting the godless Frenchies.

But his mouth dried on the words. And his throat parching, Georgie swallowed. "Yes, my lord, it was all very pleasant," he lied. And the moment was gone. Just like that. And the knowledge of its passing left him suddenly bereft of breath, like a blow to the solar plexus.

"Good, good," Lord Castlereagh declared, taking no notice of the skin whitening and tightening of around Shuster's mouth. "Upon my word, I knew they would be delighted at the sight of you. How could they not? To be sure, how could they not?" Then, as if his mind had been elsewhere, he said, "Dear me, what am I thinking, come and take a seat, Captain."

Planta brought in two glasses of burgundy on a tray and presented them, one to his lordship and the other to Georgie. Lord Castlereagh took his with vague thanks, sipped at it, set it down then heaved another deep sigh. "…I thought you would wish to know, Captain…I have arranged for that fellow Fitzroy…Colonel Fitzroy, wasn't it?" He glanced up to see Georgie nod. "To be transferred to somewhere in Wales…The exact location escapes me for the moment…"

Perching on the edge of the seat, Georgie stopped, perplexed and blinking. "Wales, my lord?" he asked. And searching for an answer to why Wales, he found none. "What," he began charily, "…if I may, sir, is in Wales?"

"Good Heavens, nothing that I know of," Castlereagh said mildly. "Which shall, one sincerely trusts, limit the damage he is able to inflict upon our efforts." He paused, refocusing his attention on another map. He turned the page over, then returned his attention to Georgie, and said with one of his genial smiles, "I did feel that he ought to face a court martial for his negligence over that fellow le Brun, but the fellows in Horse Guards refused to consider it…his wife's relations are too powerful, it would seem." He sighed heavily. "So Wales it had to be."

So, it was meant to be a favour then. "Thank you, sir. That's very kind…"

"Not at all. Not at all." Then, seeking some comfort or diversion, Lord Castlereagh turned his attention to another stack of opened letters and eventually to a flattened map of Holland and Westphalia. He studied it, then his thoughts appeared to move on, for his gaze narrowed and he rubbed at his chin. "Do you know, I have been looking and looking at this map of the German states for days now, trying to imagine what has become of the boy," he explained.

"What should have happened to him?" Georgie asked carelessly. Boy Tirrell was an impudent little cock and heaven only knew what he'd get up to.

Castlereagh regarded Georgie obliquely. "Nothing! Nothing at all! But with le Brun still on the loose I cannot help but remain uneasy!" he snapped.

"Where is he meant to be?" Georgie asked, rising from his seat and coming to the desk to peer at the maps upside down.

Castlereagh put his finger on the dot marked Hohenkirchen. "He was meant to land here. And to stay out of France. Specifically, out of Paris."

Georgie turned his head sideways to regard the map. "Then he will have landed in Hohenkirchen and kept away from Paris, I should have thought." He studied the map more closely. "And then, he'd likely be following the French army or interfering with their supply lines…or doing whatever it is he does to make himself so deuced unpopular that they send assassins after him."

Castlereagh frowned with displeasure. "But is he safe, do you think?"

"No, sir," Georgie said bluntly. "None of us are." Then, more heartily: "But he knows the risks as well as any, Boy does. And no one is more adept at the art of disappearance. No one. And if he said they'll not catch him twice, then there's an end to it. They'll not lay hands on him again. I'd stake my life on that." Then a thought: "But…do you wish me to go after him, sir? I can, you know. Upon my very life, I'd be more than happy to." Action, he would see action again. "I know Boy has always worked alone, but I'd not get in his way. And I could protect him, I give you my word." Hope soared at the thought.

Lord Castlereagh continued to ponder the map. Finally: "No…"

The delight and anticipated happiness of harassing the French lines, of picking them off, one by one, the thrill of fear and of danger, dissipated upon the word.

"No, but thank you, Captain."

He was meant to be kept here then. Doing nothing. Wasting his time and energies on…

"I confess, I allow myself to become overly concerned with such matters," Castlereagh admitted. And he seemed, for the moment, to be satisfied, or at least less fretful and dispirited. Then, looking up, and with his elbow upon the desk, he rested his chin in his hand. "Hmn, yes…" Then: "Remind me again, Shuster, how well do you know Dunphail?"

His attention still upon the map, upon where he might have gone to encounter the boy, and the French, Georgie raised his eyes and shot him a cautious glance. "My lord? Dunphail? Johnny Dunphail?" he groped.

"Yes…" The Foreign Secretary smiled broadly, affability and expectancy playing across his features. "Yes. Dunphail. That is to say, you knew him at school, did you not?"

"Yes. But…I do assure you, my lord, it is as I've told you, I barely know him…" Georgie stalled, straightening. Then returned to his seat. "To be sure, we was at school together, but…

"Yes! That is what I remembered. Excellent. Well, well. That'll do. Yes, that'll do. I wish…" His dark eyes now sparkling with excitement, Castlereagh paused briefly in thought, as if considering or choosing his words. "I wish for you to rekindle your friendship with him." The depression had been banished, replaced by that fearsome articulate intelligence.

Jolted, Georgie felt a sudden unexpected spurt of confusion or rage. Dunphail? His mind rebelled. Hell and confound it, it was another non-assignment. Just like damned, bloody Nottingham! "But, 'pon my word, sir…I know nothing about him!" he protested. "'Struth, we was barely acquainted at school. He was always Myddelton's friend, and Pemberton's. They was always together. He passed his time with them, and his cousin!"

Castlereagh waited. Waited, listening. Weighing even. Then said carefully and evenly, "Yes, yes. But…I may not have mentioned before, Captain, I cannot employ Myddelton for this. I have, of course, considered it, but I need him here, or at least close enough at hand so that I may call upon him when I require his services. I know you will understand."

Instantly, Georgie stilled. All further protest died in his mouth. Since he returned to England it was the first reference anyone had made to what had occurred in France before he was recalled.

"And I do require him here in any event, do you see?" Castlereagh continued. "His cypher work is unequalled, as I believe you must be aware." Then more rousingly: "But the shooting season approaches, does it not? And the stalking season? Jesuadon has kept me informed, so I know that Dunphail has remained in London and has not, as was his wont, returned north for the summer. To be sure, I am conversant with the fact that Dunphail's family has held Jacobite sympathies in the past…" he paused, delicately, allowing the information to penetrate. "Yet I am equally confident you will find a way to circumvent that loyalty." His gaze dared the Captain to disagree.

Dumbly, Georgie found himself staring. He meant it.

"So. I wish you to get yourself invited up to his hunting lodge in Inverness," continued his lordship. "Indeed, I am convinced you shall have no difficulty with that, for if I am not mistaken, you are a keen shot. Yes?"

Georgie swallowed tightly. Not bloody Scotland again. "Yes, my lord," he agreed.

"Excellent. And then…then, upon your return, I shall wish you to bring him in…" he declared, his gaze narrowing.

"My lord?" Georgie exclaimed, now unable to compose his features into anything other than stunned amazement. Bring him in? What in the name of all that was holy could Castlereagh want with Dunphail? He was nothing but an infernal Scottish…

Lord Castlereagh regarded him shrewdly. "And that is an order, Captain." It was gently said.

Blinking his bewilderment, Georgie rose to his feet, the air squeezed out of his lungs. His mind was still reeling, yet all disagreement was done. "Yes, sir." It was an order. There could be no mistake. It was an order. Dunphail, of all things! "My lord," he said firmly. And bowing, made his obedience.

Chapter XIV

1

Barnet said they were looking for Lady Wilmot in London now. Since they'd had no luck in Portsmouth or Southampton, they'd begun to search here. Making discreet enquiries in the better end of Town. Though there had been a few questions asked here in Charing Cross, too. And that he would need to tell the Governor. Soon.

Jesuadon leaned out of the open window looking down upon the street, crowded in the midday glare, a milling crush of travellers, costermongers, porters, and thieves—in the air that morning there had been the first hint that autumn was not far off, something in the smell of the dawn or the wheaten colour of the sunlight it was. Yet below, among all that throng, he could see no one matching the description Barnet had given—a rake-thin shabbaroon with bad teeth. "Wears a buff-coloured coat. Thinks he has a way with serving girls, which he ain't…" had been Barnet's pithy assessment.

No, there was none matching the description of Wilmot's man. Not that he could see.

At the corner, there was his own watch—the crossing sweep in his pay.

But with them now looking here, should he double the guard? And put Sparrowhawk on alert?

And should he tell her?

He turned away from the window to consider Lady Wilmot, sitting straight and quiet, sitting as she often did, in the lightfall but not near enough the window to be seen, sewing, the inexhaustible supply of unmended linens on the floor beside her. Od's truth, she was a pretty little thing.

She could not return to Wilmot now. She'd all but indicted him for treason. And even if she hadn't, the infernal brute would assuredly beat her to death. God's teeth, what a midden-mess it all was. They had been fools to involve her in any of this. Mad fools. And that plaguey lolpoop, Ladyman, the maddest of all. But there was no going back for her. Not now. Not to Wilmot, that limb of Satan. 'Struth, not even to her family, for now. Perhaps later. But not now.

So what, in heaven's name, were they to do with her? Always providing, of course, that Wilmot's bloodhound picked up her trail? Or even if he didn't?

She raised her gaze to meet his, and blinking, smiled her tremulous smile. "Is there anything the matter, Mr. Jesuadon? For…" She hesitated. "For you seem most preoccupied today, sir."

"No," he reassured her. "Not at all. Nothing. Thinking. Just thinking." He could not tell her for it would increase her fears to know that the hunt was on. Which would accomplish nothing to the purpose.

Accepting his answer, she nodded and bent her head over her stitching. "Was the list I gave you, was it of any assistance to you, sir?" Again, she raised her eyes to meet his in a gaze of growing levelness.

"Yes. Yes, thank you. I believe it may prove so, ma'am. It is too early to tell."

"Oh, yes," she breathed. "Yes, of course, And, if I am not mistaken, you must not tell me in any event. Is that not so?"

It was a whisper of a smile he gave her. "Yes, you are perfectly right, ma'am. It would only serve to upset you. And that would be to repay your help with gross unkindness. I would not do it."

"Oh…yes."

He would not tell her. Not today. Not now. There was no point to it.

"I should leave you…

"But…" he hesitated. Should he say anything at all? He must. "But, you will remember to always stay away from the window, ma'am, promise me that?" He had never said so directly before. But now, now with them looking, there must be no mistakes, no slip-ups. Not any.

"Yes," she nodded emphatically. "Oh yes, I promise. Of course." And if she wondered at his asking such a thing, she did not say so.

"Excellent. Then I shall have no fears for your safety. I shall leave you now." He bowed, suddenly anxious to be quit of her company. For he was growing to like her—she with her soft voice and sweet ways. And that must not be allowed to happen. It would endanger them both, and he knew it.

But there had been something in his voice, something different she had noticed, so instead of bidding him farewell, she said all in a rush, "Have you…forgive me, but have you seen him, sir? My husband, Sir Robert? Have you seen him?"

He would not lie to her. Not if he could avoid it. "Yes, I have seen him." And he saw that she was now, as she had done when he had first come to meet her, darting quick nervous glances between her hands and the work she was engaged in and his face—as if she feared to look at him plainly and openly, fearful of what she might see, of what she might learn or what she might inadvertently reveal.

"And…did he mention me?" There was the veriest quaver in her voice.

He spoke truly. "No."

She nodded, her brow furrowing, and bit her lips together. She bowed her head over her mending.

But he saw that her breathing had quickened. "No, he did not mention you," Jesuadon reassured her. And remained, studying her for a long moment. In her dark, serviceable gown, one could too easily forget who and what she was. But for now, she was safe. "Not at all. You may be easy…I shall…I shall return on the morrow, ma'am. Good day to you." And bowing, he quitted the room.

And, locking the door behind him with certain care, he walked slowly down the three flights of stairs to the connecting door, panelled antechamber and hallway which by circuitous means led to his own apartments on the other side of Sparrowhawk's labyrinthine premises.

It was a damnable coil, this. Damnable.

He unlocked the door and went in.

"Christ, what?" he snapped.

For Barnet was waiting for him. There, in the shadow of the far corner, standing by the empty hearth, his hat in his hand, flushed with the heat of the closed room, waiting.

Jesuadon shut the door and shot the inner bolt. "What?" he repeated, his wearied contemplation replaced by an impulse of ragged impatience.

Barnet's full moon face gave away nothing. "It's about the maid."

Jesuadon shook his head. He was too wearied today. And was wanting his bed. Not another report of another cock-up for which Castlereagh would blame him—when he told him. He looked away toward the dimity hung window. "What maid?" He went across to the window and threw it open to look out upon the busy innyard, the noise of which would obscure any sound of conversation from his chamber.

"The abigail," Barnet explained as if that made all clear. He hadn't moved.

Jesuadon turned on him. "What bloody abigail? London's full of the whey-faced creatures!" And then he paused, noticing, as tired and bleary-eyed as he was, some element of fear or distaste in Barnet's usually placid countenance. And his senses sharpening now, he asked again, but quietly: "What abigail?" He regarded Barnet's sonsy face. "Why? What's happened?" And suddenly, he thought he knew. Even without Barnet telling him. Even without a word.

Barnet raised his eyes toward the ceiling—beamed, plastered and surprisingly clean—in the direction of the safe chamber. "The abigail. Lady's Wilmot's woman that was. They found her with her head and face beaten in. She's dead."

Jesuadon felt the breath shaken from his lungs. Briefly he closed his eyes. "When?"

Barnet shook his head. "Dunno." Oddly fretful, he rubbed at his bald patch. "Last few days. She was only just found. Foxes hadn't been at her yet, so it can't have been that long," he reasoned.

Silent now, contemplating, Jesuadon went to the cupboard beside the fireplace, opened it and removed a plain stoppered bottle and two glasses. Setting them on the table, he poured two glassfuls of liquid—clear Hollands, it was. He handed one to Barnet who tossed it off. Jesuadon drank his and, still cradling the glass, went and slouched down in one of a pair of worn and patched wing chairs. It was a long moment before he spoke. "Tell me."

Barnet returned his glass to the table and came and then sat down, perching his large frame uneasily upon the seat's frayed edge. "I set a watch on Wilmot's place...like you said. Which weren't easy. Outsiders in a place like that, everyone notices 'em!" He shook his head over it. "But I managed to get a lad in place. One of Warne's lads, he is. Anyroad…the abigail. Once they knew who she was, they brought her back there, to recover her health after the fever left her." He was not laughing. Not as he had been when last they spoke of her, after the hold-up. "Then, sometime on Saturday it must have been, she went for a walk. No one knows for certain when she left the house. She kept herself to herself. Didn't talk much to the other servants. Sometime on Sunday it was, they noticed she'd gone. Wasn't in her room…hadn't come down to the kitchen, that sort of thing."

"When was she found?" Jesuadon asked, his grit-in-the-eye fatigue retreating before such facts.

Blinking rapidly, Barnet shrugged. "Monday night…dawn Tuesday. A ploughman lad tripped over her on his way back from the local inn. Or his sweetheart. Difficult to say really, he don't tell the same story twice."

Barnet sat for a moment, peering at his large workman's hands. "It's him," he said with finality. "He's back in the country."

"Who?" Jesuadon demanded, perhaps already knowing the answer. Fearing it.

Barnet didn't answer at first, but shifted awkwardly on the chair's edge, his expression far from happy. "John Brown."

Jesuadon sat up, instantly straight and alert. "What?" he bellowed. "You're bloody joking! How can he be back? How can he be back and we know nothing about it?" He screeched. "Christ!" He caught his face in his hands. "Christ's wounds," he ground out.

But gathering his distracted, angry wits, Jesuadon refocused his shrewd gaze upon Barnet's tanned and flushed face. "Are you certain? Are you certain it wasn't some local? Or the ploughman?"

Barnet wiped his mouth with his sleeve. "Yes," he said. "They found her with her face was beaten in. Just like young Bretherton."

Jesuadon exhaled slowly. "You're certain?" His voice had deadened. "Anything else? Had she been raped?"

Barnet shook his head. "Hard to say. I couldn't tell from her clothes, which was all mucky with blood and mud. An' I didn't like to ask. They was all strangers. But it looked to me like John Brown's handiwork."

Jesuadon sat quiet, contemplating the death, its implications. For all her bile, the woman had not deserved such a fate. And, there was also the unwelcome return of John Brown—without his knowledge. His or Flint's. Which would take some explaining. And suddenly incandescent with the force of new anger, he refocused his attention on Barnet. "You've seen her?" he said in a voice just above a whisper. "You left your cover to see her?" he exploded, bounding from his seat. "You went down there? Have your wits gone begging? Have you gone mad?"

"I had to, Guv! There was no other way! No one but you and me knows what Bretherton looked like after he'd been basted. I had to see her! How could I tell if it was our man otherwise? No one saw me though! I did take care. I'm not that stupid!"

Jesuadon drew a deep shuddering breath. He was shaking with rage. Christ, it was all unravelling. But who was behind it? What sodomising devil was driving it? "And what if Brown was watching, eh? What then?"

"Bloody hell," Barnet muttered, whitening, and shook his head. "If Brown was watching, then I'm next," he said plainly. And rose from his seat to refill the glasses. "Here." He waited while Jesuadon emptied his glass, then he drank his own down.

Jesuadon dropped back into his seat, and sat for a long while, rubbing at the bridge of his nose. Finally: "You're certain it couldn't have been an accident? She couldn't have been run down by a horse? Or did she slip out to meet someone?" Pondering, he bit at his upper lip.

"You're asking me if I think she knew him, ain't you? I don't know," Barnet shrugged. "Who would be daft enough to go out to meet that?

And it ain't possible to say. But I shall tell you this, Thos, this is Wilmot's doing. I'm dead certain of it."

"What?" Jesuadon exclaimed, peering at him in disbelief.

Barnet wiped again at the sweat from his brow with his sleeve. "No, Jes, listen. For I reckon it's the link that'll hang him. Wilmot's wife's been gone for how many weeks is it now? And he can find no trace of her. Not anywhere. And there's her family—when will they start asking questions, eh? And there's the maid, rabbiting on, every time she opens her stupid gob, about how she was treated and how Lady Wilmot run away with a highwayman. Makin' it all worse, do you see? It *was* Wilmot who gave the order. Had to be. And it's our link. It's the link we've been looking for. Between him and our John Brown. It proves that Wilmot's in with him."

Jesuadon sat still. Blinking. Listening. Thinking. Pondering. He gave the bridge of his nose a final rub. And said at last: "It could be."

He stood up suddenly and looked away—again toward the window where the afternoon sun was bright through the faded fabric of the curtain. "It could be…" Biting at his bottom lip, he took a turn about the room. "Double the watch on him, will you? Today. And I want a record of everyone he talks to. And then I want maps. Maps tracing every step he takes. Every shop he calls in at. Every brothel. Every pie shop. I want to know where he goes and who he talks to. Because somewhere, in all of this, somewhere is the man who gave the order. Unless it was the maid herself. And now he's got rid of her. But if you're right, Barnet, if you're right…if this ain't just a terrible coincidence and she was in the wrong place when our John Brown was out looking for amusement, then somewhere there is a man who is giving the orders to John Brown. And Ladyman will be next. Or the boy…" He exchanged a glance with Barnet—they both knew what that would mean. "And after that…after that, it'll be Lady Wilmot." He rubbed his face and sighed. "Or you." He heaved another great sigh. "I shall need to get word to Warne."

"And Flint?"

"Aye, and him too…" Jesuadon agreed. "Him, too…You get the word out on the streets too, right?"

Then with a return of his roiling anger, Jesuadon continued: "And as for you, don't you dare to leave London again, d'you hear me? And don't you dare go out unarmed. Not ever! And if he comes for you, Barnet, I don't give a good Goddamn what the Guvnor's orders are, you take him down, d'you hear me? Slit his damned fuckster's throat." His expression was fierce. "And then slice his balls off. For Shuster will want to see 'em."

Chapter XV

1

Silent as stonework Georgie Shuster stood, gazing into the expanse of limpid blue sky, his eyes trained upon the still riding of a bird of prey—wings spread, gliding aloft upon a crest of air high above the clearing, held and lifted and serene. At this distance, it was impossible to tell whether it was a merlin or a kestrel. Watching, he stood, admiring the falcon's effortless mounting of the breeze, its cruciform dark against the paler sky.

Away to the west the purple hills, spanned and seamed with bracken, shone as dusk in the afternoon light, their stepped and steep sloping horizon lines unbroken by the silhouette of horse or cannon. Above, the distant clouds were too high to bring rain. And when he looked again, the falcon was gone.

Then, with a final glance all about him, his eyes readjusting, Georgie continued his loping walk down the granite and heather-strewn hill toward the glen and the near wood.

They had been up early that morning, he and Dunphail, to walk out upon the moors as the mist lay in random swells upon the mounds and furrows of heather. Before them walked the gillies, beating the heather and bracken and earth, raising the birds that they skirred upward, above the shredding blankets of mist, to be shot down, and retrieved by a liver and white spaniel.

As Dunphail had promised, the sport was grand, with the familiar thunder of the guns—their fire muffled by the heavy air—booming into the quiet, a homely sound after the years in Spain. Pleasant too was the employment of the heightened alertness and restless energy, the sharpened hearing and searching vision which had spelled his survival in the Peninsula and elsewhere—whether perched in a sharp-shooter's position between the rocks and mountains, or out, alone, riding information.

At last, their bags full to bursting, with nearly a dozen brace taken, they'd stopped and made their way back to Dunphail's lodge in the pleasant heat of midday.

But for the afternoon, Dunphail was engaged upon business with his grieve, so Shuster had come away from the stone fortress of a house, straight-sided unwelcoming walls of granite rising square and unyielding to the heavens, to walk. To walk with Comfit, the spaniel who had attached herself to his side from the moment he'd set foot in the lodge, through the home wood and down to the stream which ran along the bottom of the valley. To walk in welcome solitude, silent and without desire, peaceful in the security of this green and lavishly heather-stained and bracken-browned land.

"Comfit!" He gave a shrill whistle through his teeth. Obligingly, she dashed out of the undergrowth to trot at his heel. "Come along, Comfit. Leave the coneys be." An admonishment which she greeted with an increase in the velocity of her tail wagging.

Overhead, a dense flock of starlings cackled and called.

Georgie pushed a branch aside and continued down the path toward the stream—strath, Dunphail called it—that ran along the foot of the wooded glen.

He caught sight of the chestnut crest and black mask of a waxwing. 'Struth, it had been an age since he last walked through a wood like this. Walked, unafraid and unharried, through stands of yew and holly and oak with sunlight dappling the ground and the tree trunks, and underfoot a carpet of wild thyme, garlic and moist decaying leaves, their scents crushed together by his boot. Without having to run—crouched over and silent in his breathlessness—wondering when some Frenchie's bullet was going to find its way into his gut or his head. Without fear of stumbling across the corpse of a soldier or a child, half-eaten and decayed. Without listening for the sounds of pursuit or the murmurings of vagabonds or the unnatural silence of waiting bandits. For here there was nought but the incessant callings of the birds—wood pigeons and woodpeckers, robins and thrushes—and the rustling, grunting enthusiasm of Comfit at his heel.

He had forgot how green was Scotland. Lush as a clipped velvet coat, it was. Not worn nor frayed like the decaying chair covers at Castlehouse, not bright as new paint, nor parched and browned like Spain. Or scorched and blackened where the earth still held the memory of the Vendée's Infernal Columns. Green. Welcoming and soft, redolent of life. Comforting as the yielding tenderness of a woman's breasts. After the four years spent in the dust-coated plains and war-ravaged mountains of the Peninsula, it was a paradise.

In the end, it had taken nothing more than a casual mention, over a game of piquet, that he'd not seen good shooting since Spain to gain Dunphail's invitation—the invite Castlereagh had been so determined upon. For at the mere mention of sport, Dunphail had called for another bottle, promising that the shooting in Scotland was excellent, the best in the world. And with that Dunphail had capotted him—which was not surprising. Piquet never had been his game. Still. Would that all orders were so easily dispatched.

But as for Dunphail…well, Christ alone knew what Castlereagh would make of him when he gave in his report. For he was a dyed in the wool Jacobite if ever there was…Though you'd not have guessed if you'd only met up with him in London—at White's, for instance. They all were though. All the Scots lads he'd served with in Portugal and Spain had been, that much was sure. Bonny fighters, they were. Diehards to a man. He'd rather have a regiment of Scotsmen at his back than anything, if it came to a fight. They never let you down. But still, Dunphail? What in the blazes could Castlereagh want of him?

For each evening as the cold from the North Sea blew in fresh and raw and settled over the land, they sat before the hearth where a fire roared and popped and spat, drinking and laughing. But Dunphail drank like an officer trying to expunge the memories of Corunna…and all else beside.

"Comfit…where are you now, you thumping…"

He heard her voice first.

"*Wi' my dog and gun…*"

And halted to stand spyman still.

"*…through the bloomin' heather, for game and pleasure I took my way, oh I met a maid, she was tall and slender…*"

It was clear as polished silver or glass, that voice. Clear and pure. A shining voice, if a voice could be said to shine. It drifted to him on the breeze, sifted through the shivering of the leaves, sometimes close, sometimes farther away.

"*I said, Fair maid, do you know I love you? Tell me your name and your dwelling also. Oh excuse my name, but you'll find my dwelling by the mountain stream where the moor cock crow.*"

A low sweet voice, but with a range that soared to greet the highest notes of the melody. God's truth, a man could fall in love with a voice like that. Or be seduced by it—was she ever so bracket-faced. Georgie ducked under the sweep of a yew's low branches into a small clearing by the stream and looked about.

And there she was. Sitting just upstream on the largest of three granite boulders, tracing patterns on the water's surface with a long stick.

"*I said, Fair maid, if you wed a fermer, you'll be tied for life tae one plot of land…*"

She was very fair. With hair the colour of ripened apricots twisted up at the back of her head and soft tendrils falling against her temples and neck, her skin the colour of bleached linen. Georgie's breath caught in his breast. And the words came to his mind, "Let me take you now. Let me kiss you. Merciful heaven, lay me down and love me…"

"*…I'm a roving johnny, if you come wi' me, you will have no ties, so gie me your hand.*" She seemed to be laughing to herself as she sang.

She was simply dressed in a gown of white muslin and the faded print shawl draped about her shoulders. Her ankles were neat and trim.

And the blood thumping through him, Georgie stashed his hands deep into his coat pockets and strolled closer.

"Ah, but if my parents knew I loved a rover, it is that I'm sure would be my overthrow..."

Comfit let out a yelp from somewhere behind.

The girl stopped singing and looked up.

From out the shadow of her boulder, a great rough-coated dog rose, stretched itself, and yawned before casting a tranquil eye on Georgie. Unimpressed by the man and seeing no other canine, the hound eased itself back into the shade of the rock and began methodically to lick a front paw.

"Good afternoon," Shuster bellowed.

"Good afternoon to you then," she called back. Then she smiled and bowed her head.

Georgie came and stood opposite her. Only the stream lay between them. Her eyes were blue, clear true blue. Her mouth was rosy and her bottom lip softly rounded. She was everything he desired. "I heard you singing. You have a beautiful voice."

"'Tis no wonder you're not bothered, Angus," she said to the dog, just loud enough to be heard. "'Tis nought but a poor wee Sassenach." Then looking up, wrinkling her eyes against the sun, or in laughter at some unshared joke, she said, "Aye, so they tell me."

Georgie narrowed his eyes and took in the long line of her throat and the swell of her breast, the pale smoothness of her skin. His breath shallowed. "It's a beautiful spot you've chosen. Do you live near here?"

"No. I'm no' but a visitor, like yoursel'." She hesitated. "Though I've not come so far as you."

Her unflustered mastery of the situation was new to him. Georgie smiled back at the challenge he read in her eyes, her smile, her voice. "No. Perhaps not." He paused. "Will you allow me to present myself? Captain Sir George Shuster, at your service." He performed a slight bow.

"Oh aye." She favoured him with a raking glance, but the smile on her lips and in her eyes never altered. The niceties of his refined speech, of his fine tailored coat and breeches seemed to leave her unmoved.

"Will you not tell me your name?"

She chuckled, then sang out: "*Oh excuse my name, but you'll find my dwelling by the mountain stream where the moor cock crow.*"

"Is that where you live?" he asked too quickly. "By a mountain stream where—what was it? The moor cock crow?" 'Struth, what he'd not give to twine his hands through the tangle of that soft hair…and trace the line of her arm to her hand. First with his fingertips, then with his mouth. Then to lay himself down atop her, lift her skirts and feel her yielding beneath him, soft and welcoming.

She laughed. "No." She shook her head. "More's the pity. I'd quite like that."

She crossed her ankles, revealing the lace edging of her petticoat. He could not look away. "May I join you here?"

"Suit yoursel'" she said indifferently. "I'd invite you to share my rock here, but I'm no' sure Angus would approve. He's not o'erfond of Southrons."

"Southrons? Ah. Is that what you call us?"

He knew very well that it was. But anything to make conversation with her. He lifted the tails of his coat and settled himself onto a felled log. Comfit emerged briefly, sniffed at Georgie's boot, gave it a brief lick, then ambled back into the undergrowth.

She watched as he seated himself. Her eyes full of that teasing laughter, she answered, "Aye, that an' other things."

"Like what?" he asked. As if he didn't know. There was a recklessness about her, a breathtaking, fearless recklessness. 'Struth, she was lovely. He wanted to smell her, her hair, her throat, the nestling curve of her collarbone, the warmth between…

"Oh…Well…" She made an expression as if to consider her answer. "Sassenach." Her smile grew. "Bletherskate. Lummox. Great dafties. All of them highly complimentary, I do assure you." She was pressing her lips together to quash her laughter.

'Struth, he longed to taste her mouth. "Of course," he agreed congenially, nodding. "To be sure, we have some very pleasant terms for you, too. All of them equally complimentary. Though, I, ah, must confess, they escape me…for the moment."

"'Tis nae doot, for the best," she said. "For they'd go direct to ma head and where would we be then? Not a milliner in all Edinburgh could fashion me a bonnet to fit…an' no bonnet, no kirk on Sunday, and we couldnae have that." Her expression grew serious and her eyes grave. "An' what would my grandfather say then?"

Dazzling, simply dazzling. "A strict churchgoer, is he?" Georgie said, coming through what he considered an awkward moment smoothly. Her face, her laughter, her speech stole his breath away.

She gave a sudden spurt of laughter. "M'grandfather? Well, no, not exactly…But what's a braw laddie like yoursel' doing up here the now?"

He noticed that she refused to use his name or give him his title. Or had forgot them. And liked her better for it. Wanted her more because of it. Wanted her now. This instant. Underneath him on a bed of heather and soft moss. Or lying soft in a feather bed beside him, while he lingered over the soft pale skin of her arm, her throat, her hip… "I am a guest at a nearby house."

"Oh aye," she nodded. "An' how do you find Dunphail's wee housie?"

Her foreknowledge startled him. "Very fine. Most comfortable. All that is pleasant." His eyes narrowed on her face as a throb of desire thumped its rampant way through his stomach and groin. Christ, what wouldn't he give to take her in his arms? To press against him, her face and mouth beneath his, her breath warm against his shoulder…

She chuckled. "Oh aye. I'll be sure to tell Dunphail that when next I see him. Nae doubt he'll greatly appreciate the compliment."

A pink flush crept into his cheeks and Georgie wondered if she knew the full extent of his reaction to her and was enjoying it. "You should not mock. It is the pleasantest place I have been in a long while."

She sobered. "No. You're right. I shouldnae mock," she said, as if she knew more than she was admitting to. Then, she favoured him with that teasing smile again and opened her eyes wide. She hopped down from her seat on the boulder. "I mun' be off." She flashed him another sparkling look. "Before you begin to think you've got farther than you have…" She had missed none of his longing, none of his discomfited hope. "I should hae warned you, sodger laddie, your Sassenach wiles are wasted on the likes o' me. Or perhaps you were hoping I might take pity on you? Up here, all alane, wi' nane but Dunphail tae ca' your guid friend," she teased, lapsing into Lallans.

His flush deepening, Georgie could only laugh. "'Struth, you sound just like him." Then: "You could overlook the Sassenach bit," he suggested. "'Pon my honour, we are never so black as you paint." He offered her his purest smile. She was so beautiful. "Please, stay."

She was not taken in. "An' why should I?" she stalled. She cocked her head to one side and gave him a long considering look—a look similar to those he'd seen on the servants' faces in Dunphail's house when he didn't understand them. "To teach you how to speak proper Scots? So that you'll understand Dunphail when he's unco' fou? That's three sheets to the wind to you, Captain. As for you being a Southron—there are some defects a body cannae overlook." Her smile was sweet and direct.

Startled, Georgie sat up straighter, but laughed all the same. "I believe I shall do better to ignore that last comment…But why do you say I cannot understand him? I've served with many of your countrymen in Spain, you know. They are the finest of soldiers."

She perched upon a low rock, closer to the edge of the stream bed, and with great care, arranged the skirt of her gown about her ankles. Sunlight slanted through the trees making soft flames of her hair, paling her skin to milk. She shrugged. "You're a Southron laddie," she said kindly.

He closed his eyes against the urgent desire. If only he could just take her hand…

Gracefully, she rose. "No, I really mun be off." She smiled. "Give Dunphail ma best." She started up the path, then turned.

"Do you come here often?" he called after her.

She laughed, reading his thought. "More often than you, sodger laddie."

"Then I shall come here. Tomorrow. In the afternoon. And hope to see you!" he called. "Will you come?"

She paused. "I cannae say. Fare thee well, Sassenach laddie. Come, Angus." She ruffled the shaggy fur of the deerhound's head, and resting her hand on his back, climbed the path out of sight. "*So I'll stay at home for another season, by the mountain stream where the moorcock crow…*"

Listening, Georgie watched her go, watched until he could hear but not see her. Then waited a while longer before he too rose, determined to walk another mile or two while his ardour cooled.

And when at last he returned to the house, stilled and quiet again, there were voices echoing through the old great hall. He closed the door and paused to remove his hat, and to listen. Two voices. Dunphail and…a woman. At least one. Dunphail's aunts, he supposed. Dunphail had said they lived nearby. Comfit wandered on ahead.

And his boots making little sound on the stone floor of the passageway, Shuster came through and crossed the empty vaulted chamber with its great stone hearth toward the few steps that led to the Drawing Room—for the voices came from there. The door stood open.

Sweet Christ and all saints, it was her. Standing near the fire beside Dunphail, with her arm drawn through his.

Dunphail looked up. "Oh, Shuster! You've come in, have you? Excellent. Come now and meet my cousin…" He smiled genially.

Piss and cock, she was no farmer's daughter; she was Dunphail's cousin.

"Ailie, m'dear, may I name Captain Sir George Shuster to you."

Her name was Ailie. A knot of lust caught in his chest.

"Shuster, my cousin, Miss MacDonald."

"Miss MacDonald," Georgie repeated. And hearing and holding that name, her name, Ailie, he stepped forward and bowed.

She performed a civil curtsy. She gave no sign of their earlier encounter.

Silencing his longing, he waited for her next words. The words that would expose him. Tensed and readied for them.

"How very good to make your acquaintance, Captain."

Was it possible she'd say nothing?

"…But have I not seen ye before?"

No! Od's blood, here it came. And he, a guest in Dunphail's house. Hell and confound it, she had to have been a relation, a cousin, hadn't she? Castlereagh would have his guts for garters.

"Did I not see ye in Dunbar, some weeks past?"

Startled, Georgie stopped dead. And blinked as his mind tripped and stalled, stumbling over the events of the day in Dunbar. His heart was thumping wildly again. "Forgive me…"

"You were riding through the town, were ye not? Wi' another sodger. And lifted your hat to my companion and me, did ye not?"

And blinking rapidly, his mind floundered still. For suddenly all he could see before him, in his mind's eye, was the poor widow Ramsey and her broken face, blinded and weeping. And he did not know whether she lived yet or no. But…He shook his head. But…yes…yes, there had been a girl. Two girls…both pretty…out walking. The one had hair the colour of ripened apricots but Fletcher hadn't known her name. Piss, how could he not have remembered? Hell and confound it! "Yes," he fumbled. "Yes. Forgive me, I do recall it. Forgive me, I was on a duty call that day which drove all else from my mind." And he knew his smile was tighter than it should be and did not reach his eyes.

And he saw too in that instant that Miss Macdonald was regarding him quizzically now, as if she did not understand, but had caught something of his confusion and would not press him.

Dunphail was looking from one to the other, wry in his pleasure. "What? Do not tell me you've met before. What a coincidence!

"Ailie's come to stay with my aunt while her sister's awa' in Perth with a friend…" Dunphail said to Georgie by way of explanation. He turned then to look upon her. "Are you sure you'll not stop for dinner, then?" At the shake of her head, he continued, "Well, if not this evening, then tomorrow. I'll send the carriage at four. No, I insist. You must come. She'll drive ye out of your wee mind with all her claik. You know it to be true."

She darted at Georgie another of her whistling, daring glances and tucked her hand closer about her cousin's arm. "Aye, then. Aye. That'd be fine. What a guid laird you are to a body," she teased.

Dunphail let out a laugh. "We'll hae a dance too. Not tomorrow. But before you go home to Wester Ross. A bite of dinner and then a bit of a ceilidh."

"Aye. Aye, then. Or ye'll rabbit on at me, till I say aye."

"Guid," Dunphail beamed. "'Tis settled then. I'll fix on a date and tell you tomorrow."

Georgie watched, his breathing slowing. She was not without

protection and her relationship with Dunphail was close. Far too close for the tumbling sport he'd been imagining for the past hour. Lud. "If you will both excuse me. I must go and wash off my dirt. Miss MacDonald." Georgie bowed.

Miss MacDonald did not shoot him another of those glances of suppressed laughter, but curtsied demurely. "Until tomorrow, Captain."

Quitting the room, Georgie drew and released a deep breath. And then another. Then slowly mounted the stairs to his chamber, needing now to cool his ardour for the second time that afternoon.

Chapter XVI

1

Jesuadon was an infrequent visitor to the offices of the Foreign Secretary. As much by inclination as by wisdom. And presenting himself, unannounced, in Planta's small and orderly domain he remembered why.

Planta, precise as ever, was at his desk totting up the columns of figures in a wide leatherbound ledger.

"Planta." Jesuadon greeted him with a nod. "Is the Governor in?" It was said civilly enough.

Folding his lips together, Planta eyed him with certain misgiving. "Yes." He laid aside his pen. "I'll just tell him you're here."

Jesuadon held up his hand. "No." He crossed to the window and stood with his back against the white, opened shutter, scrutinising the street below. "Don't." There were few hawkers, but a closed carriage, a hackney, and the usual foot traffic. "I'll not stay long."

Planta watched him as he studied the scene outside. At last, and silent still in his self-containment, Jesuadon went and admitted himself to the inner sanctum.

His lordship was writing. "Planta, is that you with the ink?" he said upon the hushed sweep of the door opening. He dipped his pen into the open standish and did not look up.

Jesuadon closed the doors. "No," he said, and again went to stand near to the open window, even as he had in Planta's office, leaning against the open shutter, carefully out of sight of anyone who might be below.

A swift medley of expressions, from surprise to heightened alertness, crossed, recrossed and vanished from the Foreign Secretary's countenance, finally replaced by a guarded intentness. Drawing himself up, he finished writing and then raised his eyes to regard his visitor. Without a word, he raised his elbow to the desk to cup his chin in his hand and to wait.

Jesuadon did not move but remained where he was, his attention wholly taken up with the street below and every movement and every glint of light on the windowpanes of the buildings opposite. Eventually, his expression unaltered, he said, "Wilmot's men are out looking for her. Here in the city now."

Castlereagh eyed him shrewdly—for today everything about Jesuadon seemed heightened in reverse. Drab he was, neither dressed in the soil of his dissolute evening pursuits, nor as the gentleman he occasionally remembered he was. Everything about him was indistinct, unremarkable, lost or blurred. Even the red-gold of his hair had been dulled rather than offset by the dreariness of his dun-coloured coat. "Are you certain?"

"Yes." It was unequivocal.

"They have been for more than a sennight," Jesuadon continued, now allowing his gaze to wander over the segmented rectangles of sunlight which lay upon the Turkey carpet, light outlined by darkness, bounded and squared within the black perimeters of glazing bars. He blinked. "They shan't find her, of course. But there's too much at stake and I don't like the risks. Not to Sparrowhawk's business, nor to Barnet and his lads. To be sure, I could have them eliminated, but that would hardly serve our purposes, now would it? So I shall have to move her." Jesuadon's eyes were bloodshot.

"Ah. Yes." Castlereagh waited. "Yes, I see. Did you have a location in mind?"

Jesuadon pushed himself away from the opened shutter and went to stand by the map-laden library table. He studied the unrolled map on the top of the pile, its corners weighted down by brass weights. It was of Prussia. "Yes. My aunt's," he said casually. As if it hardly mattered. "In Cleveland. She will be safe there."

"Is that a hope? Or a guarantee?" The Foreign Secretary did not raise his voice. He did not need to.

"She cannot stay here. Wilmot's men are sniffing about Charing Cross even as we speak, and there's too much at risk. I have to get her out." Neither did he raise his voice.

"Yes. Yes, I do see that." Lord Castlereagh paused, sat back in this chair the better to study Jesuadon. "However, this remains an awkward business. Her family is from Norfolk, as I dare say you know…"

"Yes."

"…and are on visiting terms with my wife's family up there."

"Yes."

"But she has been of great assistance to us. And I want no harm to come to her."

"I understand that."

"And no scandal, inasmuch as that is possible."

Jesuadon answered on an exhalation of breath. "Yes."

"And you are certain she shall be safe with your aunt?"

"Yes." Jesuadon lifted the map and idly regarded the map beneath. This was of Spain. "But every day that she remains here becomes more dangerous. For her and for us. There is always the chance, small perhaps, that someone lets a word drop, or someone in the street catches a glimpse of her. That's all it would take."

"Yes." Castlereagh rubbed the bridge of his nose, considering. "So when do you leave?

"As soon as I can arrange it. I shall leave Barnet in charge." Still Jesuadon showed no emotion.

"You are escorting her yourself?"

"I am. Do you object?" Jesuadon queried, knowing that he did. He looked up for the first time.

"No. No," the Foreign Secretary repeated reassuringly. He hesitated. "Has her family been informed of her disappearance yet, do you know?"

Jesuadon shrugged. "No. Barnet tells me not."

Shaking his head, Castlereagh leaned back in his chair. "All right. But I do not like it, Jesuadon. I do not like it at all." His volume rose. "She should never have been involved. Never. And with Shuster away! It leaves us too exposed."

"We was always exposed," Jesuadon said tightly.

Castlereagh slanted him an angry glance. "Do you want me to call in Bayard?"

Jesuadon scowled. "No. 'Struth, no. He's too well-known a figure. You call him in, and everyone from Savary down to the potboy will know something's amiss."

"And ain't it?" Castlereagh snapped.

Jesuadon looked up, grey with patient fatigue. "No," he murmured. "It may be. But it ain't yet…"

Castlereagh regarded him steadily, then grumbled, a low growling sound deep in his throat. And returned his attention briefly to the letter before him. "Yes. Yes, all right," he consented. "Keep me informed, yes? Have Planta supply you with funds…Whatever you need."

2

Jesuadon was in the rear garden of a house in Kensington when Barnet finally found him—a walled garden, upon the ancient brick of which were climbing late roses, their boughs laden and bent with fragrant sprays of small blowsy pink and paler blossoms. Jesuadon was seated in the sun, his feet propped up upon a rustic table, drinking. Lazily, at the sound of the creaking gate opening, he turned his head.

"Ah. So you've decided to join me, have you?" he murmured. "At last."

Looking about him with interest, Barnet shrugged. "It took me a bit to get away. I had things to see to."

"What things?" Jesuadon enquired. Then, as if mellowed by the sun and the drowsing of bees amongst the roses and Michaelmas daisies, he added softly, "Never mind…" He took a long drink from the bottle he had been cradling against his chest. He gestured to the opposite bench. "Sit."

Barnet ignored him and strolled about the garden, incuriously regarding the displays of mixed flowers, the pair of fruiting trees, the climbers upon the walls. At last he came and slouched down on the bench and drew a deep breath of the untainted country air. "It took me a fair bit to get here." Pushing his hat back from off his forehead, Barnet tilted his head so that sunlight fell upon his already reddened face. "What are we doing all the way out here?" Then liking the warmth, here in the open, he took his hat off and tossed it on the table.

Jesuadon finished the contents of his bottle. "I'm being followed."

Barnet grunted and straightened. "I don't believe it."

"I don't like it." Jesuadon pronounced, as if he had not heard Barnet. He drew another bottle from out of his pocket and removed the stopper with his teeth. Then spat out the fine bits of cork which had crumbled in his mouth. "I want you to take care of it."

"Yes, all right…" Barnet nodded though there had never been any question.

Jesuadon took a long swig. "There are two of them. Possibly three."

"That's the reason you've had me come way the hell out here, is it?"

"Yes."

Barnet rolled his eyes, then nodded in tacit agreement. "When do you want it done?"

"Tonight. And find out who they work for." Jesuadon glanced briefly up at him, then put the bottle to his lips and drank.

"And then? The river?" Barnet was hardly paying attention.

"No." He said it so softly Barnet had strained to hear the word. "No, I'm tired of death."

A mass of silver clouds, well-charged and mountainous, drifted across the sun, turning the afternoon to sudden chill. And then, just as silently, as unharried, slid away again. Jesuadon appeared not to notice, but continued staring straight ahead at the flowers or the bees or the motes of dust and early leaf-fall caught upon the currents of air and wind.

"Have them taken to Spithead. 'Struth, they're always in need of more boys to serve in His Majesty's Navy. Mind they're signed on to separate ships though. We don't want them comparing beatings." He produced a languid half-smile.

Barnet beamed at the thought of their intended future. He chuckled. "Right…And after I've learned the name of their master? What then?"

"Turn him." Jesuadon remained as he was, but the languor was gone; the harshness returned. And only one who knew him as Barnet did would have noted it.

"And if he resists?"

"Circumcise the bastard."

Barnet's eyes widened. "What?" he muttered.

"'Struth, you heard me, jolter head. Circumcise him. He wants to cock about with me. Show him the cost in a way he's most like to remember." Jesuadon narrowed his eyes. "Or perhaps, just at first, shave off half his foreskin. But I want him not to forget. So that every time he goes to take a piss, every time he fancies some whore, there's a little reminder of who owns him now."

"Right…" Barnet said, disliking the order. "Anything else?"

"Yes. I want him branded." He did not look up to see the expression in Barnet's lashless eyes. "Or tattooed. I don't much care which. With a symbol of the French royalists, do not you think?" he asked quizzically. The line of his jaw hardened. "So that he fears the discovery of his being turned more even than he fears me."

Barnet drew a deep breath, squaring his broad shoulders. He took his hat into his hands and holding it by the brim, turned it round and round. "I'll see to it." He waited while Jesuadon finished his last bottle. "And Wilmot?"

"Ah yes, Wilmot…Amiable patron of the Macao Club and my favourite companion of the evening," Jesuadon sneered. "I want him set upon. This evening. Some time after I take my leave of him. Perhaps a boxing of the watch gone wrong?" he said, slanting a malice-tainted glance at Barnet. "Or a gang of thieves? Your choice. But I want both his eyes blacked out and swollen shut. Steal his purse if you think it will add to the illusion. But don't break his nose. You'll want to leave something for later."

Barnet gave a silent laugh.

"But by all means, break a rib or two if you like. I shouldn't him permanently harmed. Not yet. But it must look credible. And disfiguring and painful enough so that he keeps indoors and denies himself to visitors—for the next several days. Do you understand?"

"Right." Barnet nodded. "Hmnh, I shall enjoy that," he admitted. "And then?"

Having sat so long in one position, Jesuadon struggled to right himself. Sitting upright, he drew a deep breath. "I'm away on the tide the day after tomorrow. With her. I shall need you to keep a tight handle on things here while I'm away."

"Aye." Barnet sat for some time and did not leer. Sat and watched the perpetual movements of small birds among the rose branches as if he had never encountered such a thing before. But after a suitable interval, he said, "The boy, Guvnor? Young Tirrell?" He hesitated. "Where's he got to then? Is he safe, do you reckon? Because I ain't had a mention of Brown anytime these last few days…"

Jesuadon belched loudly and drew a deep breath, then peered up at the sky. "His lordship forbade him to set foot in Paris, but said he'd a mind to send him to Spain…So by my reckoning he will have stayed clear of Paris and…" He burped. "…By my reckoning, the infernal saucebox will have headed as far in the opposite direction from Spain as he could reasonably manage." The smile he produced was little amused. "So Prussia, perhaps? Following Bonaparte and his pestilential army of scavengers? He travels fast, the brat does, so by Christmas I should have thought he will have run almost all the way to India, do not you?" He shook his head. "Infernal nocky boy."

Chapter XVII

1

Lady Wilmot had not been outside the walls of Sparrowhawk's rambling Inn in over a month. Indeed, she had not once been outside of the locked garret chamber in all that time. Not since that first night when Sparrowhawk had escorted her, exhausted and trembling, up the narrow staircase and through the maze of passages and hidden doors to the room under the eaves. And during the past of those lost days and nights, what she had seen of the sky and its changeable, London fog-bound moods had been framed always within the borders of the upper casement window, near which she was not permitted to stand. Not even to look out upon the moon and the never silent city. Not to feel the sun warm and strong upon her cheek.

But standing now just without the kitchen's threshold, she paused and looked up to regard the great expanse of London sky, blue and spectacularly cloudless. And caught her breath. And holding that intake of breath within her as a secret, she gazed upon the sky with a kind of wonder, looking up and glorying in this bright moment of freedom, upon the rooks wheeling overhead, and the street sparrows perched upon the gutters' edges, gazed with unparalleled pleasure and an awe which made her heart quail. And she would have stood thus the whole morning, emptied of thought or expectation, just watching in open wonder and private contentment the threading drifts of cloud and paling blue and the unfettered birds which flew as winnowed meal. But then, a touch on her shoulder reminded her that she could not linger, that she was not safe. And thus recalled to mind her precarious position, that today she was to be spirited away, she glanced up at Mr. Jesuadon's face and her heart began to thump. Suddenly, she noticed the bustle and hum and roar of the crowded street beyond the inn yard, and the brewing heat and stench of the sun-drenched day. And again she caught her breath. And lowering her gaze, she pulled the heavy veil of the black bonnet over her face and took his arm. And without even a glance at the coach or driver, she allowed him to assist her into the dark interior of the closed, unmarked carriage.

It had only been two days before that he had come to the upper chamber, as she thought, to drink tea with her. He had been no more nor no less taciturn than was his wont. But had stood at the open window, observing as he always did the street below. Until finally he had turned to her and said, "It is no longer safe for you here, ma'am."

At that she had looked up and saw that he did not dissemble. And she froze with a newborn fear.

"I have brought everything that you shall require," he continued. "Anything that you had with you when you first arrived here, you must give to Molly. There must be nothing left to link you either to Wilmot or to this place. Do you understand?" It was not unkindly said.

"Oh…Oh…But what has occurred?" she whispered. And she had blinked rapidly as she struggled to comprehend what it all might mean, such an announcement, there on that placid afternoon. She searched his eyes and his still, fair face. "Where am I to go, sir?"

"I have arranged for everything," Jesuadon said. "We travel by sea from Greenwich in two days' time. You will be safe.

"There are clothes…I shall fetch them. I believe you will find everything you require. You and Molly may wish to make some alterations or adjustments—I shall leave that with you. But from this day, there is no more Lady Wilmot."

And nodding, blinking rapidly—she was not after all to be turned out or abandoned—she had begun finally to perceive, for the first time perhaps, what she had done since that night when she had run away.

Then, all that had once been hers had been taken from her—undergarments, stockings, her monogrammed handkerchief, shoes. And at last, every stitch of her former life removed, and redressed in the black of deep mourning, she had given to Mr. Jesuadon the wedding band which was all that remained of Marianne Wilmot. He had taken it without a word. And soberly, he had replaced it with a worn and simple band, a plain band which better befitted the modest military widow into which she was transformed.

She did not look out of the coach's window as they left the Inn yard. But kept her eyes fixed on the seat opposite or on her hands in her lap as the carriage slowed and speeded, jolted and shook over the clay and grit roads and the uneven cobbles as they travelled toward Westminster Bridge.

Beside her Jesuadon sat, dun-coated, taut, still and austere. Carefully, as ever, not touching her. Though she had felt the unyielding lump of a side arm in his pocket as he'd settled next to her. She saw there was a knife in his boot, and another pistol, like one of a pair of duelling pistols, in a holster near the carriage door.

And so they travelled not by the most direct route to Greenwich, which was by water, but across Westminster Bridge and through Lambeth until they picked up the Old Kent Road to journey cross country. For Jesuadon had said he would not expose her to risk of discovery on the open river; he could not guarantee that she would be hidden from view along the riverbank or from passing vessels, even with an awning on a scow's deck. Too much could go wrong. Accidents could too easily be contrived.

He had promised there would be outriders with them throughout their journey. That he had dispatched his own men to watch along the route. He had prepared for everything, it seemed. Yet with each assurance of her safety, her fears had multiplied.

By the time they came to a halt at Spread Eagle Yard, the point of entry for all carriages into Greenwich proper, she had lost all track of the hour. But the toll paid, the carriage once more lurched forward into the press which clogged all those roads leading to the docks.

Jesuadon had been silent during their journey. But now, the carriage halting near the quayside, he turned to her. "Are you ready, ma'am?" She saw that he was paler even than usual.

She bit her lip, but with her nod, he said, "Stay close to me at all times. Do not lose hold of my arm. No matter what. Do you understand? I will take care of everything."

"Yes." She spoke so faintly, he had to strain to hear the word above the din outside. "Yes," she repeated, nodding, struggling for courage.

He regarded her gravely, then opened the carriage door and stepped down into the quayside traffic. And stood for a moment to behold the river where the sun glittered upon the surface like cloth of gold against the obsidian shadows, then scanned the dockside for his own men, and measured the distance between the coach and the waiting chasse-marée, and the distances between each of his men. Searched too for any of Wilmot's. Then reaching for her hand, he drew her forth into the sunlit afternoon and the swarm of beadles and warrant officers, dock workers and wherry men, all of whom were shouting and gesturing as they pursued their many jobs.

She had never been near the docks before. Nor so near to the sea. The noise of it—the yelling of so many men, so many voices, and the harsh cries of the herring gulls as they dipped and dived, and the smells, the heavy dank smell of the tidal seawater, the smell of the wet hempen ropes, of the produce and manure, all caused her to stop, recoiling and faint, as Jesuadon drew her hand through his arm. She looked at him through the dark scrim of the veil protecting her and did not cry out. And she remembered that she must not lose hold of him and her hand tightened about his elbow.

Stopping every few feet to allow the lumpers to hoist and load and shift the crates of cargo ahead of them, stepping aside to avoid the coils of rope and the warrant officers with their notebooks, slowly and carefully, her hand clutching at the crook of his arm, they made their way along the quayside. Past the wherries and lighters and cockleshells which crammed the waterway and drew alongside the moored craft—the yachts, the schooners and smaller Indiamen—until she saw a three-masted boat which lay moored and readied, the gang-board down in expectation of passengers or more crew.

Yet with each step, Jesuadon could feel her courage flagging as her grip on his arm tightened; he bent near to her ear. "We are very nearly there, ma'am." And scanned, as he had done since arriving, all those near to them, and those farther distant.

At the side of the carriageway, two teenage crossing-sweeps, his own men, disguised by their native covering of grime, leaned upon their brooms, appeared to be making idle conversation. Beyond them, one of Wilmot's men—the narrow-faced grey man. With a sharp glance, Jesuadon caught the eye of Barnet, lounging near a stack of empty pallets.

Interpreting the darting glare and following its lead, Barnet stood, and wiping his brow across his sleeve as though he'd had too much sun, wandered off in the direction of Wilmot's cullion.

Ahead was a trio of gentlemen, dandies, sauntering and out of place, all pomade, high collarpoints and languid pride, the one regarding the gold handle of his cane.

Jesuadon felt her stiffen. And heard her breathless gasp.

Then catching her heel against the corner of a cobblestone, she stumbled, colliding with the tallest dandy's back.

Jesuadon's arm snaked about her waist, hauling her upright.

The dandy turned, sneering, ready to administer a rebuke.

Again Jesuadon heard the catch in her breath. Saw her frightened almost raising of her hand against the stranger. And, reading panic in that raised hand, he bent and scooped her up into his arms and he felt her tense and almost faint against his chest. "Your pardon, sir," he soothed. "The lady, she faints..."

The dandy paused. Hesitated. Regarded for too long an instant the heavily veiled creature and the gentleman whom he knew by reputation though not acquaintance.

Barnet was too far away for use.

The dandy stepped to one side and bowed. "Of course. My clumsiness. My apologies, sir. Ma'am."

Cradled in his arms, her face pressed against his shoulder, Jesuadon could feel her heart pounding through the layers of her clothing. Could feel her shaking and fraught. And registered through a fog of icy rage the cod's head who had caused for whatever reason such distress: his face, his height, his mien. Not to be forgot.

The trio stepped to one side to allow him to pass and he strode forward to carry her up the gang-board as the two sweeps came behind, blocking the gentlemanly trio's path.

Within moments of their boarding, the gang-board was drawn up.

"It is over now," Jesuadon said, bending his face close to hers. "I have you. You are safe," he murmured. "Mr. Matlock, can you take our guest below?" he called out, and handed her into the care of the First Mate, who took her as if she were a child, to carry her down into the cabin.

Captain Fiske, having watched as the seamen drew up the gang-board and the ropes were untied and cast off, came to consult with Jesuadon as the breeze filled the foresail and the lugger slipped from the dockside upon the tide. Beside him Jesuadon stood, only half-listening, his eyes fixed on the spot where Barnet was, where there was no longer a thin-faced grey man.

"Sir?"

Jesuadon turned. It was Matlock, the large Yorkshireman.

"It's Mrs. Tomkins, sir. She's not well. Will you go you to her, sir?"

Jesuadon paused. Hesitated. And gave a final glance at the slowly passing shoreline. Barnet was now lost to view. "Yes."

"Just this way, sir. And mind your head belowdecks," he said, leading the way down the companion way.

As if it were still the Captain's private quarters, Matlock knocked on the cabin door, then opened it wide for Jesuadon without awaiting a reply. "Sir."

She was standing in the middle of the neat lamplit cabin. She had removed her bonnet and pelisse, but now she stood, just stood, her hand on the bunk to steady her and her face drained of all expression, all colour. He saw that she had been weeping.

Jesuadon closed the door behind him and stood with his back to it to look about at the dark panelled walls, the two wall-lanterns, and the washstand with its jug and basin. Her trunk had been placed at the foot of the bunk. "Mr. Matlock says you are not well…Shall I…fetch you some tea, perhaps?" he said, offering her the chance to regain her equanimity, for he noticed too that she hardly dared look up.

"Oh," she whispered. "Oh yes...that would be very kind, sir," she said.

Jesuadon regarded her steadily, unhappy to see her rendered so fearful as she had been when first he met her. And wishing to apologise for that to which she had been exposed today and for taking her from Sparrowhawk's where she had been safe, he came, and though he knew he should never do so, he took her hand. Then did that which he also knew he must never do. Holding still her small hand within his own, he placed his arm about her to draw her close. And his arms comforting around her, she gave way to tears.

Stroking her hair away from her face, he found it soft. Then just this once, he laid his face against her hair and found that it smelled vaguely of lavender or pinks. He allowed himself the brief pleasure of just inhaling that sweet, soft scent. Just this once. "The gentleman who stopped you. Did you know him?"

She hesitated. He could feel the anguish in her hiccoughing intake of breath. "Yes, he is called Waley, George Waley," she said on a sigh.

"He is...or he was...Sir Robert's lover."

Slowly, Jesuadon drew in a deep breath. And did not react. Tenderly his hand sought her cheek, to lift her grief-washed face to his, and he gazed down upon her, studying her pale beautiful face. Weighing her answer, he found honesty. Then he did that which he must never do, which broke every rule, which he would not permit himself to think on, though the dreams kept coming night after night, that which came natural to him: he bent and gently brushed her mouth with his.

Her mouth was soft and still beneath his. Lifting his head, he brushed the soft curls from her face, and bent to kiss her again. And tasting her mouth, found it as sweet as he had imagined it would be—tentative as if she had not been much kissed. And kissing her, he tangled his fingers among her hair as it tumbled down about her shoulders. And he kissed her again, tenderly and gently.

Her face, her hair, her mouth, Jesuadon kissed them all. And starting thus, there was, there could be no stopping. And still he kissed her...as if he would banish all trace of Wilmot's gross unkindness and expunge his shaming infidelities. Knowing he had long since forfeited all right to one such as her, gently, softly, tenderly, Jesuadon kissed her.

He knew he must stop. That he must stop and remove himself from her. That to remain there was to break with every code of honour, to bring disgrace upon them both. And smoothing the fair skin of her throat and her collarbone as if it were the rarest treasure, he bent his head to kiss her as he had dreamed of doing since he had first seen her.

But then her arms went about him, hugging him to her breast, pressing him close. Jesuadon raised his head and saw in her eyes a look which he had not expected ever to see in the expression of any woman. And seeing in the slope and fall of rose upon her cheek, in the gentleness of her gaze upon him the invitation to love and to be loved, he tightened his arm about her against the increasing motion of the boat. Hesitant still, but with whisper of her breath soft upon his face, he traced a tentative finger down to pull at the ties which held the fall-front of her bodice. And she watched as his fingers closed over the ribbon-end and pulled it free.

She gave a sharp intake of breath. Looking up at him, sudden fear writ large in her dark eyes, she closed her hand over his, halting him. She was shaking.

He searched her face and would have begged her forgiveness. But trembling still, her hand fluttering against his chest, she reached out to unfasten the buttons of his waistcoat. And answered, he began to kiss her once more, all hope of restraint now wholly lost as much as if it had been thrown to the waves.

His waistcoat falling open, she laid first her hand against his chest, and then her cheek. He closed his eyes to savour the warmth and smallness of her presence there in his arms. To hold it as a memory, etching it against his mind. And he caught her hand to kiss, to twist and then to kiss again, her palm, her fingers, her wrist. Then she allowed him to draw back from her just long enough to remove his coat and waistcoat. And he stood, still with unquiet longing, while she reached up and untied the knot of his cravat and loosened the starched fabric from about his neck until it fell away and his shirt collar fell open to reveal the fair skin of his throat, and she laid her fingers gentle against the pulse that beat there.

And as the boat slipped past Woolwich and then Dartford these were passed without notice. For he had bent to kiss her and kiss her again. And he knew that whatever the consequences, there was no stopping.

For though there remained in her eyes a shadow of some fear, she captured his hand and returned it to the remaining tie upon her bodice, then stood, her hands raised to the side, presenting herself to him to undress. He pulled free the other tie, then traced his finger along the lace edge of her bodice until it fell away to reveal the thin lawn of her chemise.

Solemnly, he stopped to look upon her as if she were a gift, golden in the lamplight, that he would never have enough of, and he brushed the surface of her chemise across her breasts with the back of his hand.

Kissing her still, he looped his fingers through the tapes which held her skirts in place, and loosing them, drew them through his fingers, as the black muslin of her gown slid rumpling in its weightlessness to gather about her knees. And soberly, he stood to gaze upon her beauty, the fairness of her skin, her breasts, still held high and round by her corset. He ran one exploring, lingering finger along the lace edging of her chemise. He had no breath; it had all been stolen from him.

Then, fixing his gaze on her corset, carefully, methodically, he loosed the lacings of her stays until that too came away and she stood before him in nothing but her chemise.

He drew off his shirt to drop it on the floor. And finally untying the ribbon at the neck of her chemise and drawing it from her shoulders, he kissed her where first he had seen the marks of bruises upon her. Then reverently he laid his hand upon her breast and held it.

Lifting her, he placed her on the bunk which had been made up with fine linen as he had requested. And their clothes in a heap on the cabin floor, he told her with his mouth and his hands all that he had never spoken. Holding himself in check, he kissed her gently, touched with soft patience as she clung to him, kiss upon kiss, touch upon touch, caress upon caress. And sacrificing his desire, in his ears the litany of her love-sighs and murmured pleasure, her arms twined about his neck, he would have held back all day and all night, for he was determined that nothing she had ever known would rival this. When at last he pushed into her, the shuddering welcome of her happiness washed over him and defeated his control. And broken, yielding to her delight, he took her as a man possessed and possessing.

And with each passing mile, each passing landmark, he held her as afternoon passed into evening, kissing her, teaching her her beauty, while the heave of the waves increased and the boat rocked as a child's cradle upon the estuary's widening mouth and another sail was raised to speed them toward the open sea.

It was dawn or a dim morning when she awoke, sheltered still within the warmth of Jesuadon's arms—face to face and skin upon skin. Held there. Loved there. And protected.

And in the murky light which stole through the porthole and made a pattern of watery shadows upon the ceiling, she touched with one wondering finger the fine red gold hairs upon his chest, and gazed upon his face, still and calm in sleep. Listening to the rhythmic pattern of creaking from the wooden vessel about her, she breathed deeply with a quiet unexpected happiness. For after a night in his arms, in this dawn light, she was unbruised, and well. There was no pain, not from rough handling nor cruel misuse. Nor any weeping neither. Instead, there was a joy such as she had never imagined, the essence of kindness and his pleasure in her. And she wanted to take his dear face between her hands and tell him. She breathed in again, smelling his scent, feeling his breath warm and deep on her face, as his hand resting on her hip drew her closer even in his sleep.

Chapter XVIII

1

The rain that fell upon the wide plains of Poland and in the Sudeten of the south was different. Different from the cold squalls that scudded fast across England and chilled a soul to the heart. Here, you could see it approaching, crouching first upon the horizon, then sweeping slowly over the open fields like a curtain, muting the colours of the distance to shadows. You could hear it coming too, stealing up in a pattering hush, field by field, frond by frond, blade by blade. And it was warm—just as wet, but warm. And soft. Here, you might put your face up to it to wash away the dismal stains of soil and tears. Or open your mouth to it to drink it in, drop by drop.

Boy stood, his eyes closed, his face lifted to the clotted grey sky, rubbing at the weeks of grime as the rain splashed on his head and face, as the water dripped down over his cheeks and chin and slid between his fingers.

He had buried Pater Wilhelm three days past. He and a stout, blotch-faced peasant, together scraping out a grave from the crumbling ground and gathering great stones to cover it, while the child sat beside the body, looking on, her face a still pocket of loss. Buried him with his rosary laced through his stiffening fingers, in a shallow grave in the churchyard of a tiny hamlet just over the border in Poland. And overhead the clouds had amassed, weighty and dark, and crows gathered in the nearby trees or took to the sky in waves, clattering and cawing, an even blacker cloud upon the earth.

Boy did not know the hamlet's name. Nor did it matter. The churchyard was consecrated ground. And that was all the sick old man had cared for in the end.

Pater Wilhelm. The priest who, risking torture and a martyr's end, had taken him in after his own father's death, hiding him from the French and their hordes of collaborators. Now he too had been broken by this war of wars, broken by the long journey to safety, down the length of Poland.

For the journey from Kovno had taken not days but weeks. Weeks of walking through a country left pillaged and consumed. Past the fields where no harvest was, nor would there be. In hamlet after hamlet, town after town, nothing but wreckage. The houses with their walls half-demolished, their broken furnishings strewn across the landscape and all windows smashed, the rough roads glinting with the fragmented particles of glass.

Across the countryside, as far as the eye could see and beyond, barns had been torched and the land spread with the carcasses of dead horses and abandoned wagons and with the unwanted heads and hides of butchered livestock, now half-gnawed and left to rot. And everywhere, the dispossessed, those who had once worked the land or lived in merchant's houses, everywhere, dressed in their tattered past, huddled families of them with lost eyes, unwashed and hungry and forlorn, refugees of an earth scorched by their allies.

It had been Pater Wilhelm's cassock which had bought their survival. For all those wretched creatures who saw him craved a blessing or a prayer. Or pleading and begging in the Polish which he did not understand, they would lead him to a nearby church—desecrated and robbed by the French—and there he would offer them the succour of their Mass among the ruins, and dying himself, he prayed for their dead. Farm to farm, ruin to ruin. With the harvest and seed destroyed, the only yield now and for years to come dearth and starvation. And so they, he, Pater Wilhelm and the child, like all the others, had survived on meagre bowls of buckwheat gruel. That, and bad kwas which Boy drank without hesitation, though made from fermented bread, it was the vilest of spirits and left him in a distending haze of drunkenness—his only respite from the misery.

But every night spent sleeping on the cold ground, clutching the child to him for warmth and comfort, weakened the old priest. And each morning he was stiffer in his movements, his steps slower, and his breathing more laboured and difficult.

Even the donkey Boy had found to carry him and the child into the mountains of the Sudeten had made the plodding journey little better. And as the remnant summer eked into autumn, and the nights grew colder, the old man had weakened until Boy believed each day must be his last. Across the miles of long, burnt grass and scrub that lay at the feet of the hills, staying to the whitened well-trodden paths, through the stretches of fern that softened the lower reaches and foothills, while the mist hung like cannon smoke over the spruce forests of the higher peaks. Yet the only hope of any kind of safety, any rest, lay across the border in Bohemia, the northernmost reach of Austria.

So each day, hungry or fed, Boy led them farther south, stopping only briefly among the wreckage of Warsaw to gather firsthand the accounts of the French iniquities and the profligate folly of Napoleon's own brother, Jérôme. Warsaw, where the already insolvent government had been beggared by Napoleon's demands and those of his looting soldiery. Where in the streets, the books from pillaged libraries lay trampled in the mud, a littering of darkening autumn leaves—of scarlet, ochre and brown—their tooled leather spines torn or crushed and their pages soaked and bleeding; where the wooden fragments of a fortepiano lay broken upon the ground, scattered, the ebony keys creating a random parquet amongst the muddy cobbles. And from there across the Varta and the Oder—haggling with the barge owners until they agreed to tow the donkey too across the wide stretches of water, scrounging cabbages or windfalls from abandoned garden plots and handfuls of grass for the donkey.

And each night, slipping away from the sleeping priest and the child, Boy ran across the blackened landscape, to wherever he might have hope of obtaining information or more food and to leave his mark in the sand.

Returning before dawn, he would wait, his knife at the ready; and drinking kwas against the despairing cold, he would watch as through a blur the outline of the distant peaks of the Sudeten, shining turquoise, azure and aquamarine under a cloudless sky, the peaks which they must cross.

On, he led them into the harsh higher reaches, upon paths wide enough only for one. One and a sure-footed donkey. Amidst the summits of mottled sandstone which towered over all, their stratified grey features pitted and carved by the pitiless fingers of rain over the centuries. Keeping where he could to the lower trails and to those hidden amongst the dense covering of spruce and scrub, where they might pass unseen by any patrol—Polish or Austrian. Avoiding too the focal points of the many fortresses which lay upon the heights and the summit levels like a spattering of whitewash, glinting like sugar in the sun, speckling the whole of the Sudeten with their square, white towers and thick defensive walls.

On, the child secured to the donkey with a rope around its middle, finally leaving Poland behind and crossing the uncertain border into Bohemia. On, buffeted by the sweeping gales, immune to the grandeur of the crests, the small beauty of the seeding flower heads which drooped from the fissured rocks, and the stark majesty of the looming stone monoliths, grey and tall as any house. On, looking neither on the prospects before or behind. For each mountain was nothing more nor less than another day's climb and descent.

Washed and wet, Boy went to kneel beside the sleeping child, her slight form dwarfed within his coat which he'd wrapped about her days since—as the weather cooled and the wind shrieked and leaves turned and fell. Gathering her up, he tucked her nodding head against his shoulder. And leading the donkey, he began the slow walk through the falling mist of dusk, the air heavy with the scent of the spruce after the rain.

The house when he came upon it was better kept than those in Poland. For here there had been no soldiers to steal and loot.

He regarded the thick walls of the enclosed farmyard, the patches of exposed stone where the aged rendering had cracked and fallen away.

The child in his arms stirred and her hand crept about his neck.

Gently, he placed her back onto the donkey and tied the lead rein to a shrub. And briefly he placed his hand over her mouth. Silent, she laid her head down with her cheek against the donkey's soft neck and reclosed her eyes.

And his movements lost in the falling night, any sound lost in the familiar stirrings and snortings of the livestock, Boy crept into the yard and edged his way along the wall, his eyes fixed on an upper window from which a soft light shone, soft like that of a bedside candle. Stopping beneath a head-high window, he paused to shut his eyes against the knowledge of what he did there, then crouched down to write with his finger in the dust of the ground. Then keeping low, he ran to lean against a corner of the building, to lean and to wait, every sense alerted. To wait with his hand resting upon the reassuring handle of his knife.

He shrank further into the shadow of the corner.

For the door was opening.

From within, a lantern was lifted high that the light might fall over the sign in the dust. The man holding the lantern paused. And looked again upon the symbols on his doorstep.

Boy closed his fingers about the knife and slid it free from his waistband, ready to throw.

Lifting the lantern still higher, without fear or hurry, the man looked about, searching the shadows of the yard, peering upon the closed stable door, the tumbled piles of wet leaves, and the barn door left half-open. Looked, searching the gloom, until his gaze fell upon the near corner where Boy waited.

Within the fall of the lantern's light, the man was fair, tall and unafraid. He gave a brief nod. "Nun dann…Komm herein." And gestured toward the open door.

"Nein," Boy said quietly. "Hier sind ein Kind und ein Esel."

"Ein Kind und ein Esel? A child?" The man frowned. "Go, fetch it in. You have come from Poland, ja?"

"Ja."

"How is it?"

"Schlecht. Bad. Very bad."

"Ja. But I have heard it is worse in Russia. Much, much worse. Fetch the child."

2

It had all been arranged by Herr Zimmermann and by others. And it was a detail which Boy had been content to leave in their hands. For what did he know of the disposal of small children?

He spent the morning washing her though. Heating the water in the great hearth of the kitchen, with its low ceiling and blackened beams in this house without a woman. Pouring kettle after kettle of warmed water into the tin tub Herr Zimmermann had brought in from the barn. There was no soap. So with a cloth, he rubbed away at the unknown months of grime streaked upon her child's face, down her legs and matted into her hair. And she was as she had always been. Silent. Her expression as empty of colour as the ruin of the church in which he had first seen her. Emptier perhaps now. And even as he had lain her back into the water to rinse the dust from her head, she remained quiescent, closing her eyes as if she expected him to hold her head under the water. And if that were so, that would be, and she would not resist.

The water streaming from her hair, Boy lifted her from the bath and wrapped her in an old bed sheet. Her hair washed free of the miles of dirt was blonde and fair, fairer even, now that her face and limbs were brown with the weeks of travelling. And redressing her in her soiled gown, mottled and blackened with smuts, he wrapped her in an old woollen shawl which Herr Zimmermann had found among his things.

Then, kneeling beside the tin tub, Boy bent to wash his own face and neck and head. And rinsed, wet, clean, he rose and dried his face as he had dried her, then put on his coat, its wool stiff with grime and sweat. Gathering her to him as he had from the beginning, Boy carried her into the yard where Herr Zimmermann was giving the donkey an evening feed.

"I will come with you, I have decided," Zimmermann announced. "It will be better that way."

Leading the donkey out through the archway, Zimmermann said,

"Her name is Frau Schmidt." He gave a nod of approval, adding eventually as they walked along the silent road, "She lost her husband at the battle of Schöngraben—just over three years ago—and their daughter, last year. She will be a good mother to the child."

Above, a harvest moon shone through the dark waftings of cloud across its face, which spilled and shifted like billowing ink released into a jar of clear water.

"It is a bit out of the way, her small farm, which will protect the child. There will be fewer questions," Zimmermann added, now taking a turning from the rutted mud road, down a narrower path, lumpy and well overgrown. "The brethren will make sure she does not go without."

The woman, Frau Schmidt, was waiting for them within her small lime-washed cottage where there were no haloes of light, only the uncertain guttering of a single candle in a lantern, casting a hesitant glow through the cross-barred windows. A scattering of weeds grew, trailing and lank, from between the loose shingles at the edge of the steep wooden roof. Yet dappling the indistinct dark of the garden, where green turned to shades of grey in the falling of evening, where the shapes of several fruit trees were only a blackening presence, the white petals of marguerites growing plentifully glowed pale.

Patiently, she stood just inside the opened door, her tightly pleated hands held at her breast, her pretty, eager face marked by years of loss, struggle and no hope of comfort. Yet as she saw the approach of Boy with the child, a look of wonder came over her—as if by some accident good had lost its way and instead found her door. Still she waited, watching their approach, while her hand crept to cover her mouth so that she would not cry out.

"Guten Abend, gnädige Frau." Boy stopped short of the doorstep and bowed his head.

Wordless, she dipped a curtsy as to her better. She curtsied a second time to Herr Zimmermann.

With his gaze steady upon the widow, Boy laid his face alongside the child's ear. "Liebling," he said, stroking the hair dried soft and curling. "Liebling, höre mir zu…Listen to me, mein Schatz. Das ist deine Mutti."

There was no response. Nor had he expected any. The child

remained as she was and did not lift her head from Boy's shoulder.

Frau Schmidt caught her breath. Tentative, doubting still that this good thing had come to remain with her, she extended her arms, reaching out for the child, longing and fretful hope playing upon her rounded features.

"Liebling," Boy repeated. "Höre mir zu. Das ist jetzt deine Mutti. Do you hear me?"

For the briefest increment of a moment, the child's small hand clutched at his collar.

"Ja, ja," Boy said gently. And so silent, it was less than a breath, he whispered as he nestled his face against her hair, just once, "Weine nicht, mein Schatz. Weine nicht."

And with that he handed her, the small soul he had rescued from the charnel house through which he had passed, with her fragmented spirit and empty eyes, into the waiting arms of Frau Schmidt. Who did not weep, but clasped her to her breast, cradling her as a mother. She kissed her head, smoothing the fair hair.

"Bitte…What is her name, sir?" Frau Schmidt asked softly.

Boy looked at the ground, then up at her, his eyes now drained as the child's. "She has no name.

"Pater Wilhelm called her Liebling. That is all I know."

Frau Schmidt nodded, accepting as they all accepted.

"Her parents?" she said fearfully, her face, even in the darkening gloom, crumpling.

Boy shrugged.

Frau Schmidt blinked as if at sudden tears. Then, still smoothing the child's soft baby-hair, now unmatted, from her face, she nodded. "Ja…Liebling," she murmured. And gave a tremulous smile. "Liebling," she repeated, catching her bottom lip between her teeth to stop its trembling. "Ja. Na gut. But I…I shall call her Anna, if that is all right with you."

"Anna is a good name," Herr Zimmermann said.

Still stroking the child's head, Frau Schmidt looked from Boy to Zimmerman, then lowered her gaze once more.

Boy gave a nod of approval and shifted his weight from one foot to another. "There is a donkey too." He gestured at the ambling soft creature which he'd tied to the rickety gate.

"Wie bitte? Ein Esel?" Frau Schmidt exclaimed, blinking rapidly. "I beg your pardon? A donkey?" She shook her head as if to clear it.

"Yes. A donkey. It is yours now," Boy said.

"Ein Esel?" Frau Schmidt marvelled, struggling against the tears which threatened to overcome her. A surprised fearful smile broke forth. "I have never had a donkey!" she declared. "Oh! Thank you. It will make everything so very fine! A donkey?" She whispered the word against the child's head as it rested upon her shoulder. "Ach so. A donkey. Danke schön, mein Junge. We have a donkey, Anna!" she burst out, unable to keep her simple tears from falling, and clutching the child to her, she bowed first to the one and then to the other of them. "Danke schön, mein Herr! Oh!"

But then, she wiped at her tears and her expression troubled, she said carefully, "But, mein Herr…what can I give you, young sir? Can I not give you something? A meal? A bed for the night? Or for as long as you need?" She hiccoughed. "I have clothes…" she nodded tearfully. "Good clothes. For a young man, they are…They…They were my husband's. They would keep you warm. Please, let me…"

"Nein," cut in Herr Zimmermann. "It is all taken care of, Frau Schmidt. He comes with me." He softened his tone. "It is better, gnädige Frau. I shall see that he is fed and kept safe. But thank you."

Boy could not see past her into the small cottage, where in its single room, the child would never be alone. And this he knew was best. "Yes, it is better," he said plainly, his face now a blank. "But thank you."

"Ach so." Frau Schmidt nodded, understanding what no one would explain. "But…mein Junge, if there is ever anything you need…anything. Ever." She hesitated over her next words. "You will come back to see her?"

"Nein. Ich kann nicht." Boy squared his shoulders. "She belongs to you now."

Frau Schmidt nodded slowly. "Ja. Ja. Danke schön," she whispered, and fingering the fair hair, she kissed the child's head. "Danke schön…"

And with his hands pressed flat upon his thighs, Boy bowed to her, bowing as her countryman, not as what he was. Then he turned to follow Zimmermann into the darkening gloom as it turned to the limpid inkblue of nightfall covered over with cloud.

He slept in a bed that night, covered by an old quilt. Fed on sausages and cabbage and weak beer, he slept.

There would be snow upon the peaks in another week.

Chapter XIX

1

The paths through the pine forests above Linz were deep with a silencing floor of fallen needles which lay flattened, tan and brown and broken, beneath Boy's swift running footfalls.

Across the northernmost tip of Bohemia, heading west for Teplitz, he had run. Down across the fir-clad mountains, across the rolling hills and plains, beside the harvested fields. Walking on rutted village lanes, dragging his hand along the walls of the lime-washed houses till his fingers turned blue with the crystalline tinting. Until he learned that the Maestro was no longer in Teplitz, but had departed for Linz.

And so he headed south, to run without anger, without even grief—the cold branches of yew slapping at his face and brambles tangling in his hair and snagging at his clothes. Catching the drops of mist in his mouth, the light and rain percolating through the filter of boughs and fir cones to hang, pendulous as crystals, from every twig. Ducking, still running, to keep from hitting his head. Always running, hurdling over fallen branches and past flapping, skirring wood pigeons disturbed in their feeding. Running silent as a native hunter seeking deer. Running without loss, with almost pleasure and with small spurts of delight in the speed of a hill's descent as he ran along the field-edges of stubble. For this one thing he could do. Run. Buffeted, or swept forward by the wind at his back.

And it did not matter that there were few safe houses here in

Austria. For here none knew of him. Nor were there any to catch him. And here, after nearly two years of peace with the warring, godless French, the harvest had been good, plentiful. Upon the ground lay handfuls of wheat, hazelnuts and apples. Falling from carts and wagons and after the markets, there were vegetables and fruit to be gathered up. And as ever he, a bland and brown boy, was invisible. Untracked and untraced. Unnoticed. Instantly forgot.

He slept in barns and sheds, behind and upon bales of fresh straw. And running on, through the vast forests which here were free of marauders and deserters, he ran into Austria proper. To those places he avoided lest he be reminded. For they were his past and he did not wish to remember. Not the battlefields where he had watched the destruction of thousands whose bones still shone white in the wintering sun. Not the markets nor the bridges where the French had turned the river Traun red with Austrian blood. Not his father, nor his brother. Nothing of life as it had been. None of it since this decade of war had begun. Yet still he ran. Down the rolling hillsides which led to the city where they said the Maestro was.

Until finally within the shadows of the great spruce forest above the sleeping city, he waited, hovering silent and alert in the hours before dawn. Waited, wiping at his nose with his sleeve, blowing the warmth of his breath into his cupped hands. Shifting from one foot to another in the damp autumn mist while owls hunted and called. Then, as a weak light edged at the eastern horizon, walking and running, he made his way down from the hidden heights. His heels catching and skidding at the scree upon the paths, he scurried down the slope to the ancient beam bridge spanning the River Danube.

His soles soft upon the old stone bridgeway, he ran, to slip into the city before the fishermen set sail for their daily trawl upon the dark churning river. Before the rheumy-eyed watch changed at the Schloss where the steep white walls bore still the blackening streaks of fire, and now prisoners were kept. Before there were any to see or to mark him.

Wiping at his nose again, silent, Boy slowed. To walk quiet among the quieter back alleys and passages of this thrice-occupied city, where high up and low, every house carried the scars of invasion, the embedded musket balls in the cracked walls, the ruins. To walk among the streets and Plätze. And briefly to think. Till at last, beneath a sky growing murky arsenic-white, he arrived at his destination. Crouching down, he huddled hungry in the alley-doorway opposite the apothecary's kitchen, and again blew into his hands to warm them. Farther down the passageway, one of the city's few remaining servants emerged to collect wood from the yard. A striped tabby scuttled across his path. Boy hunched further into his coat, clamping his jaw to keep his teeth from chattering. And waited.

2

From that first moment of waking, his eyelids fluttering unwilling against the unwelcome grey light of morning, the Maestro knew it would be a better day. Despite the constant uncertainties of this uneasy peace and these years of unbroken austerity. Despite yesterday's scenes of tears and rage and recrimination. Despite all the stupidity of his brothers and their incessant follies—first the one thing and then another—their health, their pricks, their fecklessness. Dumm geboren und nichts dazugelernt. But today would be better. He could smell it.

He lay back against the lumpen bolster—breathing in the enclosed air, testing it—to puzzle over the vague wafting of that smell so familiar, so embedded in his thoughts of a happier time, yet almost wholly consigned to memory. Nowadays, one could only remember. But still, there it was. A gentling smell, warm and welcome, comforting as a child's laughter. He closed his eyes to breathe in deeply and to dwell, just for a little, on those lost bright days when all of Vienna had smelled so.

And only when his bladder would wait no longer, did he throw the bedclothes off himself to struggle into his dressing gown. And he sat, pondering. Thinking back. For it was still present, still there, that alluring smell, soft and sweet as Gugelhupf. He drew in a great lungful of it, wanting it to linger in his nostrils like a lover's perfume. Unwontedly hopeful, smelling it still, he went to wash his face. Yes, assuredly, it would be a better day.

His head ached a little from the poor wine of the previous evening and his gut ached more. But about him, his brother's house was silent.

No tears this morning. Or none in his hearing, praise God. Humming the new melody a little, he struggled into some clothes and—but partially dressed, his dressing gown hanging open, his linen clean but askew, his hair on end—he thrust his feet into wool embroidered slippers to lumber into the small panelled study beside the bedroom. To work.

"Dadum, dadum, dadum…da-dum, da-dum, da-dum…"

"Maestro."

The music in his head stopped. Blinking with disbelief, he stared—his hand, half-raised to conduct, stilling mid-beat.

Standing before him, within the frame of weak light which fell from a high narrow window, was a boy. "Maestro," he repeated. And bowed his head, then stood erect. And extended a serving tray upon which was placed a single cup upon a saucer.

The maestro's eyelids flittered with surprise. His nose had not lied. Even if his ears were no longer all they might be, his nose had not lied. It was not a dream. The smell was greater in here. And it was, it was indeed, the smell…of chocolate. The sweet intoxicating scent of Vienna as it had been. In his youth and young manhood. And every day until that turdish Corsican anti-Christ had imposed his damned decrees—six long years ago. And the face…the face above the tray was from the past too. It was the child. Tirrell's young prodigy of a child. He had brought chocolate.

"Mein Gott! Mein Gott," he mouthed. "Junge?"

"Maestro," Boy said proudly, and again bowed his head. "Ihre Trinkschokolade." And for once, he did not hold back, but brightened, beaming with diffident pleasure.

Yes. Yes, indeed. It was going to be a fine day. A most excellent day. Chocolate. Hot. Mixed with milk and sugar. Sugar, think on that! Trinkschokolade! And Tirrell's Schätzi.

A rare smile, a beginning of laughter, an unfamiliar sound—a rasping, coughing rattle of noise—erupted from the older man, as, not taking the cup which was meant for him—the chocolate and sugar so dearly smuggled this distance—he enveloped the boy with his arm and ruffled his damp hair. (It smelled of earth, forests and fire. Not like the old days.)

"Mein Gott! Mein Gott…mein Kind…" And bussing the boy

soundly on both cheeks, he was kissed upon his unshaven face in return. He ruffled Boy's ragged hair again and pressed him to his hard chest, thumping his back. "Ja! I had not heard of you for now it is two years. I have thought the worst. Ja, this is fine. Ho ho ho ho. Genau, Trinkschokolade, mein Schätzchen. Genau! Und du...und du." He stopped to hold the boy's face between his large pianist's hands. "You are here." His face creased into a wide smile that was painful with sudden unwept joy.

And resting there, in that close haven from his past, the Maestro's strong arm cleaving him close, Boy shut his eyes to savour this one moment. To feel...here...safe. Pleased with his reception, he looked up. "Ihre Trinkschokolade?" He gestured to the tray, now resting upon the near table.

The Maestro looked at the tray. Such luxury, such history, in one small cup. He huffed, coughed, and disengaged himself to sit at the table.

Closing his eyes upon the sparsely furnished chamber, he prepared to relish it: the smell, the taste, the texture. He had not tasted nor smelt it in three years. Not since Boy had last come to him.

"How did you get rid of that fool my brother and his servants, eh?"

Boy shook his head. "Someone's purse had broken open in the Hauptplatz, I fancy. They were all out hunting for pennies in the mud, so the kitchen was empty..."

Again, that rumbling unfamiliar sound—laughter. "Such fools. Such fools..." Closing his eyes, the Maestro took his first sip and let the taste spread, expanding smooth over his tongue and the roof of his mouth, then trickling warm down his throat, bathing it all the way into his chest. And heard as he always did, the distant strains of music playing through his mind—dadum, dadum, dadum...F, then up to the mediant—the tempo menuetto. And he did not speak again until he had finished the precious chocolate, mouthful by blessèd mouthful.

Observing his former teacher, the boy went to sit at the stool before the fortepiano in the corner: his hair was greying now and worn longer, though still as wild, and the scowl lines in his wide brow deeper than they had been.

"They came looking for you, you know," the Maestro said at last. He smacked his lips, tasting the chocolate still. Enjoying even the aftertaste. "In Vienna. Asking their impertinent questions. 'Did I know any boys?' Twice they came."

The boy straightened, sobering. "Who was looking for me?"

"Soldiers." He said the word with disinterest. "Or Metternich's little band, I imagine. I do not know. And I didn't ask. They all look the same to me—stupid."

"What did you tell them?"

A smile, sly and wise and wary, appeared on that well-known broad face. "I told them I know many boys. I teach many boys. All of them come to me for lessons. Many foolish boys always coming to me for lessons." Drawing himself up, the Maestro rose from his seat and grabbed hold of a switch he'd brought in from a country walk. "But they do not practise!" he shouted, thrashing at the tabletop several times as if in one of his famous rages. "They do not practise!" he roared. "Not nearly enough, I told them." His dark eyes, when he looked at Boy, gleamed. "Not even when I beat them!" He shrugged. "They left after that." He gave a sudden rumbling chuckle. "I think they feared I might beat them too. And I would have done. Impertinent dummkopfs. Bah! They did not return after that…"

"No," Boy agreed, his expression serious, but his eyes alight with humour. "I should not think they did, Maestro. I wouldn't."

The Maestro smiled, pleased with their shared joke. "Not if they know what is good for them, no." Not liking the world, he blew out a breath.

"How are your ears, Maestro? They tell me…"

"Today it is good. Some days it is bad. Tomorrow it may be very bad. But today it is good…So now, you will play for me. We have not, I think, much time." He went to a large, leather trunk in the corner of the room, opened it wide, and rustled through the papers there. "It is all here…The last two years. Everything is here…" He glanced up and frowned. "I do not suppose you have been practising either." He shot him a piercing glance.

"No, Maestro," Boy admitted. He lowered his gaze to rest, brief in his shame, upon the bare floorboards. He looked up again. "I will though," he said earnestly, in that one moment a child again. "One day again, I will."

"Ja…" Having found several sheaves of music, the Maestro straightened. "Ja, you will," he affirmed. "You must. Your father, he would desire it…and you must do his will. But for now, we shall make do with what we have." He came and opened flat a sheaf of music on the stand. "Opus thirty four. It is all here. Play it for me."

And sitting, resting his fingers upon the black and white keys of the old fortepiano—brought in specially for the Maestro's stay—Boy prepared to play.

Reading the first pages of the music open before him, he felt the worn surfaces of the keys smooth beneath his fingertips. And remembered.

Then, awkward at first, slower and less certain than he would have wished or would have performed all those years ago, he began with the opening chords, the gentle melismatic harmony replacing all else in his mind. He played on, until he, like the fortepiano, became no more nor less than the Maestro's instrument. While beside him the Maestro sat, humming along, beating the time on his leg, perhaps listening, hearing even, and turning the pages for him, conducting—gently patting at the air for a decrescendo, or abruptly slicing it for the sforzandi which were his trademark.

Nor did Boy stop until he had played straight through the whole of the three sets of themes and variations: La Sentinelle, Partant Bacchus La Syrie and Mozart's Opera. And only then, once he had finished, did he look up and smile. He nodded. "Ja, genau." And his smile grew, reaching into his eyes "Ja."

"Your trills have got sloppy," the maestro commented. "Very sloppy. That must change…they must be little trinkets of delight. Not this…"

There was a knock upon the door, timid at first, then louder. "Mein Herr?"

"Go away!" shouted the Maestro. "Can you not hear I have a student? Dummkopf!"

Boy looked at his lap, embarrassed, and waited while outside the door, the floorboards creaked, followed by the patter of retreating footsteps. "The trills, yes. I will work on those. Did you say there was more for me, Maestro?"

"Ja." The Maestro rose and fetched a second sheaf of music from the table. "Here it is. Opus fifty-seven. I have called it Variations for Piano in F-major." He gave a glimmer of a sly smile. "Ja, that will throw them, I thought."

And it was almost as if it had always been. It might have been all those years ago, had Boy's father been there. Listening. Leaning against the wall, or resting in the armchair, his violin at the ready. And the smile that had nearly crept onto his face fell away at the thought. Caught by his past, Boy looked up at the music and knew nothing to do but to begin to play again, from beginning to end. As they expected him to do.

He raised his hands to the keyboard again, but the Maestro, as if reading his thoughts, made a guttural sound. "Mein Gott, when I think what they did to your father." He grabbed the boy's arm and held it tight. "Tell me they did not touch his hands."

Boy was silent, though no tears fell onto his cheeks or chin. Finally he shook his head. He drew a deep breath. "Not until after he was dead," he said quietly.

Though the maestro heard. "Mein Gott, they are pigs. Swine." He rubbed his face. "To be driven over the precipice." He closed his eyes for an instant, then gave a nod. "Play on."

The morning had passed into afternoon. There was a light splatter of rain on the windowpane. "You must be going," the Maestro said at length, glancing at the darkening sky outside. "You will need to be out of the city before curfew."

"Ja." Boy rose from the fortepiano and slid the remainder of the thin packet of chocolate and sugar out of his pocket to lay them on the table. And from his cuff, a small hard block of tea, wrapped in brown paper. "Take these with you, back to Vienna." He paused. "I heard…" He bit at his lip. "His lordship is concerned and asked me to bring you this," he said, lying. He laid a small purse of gold sovereigns down. "And he wishes to know if there is anything else I can bring you the next time I come?"

"That is kind," said the Maestro. "More than kind. Thank him for me.

"I have been thinking…my hearing is not improved…And Prince Kinsky is dead, you know. He fell from his horse…"

"Yes. I'm sorry."

"So I thought I might travel to England, with Maelzel…There may be better doctors there."

"That would be fine!" Boy exclaimed. "I shall tell his lordship to look for your letters."

The Maestro nodded. "Ja…Ja. What is it like out there now…in the world?"

He knew what he was being asked. Boy shook his head. "The same as ever. Wherever the French have been, the towns have been looted and pillaged…the women all raped…and the crossroads resemble a churchyard, so full of graves are they."

Regret passed over the Maestro's face, an expression of vulnerability and perpetual bereavement. "That is what they will do to you, Schätzchen. Kill you. Or rape you until you do the job for them. When they catch you."

Boy lifted his chin. "They shall have to catch me first," he said fiercely. He paused. "Metternich?"

"Tell your master not to trust him," the Maestro said softly. "He is an oily popinjay. The Emperor believes he works for Austria. He is wrong. Metternich thinks only of himself."

"Yes, Maestro. I shall tell him…

"They are saying, you know, they are saying there was a great battle somewhere near Moscow—greater than all the rest—and that the Russians are defeated. And that Napoleon has conquered the city. Or he would have done, but it was set alight. And Moscow is now destroyed."

"Wie bitte?" the Maestro exclaimed. "But Moscow was a great city. What else? How many were lost? Tell me! How many more?" he raged, suddenly overcome.

"I came through Prussia. There is little left there…"

"Bonn?"

Boy shook his head.

The Maestro covered his eyes, striving, as they all strove, to comprehend. And to counter the waves of despair washing over him, drowning him hopeless with every additional loss, every battle. Finally: "You must tell the brethren. They will need to be told. So they can prepare."

"Ja. I will do so.

"I must take my leave of you, liebster Maestro." And standing, Boy took the master's fine hands in his own and bowed low, resting his forehead on the the great man's fingers.

The Maestro stood and held the boy close against him. "Geh mit Gott, mein Schätzlein. Geh mit Gott."

Chapter XX

1

They slipped into Whitby harbour at the mouth of the Esk just after dawn, with only a capful of wind beneath a watchet sky and all hands on deck. On the foredeck Captain Fiske stood with Jesuadon beside him—the one dressed in his uniform, the other as a gentleman. Together watching as they slid past the great granite cliffs a-lee where the waves breached the rocks.

Beyond, in the North Sea, the flotilla of fishing boats had been about their business for hours since. Ahead, coal ships were being loaded and merchantmen unloaded into the tall warehouses that crowded the quayside and clung like barnacles to the steep rise of the hill. And up on the headland, the stark ruin of the Abbey towered over all, haunting and roofless, its vast arched windows long-emptied of glass, though its traceried spires pointed still heaven-ward. Yet the noise was that of any bustling port—a cacophony of men and a shrieking of herring gulls.

Below in the after-cabin, Lady Wilmot sat, her hands folded in her lap, gazing blankly about her. She sat silent, listening to the smacking of the water against the hull, and the rapid thumping of the sailors' steps upon the deck as they readied for mooring. She braced herself against the jolt and bobble of the chasse-marée pulling up along the pier and the rolling pitch as the hawsers were lashed to the quay and the gang-board laid down.

It had been early, early that morning, well before the light had broken as they lay anchored off-shore, that Jesuadon had risen. Quietly he had left the small cabin to wash and to shave and to dress himself. Some time later, he had brought her tea. And it was fine China tea.

Again he had left her, only to return carrying jugs of heated water.

Then as her servant in the cramped cabin, he had washed her. Holding her hand while she stood in the low copper tub. Carefully as a new mother, he had smoothed the fine-milled soap from her shoulders over the soft skin of her arms, over her elbows and the palms of her hands, along each of her fingers and the insides of her wrists, handling her as if she were finest porcelain and he a connoisseur of rare and precious objects. Lifting her hair away from her neck, he had soaped her nape and throat and her back. Inch by tender inch. To wash away the traces of himself and the tang and film of the sea-air. Then taking up the sponge, he had rinsed the soap and lavender-scented lather from her, refreshing the sponge frequently, easing it over her skin. And like the dew falling, all noiseless and unseen, she had felt his breath soft and warm and close. Kneeling before her, he had washed her legs, the pristine white of her, her knees, her ankles, and finally each small foot, tending to them as he had her hands.

Still without speaking, just as carefully, he had helped her to dry and to dress in the clothes and undergarments he had purchased for her. In each touch, she had heard a word. In each service, an avowal of his devotion and self-abnegation. For all that he did and had done all these days whispered that she was his dearest of cargoes and he her servant and slave.

Each night of the journey they had lain together too. Face to face, breast to breast, his arms about her, about her waist while his other hand caressed her hip, her mouth soft beneath his when he sought her in the comforting dark. With his hands upon her and his kissing of her, each midnight and daybreak, he told her all his thoughts of her. And his silence was the loudest declaration of all.

Yet only this morning as they lay in that hour when the darkness seeps from the sea's horizon, even then in the limpid contentment of after-love, she had looked down upon his chest rather than at his face. "Can you not tell me where you are taking me?"

Kissing her temple, he lifted a curl from off her throat and rested his mouth upon the slope of her cheek. "To my aunt."

Surprised and confused, she did not reply, but moved her mouth in mute repetition of his words.

He raised himself on one elbow. "She is all the family I have left—or who will acknowledge me. And I would entrust the care of you to no other…"

She studied his face, now tanned from their days at sea, and his eyes—amber and green and unguarded—puzzling over this. She knew so little of him, nothing at all really, only his great kindness to her. But at last she said: "Does she know?" She had never spoken it. Never mentioned it.

Deliberately, he misunderstood. "What? That I am a gambler?" He dropped back against the bolster. "A wastrel? Debauched?"

She hesitated. Because the truth did not much matter. Not to her. Not any longer. "That cannot be right," she ventured.

"'Slife, it must be. 'Tis what they say," he mocked.

Undaunted, she persisted: "But you work for someone…"

"Yes."

"Are you a spy?"

He gave a rare smile. "Yes." His eyes glistered dangerously as if he enjoyed the admission.

"For the Government?"

Again that smile which few had seen. "Yes."

At that, tears sprang to her eyes and she smoothed the red gold hair from his forehead.

"No," he pleaded as her tears of fear for his safety fell onto the pillow between them. "Marianne, 'struth, no. Do not cry. Not for me." The tenderness in his expression made her face buckle. "No," he said again and he kissed her—her tears, her forehead and her mouth, all salty-flavoured with her grief.

"You are the best of men," she protested.

"No," he said firmly. "No, I assure you, I am not." And he said it with such untroubled conviction that she wondered at it.

Now, just outside the cabin, she could hear his tread descending the companion way. Opening the door wide, he stood before her. "It is time."

And taking her in his arms, he kissed her. Without hesitation, with all devotion, her mouth, her face, her hair. Kissed her knowing that this might be the last time he might ever do so. He closed his eyes and held her against him for a final moment. "We must go," he said.

She nodded. And with a last look upon the small, kind cabin where she had learned what it was to be loved, she followed him out.

Upon the quay, an anonymous black carriage with a team of fast horses had been brought close by to the dockside. Nearby, three mounted outriders, dressed in drab greatcoats, sat ready on their tall bays, their reins held slack as they talked among themselves.

Emerging into the opalescent light of morning to debark, Jesuadon escorted her up the gangboard and onto the stone pier. About and above, kittiwakes and terns screeched as they dived and skidded, searching for a meal among the flotsam and bubbling swells that slapped the harbour walls.

Disoriented and unused to the unrocking stillness of dry land, she stepped onto the uneven cobbles and stumbled.

About her waist, Jesuadon's arm tightened, keeping her upright.

She caught hold of his free hand, large and assured about her own as he drew her closer to him—an intimate gesture, intimate in its understandings and assumptions. But none noticed. And this time, she was unafraid. Or nearly unafraid. It was only a few steps to the waiting travelling carriage. And none here had ever heard of Lady Wilmot or her dishonourable abandonment of her husband.

About them, braying, harsh even against the harsher wind from off the North Sea, were the shouts and calls of the men who worked the port. Listening and alert, Jesuadon saw and heard it all, his eye seeking out the shadows of the scene, the activities, and above all, the faces—those that belonged, those watching from behind windows, and most importantly, those which did not fit. At this hour of the morning there should be no loungers, no saunterers. Only the keel bullies and broad-faced sailors, the port officials and the clerks with their lists, overseeing their loads. He searched the scene for who did not belong. Finding none, he knew a brief minim of satisfaction.

Beside him, he felt her pause, catching her breath as she stopped to take a final look at the chasse-marée and Captain Fiske, at the sunlight falling like a handful of pale gold shingles tossed upon the chopping waves of the inner harbour where the gulls floated and swam. She took one last lungful of the sharp sea air. Then leaning upon him, she allowed him to escort her to the closed, unmarked coach and help her inside. It smelled of worn leather and must. And as always when he settled beside her, she sensed the unyielding butt of his side arm in his greatcoat pocket, and the length of him, hard and warm and taut beside her. His features too had resumed the watchful, stern lines of his profession. He was become again as she had first known him.

With the iron-shod hooves of the team and outriders clanking and ringing on the cobblestones, yet ignored by all, the carriage pulled away from the quay along the pier, then turned to lumber up a lane deep in morning shadow and so narrow that she could have reached out and brushed the stone sills with her fingertips. Still climbing, the carriage juddering and creaking, it turned down another such sunless street, where the pale lime-washed houses of sailors jostled close against those of clerks, then turned again.

At a town-gait, they passed the neat stone-cornered merchants' houses with their small orchards and gardens bound within picket fences, all still quiet, and beyond, the rising banks of grass on either side. Until at last gathering speed, they left the town and its early morning slow traffic behind to pull out onto the open road.

The driver cracked the whip and the team broke into a quickening trot.

Jesuadon scanned the scene outside the carriage window, the sheep and cows grazing the hillside pastures, the shuttered sleeping farmhouses in the far distance with their red tile roofs, and the outrider occasionally riding into and falling back from view. "The journey is a little over four hours. You should try to sleep."

She wanted to take his hand. To hold it. "Oh. Oh, yes. Where… where is it we are going? Your aunt, where does she live?"

"Guisborough." His thoughts were elsewhere.

"Guisborough?" she repeated, blinking. It meant nothing to her. "And your aunt, she is…"

"A gentleman farmer," he said with a wry scowl on his face. "In every thing but the breeches."

"Oh." She tried not to sound surprised. "Then…"

"Her name is Richards," Jesuadon continued easily. "She has a voice which carries like a tantwivy over three hunting fields, a manner which would sit ill in a London Drawing room though she's as well-born as the whole lot of 'em packed together. And she is as fine a soul as ever breathed air." He was still looking out of the window, away from her.

"Oh," she exclaimed, nodding again, and not understanding. Though Jesuadon rarely spoke of anyone else and never with such approbation.

"She will take good care of you."

"Thank you," she said, still nodding. "Thank you."

She tried to be as calm as he was, as distant and self-contained. On either side of the carriage, across the whole of the sun-drenched horizon, the violent purple of the heather flowers had faded to nothing, leaving a clumpen wiry green carpet and the dull scrub blanketing the steep and endless hills. That, and the bracken, mottled like a spilling of paints—ochre and umber and raw sienna—as far as the eye could see, spattered over the fading green of the moorland grass and the outcroppings of granite. Outside she could feel the wind increasing, buffeting the coach, though the horses did not slow for it.

She looked down upon her lap. Then earnestly up at Jesuadon, at his profile stern in the shadowed interior and wished she knew even his Christian name. His gaze rested upon the moors beyond. "I must say this, Mr. Jesuadon, I must," she began. "I have never in all my years known such kindness as you have shown me over the past weeks. I had not ever believed…"

"No," he interrupted, facing her, stopping her. "No. Do not tell me," he said fiercely. He kissed her hard. "It will only make me want to kill him more than I do now."

"Oh…" she whispered against the noise of the carriage. Yet that exhalation of breath had less to do with the prospect of her husband's death, than with the twin facts of Jesuadon's care of her and the violence of his nature from which he had always sought to shield her. "Oh…" she repeated, subsiding, understanding less than ever. She would have studied his face for an answer, but he had once more turned from her, to watch.

On the box, the driver cracked the whip and the team lengthened their strides into the steady canter that would speed them over the barren road across the top of the moors. Wrapped in their greatcoats, the hard-riding outriders increased their pace to match. As the coat of one fell away as he rode, leaning forward over the horse's neck, she saw that he had a pistol strapped to his thigh. She looked to see his face but it did not look like the face of a killer to her.

And across this peopleless landscape of ceaseless green and yellowing moss-coated hillsides, where the clouds laid their blackening shadows upon the land, the hooves of the seven horses beat their time against the shuddering earth. Hastening, climbing all the while toward the moorland heights where no trees grew, they neither slowed nor slackened, not even when they passed at speed another coach upon the way. Within, Jesuadon watched, wary and still, never taking his eyes from the scene without, the country of his childhood, the home of his disgrace. He had not been back there in five years. Beyond the carriage—a moving speck of black upon the landscape—the stark immensity of it was spliced into parcels by the weathered grey of the crumbling dry stone walls.

When it was, she did not know, but she awoke with her head leaning heavily against Jesuadon's shoulder. Awoke to the oppressing, musty smell of the closed carriage and the endless bobbing and swaying over the pitted road. And was instantly ill. And with Jesuadon supporting her in the sharpening breeze, clambered from the carriage and was sick upon the verge.

The wind whipped her skirts about her, causing them to billow and slap like sails of canvas, while they waited for her dizziness to abate and Jesuadon scanned the horizon and the near and distant fells. Above, the moorland birds swooped and soared but she did not know their names. A way off the dismounted outriders huddled together, their reins draped loosely from their hands while the horses rested and grazed; and she saw that another of them had a knife strapped at his back.

Seated once more within the closed carriage, Jesuadon reached into the depths of his greatcoat pocket, and handed her his flask so that she might wash the taste of bile from her mouth.

Unstoppering it, drinking gratefully, she stopped to exclaim, "It's watered."

Jesuadon looked up. "Yes."

"But…"

He slanted a mocking glance at her. "Did you honestly think me drunk all the time?"

A smile spread over her face. "I should have known," she said at last. "I should have suspected." She gave a weak laugh, and returned it to him. "How foolish I am…"

She was not ill again. But as the coach began the descent from the moorland wilds, and she began to contemplate what little he had told her for his aunt—of her character and occupation so alien to all that she had ever known—a mist of unquelled desolation crept upon her. Anxious lest she sicken further and increasingly distraught over losing the security of Jesuadon's still, unyielding presence, she did not notice when the outriders left the carriage. The dread of what lay ahead in this barren place, so far from home, from him, from all that she had ever known and the quiet kindness of Sparrowhawk and Molly, laid waste to the now fragmenting tatters of her remnant equanimity. The fear of discovery, of revelation and exposure, the necessity of concealing of her identity and her past—and her growing affection—weighed like millstones upon her flailing spirits. Nor could she see that there was any help for it.

Beside her, Jesuadon was taciturn, his face unreadable. She plaited and unplaited her fingers and admonished herself against her frailty. And by the time they had pulled off the main road and onto a narrowing country lane between high and deep hedges, even his unspeaking presence could offer no comfort.

"We're nearly there," he said, patient, straightening beside her. His voice was devoid of emotion.

As they pulled into the fine surrounding park of Roseberry Lodge, eventually halting before the sprawling grey stone manor, Mrs. Tomkins knew of a certainty she could not walk even so far as the front door.

Even before the coachman had applied the brake, Jesuadon was unlatching the door to put down the steps and climb out. He stood for a moment, to stretch and to regard the house before him—it was exactly as it had been—then turned to extend his hand to her.

Holding tight to the mounting strap, she looked upon his face and wished that once, just once, she might see his rarely given smile again. She pressed her free hand to her mouth, swallowing hard against the remittent waves of dizziness. "Your aunt, what will she think? Forgive me…" she murmured. Then her legs gave way, and swaying, she crumpled forward.

Staggering a little, he caught her, gathering her to him as she fell, and swung her into his arms to lift her away from the coach. His face bent close to hers, he carried her up the lichen-stained stone steps and through the door, now held open by a middle-aged housekeeper.

"Hallo Matcham," he said negligently to her servant's curtsy. "…Mrs. Tomkins was taken ill on the journey. Tell my aunt we've arrived, will you?"

He nodded his understanding at the broadly spoken direction of which bedroom Mrs. Tomkins was to have, and brought her straight through a painted and panelled hall and up the wide oak staircase. Clinging to him, embarrassed by her weakness and ill-mannered arrival, Mrs. Tomkins whispered against his chest, "Forgive me. Please…"

"Hush," he murmured against the pallor of her cheek, then brushed her temple with an unseen kiss. "It's nothing but carriage-sickness. I shall present my aunt with your apologies. She will understand." He gave a dry laugh. "And probably berate me for my thoughtlessness in making you journey so far."

Nodding against the folds of his cravat, she held onto him, her tears soaking into the folds of his collar while he carried her up the broad stairs, and from there to a large west-facing chamber hung with blue India chintz where he settled her on the tester bed. Gently, he helped her to remove her bonnet which he threw carelessly into a chair, to be followed by her pelisse and her half-boots. Ignoring her protests, he reached to unfasten the hooks of her gown.

"No," he soothed. "Don't be silly. Let me…" Without touching her, without even grazing the underside of her breast with the back of his hand, as a genderless servant beyond and without desire, he untied the laces of her stays and loosed them, easing the garment away from her.

Shaken and ill, she allowed him to lay her against the pillows and to spread a quilt over her. For a long moment, he held her hand and looked upon her pale face.

"I must be off," he said softly. "But remember, you are safe here. Sleep now. I shall have some tea sent up before I go." Then, standing for a moment, austerely regarding her, he bowed. "Ma'am." Then, he quitted the room, closing the door behind him.

His aunt was not waiting below in the hall as he came down the stairs. Instead, he heard her bellowing, her voice amidst the frantic barking of a terrier and the deeper resonating yelps of a mastiff echoing through the hall and passageway. "Thomas…Thomas!"

His steps sounding on the scrubbed wooden floor, he came through the hall and down the passage into the shelf-lined estate room to see his aunt, arms akimbo, grimacing at a ledger on a top shelf which she could not reach. Upon the walls there were several framed maps of her lands. Her desk was likewise piled with ledgers and land agents' reports.

She turned, her eyes alight with pleasure at his presence. "Tom! There you are, at last! Reach up and fetch me down that file, will you? I've been waiting these two days since for you to get it, you know."

Barking and running, the dogs came to prance and weave about his legs. Ignoring them, he came and reached easily to the shelf to retrieve the file.

"Aunt." He bent to kiss her cheek, then handed the file to her. "I trust you are well." She with her face a mosaic of wrinkles, a fine starched cap upon her unruly grey curls, yet her dark hem deep with a speckling of mud from the farmyard which stood between the kitchen and the barn where her best milkers were housed. She was no thinner than when he had last seen her, but stoutly robust and bright-eyed as ever. Just as he remembered her.

"Why is it that you tall creatures are never about when you're wanted?" she demanded to know, beaming at him.

Jesuadon gave a wry half-smile. "I cannot stay, Aunt."

Instantly, her face rumpled. She sighed, the child's delight in her eyes flaring and fading. "That is most unfortunate for I have a thousand things that you might do for me, tall creature."

"I have taken the liberty of taking Mrs. Tomkins upstairs. She became very ill with the length of the journey..."

"Did she? Oh...oh yes." Her face fell still further. "Of course she did. Yes. Of course, poor child. You did quite right." She bustled toward the desk to lay the file upon it. "Why must you always travel at such a pace?" she fussed, blinking with uncertainty. "Shall we wait for her to feel well enough to come down when she's ready...and then dine?"

He regarded her for a moment, seeing her unvarying kindness, knowing that in all these years he had done little enough to deserve it. "If you could send her up some tea in an hour or so, that would no doubt revive her."

"Well, yes, of course. But surely you'll take some luncheon, my dear..."

"No. No, Aunt, I'm sorry. I return at once. We sail again on the tide. And I've no doubt there's a storm brewing."

She nodded, though she had clamped her lips together. Perhaps she did know. "Well at least stop in the kitchen for a tankard of ale...to wash the dust from your throat."

"Thank you."

She reached up, cradling his face in her warm gnarled hand. "Thomas," she said at last. "Promise me this—she is not your mistress, is she?"

"No. No, of course, she is not," Jesuadon said evenly. "I give you my word." And bowing correctly as a gentleman, he took his leave of her.

Chapter XXI

1

Barnet stood within the corniced shadow of a darkened doorway and porch—a shadow made still longer by the uncertain light of a street lamp—and counted out against his leg the days that Jesuadon had been gone. The chilling night air made mist clouds of his breath. Ten. Jesuadon had been gone for ten whole days and nights.

Barnet didn't like it.

He sucked in another breath of cold air and held it before expelling it slowly in small puffs that left no trace.

Captain Shuster had been absent from Town still longer. Though for how long he didn't know. He didn't like that either.

Across the quieting road, with shutters all closed to prying eyes, the tall, elegantly fronted bordello of dark brick that he'd seen Wilmot enter some two hours previous opened its door to belch forth a bevy of damme boys and dandy prats—a pair of them with their breeches bewrayed, and all swearing, laughing and singing. The door slammed shut behind them and the street was once again reduced to the glimmering murk of a cold autumn evening, as tripping and staggering down the front steps, they landed in the sudden gloom. One of the chubs, a great hulky fellow he was, doubled over to flash the hash in the gutter. Wilmot wasn't among them. Barnet liked the last even less.

This particular vaulting school at the wrong end of Bury Street had become a frequent haunt of Wilmot's over the past sennight. He'd been visiting the pestilential place nightly, sometimes with the dandy poet, sometimes without.

Barnet reached into his pocket for his flask, an ugly impatience settling over his features. Hunching his shoulders against the lowering fog, he drew further away from the light, shrinking his farrier's shoulders into the shadow, and swiped at his nose with his sleeve. He supposed he might try to get someone on the inside—a servant perhaps, or one of the baggages who plied their trade within. But Jesuadon was better at that sort of thing, especially in this end of Town.

Farther down the road, one of Jesuadon's sweeping boys, a mite of a dust-coloured street arab, was leaning on his broom, watching the giggling, drunken toffs as they jostled and stumbled on unsteady feet all the way down the street. Barnet felt a nagging desire to cosh one or other of them, but did nothing. He sniffed hard, drank down the last swallow of sky blue in his flask, then returned the object to his pocket.

Ten days. It was too long. And he didn't like it.

It was too quiet too. Which meant the damned Frenchies was up to something. Planning. Or waiting. But Barnet didn't know for what. And Jesuadon would want to know why.

Flint had said that the Guvnor was growing resty too. Edgy, he'd called it. He was missing Jesuadon. Wanting the security of Jesuadon's presence and his net. Or that's what Flint thought.

In the morning he'd pay a visit to Hatton, the hard-faced bastard who'd set the watch on Jesuadon, to see what he had to say for himself. He'd been hard to break, sure enough, red-faced blaggart that he was, and had remained full of oaths and swagger until the branding iron had been brought forth. Then in the gloom of the vacated smithy near the Devil's Acre, he'd leaked and cackled all—he didn't know his master, swore blind he'd never met him…he received regular payments to carry messages to Wilmot, it was true, but he didn't know who sent them and he didn't know who it was who'd wanted Jesuadon watched. It wasn't enough to stop Barnet carving off half his foreskin, just as Jesuadon had said, though he'd pleaded and begged and in the end had cried like a woman. Fancied himself a coming man, no doubt, the fool. So Barnet had promised to take his helmet the next time—if he didn't find the name of his agent soon, or ever forgot who owned him now. Not that it was likely. Not now. Not when he was reminded every time he took a piss or tried to sit on his branded backside.

Across the way, the door half-opened again, spilling a rectangle of light onto the darkened street, but without the tuneless accompaniment of drunken caterwauling. Silhouetted in the doorway, a man gave a final buss to his companion of the evening and helped himself to a final grope of her ample breast. Then, pausing to adjust his hat, he stepped into the street and the door was shut upon him. It was Wilmot, the prinking jackanapes.

Barnet inched forward from his position against the wall and gave a slight nod. Watching for the signal, the sweeping boy nodded back and began shuffling his broom against the cold pile of horse muck near his feet.

Ten days. Or was it now eleven?

Chapter XXII

1

They had been drinking for three hours. Drinking and dancing and eating. A full complement of Dunphail's relations, tenants and friends, dressed in their country finest, each of them wearing a clan badge and adorned with a presence of their plaid. Some even, like Dunphail, grand and noble, wearing the kilt with their cropped jackets. Lumpish or lathy, ginger-pated or black Scots, their cheeks patterned with chilblains or flushed with drink. Great braw lads like those of the Gordon Highlanders, and pretty girls. Filling the whole of Dunphail's great stone hall with their laughter and courting and singing, their voices echoing up to the rafters as they sat at trestle tables laden with dainties and the bounty of the laird's harvest—venison pies, pheasant puddings and bottles from the laird's own still. Alone among them, Shuster was English and a serving officer in King George's army. Though this evening, he had done nothing to draw attention to the fact.

Two pitch-tipped torches flared and burned on either side of the carved stone hearth where a conflagration of logs shifted and collapsed into a great flaming heap. A burly servant threw another armful of logs onto the grate.

In the corner beside the stairs, a single fiddler was idly bowing his instrument while his fellow musicians refreshed themselves. A group of lads, just returned from answering a call of nature on Dunphail's front lawn, began to stamp their feet with impatience. Standing beside the fiddler on the second step, with every eye upon her, was Miss MacDonald. In the torch and candlelight, her hair, all dressed in plaits and curls for the occasion, was the colour of summer peaches. She was gowned in her customary white, with her tartan over her shoulder and knotted at her waist like a sash. Tonight, there was little doubt who she was.

She looked out over the assembled guests and smiled—that breathless, daring smile that made Shuster's blood overheat every time he saw her—and even when he didn't see her, but wished he might. Unflustered by the stamping, the whistling and calling, she laughed, then wetted her top lip with her tongue. The audience hushed, and every ear tuned to her as she drew her breath, then opened her mouth to sing, her voice beginning to rise and dip, to speed and slow to the accompaniment of the single fiddle.

"As I ga'ed doon the Ettrick Valley
At the hour o' twelve at night,
Who did I see but a handsome lassie
Combing her hair by candlelight.
'Lassie, I have come a'courtin'.
Yer fine favours for tae win,
And if ye'll but smile upon me
Next Sunday night I'll call again.'"

And Georgie thought as he always did how he'd like to kiss her. Long and slow, with her mouth sweet and tender beneath his. And then touch her...the smooth skin of her arm and her throat…He closed his eyes to let the sound of her voice seep through him, like a golden-flavoured wine tasting of apples and sunlight.

"Fala tala rudum rudum rudum fala tala rudum rudumday..."

A second musician began to pick out a counterpoint melody on his tinny-sounding cittern.

"'So tae me you've come yer courtin'
Ma fine favours for tae win,
But it wud give me the greatest pleasure
If ye never did call again.
What wud I do when I go oot walkin'
Walkin' oot for the Ettrick view?
What wud I dae when I go oot walkin'
Walkin' oot wi' a laddie like you?'
Fala tala rudum rudum rudum fala tala rudum rudumday..."

A rustling of muffled laughter rose and died.

First to kiss her and then…God's garters, and then…Georgie swallowed and tried to quell the ungovernable rush of blood in his stomach and groin.

"'Lassie, I have gold and silver.
Lassie, I have houses and land.
Lassie, I have ships in the ocean.
They'll be all at your command.'
'What do I gie for yer ships in the ocean?
What do I gie for yer houses and land?
What do I gie for yer gold and silver,
When all I want is a handsome man?'
Fala tala rudum rudum rudum fala tala rudum rudumday..."

There was that smile again, undaunted, elusive as quicksilver. The second fiddler began now to add his flourishes to the tune.

"'Did ye ever see the grass in the morning,
All bedecked wi' jewels rare?
Did ye ever see a handsome lassie,
Diamonds sparklin' in her hair?'

Did ye ever see a copper kettle
Mended wi' an auld tin can?
Did ye ever see a handsome lassie
Married off tae an ugly man?"'

She laughed a little as she started the nonsense words of the refrain, slowing then deliberately, as if to savour each syllable, rolling them off her tongue. *"Fala tala rudum rudum rudum fala tala rudum rudumday…"*

The audience was laughing now, jostling each other and clapping their hands.

Her cheeks were flushing with the heat and with excitement as she repeated the opening verse. *"As I ga'ed doon the Ettrick Valley…"*

But now the louder guests had joined in, shouting and singing, for the final chorus. The formality Georgie associated with dancing parties had long since been abandoned. And she finished with the guests, her friends and relations, erupting into applause and shouts of laughter, as if it was all some great joke.

In the far corner, away from the hearth where Dunphail stood, a skirmish of some sort had broken out. Georgie strained to see, but he hadn't seen it start and couldn't see what it was. Only some fellow's dark head and darker scowl. Then the scowler shoved his way through to the door and pushed his way out. From across the hall, there was more laughter and a call for the fiddlers to play again.

Amidst the heaving crowd and their roaring laughter, Georgie made his way to her side to lean his face close against her apricot hair, to smell the sharp, clean, soap-scent of her. "Dance with me, Ailie," he murmured. He was drunk.

She threw a daring glance over her shoulder at him.

"Dance with me," he insisted again, for her ear only. "Or am I not handsome enough?" He wanted to kiss her. Just kiss her. Unnoticed, he captured her hand and held it for an instant, keeping hold of her smallest finger for a minute longer. No one saw.

The three musicians in the corner were retuning their instruments.

She had already danced with him twice. And had been besieged by others for the same favour.

About them, her clansmen and neighbours, their tongues liquor-loosed, argued and chatted and jollified—understanding but one word in five at the best of times, Georgie understood still less now. But a harvest supper of roast venison followed by the laird's own distilled whisky made for as fine an evening as ever there was. The music was beginning again.

It was a strathspey. And she never ought to have danced it with him. She ought to have danced it with her kinsman and never with an Englishman. But she did. Hand to hand, their arms entwined together as if bound, their eyes fixed upon each other, circling and intent, her arm arched over her head, fingers held as the stag's horn, a mirror of his—just as she had taught him on those many sun-washed afternoons by the strath, his hand tucked about her waist, and hers about his.

Her cousin was waiting for her when the dance finished. As couples lined up for a country dance, the men on the one side of the room, the ladies on the other, the fiddlers struck up a reel.

His dark brows drawn together, Dunphail tossed off a tot of whisky. "He'd be a guid match for you, Shuster would," he remarked temperately. He had not taken his eyes from Georgie, the Englishman in their midst, standing near the trestle where the kegs of ale were still in full flow. "The money's not the best, but it's a guid enough family. And you cannae stay here after what you've just said to Johnny Campbell…"

She followed the line of his gaze, but now she neither laughed nor smiled. Nor did she flinch at the rebuke in her cousin's voice, but chose to ignore it. "He is a Campbell." She needed no other reason.

"Aye, well. So he is. But he is also my guest."

She shrugged. "I didnae like him skulkin' about, always actin' as if he a'ready owned me. He doesnae. And I'll no' marry him. Not now, not ever. No matter how many times he asks me."

Dunphail raised an eyebrow as he considered her. "'Struth, there's no chance of that now, I should have thought. Not after what you just sang at him, puir wee beggar…"

Miss MacDonald was unimpressed. "He'll recover. And he is. Ugly."

Dunphail gave a reluctant chuckle. "Aye, well. 'Struth, there's no help for that, is there? But you didn't need to tell him so in public."

He waited a moment longer, still regarding the Englishman, his other guest, studying him. “Dinna look at me so, Ailie. It’s my duty to see that you’re looked after. And if Campbell was bothering you, you should have told me,” he stated equably. “Still…if you decide to take yon’ Sassenach, I’ll see to your bride portion. You know that, aye?”

She regarded him strangely. Then, she did smile and tucked her hand through his arm as he liked. “No, I didnae,” she said quietly. “Thank you.”

“Aye, well,” he said, patting her hand. “Now you do. It’s my duty. My pleasure too. ’Slife, if you’ve a fancy to be a soldier’s wife, he’s as guid as any.” He gazed down at her with affection. “And I’ve no doubt but he’ll dote ye kindly…” He smiled then. “’Struth, he dances well too,” he teased. “He tells me that when they’re in winter quarters in Spain, Wellington makes a point of seeing that they all can dance. Can you imagine that…” He puffed out his cheeks and shook his head, thinking on the incongruity of it.

2

Alone, Georgie sat in the hall, gazing into the great hearth as slowly the fire burnt down, the logs shifting and collapsing in upon themselves, the ash falling through the grate onto the stones below. He had been in Scotland for over a month, longer than he had meant to be away, longer than Castlereagh intended certainly. In his pocket now was Planta’s letter recalling him back south: Castlereagh trusted that he had accomplished all that he’d set out to do.

Assuredly, the ten days spent in Edinburgh questioning Jean le Brun’s former cellmates had confirmed what he had suspected. That there had been a prearranged signal. Quizzing them daily, he had learned that le Brun made his escape just days after receiving a parcel. A book it had been. No, they didn’t recall the title nor who had sent it. Perhaps le Brun hadn’t said. But it had been wrapped in a London newspaper, of that they were certain.

Dunphail was somewhere about. He may have gone to bed, Georgie didn’t know.

The guests had gone too. Most had left late, tired and happily drunk after all the dancing with the fiddlers, vying to impress the company with their energetic sawing and interwoven melodies, and everyone joining hands and dancing and twirling together.

And in the morning, he would be gone too, returning south.

Every day, he had seen her. Every day he had walked to the spot by the stream to wait for her, to wait for that moment when he would hear her voice and be dazzled by her. And every fine day, she had come. He had even held her, albeit briefly, each day, for he'd pleaded with her to teach him the Highland dances that he'd need to know for Dunphail's ceilidh. And she, knowing no better, had obliged. He hadn't told her that he knew the steps and turns already on Wellington's orders that all staff officers learnt such things.

He sat, unthinking, silent, his gaze upon the fire comfortably softened by the whisky he'd drunk, aware only of what he craved. She had become a roaring in his blood.

Suddenly, abruptly, he arose and went through to the side door. Snatching his oilskin cloak from off its hook, he wrapped it round himself, grabbed his hat to pulled it down over his brow. And went out.

The storm that had been gathering all evening had broken, the rain plummeting down upon him so thick he could barely see. But he did not stop, but strode out, walking as briskly as he could on the sodden earth, across the lawns and beyond the grounds, down the footpath toward the valley. Still the wind howled, the rain beating against him. Wrapping his cloak more closely about him, he bent low into the wind's face, to press on.

He had marked the path many times over the past weeks as he and Dunphail had walked out, and upon their return from the day's shooting.

Water spilled off his bicorne and dripped down his collar. It dripped down his throat and streamed down his cheeks and blew against his breeches. He quickened his pace as he headed downhill. Somewhere near, undaunted by the rain and the violent gusting of the wind, an owl hooted. Over and again, Georgie slipped, sliding on the sodden grass and fallen leaves and mud, stumbling, catching himself with one hand before he fell, then scrambling to regain his balance, he strode on.

He paused as he came upon the storm-hidden shadow of the stone house. There was still a light burning from one window.

Silent as a stalking rifleman he approached and leaned against the window pane to peer through the crack where the curtains did not meet. It was Miss MacDonald. Ailie. Her hair was down, all unbound about her shoulders. She was alone, wrapped in a tartan shawl, reading. Even her dog appeared to be absent.

Laying his cheek against the glass, discreetly, Georgie tapped against the pane.

Miss MacDonald checked, still, her head half raised as she listened, wary.

Again, Georgie tapped.

Fully alerted now, her every sense engaged, she jerked about to look toward the window. She checked again, uncertainty or indecision in her face. Then, tucking her shawl more tightly about her, she rose from her chair and went from the room.

He was at the front door almost before she unbolted it, resting his full weight against it. Even as she opened it to him, he pushed against it to fill the doorway with his great height. Unspeaking, clasping her to him, he slid one hand into her unbound hair and bent his head to kiss her, to wrap himself about her and to kiss her.

She could taste the whisky on his mouth. "You're drunk."

"Yes."

Finally, his breathing harsh and fast, he leant against the door to press it shut, and laid his cheek against her hair. "Marry me," he whispered, his breath rasping in his throat and his blood thumping its way to his groin. "I must leave in the morning. Come with me."

She paused, lifted her head, and searched his face. "Ye're wet," she declared in simple surprise. And with that same teasing smile lighting her eyes, she began to push his cloak from him, to cast it aside. She lifted his dripping hat from off his head and dropped it on the floor.

He wanted to make love to her so badly it was madness. "Yes," he laughed. "Drenched to my skin," he admitted, caught between happiness and dizzying lust. He took a lock of her hair between his fingers and held it there, learning its texture.

"Daft creature…" she murmured as he bent close to her throat.

"Sassenach," he corrected breathlessly, tasting the scent of her. "Daft Sassenach…" he said, kissing her again, holding her close as close. "Marry me. Come with me," he pleaded. He could not stop his kissing of her, he had waited so long for her, to touch her, to hold her, to feel her soft and close against the length of him, had dreamt of her night after night, waking over and over, aroused and shaking.

Then he felt her hands against his chest, not to push him away, but to work her fingers up about his shoulders and into the wet hair that clung to his neck.

He raised his head again to read the answer in her eyes.

"Where?" she questioned. "Gretna Green?" She smiled.

"I don't care. Wherever you like…To be sure, I don't know your laws. Just say yes…I can keep you, I'm not rich, not like Dunphail, but I have my prize money. I swear you'll not repent it." He kissed her hard again. "I swear to you…" His hand had crept below her waist to cleave her against him. "Or am I not handsome enough?"

She gave him a half-smile. Then she stopped, and as he opened his mouth to ask her again, she laid her fingers against his lips, silencing him.

Her dressing gown had come untied and hung open, revealing her night rail, now wetted from pressing against him and clinging to her. In the light of the single hall candle, her skin was whiter than pale. He was nearly unmanned by desire. She took his hand to draw him further into the house.

"Mrs. Elgin?" he questioned.

"Her pug snores," Ailie said simply. And led him into a darkened hallway.

His eyes adjusting to the total gloom of the house, he found she had brought him to a bedchamber. He stood in the doorway, and looking about in the eking light of the embers of a small fire, saw the gown she'd worn earlier thrown over the back of a chair. And knew that the uncanopied bed before them was hers.

Silently, carefully, she closed the door behind him.

Chapter XXIII

1

Though the fog had been cut away with the dawn, by mid-morning the sharp glare of autumnal light had been overlaid by a horizonful of heavy cloud—a watercolourist's palette of leaden grey and Prussian blue upon slate—borne on a cold northeasterly.

Planta leaned forward to twitch at the curtain's fraying edge, and eyed the row of gulls sat upon the tile ridge of the roofs opposite and perched upon the adjacent chimney pots, their feathers ruffling in the wind. The house martins were long since departed for warmer climates. From out one of the chimneys a column of black smoke shot upward, soiling the sky.

Planta shifted his weight from one foot to the other, and wetted his bottom lip. He darted a glance toward the gilt mantel clock sitting amongst the quills and standish on his desk. Gone ten.

Lord Castlereagh was late.

Leaning toward the window, he peered anxiously down through the darkening morning. A handful of the last autumn leaves was whisked from somewhere to spiral down upon the opposite walkway and collect in the gutter. Chewing at his lip, he looked up the street. Then down. Then up again. Among the brown-coated pedestrians, the horsemen, the sweeping boys, no sign of his lordship. Nor did any of the hackney carriages stop to let down a passenger.

Lord Myddelton had been in the office when he'd arrived. Making copies of the coded letter he'd spent all night deciphering. The original of which Planta now held in his hand.

Planta stepped away from the window, and holding his bottom lip between his teeth, apprehensively examined the first page. He edged to the window again to survey the street once more. The sky had grown still darker, charging and changing the atmosphere. Regarding the deepening layers of ash-coloured sky, he pictured the days ahead, marked out and measured by the weight of the drumming rain which would beat upon the houses and streets and horses, drenching the city, flooding the Mint, dripping through the roofs, flushing out the gutters, spewing forth from drainpipes and gargoyles' mouths, turning all to drear beneath it.

Drawing a deep breath, Planta considered the missive, wiped at his mouth, then paced to his desk and laid the pages down. He fingered the knot in his cravat, reassuring himself of its starched perfection. Perhaps he should he send for Flint.

He leaned over the desk to read it all. For the fifth time. Then raised his head, to glance at the door, to listen for the approach of his lordship's step. But could detect nothing. He rubbed at his forehead and returned to the window to watch. Even though his lordship never entered the building by the front door. Still.

The fire had been lit in the main office an hour since to offset the cold and the damp.

But where was he?

Planta looked again at the pages of Myddelton's neat copperplate, now lying white and pristine on his desk, and clenched and unclenched his fist. Then studied the street in both directions. He sucked at his bottom lip. His lordship was never this late. Never.

There was the click and sough of a door opening.

Planta jerked about. "Sir." A sweat of relief broke out on his upper lip. "Sir!"

Lord Castlereagh halted to patiently consider his secretary, regarding him with curiosity. "Yes?" He smiled. "It is I…" he said affably, as if to a child. "What is it?" His cheeks were flushed with exercise and exposure to the wind and air.

"It's this, sir!" Planta exclaimed, crossing the room in three strides to snatch up the missive. "Lord Myddelton brought it round at first light!"

Leaning on his cane, the Foreign Secretary shut the door gently behind him. And as Planta came to help him to remove his greatcoat, he took the pages. Shrugging the garment from his shoulders, he began to read.

"Dear me!" he murmured after only a paragraph. "What?"

Reading on in rapt attention, his mouth fell slightly ajar. He lifted his head, his expression sharpened. "Dear God in heaven! Planta, can this be true?" he murmured. "Malet has escaped from La Force and sprung a coup to overthrow Bonaparte? He's done it?"

Walking awkwardly, he laid the pages on Planta's desk while he removed his hat and gloves. His face above the stark white column of his cravat and collar had drained of colour. "Where is Myddelton now?" he asked quietly.

"With Sir Charles Flint, I believe, sir."

Castlereagh nodded, and collecting the pages up, limped toward the inner office. "Send for him. Find him now. Has he informed the Home Office? And the Foreign Letter Office? And Liverpool! This all happened on the 22nd—have we no other news of it than this?" he demanded, his breath shortening.

"I don't know, sir," Planta confessed, hesitating.

"And where is Jesuadon?"

"Just back from the north, my lord."

"Get him here. On the double."

"Yes, my lord. Anything else, my lord?"

Shifting the pages, the Foreign Secretary stopped to scan the second page of the decrypted letter. He paused, raising his eyes for a moment. "Pasquier and Savary both placed under arrest and sent to La Force! Good! Excellent. Napoleon's death in Russia was announced in the Senate…do we have any independent confirmation of that?" Keenly, he turned the page over to continue reading. "Guidal… Lahorie…yes, just as they've planned…de Puyvert too?" He stopped. "What? I don't understand…Pandemonium throughout the city? But…?" he spluttered. "Good Christ, I don't understand. What can have gone amiss?" he cried.

Lord Castlereagh looked away, then stared up at the small room's over-elaborate cornice, its upper surface dirtied with dust and cobwebs. Then continued reading. He swallowed. "It says here that Savary and General Laborde rounded up the plotters almost immediately. Within hours. All twenty-four of them. And that they've been shot. What, all of them?" His eyelids fluttered with uncertainty as he struggled to comprehend this new knowledge, to consider and weigh it, to evaluate the ramifications. "Who is this from? Oh, Jules de Polignac…So there can be no doubt…" Then, fearfully now, and with his lips bit tight together, he read over the final page again. "And all of them dead…

"I knew this was coming. It has been in the works for months, you know. For years even. These were all Flint's agents. Which is why I told Boy to keep away from Paris."

Planta said nothing.

"But of course, he didn't listen. To be sure, it is exactly the sort of thing he would get up to! He knows no bounds, you know. He never listens…And he's known most of these men from his childhood…" He drew and expelled a great sigh, and covered his mouth with his hand. And with that, he turned his back on Planta to contemplate alone the depths of his private inner office, cornered in darkness despite the hour.

"So that's it, then. He is dead, isn't he? They were all shot. And the boy is dead."

And standing thus, silenced and still, blocking the doorway with his great height, his silvering head bowed, he closed his eyes against this new and terrible loss. To miss and to mourn and to grieve for the boy. For what might have been. In horror to envision him lying bound and broken and dead, shot through, his face white, his blood spilled and staining the cold granite cobbles of some French prison yard.

Planta swallowed painfully and shook his head. "I don't know, sir."

2

With his elbow propped upon the mantel and his head resting against his knuckles, Jesuadon stood listening, his gaze as ever upon the oriental patterning of the Turkey carpet. He did not look up.

He rather thought Lord Castlereagh had been weeping. Though he was no longer. Now he sat, quietly aloof in his grief and rage, issuing instructions even as he demanded answers that no one had.

They all had known of the plot, of course. But not who had aided Malet in his escape from La Force. Nor why it had all gone wrong. Nor what had become of the others—the other Chevaliers de la Foi. And no one knew what had become of the boy. Not where he'd gone. Nothing. No one knew where John Brown was neither. Shuster was still in Scotland.

The rain had hardened as it swept across the city, beating against the window like a shower of pebbles.

Planta hovered like a nervous peahen and did his best not to wring his hands.

Jesuadon stooped to add a shovelful of coal to the fire. And the coal dust hissing and sparking as it hit the flames, he straightened, but did not raise his eyes to meet those of the others. He had barely slept, though he had managed to wash and change his linen before coming out.

The aching silences lengthened. And still, his head lowered, Jesuadon listened. To the halting half-tried excuses, the desperately voiced hopes, the false assurances and the disbelief, until finally, all but he departed. It was none of it of any use.

The doors closed upon them, Lord Castlereagh bowed his head to press the palms of his hands against his eyes.

Jesuadon waited.

At last, the Foreign Secretary looked up. He had been weeping again. "Well?" he said, his voice near breaking.

Jesuadon regarded him steadily. "She is safe-stowed."

Castlereagh nodded his understanding. "Good."

"I'll get him for you. I'll get Wilmot and all his minions."

Again, Lord Castlereagh nodded. "Do you think he suffered?"

Jesuadon eyed the low flames snaking about the coal lumps while he considered his answer. "You mean, was he tortured?" He gave a shake of his head. "No. It was over too quickly for that. It was a botch-job."

Castlereagh clenched his jaw, then nodded too swiftly. "Well, at least that's something then…" He raised his eyes but did not look at Jesuadon.

"I should never have allowed him to carry on, you know," he said at last. "Not after they killed his father. I should have found him a proper home, with someone to look after him…not let him…not allowed him to…to return…"

"He'd never have stayed," Jesuadon said, without dissimulation. "No matter how fine your intentions. 'Struth, it was not in his nature to be so contained."

Castlereagh's face was glistening wet and pale though still as he recalled: "I was the only one he knew here back then. And he only knew me because of the music…I had played with his father, do you see? Duets. And with him. He was so very young then, just a child…but you should have heard him!

"I held no office then, of course, for I had not been long in the House…but I knew Pitt…so I effected the introduction. I suppose I should have sent him to Portland…or even Canning." Briefly, he clamped his jaw together. "But I did not. So he continued with me…because of the music." He drew a deep breath, almost a sob. Then falling silent, he cupped his chin in his hand and looked bleakly down upon the many papers littering his desk, unlit by the few candles guttering in the sconces.

Finally: "Thank you, Tom. Thank you."

3

The remainder of the day Jesuadon spent walking, with his collar turned up and the wide brim of his hat pulled low over his forehead, his greatcoat slapping and catching against his ankles. Walking as the incessant rain pummelled down upon the roofs and every thing, turning the roads to dark eddies or slurried potholes swelling to lakes that threatened the lower doorsteps. Calling in at selected taverns where the clientele was less than genteel and the strip-me-naked stung the throat. From neighbourhood to district, he strode through the puddles and mire and across the streaming cobbles, from the Foreign Office to Seven Dials, to Covent Garden and Charing Cross, down into the black recesses of the Rookery and on to Petticoat Lane. And from thence to the Docks.

So that every last one of them could see that he was back.

And as word of his return spread amongst the ranks of mud-stained boys, hunched sodden and impassive on the street corners with their brooms—the eyes that saw all comings and goings and heard all manner of secrets—others crept from their darkened corners to catch sight of him, of his pale face damp with spray, and perhaps to earn a glance in their direction, or even the intimacy of a nod for their efforts. And on he walked, spotting those who had cause to fear him. Listening for any word that might reveal something of the doings in France. About which they'd heard nothing.

All except amongst those in St. Katharine's, where news was plentiful but varied.

Aye, they'd heard that there'd been a coup, but that Malet hadn't held his nerve, had he? Lost it, hadn't he? Perhaps Boney was dead, just like he said. Even though that Savary said he wasn't. But he would say that, wouldn't he? More than his life 'ud be worth to say otherwise…Never did speak an honest word, did they, damned Frenchies...? But aye, Savary had his lads out everywhere. Worse than before, it was. Still, it was only a matter of time, wasn't it? Didn't have men enough to guard the coasts, did they, so aye, the smuggling was good…did he need summat delivered? Or p'rhaps brought back, neat and quiet-like?

About the boy, nothing.

At last, his pockets emptied of pennies, he idled his way back through the darkening streets to St. Giles to the King's Head to wait. And to dry out. Appropriating for himself the long settle within the large inglenook, he called for a quart pot of flip, heated through.

About him, the low cavern of an inn was crowded, airless—rank with the smell of wet wool and wetter shoddy—and crammed with the dowdies and golumpuses who had stopped to escape the rain and had stayed on, their faces distorted into lubbering caricatures by an evening's drink.

Jesuadon leaned his head against the corner of the wooden settle and regarded the sodden leather of his boot, propped up before him on the seat. The expression on his face did not invite interruption. Even those in their cups could see that, even in the firelit gloom of the place.

Across from him, perched on a three-legged stool, Barnet was nursing a rum toddy and a cold. Drops of wet glistened and beaded and clung to the felt of Barnet's low crowned hat, placed on the table beside the pooling light of a single tallow.

"It's certain then, the boy's dead?" Barnet asked, without looking up. There was no need to lower his voice. For who could hear anything above the roar of the alehouse laughter from across the room? Barnet took a long drink, then lapsed into an extended fit of coughing.

Jesuadon shrugged. The shoulders of his coat were only just beginning to dry now, even with the near heat of the fire.

Barnet frowned. "You're a hard bastard, you are," he commented, though without rancour.

"'Sblood, there's nothing I can do about it one way or the other, so what can it matter?"

Barnet risked a sideways squinny at his face. For there was something about Jesuadon this evening. It had been there since he'd returned. A deepening hardness. A ruthlessness. He'd noted it almost at once.

"Tell me about Wilmot?"

Barnet screwed up his face and drank his toddy. And coughing again, spat a gobbit of phlegm onto the plank floor. "I wrote it all down for you. It's with Sparrowhawk. But there's little enough to it." He stopped to blow his nose into a raggy checked handkerchief. "Most evenings it's the Macao Club and then, this past week or so, it's been a stop at that vaulting school on Bury Street—run by a Mrs. Somers. And then he toddles off home."

Jesuadon took a long swill of flip, then regarded the tankard on the table. "Have you seen him with a fellow called Waley?"

"Waley?" Barnet shook his head. "Don't think so. Who's he then?"

"Wilmot's lover, it would seem." The tone of Jesuadon's voice was deceptively mild, and so soft that Barnet wondered if he'd misheard.

He looked again at Jesuadon to see that he had not misunderstood. Then: "Oh Christ, no!" he said, shaking his head as he did. "You're not telling me he's a Miss Molly…"

"It would explain the friendship with the poet..."

His eyes red-rimmed and rheumy, his face flushed, Barnet shook his head. "No..." he murmured to himself. He rubbed the sweat from his head. "Poxy bastard. I'll see what I can find. But I'm never tellin' the lads." He'd begun to hack again. "And I'm not sending 'em down the Molly-walk neither," he stated emphatically. "They'd kick the pair of 'em to death, you know."

"Sounds ideal," Jesuadon said with quiet pleasure.

Barnet ignored him. "So what d'you want me to do?"

Jesuadon appeared to consider. "Tell your little band of cutthroats that none of them are to go out singly again. Not even to take a piss. Tell them I want them out in pairs. Or better yet, three or four of them together. Is that understood?"

Troubled, Barnet nodded. "I'll tell them. But why?"

Jesuadon sat silent, staring blindly ahead. Then: "Because after that cock-up in Paris, Savary's going to want his revenge. And it does not matter whether the boy was there or not, whether he's dead or not, Savary will know he had a hand in it. And I'll sacrifice no more of my lads to that poxy bastard's little games. That's why.

"Set a watch on Waley. Find out where he lives and if he has access to a boat, or a yacht."

Barnet straightened. "All right...And then?"

"Get rid of that bloody cold."

Then rising, shaking out his coat, Jesuadon clamped his teeth together, baring them. His eyes glittered with menace, or rage. "And now *we* play."

Chapter XXIV

1

The fog that lay thick as lambswool over the fields was rolling away with the breeze and late autumn sun, yet still the air hung dense and damp, laden with the scents of fallen leaves and wet bark, of wood-smoke and cold. But at least it wasn't raining. And Georgie said the walk would do them good. A perfect cure for cropsickness, he'd said, as he hauled Harry out of bed, demanding that he wash, shave and dress.

God's garters, he was mad as a whole street of hatters. But there was no point in arguing, so Harry, now washed, decanted into his clothes and with his head throbbing, followed his brother down the High Street.

Fancy, driving all the way from London to Godalming at some infernal hour to rouse a brother from his bed merely in order to walk. Mad, quite mad.

There were few people about—only a few tradesmen and a little maid washing the windows and front steps of the village bakery.

"'Struth, Georgie, are you trying to ruin my boots? I've just had these from Hoby, you know," Harry grumped, lumbering behind. He wished he were back in bed, with the curtains drawn and his head half-buried beneath a bolster.

"Have an apple, Harry," Georgie said, still repellently cheerful. Striding on, he retrieved an apple from his pocket and tossed it over his shoulder in the expectation that his brother would catch it. Which he did.

Always had, always would.

Harry ate the apple. It didn't help.

The mud beyond the stile which led onto the adjoining common was deeper still, unharrowed, and poached by the grazing herds. And this, at last, forced Georgie to slacken his pace, while he slipped and stuck in the lumpen black mire.

Harry gave over thinking about his ruined boots and, catching hold of fence posts and near branches, concentrated on remaining upright.

Ignoring the beauties of the morning, the Constable sky, the overgrown hedgerows and the myriad flame colours of the leaves on the bordering beech and oak, they trudged on, oblivious too to the bird-song—those sharp shrill bursts which precede well-charged clouds unloading their wares upon the heads of those below. Neither did the herd of milkers in the far corner, clumped together under a stand of blackthorn, raise their heads to notice the human intruders.

"You want your head looking at…" Harry grumbled as he stumped along the bottom of the next field, only recently harvested, the ground churned thick as the mashed turnip swill they fed to pigs and schoolboys. "Does Wellington know you're of unsound mind?" he called, but Georgie wasn't listening.

Still behind, Harry turned in the far corner to see that the stream, which apparently Georgie had meant for them to cross, had burst its banks. "Oh Sweet Christ," he swore. "Georgie, you lunatic! What the devil have you brought me here for? Have you taken complete leave of your senses?"

Laughing without concern, Georgie turned back. "No." His smile was broad. "I just wanted to speak to you without the prospect of an audience."

"Oh," Harry subsided. "Right. What for?"

"Well, the thing is…" Georgie began. "I wished to tell you…I've got married." And his face was as bright as a new-minted penny at the thought.

2

On either side of the road, the threshers were making the most of the dry day to gather in the last of what was a late harvest. A lean harvest too. It should have been in weeks earlier. And but for the bad summer, it would have been. The codders were long gone, and the hops were in, to be sure. And now, the corn.

The heavy wains stood, the draft horses patiently waiting and used to waiting, while the men pitchforked the corn into stooks and onto the smaller carts, and the women and children, their skirts hitched knee-high, came behind, gleaning. Gleaning and singing and working—and warm even on such a cool morning. Before the frosts came and ruined it all.

A clutch of birds, tits, chaffinches and other land birds, darted from the hedges, lighting and pecking at the grain and corn dust upon the field's surface away from the harvesters, then flitted to perch upon the top of a hayrick. And swooped down again.

Boy stopped to collect a handful of blackberries from the hedgerow—grazing his hand against the serrated leaves already turned damson brown—and ate them. Ahead, a harem of hen pheasants, drab and foolish, tumbled onto the road and skittered away, running from side to side, unable to fix upon a direction. Behind them, a cock pheasant strutted for a few steps, then took fright at nothing and launched noisily into the air. Boy gathered another handful of fruit. His expression softened, and he walked on, safe. Life as it was intended to be and not as he knew it. Safe enough to venture out and walk openly. Upon the lanes, upon the byways. To feel the sun on his face as he was meant to. Almost smiling, his breakfast finished, he thrust his hands into his pockets and ambled on.

He crept into London just before daybreak on the fourth morning. Just after the hour when Barnet's heavies lowered their bulks to their beds and before the time when Jesuadon's boys would begin their watch. Crept in quiet and unheralded amongst the horse-traders, farmers and goose girls bringing their noisy, ungainly broods to market in the thin mist and uncertain November light. Through streets washed clean of offal by the rains, past the stonemasons' carts and half-built, scaffolded squares, he made his way to the Foreign Office. And there, in the silent twilit tomb that was the inner chamber, he removed the manuscripts and messages from the secret pockets in his coat. And laid them out, neat as wares in a shop window, upon the Foreign Secretary's desk. Then, arranging the pages of foolscap on the writing table before him, he perched on a chair's edge, and dipping a quill into a full standish, began to write of Prussia. Of the poverty, of the echoing emptiness with none but the plaintive cries of the cranes to fill the silence, and the scores of soldiers along the roadsides, dead in their thousands.

He had stopped briefly—tracing in his mind his path, and the places where he had left his mark in the sand, when he heard the Foreign Secretary in the outer office, humming, the sound of his tread uneven upon the wearing carpet. Laying aside the quill and closing the standish, Boy stood, to attention and with his head bowed.

The double doors opened, but in the curtained half-light, Lord Castlereagh saw only his desk. His brows drawn together, his jaw stuck out, he regarded with a dour expression the stacks and files which had accumulated there overnight.

"Sir," Boy said, making his obedience.

His hand tightening imperceptibly on the door handle, Lord Castlereagh raised his eyes to the scruffy figure in the shadows.

"Boy?" he ventured, for assuredly it was his voice. And his face paling to ash and tallow, blinking in disbelief at his own vision, he hesitated, afraid. "Boy? Is that you?"

Boy straightened. "Yes, sir."

"Boy!" Castlereagh exclaimed and rushed across to embrace him—his limp forgot, his eyes pricking with tears. "Oh dear heavens," he said, laughing with joy and relief. "My dear heavens! You are here!" he declared and clamped the boy to his chest, thumping his back, pressing his face against his shoulder.

"Oh dear blessèd Jesu!" he whispered. "Ha ha ha ha!" And taking the boy by the shoulders, he held him away to gaze upon him. "Let me look at you! We heard you was dead, child. We heard you'd be taken...de Polignac said...But how came you to escape? What happened? Were there others saved too?" he demanded in a rush. "But here you are! Here you are!"

Lord Castlereagh stopped to gaze briefly at the ceiling. "Dear blessèd Christ, you are here…" he said feelingly. And then stopped. And pulling away, his eyes narrowed with sudden intelligence, his concern and surprise transformed. "But what…what the devil was you thinking, playing off a stunt like that?" he now demanded. "We all thought you'd been shot." His voice had hardened. "We thought you was among those who'd been caught. What happened to them? What happened to the others?"

"What?" Boy exclaimed finally, dazedly, and took a step backward. "I beg your pardon, sir?" he faltered.

"Had you taken leave of your senses? Throwing your lot in with that idiotish band of mar plots and Royalist fools?"

"What?" Boy repeated in confusion.

"How came you to do such a thing? Had your wits gone begging? How came you to be so foolish? To put so much at risk? How can you you not know how much is at stake? To throw your lot in with Malet? When I distinctly told you to stay out of Paris!"

Staring in confusion, Boy protested: "But I haven't been in Paris, sir. I haven't been anywhere near it. You told me not to," he insisted. "I…I could never disobey you, my lord! Never!"

Lord Castlereagh stopped to regard him closely. "What?" he barked. "You wasn't in Paris?"

"No," Boy said bluntly. "You said not to, sir," he repeated.

"Then where the blazes have you been?" Castlereagh raged.

For an instant the boy was still. Perfectly still. And it seemed in that dim light as if his eyes lost their colour too. "Prussia, my lord." He said it so softly, and hung his head, as if the memories were perhaps too difficult. Even for him. He who had seen everything. "And Poland…" He drew a deep shuddering breath. Then turned to collect up a sheaf of music from off the table. "And getting you these, sir."

Straightening, Boy handed over the pages of neatly copied music. "From the Maestro—a full report. Opus thirty-four, which is three sets…" he faltered. " …of themes and variations: La Sentinelle, Partant Bacchus La Syrie and Mozart's Opera. And opus fifty-seven, Variations for Piano in F major." The dull, flat tone of his voice was a rebuke.

Lord Castlereagh took the proffered sheets of musical manuscript, then again looked upon that still, unblemished face. "You have been to Vienna?" He too had quieted.

Boy shook his head. "No, my lord. He wasn't there. He was in Linz, with his brother. He sends his warmest greetings and hopes that he may see you in the new year," he finished and bowed as with the Maestro's compliments.

Lord Castlereagh looked longingly upon the music, then at the boy's open face. "Then you had nothing to do with it?"

Again, Boy shook his head. "No, my lord," he replied. "I do not even know of what you speak, sir." And he stared straight ahead, his eyes emptied of all emotion.

Mystified, Castlereagh pondered the music in his hand. "Paris," he said by way of an explanation. "Paris…" He shook his head.

"Come, Boy…sit down…" He went to place the music upon his desk. "I shall have this translated this afternoon…a pity I shall not hear it played then…"

Puzzled and puzzling, Lord Castlereagh came across to his favourite wing chair and deftly lowered himself into the seat. "There was a coup," he said on a sigh. "Organised by Malet, we think. He escaped from La Force by pretending to be ill. And together with de Puyvert, Lahorie and a handful of others, had it announced in the Senate that Napoleon had been killed in Russia. They seized power, declared a Regency for the King of Rome. They even had that demon Savary thrown in La Force for a few happy hours!

"But Malet lost his nerve and it all went to pieces." A shadow of regret crossed the Foreign Secretary's face. "By the next day, Savary was freed and he and Laborde had rounded them all up. And we thought… we assumed you were among them. We were certain that it was…that you must have had a hand in it…and when we didn't hear from you…"

"No, my lord," Boy said softly. "Who else was killed, sir? Besides Monsieur de Puyvert?" And looking down on his hands, he murmured, "He was a friend of my father's…"

"I'm sorry. I am so sorry…" Castlereagh shook his head. "I don't recall. It was all in a letter from Jules de Polignac…" And sighing heavily, as if the weight of his office had suddenly become too heavy, he rose and limped to his desk to sit again. He looked down upon the music, then up at the boy—plain-faced and earnest—seated motionless, with a hand on each knee, at the writing table, and sought to rearrange his own thoughts to accommodate this new information. He blew out a breath, then rested his forehead against the heels of his hands.

"We must think what to do…This I had not foreseen…" he said, still reordering in his mind the ramifications, the connections, the assumptions. "Because…because, you see, if I believed you to have had a hand in this coup, then it is certain that Savary will think it as well." He propped his elbow on his desk, resting his chin upon his fist. "Upon my life, I must find you somewhere safe…"

Then, distractedly, he looked up. "Did you say something?"

"There is nowhere safe, my lord," Boy said baldly. "Pater Wilhelm is dead."

Castlereagh's face fell. "Is he?" He closed his eyes. "Oh, Boy, I am so sorry. So grievously sorry." His tears were returning. He blinked them away. "To be sure, it's worse now, ain't it? It is worse. This latest campaign of Napoleon's has been worse…"

He did not raise his eyes to see Boy nodding. He did not need to.

"Another life…another death…How many…?" His voice broke. "How many do you suppose he's killed this time? Thousands?"

Boy shook his head. "Oh no, sir. No. More. Half his army was dead before they crossed the Nieman into Russia." He did not pause upon his lordship's gasp. "That's what I heard, and that is how it looked to me."

Castlereagh slumped against the back of his chair and stared. "You was there?"

"Yes, my lord." His voice had thinned. "I spoke to those in Bohemia too," he said distantly. "They had heard the same. And that there was a great battle, bigger than all the rest. Greater even than Austerlitz. But I can assure you, at least half of Napoleon's troops had starved to death before they ever fired a shot."

Stunned, Castlereagh sat. And this time could not think what it all might mean. "He is a monster," he fretted. "And like a monster, he has consumed all of his children…

"But he shall not have you. By God, he shall not have you!"

Chapter XXV

1

The Morning Room of White's Club was not unfull of members on that dull November day, for what person of sense would chose to remain at home suffering the inconvenience of a smoking fireplace, or worse still, draughty bachelor's chambers, solitary, when the several comforts of amiable company, a full selection of the day's newspapers and a roaring fire might be had for the price of a short walk down St. James's? To be sure, a partial flowering of Society's bucks and beaux had departed to strut and preen in Hyde Park. Yet still there there remained enough members present in that large, pleasant, candle-lit room to lend an impression of convivial fellowship on a chill afternoon.

Alvanley sat adoze in his wing chair.

A clutch of Bloods emerged from the Coffeeroom talking loudly of the Hunt, looked over the room for their acquaintances, then hurried up the stairs to the Gaming Room.

Alone, Lord Castlereagh stood in the foyer, handing over his hat and gloves to the porter, then allowing this individual to assist him off with his coat while he surveyed the room and its occupants. He did not relinquish his cane, but limped further into the Morning Room, nodding his greetings to one and all, to stand for a moment beside the hearth.

Back from the gunsmith's, having enjoyed the traditional marriage toasts on the previous evening, Georgie Shuster wandered in—at ease and out of the threatening rain—discussing with Dunphail the several pairs of carriage horses they had seen at Tattersall's.

Seeing Shuster approaching, Lord Castlereagh hastened toward him, his hand extended in greeting. "Captain Shuster, my dear fellow, I hear I am to offer my felicitations on the happy occasion of your marriage. This is very good news! Very good news indeed. I am heartily pleased for you, George. May I wish you every joy…"

"Thank you, my lord, thank you." Georgie said, grinning and bowing. "I shall convey your compliments to my wife."

"Oh, yes, you must do so! And you and Lady Shuster must join us for dinner one evening."

"Thank you, sir. We would be delighted…"

Lord Castlereagh turned to Dunphail. "And you must come too, Dunphail, for it is not true that the the new Lady Shuster is a relation? Or was—until Shuster carried her off like young Lochinvar, eh?" He laughed. "We shall make it a family dinner…"

"How d'ye do, sir…Yes, so she is. "

"Very well, indeed," the Foreign Secretary responded. "Except for a touch of the gout…" He looked down his great nose upon his foot, peering disconsolately at his shoe. "Miserable weather, ain't it? I, for one, am glad to be out of it this afternoon…" He cast a glance at Georgie. "But you are new-married and therefore impervious, I make no doubt…"

Another trio of gentlemen, all of them dressed for riding and smelling of horse, bestowed a cheerful nudge or clapped Georgie on the shoulder as they passed on their way to the Coffeeroom.

Straining to hear, Georgie lifted his head for a view of the far end of the room. "Sir, Dunphail, excuse me for a few minutes, will you? I believe I've heard my brother's voice in the Coffeeroom and I have promised myself the, er, pleasure of a word with him," he said, and rolled his eyes, before heading off across the room.

Chuckling, Lord Castlereagh observed: "He seems most happily wed."

"Aye, he does," Dunphail agreed. "Do you care to join me in a glass of wine? Or do you go to the House now?"

"Yes, yes…the House. But I do believe I will stop. Thank you, yes…And the lady, she is your cousin, so kinsmen, as well as friends. How fortuitous…" Castlereagh continued. He paused to look over the room, while they settled into a pair of armchairs near the fireside, then fell to smoothing his thumb along the calloused tips of his fingers. "I am most glad to see young Shuster wed, you know. Very glad indeed. He was one of Wellington's most trusted aides in the Peninsula, before he was wounded, of course…"

"Was he?" Dunphail shook his head. "'Struth, I'd not known. Only that he served. He does not speak of it…"

"Oh, yes. Yes, indeed," Castlereagh nodded. "Upon my word, he is a hero amongst his peers for his efforts for King and country. Courageous to the point of folly—and on that I speak from experience. For the Duke has kindly lent him to the Foreign Office, for the nonce."

Dunphail gave a courteous nod, then raised his glass in salute. "To Captain Shuster."

"Captain Shuster," Castlereagh repeated and drank the toast.

For a long moment, Lord Castlereagh gazed about the room, savouring the ease of the place, the contentment, and sipping at his wine. Then: "Do you know, I must tell you…" he began. "I have been wishing to thank you for some little time for a service you provided for the Foreign Office…a few months ago, it was. And while it may have seemed nothing to you, I can assure you I was most grateful."

Dunphail raised an eyebrow. To his certain knowledge he had never had anything at all to do with the Foreign Office—outside of his acquaintance with Myddelton, that was.

"I believe you rescued a boy from being beaten, is that not so? In Kent, it was…" Castlereagh's smile was at its most affable.

Dunphail shook his head in surprise. "'Struth, did I?"

"Yes. And brought him safe to London. And for that I must personally thank you, my lord."

Dunphail tilted his head to one side, recalling the incident as best he could. "Ah," he said, groping for words. "Aye…well then. I was…ah…glad to do it. I trust the boy…he'd taken quite a basting, hadn't he?" he faltered. "He sustained no lasting hurt?"

"No. No, no…he mended well. Very well indeed, thank you…"

Castlereagh said, sipping his claret. Silently, he inspected the row of callouses upon his fingertips. Then: "How shall I put this?" he said pleasantly. "'Struth, I know I may rely on your discretion, my lord…Tirrell—the boy—has been in the pay of the Government for some time now, and I am more grateful than I can say that you intervened on his behalf that day."

Outside, the rain had begun steadily to fall, beating its perennial tattoo against the windowpanes.

"…Which did cause me to wonder if I might call on your kindness once more, my lord. For the boy, that is." Lord Castlereagh allowed himself a diplomatic pause and an affable smile. "There was a coup in Paris, you see…" He spread his hands. He lowered his voice. "It is not yet generally known…nevertheless…still, it appears the French authorities believe young Tirrell to have had a hand in it. Which is a nonsense, of course. But they are not always rational, you know, the French…and they jump to every kind of conclusion in their mad devotion to their emperor…"

Dunphail blinked and stared.

Still the smile. "…So it came to me to wonder whether I might be able to persuade you to offer him the safety of your house in Mount Street?" Pensive now, Lord Castlereagh pressed his fingertips together, resting his chin on his middle fingers. "I know Mr. Hardy is no longer there to lend you company and I can assure you…though it would seem otherwise…the boy is gentry-born, and you need have no fear for his manners or character."

For some minutes, Dunphail had been considering whether he had, somehow, wandered into a fool's opera—with himself cast as chief fool. For this was the Foreign Secretary, Lord Castlereagh, speaking openly to him about what must surely be state secrets. Asking him to house a spy. Was that right? And this was White's. White's Club. He glanced about. No one was paying them any heed. Across the breadth of the room, no one even noticed. About to protest and refuse, gathering his jumbling thoughts, Dunphail began, "I do not…"

Holding up his hand to halt the answer, Castlereagh said, "Do you know, it is a very curious thing…to be sure, I cannot think how it came to happen, but I came across a shelf of old files which the Home Office had sent over the other day. I was just reading through them, you know. And I came across some business about your family. In the last century…"

And in that instant, Dunphail was no longer at sea. "I beg your pardon, sir…" he whispered, his eyes widening, the air knocked out of him.

"Yes," Castlereagh continued. "It is curious, ain't it, what sorts of pursuits and alliances our forebears entertained, do you not think? Some of them even treasonous…Most of it to do with the Old Pretender, of course. Or his drunkard of a son, Charlie, the Bonnie Prince, as I believe he is still called…" Castlereagh's eyes glittered with a piercing intelligence as he watched the effect of his words.

Dunphail stared. "I beg your pardon, sir?"

And observing with satisfaction the confusion, the apprehension in Dunphail's expression, Castlereagh pressed on: "As I was saying, the boy. Young Tirrell. What do you say? Will you have him?" He smiled brightly.

Bristling with rage, an indignant flush suffusing his cheeks, Dunphail said bluntly, "The answer must be no, my lord. 'Struth, I am no fit person to have charge of a boy. Nor do I think…"

"Do you so? How curious," Castlereagh soothed. "For do you know, among those papers from the Home Office, I have even found proof that many of the reparation payments to the Crown were never collected. Can you imagine such a thing? Thousands upon thousands of pounds never paid! Lands declared forfeit that were never rendered up…"

His mind now in chaos, a dull thudding having begun in his stomach, Dunphail could think of nothing to say. He was being blackmailed. For his grandfather's Jacobite sympathies and his participation in the Rebellion. There could be no question. This was blackmail. His mind stuttered at the thought, the word even. The reparation payments would cripple him—as they were meant to—if they demanded them now. His jaw clenched and unclenched. "Were they not?" he managed at last. "And, what…'struth, what, may I ask, will become of those who…"

But Castlereagh was not finished. "The French, they are without pity, you know. I sometimes believe they have lost even the veriest shred of their humanity. For, do you know, that *boy* was forced to watch as those hell-born bastards from the secret police hacked his father to death. With their bayonets. They hacked off his hands. One, and then the other. And the boy watched and could do nothing as his father screamed in agony. They nailed his hands to the prison gates too. Then they guillotined his body, even though he was already dead, so they might mount his head as a trophy."

Appalled, sickened, Dunphail stared. He tried and failed to recover his wits. His mouth had gone dry. "What did he do then, the boy?" he said quietly.

For a brief instant, Castlereagh's expression softened. "He did as his father bade him. He hid until it was safe and then he carried the papers home to England, to the Prime Minister, is what he did. What he still does…" he said, intent once more.

Dunphail swallowed, whitening. "I…I…" He was shaking his head, still overcome with revulsion. "I do not see how I can care for this lad. 'Struth, I know nothing of bairns…"

"Oh…I expect given his previous experience, he will manage to endure whatever privations you might inflict upon him." Castlereagh subjected Dunphail to a harsh, dismissing glance. "Did you think this was a nice war, my lord?" His voice had hardened. "An honourable and clean war? There is nothing honourable about the butchers and madmen who make up Bonaparte's army, my lord. Nothing."

About them, the well-bred charivari rose and subsided. Two gentlemen, a red-coated officer and his fellow, passed them, one with his head thrown back in laughter.

"And…ehm…if I agree to have the boy, as you say?" he said bitterly.

Again, arching his hands so that his fingertips rested against each other, Lord Castlereagh appeared to consider. "Planta can be so very careless, you know. Can you believe it, only last week, he slipped while he was standing before the fire, and of course, that old parchment they used, it goes up in a second…a whole file, gone! Up in smoke. Just like that."

Dunphail flexed his jaw and did not hesitate. He nodded. "I shall have a room prepared for the boy on the morrow. Will that suit?"

"How very kind. Very kind indeed," Lord Castlereagh said by way of thanks. "I shall have him brought to you in a day or two. With further instructions as to his safekeeping." The smile was again in place.

Lord Castlereagh paused elegantly. "It would also be of great assistance to me, and by to me, I mean to the King, if you was to end your liaison with the charming milliner you have under your protection as soon as possible. And then, after a suitable, but brief interval, you know…if you might—perhaps a few nights a week—spend some time at the establishment on Bury Street where the proprietress is one Mrs. Somers."

His wits wholly scattered, Dunphail's mouth fell ajar and eyes widened. A dull flush of crimson suffused his face. What did they not know about him? For how long had they been spying on him? "I do not…" he rebelled, struggling to find his voice. "I do not frequent *low* houses like that…"

But still Castlereagh only smiled. "Oh…but you do now, my lord. You do now."

Minutes later, redressed in his greatcoat, Castlereagh paused for an instant under the famous White's portico to glance up at the darkening, weeping sky and did not look across the street to where Jesuadon sat in a waiting hackney.

2

The boy had been standing before the fire in the Foreign Secretary's office for hours. Waiting. As he had been ordered. Standing to attention while the flame shadows slithered and gyved and waned upon the walls.

Planta had offered to fetch him a pie for his dinner, but he had declined. Only the candles in the wall sconces above the fireplace had been lit.

The mantel clock chimed an hour past midnight, but he had given up counting some time ago. He shifted his weight from one foot to the other and stared at the painting on the opposite wall.

Castlereagh came into the doorway. "You are here. Good." He was dressed for the evening in a black coat with satin kneebreeches.

Boy bowed, making his obedience. "My lord."

Lord Castlereagh closed the doors and went to his desk. "Another late sitting tonight," he remarked, his tolerant patience apparently little impaired. "And they're still at it, still hammering away like a blacksmith's race, of course…Lord knows they create just as much of a din. But I came away. Od's blood, how the Whigs can carry on for so long and say so little, I do not know…"

He paused to take in the state of his desk with an air of baffled curiosity. He lifted one ribbon-bound sheaf of papers and peered at the topmost page beneath it. Then, did the same with the stack beside it. He sank into his chair. "I wished to tell you that have made arrangements for your safe-housing," he announced, without looking up.

Boy blinked. "What? But…"

Castlereagh was rummaging through the piles of papers and letters on his desk, making an unholy jumble of Planta's neat stacks and ribbon-bound organisation. "No," he countered, examining a bottom-most missive, then setting it aside, a vexed expression marking his countenance. "No, it is no longer safe for you at Sparrowhawk's, so do not argue."

Boy straightened and drew a cautious breath. "Where then, sir?"

Castlereagh stood, regarding the scrambled mess of papers and folios. He frowned. Then, raising his eyes, he put the matter from him and his expression cleared. "You will recall the gentleman who rescued you from John Brown last summer, Lord Dunphail. He is to have you," he explained. He smiled expectantly.

Boy's face fell. "My lord?" he murmured, shaking his head. "No. Oh no, my lord," he countered. "Not that. No! I must go back…"

Lord Castlereagh sat back in his chair his desktop search now wholly abandoned, a chilling hauteur creeping over his expression. "I beg your pardon?" he questioned, one eyebrow raised up.

Boy rushed forward. "I must, my lord. I must. I've got to! I've got to return to the Continent, don't you see?" he said in a rush. "Those reports I brought you, have you not read them? Who knows what will happen next? And there's no one else who can get as close to the French as I can, sir. No one," he declared, his volume rising. "S'truth, they've taken Moscow, and there's been a great battle, but who knows how many they've lost or what will happen next? You must send me back. You must let me return!"

Lord Castlereagh slammed down the file he'd been holding. "I have read your reports! Every blessed word of them. Great God! I have read the Maestro's reports too. By your own account Bonaparte had lost half his army before he ever crossed the Nieman and more than half his horses. He is lost! This war is lost to him. The question is no longer how many of the six hundred thousand men he took there has he lost, but did any of them survive?"

"I could get you that, my lord," Boy said eagerly. "I could. Let me go to Paris. They won't be looking for me there…And I'll get you word. I'll send regular reports–everything I hear, I give you my word," he promised.

"No, Boy, no. They will be looking for you there. They've never stopped looking for you there!" Lord Castlereagh retorted. "Sweet heavens above, do you think there are no other agents out there but you?

"Do you think Chernyshev and Lieven don't keep me informed? No! What do you not understand, Boy? You are not going to Paris. You are not going to Russia. You are not going to Vienna or Berlin. I will not have it," he raged.

Breathing heavily, Lord Castlereagh stopped to rake the boy over with a look that stripped away all bluster and pride, beheld too all the passionate and reckless care, and took in the unhealthy pallor, the cheekbones prominent in what should have been a youth's face, the thinning fingers of his fretful hands clenching with despair. "For Christ's sake, Boy, look at you," he despaired. "By my soul, you've grown so thin the next gust of wind might blow you away. Even Planta has noticed, bless him! You will…you must remain here," he finished.

"Please, sir, they're dying out there," Boy implored. "In their thousands, sir." He shook his head against the images forming there—of men and horses, women and children—beating against the walls of his mind, and nearly wept. "In their thousands…upon the plains…or drowned. Unshriven and unmourned. I need to be there," he said, his voice breaking.

"No, Boy." Lord Castlereagh shook his head. "No. Let someone else count their dead this once."

"No, sir. I belong there, sir!" Boy cried.

Again Lord Castlereagh shook his head. "You don't know where you belong," he said quietly.

"Please, sir," he begged. "This Dunphail, he'll…"

Castlereagh raised his hand. "Enough," he said in a tone so soft it was barely a whisper. "Enough, Boy. It is arranged."

His hands dropping limp to his sides, Boy drew a half-sob of breath. Then hunching his shoulders, he turned away and went to face the fire. And with his hands now folded together on the mantel, he leaned forward to watch the dying flames. In the grate, a log collapsed, sending a plosh of greying embers and ash onto the stones below.

Lord Castlereagh fussed with the papers before him, resorting them into some measure of apparent order—for Planta's benefit, if not his own. "I have set Jesuadon to provide you with all you shall need to become a young gentleman. When everything is ready, you shall go. Until then, you are to remain out of sight at Sparrowhawk's. Is that clear? I do not forget who you are, even if you have." Silently, he perused the disordered order of his desk once more, anticipating Planta's near-silent tsking on the morrow. "Jesuadon is waiting below to see you home. Remember, stay out of sight."

The colour emptying from his eyes, his mouth still ajar, Boy went to the door. And facing his lordship, made his obedience. "My lord." He bowed.

But the Foreign Secretary did not look up again.

Chapter XXVI

1

Within the confined space of the black travelling coach, where in the deepening twilight the shadows were dense as the inked cross-hatching of a master's etching, Boy sat as far from Jesuadon as possible. Mutinous. Unspeaking. Now dressed as a young gentlemen of means, with his hair barbered and brushed, and his clothes made by Castlereagh's private tailor with extra padding to the shoulders and a pocket secreted in the back panel.

Slumped in the corner and drinking steadily, Jesuadon had affected not to notice—not the boy's meticulous removal of his person to the far side of the coach, not the refined features revealed by the application of water and soap, not the deliberate turning away of his head—or was not interested.

They had left Sparrowhawk's at noon, to journey out of the city by way of Blackfriars Bridge. Accompanied by two outriders. And now they were back again, having raced through the adjoining counties, juddering and swaying to the measured tempo of cantering horses and the perpetual crackling of the iron-clad wheels on the grit and clay roads. Having changed horses. And now with three…three *different* outriders.

Ahead, the lock at Hyde Park Corner was beginning to loosen, the two drivers who'd engaged in a mutually-fulfilling shouting match of obscenities having remounted their boxes, the coach was once more edging forward.

His eyes closed, Jesuadon removed his feet from the seat opposite and struggled to uprightness. “Act your age, you pestilential brat.”

From his corner, the boy darted him a malevolent glare.

Jesuadon dropped the empty bottle to the coach floor where it rolled and clinked. “’Struth, you should take a razor to your upper lip too. Occasionally. It’ll help create the impression that you’re older.” He narrowed his eyes with mocking pleasure. “’Slife, who knows, it may even help speed things along.”

“Shut up.” The resentment was palpable.

Jesuadon shrugged. “It wasn’t me who sent you here. If it was up to me, you’d be off in Paris or Vienna or anywhere I don’t have to see your sullen gob, you little fuckster…”

Boy thrust his chin forward, over the discomfort of the constriction of high cravat and collarpoints. “Why did he?”

Without pity, Jesuadon eyed the petulant jut of Tirrell’s jaw, the glitter of blazing rage in those limpid eyes. “You’re the bait.”

Blenching, blinking rapidly, Boy’s fury fell away. “What? The bait?” He shook his head. “For who? What?”

Jesuadon raked the young face, the unrazored cheeks, the old eyes. “Wilmot.”

“Who’s Wilmot?”

“Your John Brown’s operator.” Jesuadon spoke the words as if they were rancid.

A uneasy comprehension had settled upon the boy. “He’s English?”

“And a toff,” Jesuadon sneered. “Don’t worry, I have him in my sights, I can assure you. He’s mine. And I will have him.”

Boy shot him a nervous glance.

“I’ve a watch stationed on your doors. Both front and back. If you need anything, I’m there. Do you understand?”

Warily, Boy nodded. “Yes.”

“But for now, you insolent royster, I need you to become a young gentlemen. We all need that. Wilmot ain’t acting alone. I haven’t yet got all his minions, but I will. Trust me. And I shall need you to remember every face you see, every name you hear, every scrap of paper you lay eyes on. Right?"

Again Boy gave a nod. "This Dunphail? Do I trust him?"

Jesuadon paused. The carriage thumped into and out of a pothole. One of the horses snorted. The biggest of the outriders on a large bay was just beyond the window. "I wouldn't," he said at last. "Though I agree with Castlereagh. You will be safe as long as you're in his care." And then, drawing a breath, he added, "But keep clear of Wilmot if you can. He likes boys from what I understand."

And when they pulled up before Dunphail's townhouse in Mount Street, there were none but Jesuadon's own lads to observe their arrival.

For a moment, Boy stood before the townhouse—red, like Somerset soil, like ancient bloodstains, seeping wet now with all the rain—to measure and commit it, like everything else, to the storehouse of his memory. Then lifting his chin, he mounted the few steps to be admitted by a servant.

The sweep, lounging on the pavement with his broom, did not look up.

Jesuadon, having delivered him to Dunphail's care, left him there to wait alone, silently taking in all of his surroundings—the fine paintings on the unmarred plaster walls, the high glass lantern which illumined the neoclassical austerity of the hall, the number of candelabra, the unlockable polished doors off in several directions, the staircase rising up from the side wall.

Dunphail came into the front hall and regarded him without enthusiasm. "You've arrived, then, Mr. Tirrell," he stated unnecessarily.

Boy made his bow. Then stood, ramrod stiff. The tall Scot looked as he remembered him—the proud face, pale and flush-cheeked, the grey eyes, the beautiful clothes. He was taller than Boy remembered though. "Yes, sir. Thank you, sir," he said, his voice soft, low. "It is very kind of you to have me, sir."

Still eyeing him with disinterest, without fondness, Dunphail did not respond directly. "Your face, it has healed well, then," he observed.

"Yes, my lord, thank you."

A silence, awkward and hostile, fell between them. Idly, Dunphail withdrew his snuffbox from his pocket, snapped it open and took a few grains. "Thorpe will show you to your room."

"Thank you, sir."

Dunphail turned on his heel, then said over his shoulder, "Do you play cards well?"

"No, sir. Not at all, sir. I am sorry, sir."

"Then you must learn," Dunphail said without looking.

"Yes, sir. Thank you, sir."

"And you will need to ride. Do you ride?" And in the query there was more than at first appeared.

Boy did not balk. "I have done, sir. As a child. Sir."

Dunphail sniffed. "Then I dare say it will come back to you. You shall ride out with More in the morning. And each morning after that until he is satisfied you shall not disgrace me."

"Yes, sir. Thank you, sir."

Dunphail began to walk away. "We dine at eight."

"Yes, sir."

Bowing to Dunphail's retreating back, the boy waited until he had gone and the door at the rear of the hall firmly shut behind him. Bleakly, he watched as two footmen collected the trunk filled with his new clothes and boots to carry it to his chamber. Then, he followed the servant, Thorpe, up the steps and through the wide hall to a pale-painted bedchamber, where the candles in the wallsconces were lit, and already there was a fire burning in the grate.

A fine large chamber with a white ceiling and a fine plaster cornice, it was, the like of which had not been his since childhood. With a proper bed with heavy lined curtains, proper linen upon it and a fine quilt. And a carpet on the floor, watercolours upon the four walls, and a writing table; a washstand and a tallboy for his clothes. And a fire in the hearth.

Boy crossed to the window, his steps noiseless in the deep pile of the dark patterned carpet. Pulling aside the curtain—padded and thick—he looked out through the glass into the deepening gloom of impending fog and more rain. Two of Jesuadon's watchboys were below, one at the corner and another across the way near the entrance to the mews.

The taller of Dunphail's servants, dark-haired and dark-eyed, was puzzling over the lock on the trunk. "Have you the key, sir?" he asked. "I should like to unpack for you if that is acceptable."

Distracted, Boy looked up. "Leave it. I shall see to it myself, thank you."

Again turning away, he did not see their deferential bows. But waiting until they had departed, he went to the chamber door and turned the key in the lock. He returned to stand before the fire, remaining there, still, and listened to the near and distant nothing. And standing, felt the heat touching every part of him, sinking into him. On his face, the dryness of it on his hands, through the fabric of his breeches. At length, warm, he knelt. Then finally he lay down before it, and drawing his knees to his chest as a child, squeezed his eyes shut.

2

A rapid and low "hoo hoo hoo hoo hoo" erupted into the nightnoise of grunts and rustlings.

Despite himself, Barnet hunched his shoulders. Then felt foolish for it. About him, the ash and birch and oak of the Ashdown Forest were close in upon him, even so near to the edge of the great forest as he was. Nor was there light to be seen, not from the sky nor stars, and the moon had been lost behind a mountain of cloud hours earlier. The lingering scent of the charcoal burners' fires and the campfires of those who yearly came to harvest the willow and broom from the forest for the broomyards tainted the cold air.

"Hoo hoo hoo hoo hoo."

A thing swept up from a branches overhead and out, to float low over the ground of a nearby clearing, unearthly pale, like some monstrous ghostly moth.

"Waowk. Awaowk!" came another cry from just behind.

Barnet shivered and cursed. He glanced over his shoulder. Underfoot, the forest floor of twigs snapped and broke. Brambles caught at his ankles. Where the devil was young Ladyman?

Barnet had been walking in this devilish place for over an hour and still the pestilential nocky boy was nowhere to be found. Probably off diddling with some wench…

"Hoo hoo hoo hoo hoo..."

"An ague take you, you daft bird, will you shut your gob?" Barnet muttered.

And then he heard.

A grunt. A thud. And...another grunt. As though the air had just been knocked from someone's lungs. He'd know that sound anywhere.

Abruptly, wholly alert now, he halted.

There it was again. The thud. This time followed by a smack. Fist against face.

But from which direction?

Then he knew. And he was running, thundering through the forest, stumbling, tripping over exposed roots, righting himself and running on. Branches caught at his sleeves and scratched his face. Without stopping, he pulled a pistol from his waist and another from the strap about his thigh. His knife, strapped to his back, was ready to throw.

He crashed from the forest covering, through the gorse and fern of the heath and saw them. A fluid blurring of a writhing ink silhouette against the midnight blue of the night. A smaller man with his arms crossed over his head to ward off the blows which rained down upon him. And a great tall bruiser of a man beating him. Clouting him with repeated blows to the head.

Barnet watched as the heavy-weight brought his fist back and loosed it, backhanded and hard across the other man's face.

It was John Brown. There could be no doubt.

It was Boy's John Brown.

Breathing hard, suddenly angry, Barnet raised his pistol, and waited for the brute to draw his arm back again.

He squeezed the trigger. The spark flashed sudden and bright. Then the thick resounding pop.

The big man froze.

Missed.

Unhit, the Frenchman screwed his face into a contorted scowl and drew his fist further back to ram home a blow which snapped the other man's head back.

Barnet clenched his jaw and changed his pistol hand. And raising the second pistol, steadying his breath, took aim—careful, fierce aim—and fired again.

"Rwaaaaah!" The bruiser's scream rent the unquiet air.

Wheeling about towards Barnet, he grabbed at his shoulder. "Rwaaaaah!" he yelped again. He let go of his victim, who, staggering, dropped to the ground.

Barnet tucked the spent pistols into his pockets and drew his knife.

"Hoo hoo hoo hoo hoo…"

"Waowk. Awaowk!"

A second nightbird, eerie in its whiteness, joined its mate overhead, rolling and checking, hovering still above the open heathland.

Looking furiously about, his eyes wild, looking everywhere for his assailant, clutching his shoulder, the bruiser swung about again, then began to run. With long ungainly strides and as fast as he could, through the fern and gorse in the opposite direction.

Barnet hesitated. Then, his eyes fixed upon the running figure, he picked his way through the prickling gorse to the fallen man. And bending down, saw a face darkened with bruising, blood slipping from his nostrils and from his torn mouth, soaking into the once-white linen at his throat. There was lace at his cuffs. It was young Ladyman.

He bent close to listen for his breath. "Tom…Tom? Listen to me lad." He glanced up to see where Brown had got to. If he was returning. He'd vanished from sight, thank Christ.

Barnet put his ear near Ladyman's bloodied face. Did he breathe yet? He could hear only the thumping of his own heart and breath. But yes, there it was—a faint puff of warm mist in the night air.

Half-kneeling, he slid an arm beneath Ladyman's shoulders and another beneath his knees. "Tom? Listen to me. Don't you dare die on me, you worthless young scrub…" Barnet said, lifting him high in his arms. "Don't you dare to do it…I shall get you to a doctor, lad. Now hold fast for me, son." And his leg muscles straining, Barnet stood. "Hold fast for me. Or Jesuadon will have us both…"

Against his chest, there was a muted movement, the rasping of a breath rising and falling. Ladyman, his swelling eyelids weakly twitching, opened his eyes and held for a moment on Barnet's full moon of a face.

Then he sagged, went limp.

"Hell and confound it," Barnet muttered. "I'm for it..." And shifting the deadening weight of Ladyman in his arms, Barnet swung his body up over his shoulder.

Chapter XXVII

1

Washed and brushed and with his face set, Boy presented himself for breakfast on that first morning in the Dining Room, at half past ten. He stood, waiting, impassive, while he took in the whole of the oval chamber, the bare mahogany table, polished like the doors to a high gloss, the pale sunlight leaking through the voile curtains, the celadon walls tricked out with plaster leaves and swags like the sugar flowers on a cake in a patissier's window. And he was as distant from the life of that elegant room as ten years could take him.

From the curved sideboard came the smells of affluence, of well-cooked food, of gammon and bacon rashers, baked eggs, bread and ale.

He bowed. "My lord."

Dunphail's appearance was, as ever, point device. An unwelcoming expression on his haughty Scots face, he regarded the boy coldly. "You missed dinner last evening. Where were you?"

"I'm sorry, sir. I fell asleep." Boy did not say that the warmth made him drowsy.

Dunphail frowned. "'Slife, it was the height of rudeness. Don't let it recur."

"No, sir. Yes, sir. I'm sorry, sir."

"And do not keep me waiting again." Dunphail looked him over. "And don't sleep in your clothes."

Boy stiffened, clamping his jaw tight as an angry flush rose in his cheeks. "No, sir. It shall not happen again, sir." It was too much, all of it.

"Very well." Dunphail resumed his reading of the newspaper, folded on the table before him. "Well, get yourself something to eat."

"Yes, sir. Thank you, sir."

Cautiously, not loading his plate with all that was before him on the sideboard, Boy came and edged himself into a chair. And silent, told himself to use a fork instead of his hands, and with each forkful not to grab the rolls before him, not to steal the fruit, not to stuff himself nor to eat more than one plateful, but to wait.

"More tells me you rode well this morning, that you have a fine seat to canter, but that you had difficulties remembering to rise in the trot," Dunphail observed matter-of-factly.

His mouth was crammed with gammon. More had knocked on his door at six and commanded that he dress himself and come out to ride. And now he could barely sit because of the saddle sores. Boy gulped down the half-chewed mouthful and nearly choked. "Yes, sir. Thank you, sir." His eyes were smarting.

"You must work on that. I shall expect a report of excellence by next week."

Boy coughed. "Yes, my lord."

Dunphail regarded him for a long moment, started to say something, then stopped and said instead, and not without a measure of kindness: "Well…I shall be off now. I assume you can read, so you may find something to interest you in the library. When…ehm…I return later this afternoon, I shall begin to teach you piquet…Lord Castlereagh has said he wishes you to attend some ton parties. And that is the only way I can see to effect the introduction…at card parties." He frowned.

Suppressing his coughs, barely able to breathe, Boy nodded and rose from his seat to bow. "Yes, sir. Thank you, sir."

At the door though, Dunphail paused, musing. "'Struth, I don't suppose you shoot, do you? For I dare say we could visit Manton's Gallery…"

"Not as well as Captain Shuster or Lord Castlereagh, no," Boy said. "I'm better with the knife."

Dunphail turned sharply, subjecting him to a long, reassessing look. The knife? "Just who in the devil are you?" he muttered.

Boy straightened, his jaw jutting forward. "I, sir?" he said with a smooth insolence. "I am my lord Castlereagh's boy." he pronounced, rancour making his voice gruff.

"'Sdeath, is that so?" Dunphail barked, his brows snapping together and his eyes raging. "Well, now, my lord Castlereagh's boy…" His nostrils had flared in anger. "In that world into which your lord wishes for you to gain entree, we don't sleep in our filth like damned French peasants. A daily bath is considered no more than the natural state of things here. We wear a fresh shirt every day. And at the very least, we change our shirts after exercise."

Leaving the door, Dunphail took a turn about him, raking him, inspecting him from all sides. "So tomorrow morning, when you return from your ride, young cocky, you will unlock your chamber door for long enough to allow the servants to fill your bath. You will also hand over your linen to be washed each day and your coat to be brushed. And when we go out together, my man, Frazer, will see to your cravat. For we appear at all times as gentlemen, not as unkempt snatch-gallows," he said. And with a final stinging glance, he sniffed, adding, "And if I am not much mistaken, your arse is bleeding through your breeches. Saddle sores, I expect. 'Struth, you should have said. I shall send Frazer along with the basilicum ointment…" before quitting the room.

Boy waited, standing alone and still, until he heard the front door shut, then blew out a huff of bored resignation. He frowned. Then returned to his breakfast. Or, more accurately, to a second helping of breakfast.

And by the end of the week, there was not a room nor a drawer nor a cabinet in the house which Boy had not examined and the secrets of which he did not know. Each day waiting until Dunphail had taken himself off, as he did after breakfast, and the servants were elsewhere employed.

But everywhere he found the same—rooms prepared for a life that was not, salons and antechambers exquisitely fitted and adorned for society's most illustrious. Paintings by Ramsay, Runciman and Allan.

Upper chambers where the shutters were never opened and the Holland covers but rarely lifted. And little to interest him. Little enough to interest anyone. The clothes left behind in the wardrobe of Dunphail's cousin, Hardy. An array of patterned and embroidered waistcoats there. In the secret compartment of Dunphail's desk, a packet of vowels on aging paper from a gamester who'd shot himself. In the Library, a folio of obscene cartoons of the Prince Regent and a small mechanical toy of Napoleon with the Empress—pressing the lever, Napoleon's sword arm and his cock popped up as the Empress's jaw dropped open and she fell to her knees before the tiny figure. He'd seen better in Prussia. Behind the mantel clock in Dunphail's chamber, a love letter, writ just a sennight since by a young woman, protesting at his abandonment of her. Meticulous, Boy returned it to its place.

And only in the music room did he pause, to stand alone before the fortepiano there. Though he did not touch it. Not even to smooth his hand over the polished surface of the rosewood case. He read the music on the nearby stand; and reading it, knew it. Yet each day he returned to linger there, gazing upon the instrument with its white roses painted on the lid and the marquetry medallions at each corner, still never permitting himself to touch it, listening to the quiet, and remembering the embers of a life long silent.

Each day too, so early there were only tradesmen about to observe if they chose, More rode out with him to one of the various parks—Green or Hyde or Regent's. And there, without witnesses, put him through his paces. Barking orders at him, commenting, correcting, encouraging, damning. And there, amid the undispersed morning mists and drizzle, spattered by hoof-flung mud, along paths both beaten and unused, as More led him on one run after another, teaching him to balance in his stirrups as he cantered, to ride forward, pushing him to race as they were not meant to—one hand tangled tight in the grey's long mane—Boy forgot all, all except that extended moment of pure exhilaration, of pounding hoofbeats and the rush of wind against his face, and his heart elated. Though there was none but the laconic More to see.

So too, each afternoon with Dunphail rapping out the rules of piquet, as Boy learned the terms, the calls, the points, the sequences and the tricks. How to shuffle, how to declare, how to feint. Committing it all to memory. Until after four days, he'd had his fill of Dunphail. Sullen, he waited, brooding, considering.

At last Dunphail dealt him a hand he could play. And then, observing from beneath his lashes the muted expressions of surprise as they skated across Dunphail's face, he played without quarter, declaring his sequence, scoring his points, then taking the tricks and scoring a pique. And went on to win the next three hands and thus the Partie. Which earned him a hard stare from his host and scant approbation.

By Sunday afternoon, he could bear it no longer. The house was empty of servants for the day. Dunphail off with friends. So he went to the fortepiano. And standing before it, told himself, just this once.

Gently he lifted the lid, tenderly he laid his fingers upon the keys. Mr. Hardy's fortepiano, it was. Not his. Never his. Except in this moment. Closing his eyes, he laid his ear near to the keys as did the Maestro, and with his thumb he pressed down the a. Just to hear its tone. To feel the reverberations against his cheek. Then he played too the f, e, d of the allegretto he loved. Then the left hand—d, a, d, f. And again.

He could hear the Maestro, "Do you feel it, mein Schatz? The rhythm? Listen. It is a horse, ja? Play it…so!" And that rusty, unfamiliar sound—his laughter. And playing it now, Boy knew that it was.

2

Barnet could hear no more than a few in the taproom as he descended with heavy footsteps the inn's narrow wooden staircase. Just three of them. Filling the waiting hours with an unlaboured drone of conversation, an easy murmuring of low voices tempered by the comfortable silences of long acquaintance.

Barnet ducked his head to avoid the doorhead and the blackened beams above and came and sat alone without the inglenook. Within it, before the fire, a wizened elderly man sucked at the end of a pipe. Across from him, sat a large man with a face like a reddened oyster, his arms folded across his chest. A tall oil lamp set on the bar gave off the only other light. Outside a strident wind was whipping in from off the

Channel. And there was no moon.

The innkeeper's daughter, a likely, buxom lass who went by the name of Tetty, filled a tankard and set it on the table before Barnet. "'Ow's th'young man, then?" she asked solemnly.

Barnet nodded his head upward. "What? Young Tom?" He took a long draw of ale, then wiped his mouth with the back of his hand. "Dunno," he admitted. "Sawbones says there's nought to do but wait." Two days and still Tom Ladyman had not waked and none could say if he ever would.

"Oh…" She drew the sound out over several syllables as they did in the country. "'tis a pity." She tilted her head to one side. It was the first time he'd left the Ladyman's bedside, the first chance she'd had to question him. "So you do know 'im, then."

"Tom? Yes." Barnet passed his hand over the smooth dome of his head. "Yes, I know him."

"Oh! We thought you was bein' a good Samarry-tan when you brung 'im in li' that. Tossed over your shoulder…Thought you'd found 'im…like t'others…"

Barnet hesitated. What others? But anxious to establish his credentials here, an incomer as he was, he let it pass. He would return to it later. "No, no" he said, adopting the softer speech of his younger days. "I've known Tom Ladyman since he was breeched." He slanted a glance at the two by the fire—Miss Tetty's protectors while her pa was from home.

"Oh! Then you're from farther down the coast, are ye?" she said, nodding as if this explained everything and had bought him a measure of trust.

"Aye," Barnet said, watching her. Watching the others.

"How far did you carry 'im then?" she probed with round eyes.

"Dunno. I would ha' carried 'im twice as far if'n I had to," Barnet said.

"Young Ladyman's not from 'round here neither," declared the elderly man with a sidledywry squint. He wheezed and coughed. "'E's from the Forest…but 'e's as fine a night rider as ever there was. Should ha' been a jockey for some fine lordling an' made hisself pots of money.

But not our Tom…He's a good lad is Tom. Rides over from Yapton when the Preventive officers is gettin' too big for theirsels." He cackled lewdly at the thought.

The other man nodded in approval. "Tha's right."

Barnet drank his ale. Suddenly he frowned. "D'you know if he was ridin' the black when he come out…Did he have his horse, Black Ben, with him, do you know?"

Miss Tetty shook her head.

"That's bad, that is," Barnet said.

"Aye," said the larger of the two men.

"D'ye reckon it was took by whoever done this to 'im?" she said, bristling with indignation.

"Dunno, Miss Tetty," said Barnet, regarding her openly with his pale lashless eyes. "But I reckon he'll not be happy when he wakes if that black's not waiting for him…"

The wheezy man gave another of his lewd cackles. "Big 'orse li' tha' might be out for a wander, you know…" he said wisely and winked. "What with there bein' no moon an' all these past few nights…" He spat and stopped to tap at his pipe. "But what brings you down 'ere to meet with Tom Ladyman?"

Barnet paused, weighing the question, considering also the answer he'd just been given. He sniffed hard and wiped his nose on his sleeve. "He said he had summat to tell me. So I went along, but he wasn't waiting where he said he'd be. So I went looking for him…"

"It's tha' Waley and 'is Frenchie 'amis'," exclaimed Miss Tetty. She brushed a sweaty wisp of hair from her cheek. "You mark my word, Mr. Barnet." Her fine bosom heaved and swelled with the injustice of it. "My pa don't let me go as far as the barn at night no more, because o' that lot. No, 'e does not!"

The large man nodded in affirmation. "Tha's right."

"Waley?" Barnet mused, narrowing his eyes. He smiled up into Miss Tetty's face. "Don't think I've 'eard of anyone called Waley. But how's he get Frenchies in past the Preventives?"

"'E 'as a boat, dudden 'e?" piped up the old boy, his face screwing up with vexation. "A big'un. Brings 'em in like that, dudden 'e? Not from

’round ’ere, ’e idn’t. Won tha’ house at a game o’ cards, dudden ’e?”

“Tha’s right, Skimble,” said his companion. “Tha’s right. Three year ago, it were,” he volunteered. “Offered ’is boat to our lads, ’e did. But they dudden take ’im up, did they? Didden like the cut o’ his jib, did they?” He nodded.

Skimble muttered something about ‘fancy Lonnon ways’ but Barnet couldn’t make out all the words. He gave his easiest, most open smile and rubbed at his shiny pate. “That were a fine swill o’ ale, Miss Tetty. Very fine indeed. Might I trouble you for another such?”

Miss Tetty dimpled and smiled coyly. “It’d be my pleasure, Mr. Barnet, sir.” She drew another tankard full, then came and set it before him. She tilted her head to one side. “Will you be sleepin’ on the truckle in wi’ young Tom again tonight?” she asked softly. “Or was you wanting me to make up another room for ye?”

Chapter XXVIII

1

"'Sdeath, did no one tell you about his memory, Dunphail?" Jesuadon said, his voice laden with boredom. He sat, slouched and with his legs, encased in soiled buckskins and unpolished boots, extended. At least he was clean.

Despite the comment, Dunphail's face was still marked with surprise. No one had told him anything much, it seemed.

They had been seated in Dunphail's library all afternoon—Dunphail, Captain Shuster, Jesuadon and young Tirrell—playing whist. Whist, about which the boy had professed to know nothing. And yet, in the space of so little time, with Jesuadon reciting the rules to him, he appeared to have mastered not only the rudiments, but much else besides.

"'Od's bawbles, stop being such a cod's head, Infant, you can't get it right every time," Jesuadon snapped. "They'll think you've marked the cards. You shall even need to lose…occasionally."

The look Boy darted him lacked its usual malevolence, but made up for it with rage. Still, reluctantly, he nodded. The perfection would not recur.

"Change places with Shuster, brat," Jesuadon ordered. "You need to learn to read Dunphail like you can read me."

Boy said nothing, but rose and did as he was bade. And played on.

Slowly, watching him all the time, Dunphail began to appreciate something of what Jesuadon had intimated. As directed, observing without ever appearing to do so, Boy marked how Dunphail arranged his hand, how the faintest expressions marked his face and told what cards he held and how he might play them.

At last, a hand finished, the scores nicely even, Jesuadon stood. "That's enough for today. We'll start again on the morrow…"

Georgie likewise had stood.

Jesuadon sketched an insolent bow in Dunphail's direction. "Dunphail. Georgie, do you come?" And left, followed by Captain Shuster.

Dunphail went and poured himself a brandy and drank it down. "That was finely played this evening, Boy," he commented.

"Thank you, sir."

Surprised still, and more than mildly impressed, Dunphail turned to regard the boy with a quizzical expression. "Who taught you to play so well?"

"You did, sir," Boy said levelly.

Dunphail smiled, amused by the unexpectedness of the certainly unintended compliment. "Did I so? And do you also play chess?" he asked. For the lad would be a fine player, a worthy opponent. Despite his dislike, even he could see that.

"Yes, sir. But I should prefer not to." His voice, his response, everything about him had turned wooden in the moments since Jesuadon had left.

Dunphail eyed the young face with curiosity. It presented to him a blank. As ever. "'Struth, why would that be?"

"I played it with my father," Boy said incisively. And proud, with a courteous bow, he made his exit.

Upstairs, alone in his bedchamber, with the door locked, tired, weary, his shoulder blades and neck aching beneath the squaring padding of his fine gentleman's coat and within the unyielding starch of his encasing high cravat, Boy sat, his back to the chair legs, his eyes shut against the fatigue, closed to the present, and drank from a bottle of Hollands. Drank. Drank against the knowledge of what he must do, what he had become and what must be. Drank, preparing himself. Until the room about him was a fine, soft blur, and he lay down before the fire, and holding himself close, he slept.

And so it was every day until the trap was laid.

2

Neither the clientele nor the premises of the Black Swan had altered in the six months since Jesuadon had last been there. Except perhaps that both now carried another impermeable layer of soot. The ceiling and panelled walls were as black as they ever were, the fug as impenetrable, the denizens as rank.

The hem of his greatcoat dragging in the sawdust and spittle of the floor, Jesuadon stretched as far back in his chair as he could with his eyes fixed on the splotches of tallowy, viscous damp which adorned the ceiling, and pondered nothing.

Without his asking, the landlord brought another bottle of claret and set it on the table before him, a companion to the others there. Jesuadon struggled to uprightness and poured himself a slopping glassful. And did not drink it. But rather placed and lifted and placed and lifted the glass, creating a pattern of wet rings on the marked and scarred table top. They gleamed bright, shining for an instant in the candlelight before they dried to a sticky dun.

About him, the noise was growing. The quarrelsome landlord was arguing but with no one in particular.

Jesuadon, leaning more closely over his wine, again lifted and placed the glass upon the mottled surface.

On a draught of spiteful rain, the door opened and was slammed shut, sputtering the candles on the tables.

Flushed crimson and sweating, Barnet pushed through the jostling, gabbing tide of drinkers spouting their views on the current Parliamentary elections. "'Slife, they prate and jabber 'round here…" He took his rain-laden hat from his head and tossed it on the table.

"Where in the blue blazes have you been, you skulking bell swagger?" Jesuadon said and did not look up.

Barnet blinked and wiped his hand over his head. He let out a great puff of air. "In Sussex. Where'd you think?" he answered, unmoved by the insult.

Jesuadon raised his eyes. "What the devil were you doing in Sussex?"

"Doing your bidding," Barnet said patiently. "You wanted Waley, did you not? Well, that's where he lives. Sussex. Near the coast, as it happens, with a great yacht moored there…"

Jesuadon straightened, his amber eyes sharp and clear. He was sober. "What?" He bit off the word.

Barnet signalled to the publican, who eventually came bearing a tankard of ale and a bottle. He pushed thruppence across the table which the publican scooped into his hand like a practised thief.

"There's more," Barnet added. It was nearly a taunt.

"Tell," Jesuadon commanded.

"It's John Brown," Barnet said softly, and swallowed down a mouthful of ale. "He's back in the country."

"What?" Jesuadon ground out. And suddenly he seemed ablaze in that darkening hole of a public house, hair, eyes, visage—all bright with a keening rage. "How the devil do you know?"

"I seen him, haven't I?" Barnet said smoothly. "Giving a basting to young Ladyman."

Like a draining, ebbing tide of light, the glittering fury seemed to slip from Jesuadon's very features. His breath had shallowed. "What," he said on an impotent outrush of air. "Red hell and bloody death, we're all dead men then," he murmured, shaking his head from side to side.

Barnet paused, watching as the images seeped into Jesuadon's intellect. "I don't see that. He's on the mend, Tom is," he murmured gently.

"He lives?" Jesuadon repeated.

"He lives," Barnet said. "Five more minutes though and he'd have been hushed."

"What happened?" Jesuadon demanded.

"I put a blue plum in Brown, didn't I?" Barnet said slyly and smiled, that smile so lately admired by Miss Tetty.

A threat of admiration had crept into Jesuadon's expression. "Did you, you unholy fuckster?" He glowed with incipient malicious pleasure.

"How very…"

"He's not dead. Just winged," Barnet said, cutting off Jesuadon's delight.

"Through and through?"

A corney-faced man, toothless and wobbling with drink, meandered close by and bumped into the table, jarring the wine and ale. Jesuadon raked him with a sour glare. He backed away, stumbling into a second table, and fell, upending the table. There was a rush of outraged babble.

Barnet shook his head. "Dunno. Might just be grazed. He did bellow though, so he did," he admitted with relish.

"Better and better…" Now Jesuadon did drink down his claret and poured himself another. "What else?"

"Waley. He brings the Frenchies in on that boat of his, the locals say. He probably ferries Brown back and forth, but I don't know for certain."

"I want that stopped," Jesuadon said succinctly.

Barnet gave a nod. "It will be. On my word," he said. He drank down his ale, savouring it as he ever did, first on the tongue, then in his cheeks, then the whole of it. "You don't want Shuster to have a word with him? Right. Scuttled then, ain't he?" He lowered his level gaze upon Jesuadon. "We don't want that bugger Wilmot running off before time…"

Jesuadon eyed him and did not speak. Pensive, he smoothed the back of his hand over his mouth. And said at last, "It's all been readied. We begin on the morrow."

Barnet narrowed his gaze and saw the anticipation, the feral excitement. "The boy?"

"He'll do. Dunphail's worked wonders. Or someone has. The pestilential brat is clean, barbered and looks and acts the gentlemen. Though Shuster says he has an arse full of saddle sores and can barely sit." Jesuadon poured himself a final glass of claret, emptying the bottle. "'Struth, you'd never know it though, watching him sit there, cool as you please, playing whist in Dunphail's library…"

Barnet let out a rumble of amusement. "If I had an arse full of saddle sores, I'd be blubbing like a girl."

"Not Castlereagh's boy," Jesuadon said dryly.

"No," Barnet agreed. Then, returning to his now-favourite subject, he lowered his voice. "So what's wrong with him then?"

"The boy? Who gives a whore's bottom?" Jesuadon said, dismissing the whole. "I assume it has to do with having seen his father hacked to death by the bastard Frenchies."

Barnet pursed up his face until it appeared to have been put through a mangle. "Is that what happened to him? I thought that was just some rum story the Guvnor cooked up."

"No, I fancy it's true," Jesuadon mused. "They chopped off his father's hands. And for all I know, beat the brat as well. Probably kicked his bawbles in."

"Poor bastard," Barnet murmured.

"Yes, he is a bit," Jesuadon conceded. "I've offered to take him wenching once or twice but he always declined, so I infer that's what happened." He thought and drank for a minute, then shrugged. "Though I dare say they may have raped him as well. Some of those sodomitical bastards got a taste for raping boys when they was in Egypt. Back in '98. Buggered the squeakers, then slit their throats…"

Barnet just looked. He drank down the last of his ale. He rubbed his pate and shook his head. "Is that why he does it then?"

Jesuadon had slipped back in his chair, stretching out his legs, and was again observing the blackened ceiling timbers, the liberal splashings of discolouring wax upon the walls. He appeared not to hear any of the obstreperous din rising on all sides of him. "Who knows why the boy does anything?"

Barnet slanted him an irritated glance. "So that's why he's not grown, then?"

"I dare say. It fits."

Barnet regarded his hat, drying on the table, and sniffed hard. "Then tomorrow he'll be happy…"

Chapter XXIX

1

They left the house just after breakfast, Dunphail and the young man.

Dunphail paused briefly to stand under the portico while Boy, dressed and shod like a gentleman, preceded him down the steps. Thence to walk in an easy silence and at a leisurely pace, tall bevor hats upon their heads, the tails of their long overcoats lapping at their heels like neaptide waves, down the length of Mount Street where overnight the late-falling leaves of the London planes had collected or now drifted. Past the other stone or brick houses of equally imposing character which belonged to the Upper Ten Thousand, but where, at such an hour, most were still about their toilettes. If Boy noted those placed to observe him, he gave no indication. To Grosvenor Street all the way to the corner of Davies Street. And pleasant, for November mornings can prove chill but welcome when the air is clear and the sky unfalling, they took their time as would two relations out for a morning's amusement. Tucked beneath Dunphail's arm within a lined rosewood box were his duelling pistols.

For today Dunphail was bringing Boy to Manton's Gallery to shoot. As one would. If one had a young, male relation come up to stay, even briefly, from the country. A male relation of whom one was fond.

Boy, his customary antipathy absent, followed Dunphail into the shop where the walls were glass cases displaying the owner's genius and handiwork—a king's ransom in firearms—the flintlock rifled shotguns that were known only as Mantons. Standing cases too contained the pairs of duelling pistols and smaller sidearms in their proper boxes, walnut and mahogany grips polished to a smoothness, simple or inlaid with silver or horn, engraved escutcheons and scrolled lock and trigger plates, their rods and powder flasks laid neatly beside them.

Against the rear wall, a wooden staircase led up to the Gallery with its targets and rows of wafers to be culped or not, where it was not yet crowded and there was still plenty of space for Dunphail and Boy at the farthest end of the long chamber.

But first: "Come and make your how-de-do's, Boy," Dunphail commanded as they strolled toward the stairs. "Manton, allow me to name m'young relation, Tirrell, to you. Boy, come make your bow. Manton is the finest gunsmith in England and he will always see you right, I give you my word on it…or he shall have me to answer to."

From behind his wooden counter, spread with the inner workings of a hair-trigger, all in pieces upon a cloth, Mr. Manton, the elder, began to chuckle, and shook his head. "My lord," he bowed. "That is high praise. And Mr. Tirrell, sir. I shall look forward to making as fine a gun for you as I did for his lordship. You shall need it—and with a good sight upon it—if he is to take you stalking, young sir."

"Sir." Boy bowed. "It is a great honour. Thank you."

"As to that," Manton said. "The honour is mine, young sir. But come along upstairs and let us see what you can do to a wafer…"

And so it began.

And there amid the bang and thunder of weapons discharging, with flash after sudden flash as flints were struck and sparked, igniting the powder, they stripped to their waistcoats and shirtsleeves. Their pistols primed, they fired off round after round, Dunphail and then the boy, until about them the air was flavoured with the salty reassuring scent of sulphur and saltpetre, and the powder had blacked their fingers and left streaks upon the white of their sleeves and cuffs.

Dunphail was a most respectable shot, and after an hour, there still was not a wafer which he had not culped.

But Boy was not, and had hit only the outmost rims of the targets present. If at all. And his arm now aching, and schooling himself to a patience he did not feel, he raised the pistol and stood. Essaying to aim but without practice. He tightened his hold on the weapon.

Behind him, Dunphail watched.

Then thoughtfully, a frown of concentration drawing his dark flyaway brows together, Dunphail came to stand against him. Leaning forward, extending his arm to place it alongside Boy's, his chest to Boy's back, he closed his hand over his and said, "Here. Like this."

Within Boy's smaller grasp, Dunphail tilted the gun onto its side. He rested his cheek rough against Boy's to take aim.

"It throws left, this pistol…" Dunphail said, one eye closed, the better to focus on the target.

"Now, look along the top of the barrel…Train your eye to the centre of the target. An' then raise it just a fraction above that…Are you there? Excellent…Now then…fire."

Within the steadiness of Dunphail's cool strong clasp, the pistol did not throw, but shot true. Against the wall, the target showed a hit to the inner circle.

Breathless, a smutch of gunpowder on his chin, Boy turned to Dunphail, his eyes bright with a new emotion. "I hit it, sir! I hit it!"

Dunphail smiled. The smile broadened out. "Aye, so you did. We'll come again tomorrow then, shall we? 'Struth, you'll do even better." Though his smile was praise enough.

Surprised and confused, pink with sudden pleasure, Boy said, "Yes, sir. Thank you, sir." And, for once, he meant it. And he almost smiled as he returned the gun to its case and reassembled the rods, rags and flask beside it.

"Manton," Dunphail called out as they descended once again into the showroom. "Manton, Tirrell is in want of a lighter pair. These are too heavy for him. Will you see to it?"

Joseph Manton stopped in his opening of a case for another customer. He looked up and over his shoulder. "Yes, my lord. I shall be pleased to look him out a lighter pair. When will you be wanting them?"

"On the morrow will be soon enough," Dunphail said, catching sight of the mistrust and astonishment playing across the boy's face.

"Very good, my lord. I shall have a selection ready for you when you come in. Good day to you, sirs."

And when they returned in the morning, after a walk which was a repetition of that first—quiet and without dissension though the air had sharpened overnight—a selection of smaller and lighter pistols lay upon the counter, awaiting Dunphail's inspection.

Bearing the several boxed pairs, a servant followed Dunphail and the boy up the stairs, then loaded and presented the flintlocks, one after another, first for Dunphail to try and then for the young sir. Eventually, after an hour of observing as Boy handled each pair, how they lay in his hand, how they fitted his arm as an extension of it, Dunphail chose for him a pair with walnut grips, inlaid with silver, and horn-tipped rods.

"Put 'em on the account, Parry," was all he said, which left Boy silent, caught by an awkward delight, an unsurpressable excitement, flustering amidst this welter of unfamiliar emotion and a want of words.

Daily then, streaks of black powder and oil smeared down the thighs of their pale breeches, on their waistcoats and upon their sleeves, the sounds of discharging guns booming and reverberating about them, Dunphail stood over him, pressed calm and warm and familiar behind him, instructing him as a marksman. Hour after hour, they stood together, Dunphail's arms about him, guiding his hands. To aim. To raise or lower his sight. To feel for the throw of that particular piece. Thigh against thigh, muscle against muscle, to stand, braced against the recoil. To gauge the tilt of the barrel for the straightest shot. To squeeze a still trigger. Gently praising him too when his aim proved true and the target was holed.

Then as each afternoon drew in and the fog rolled in from the river, creeping along the passages and lanes, muffling the city and all its life with a shroud of dank mist, they returned to the library, where Dunphail oversaw Boy's meticulous cleaning of the pistols. And when that was accomplished, they played at piquet so that Boy now observed the myriad courtesies as well as the rules.

Occasionally too, Dunphail remained in for dinner. And it was only after, when he had made his way out for the evening to call in at White's for a hand of whist and later to pay his nightly visit to the bordello on

Bury Street, that Boy returned to the sanctum of his chamber. And there sat before the fire, his arm about his knees which he had drawn up to his chin, his head against the chair wing. Breathing. Waiting for nothing, while the sudden frequent light from the torches of passing linkboys threw macabre shadows upon the ceiling. Breathing only. Staring into the flames and beyond. Warm. Fed.

Or, if he found the servants were long over their dinners and the house quiet, trailing his fingers along the smooth plaster of the unlit hallways, he would go to the music room and lift the lid of the fortepiano. And there in the uncandled and unquestioning darkness, he would sit and play. He had no need to see; he could hear.

When he was next in Vienna, the Maestro would be pleased.

2

By the following sennight of their visits to Manton's Gallery, Boy's aim had improved beyond telling, and everything about him now proclaimed his competence—his carriage, his handling of the weapons, the speed and assurance with which he now primed and reloaded. Even his bearing as he took aim. So much so that Dunphail began his tuition in the gentlemanly art of duelling. How to face an opponent, how to stand, how to hold the weapon in readiness against his collarbone, the barrel resting just away from his cheek, and thence to straighten his arm and hold it still, to find his mark and to fire. All without hesitation or flinching.

Watching carefully, his eyes measuring the holes in the target at the end of their lane, Dunphail suddenly called for it to be replaced with wafers. With a patient smile, Dunphail took up his position close behind the boy, their hands held together on the pistol's grip. Soft and strong, still, Boy squeezed the trigger, just as Dunphail had taught him. And fired. The smoke cleared, drifting off to the left.

The wafer. It was his first wafer, culped.

About them, the other gentlemen and Manton's menservants began to applaud and to call out, "Well hit, young sir. Well hit!"

Boy turned, looking up at Dunphail, giving him a glimpse of that fleeting half-smile, and for that brief instant, the void of emotion in his liquid eyes was absent and no longer filled only with wariness, rage and loss.

Approaching from down the room, Captain Shuster exclaimed, "God's garters, Dunphail! Upon my word, when I heard you was here with some infant, I took it for a cock and bull story." He laughed. "But here you are." A pair of shoes, their laces tied together, was draped over his shoulder. "Who's the bantling?"

Instantly, Boy had stepped back and lowering the pistol, executed a proper bow. "Sir."

Dunphail produced a lop-sided smile. "Ah Shuster. How d'you do? Didn't think to see you here so early in the day. Ha ha. 'Struth, I thought you was in Bath. Come and meet another relation." Blithely he looked about. "This is Tirrell. Here to stay with me for a while. Boy, this is one of your in-laws, Captain Sir George Shuster. Married to your…'Struth, I don't know what degree of cousin she is…" He chuckled again. "Lady Shuster. That'll do," he laughed.

Again Boy bowed. "Captain Shuster. A pleasure to make your acquaintance, sir."

Shuster bowed and casually eyed the young man over. "And yours. How long have you been here this morning? Finished now, are you? That's a dandy pair of pops you've got there…" He lifted one, and then its mate, inspecting them. He glanced up at the boy. "These cost someone a pretty penny. Dunphail give you these?" he said softly, raising an eyebrow. He relaid them in their case. "I say, Dunphail, you and Tirrell come join me at Angelo's, why don't you? I'm just off there now for a spot of sword play…"

"May we, sir?" Boy said, turning to Dunphail.

"Whyever not?" came Dunphail's genial reply. And with that, he noticed a certain kindling, again of an emotion he had not previously seen, in the depths of Boy's still eyes.

The three gentlemen made their way along Brook Street to Bond Street, but their progress was slow. For with the later hour, the streets were cluttered with carriages and horsemen, the pavements busy with pedestrians, many of whom were acquaintances who must be greeted, who had not yet offered their congratulations to Captain Shuster on the occasion of his marriage and to whom Boy must needs be introduced.

Henry Angelo's Fencing Academy on Bond Street stood immediately next door to Jackson's Boxing Saloon. And standing aside to allow Georgie and Boy to precede him through the door, Dunphail held back, suddenly remembering the boy as he had first encountered him—his face bloodied and bruised, unrecognisable, his clothes ragged. No one and nothing in the middle of nowhere. Glancing up at the facade of Jackson's hallowed premises, he wondered if it had been here that Boy had been coached in taking those blows as he had, here where he had learned to survive the battering which should surely have killed him. He shook his head—he disliked conundrums—and followed Boy and Shuster inside.

Upon the perimeter walls of the large elegant chamber with its high, vaulted ceiling, rows of foils hung in racks, with further racks fitted into the several arched recesses of the salon. A pair of crossed foils hung in a place of honour on one pale wall, a pair of padded fencing gloves dangled from the same peg, while from high upon the other walls, portraits of the finest swordsmen of the last century gazed down. Set at an angle was a long bench, the repository for unwanted coats and hats. And throughout the room, pairs of gentlemen in short padded military jackets, wearing soft shoes, practised their fencing. Like the streets, the room was crowded with gentlemen, some there only to watch, some stripped to their shirtsleeves eager for a bout, and others just idling in their coats and with their hats still perched atop their heads.

Upon seeing Captain Shuster, a man of imposing height in a white asymmetrically buttoned jacket, grey-haired, with a fleshy face and a significant nose, disengaged from a pair he was coaching and came bustling toward them. They were expected. Or at least, Captain Shuster was.

"Captain Shuster, there you are, sir. I shall be ready for you as soon as you have changed." It was Sr. Angelo himself, the finest swordsman in all Europe, so they said.

"Angelo, m'dear fellow," Georgie laughed and bowed. "Excellent to see you, sir, at last."

Angelo clapped Captain Shuster on the shoulder. "It has been too long, Captain. Far too long! I heard tell of your injuries, of course, and trust you are well on the road to recovery. But I give you fair warning, I am determined I shall play my part in getting you fit again."

Georgie laughed. "That's all very well, Angelo. But don't go telling Wellington, will you? I shouldn't like to pack up just now…you know Dunphail, do you? Now my cousin by marriage…" His eyes sparkled wry with the happiness of it.

"And yes, I heard you was recently wed. That's fencing of a different kind, Captain…" Angelo teased, nodding. "My lord." He bowed.

Dunphail inclined his head. "And m'young relation, Angelo, Tirrell. Boy? 'Struth, where have you got to?"

"Oh yes, Angelo," Georgie interjected. "Young Tirrell here has thoughts of the army. Been practising his exercises in secret, I've no doubt. Shall we give him a go?" Georgie said, a strange glitter in his eyes. "Have you a jacket and shoes for him somewhere, do you think?"

Boy stepped forward and bowed.

But his sombre, still expression did not alter, and Dunphail could detect none of his thoughts. He had made his bow, certainly; Monsieur Henry Angelo was known as much for his strict adherence to courtesy as he was for his genius with the sword. Yet something in his manner betrayed that Boy had anticipated none of this morning's events.

A buff-coloured, padded jacket of an appropriate size was found, left by a young man who had gone to the Peninsula as an ensign, as were his shoes. Withdrawing in some disbelief to a corner of the chamber, Boy stripped to his shirt and buttoned himself into the double-breasted jacket. Then laced the shoes on. And came forward to face Georgie, who like him, was now dressed for a bout of fencing.

"You are familiar with the exercises, are you, young sir?" Sr. Angelo asked.

Boy bowed. "Yes, sir. Thank you, sir." His face cleared. "From the First Lesson, sir. Cut at Antagonist's Head. Guard your own. Cut at Antagonist's Leg. Guard your head," he recited.

Angelo's face creased into a smile. "You will do well. Now let me see you. Where is a foil? Captain Shuster, you shall be the Antagonist…"

Another of Angelo's buff-jacketed assistants brought forward a choice of swords and presented them to his master. Angelo took each in hand, testing them, measuring the weight of each, before he gave one to Captain Shuster and the other to the young man.

"Gentlemen. Salute," he said stepping back and away.

It had been clear that never having learned nor having the capacity to carry a firearm with all its paraphernalia, Boy had known nothing of pistols nor shooting. Except to avoid it. Yet now, his sword held still and aloft before his face and then brought to rest against his shoulder, Dunphail knew of a certainty that Boy possessed a long acquaintance with steel and equally that this was not the first time he had faced another in friendly combat. He saw too what he had not before seen in Shuster's eyes, a deadliness of intent. Saw it was present in Boy's eyes as well. Somewhere, someone had coached him thoroughly in the art and science of the sabre. Had taught him all the courtesies of Angelo's Exercises. And having been taught, he had practised.

Boy tucked his left arm behind his back, stilled, and waited. And then he was cutting at Georgie's head, defending his own, slashing at Georgie's leg and again guarding his head. And the air was sharpened with the shrieking clang and scrape of steel on steel, and Dunphail wondered if this was indeed an exercise at all.

Like a censorious goshawk, his dark brows in constant motion, Sr. Angelo watched them as they performed each step of the First Lesson, repeated it, and then the Second. Pacing about them, he peered at the boy's footwork, scrutinised the movements of his wrist, the extension of Shuster's arm, Boy's cuts at Shuster's head and leg and his guarding of his own.

His cheeks flushed with exertion, tricklings of sweat slid unsteadily from the boy's temple. He cut at Georgie's ribs.

A beading of moisture appeared on Shuster's brow and upper lip too.

Inserting his Master's stick between their two swords, Angelo raised it to separate them. He pursed his full lips. "Respectable," he pronounced. "Considering…" He nodded thoughtfully. "Mr. Tirrell, though he lacks the Captain's height, does well with the sabre. Come tomorrow and we shall begin again."

Their breathing shallowed, both combatants raised the swords in salute, then swept them to their sides and bowed.

Georgie bowed. "A thousand pardons, Angelo, but I am promised to my wife on the morrow." His eyes creased at the corners. "But if I may, on the day after?"

Angelo nodded. "Yes, that will be better, Captain. For you will be aching in the morning, I make no doubt. Until then, gentlemen…"

Georgie's eyes glistened. "And may we have a bout, sir? A proper bout?" His eyes were alight with anticipation.

Sr. Angelo leaned back upon his heels. Momentarily, he considered the boy they called Tirrell. "Yes, Captain, why not? To be sure, he is young and lacks your reach, but you are all to pieces and wholly bent out of shape."

Dunphail, having just taken a pinch of snuff, spluttered and choked, his eyes stinging as he suppressed a laugh.

Georgie cast him a sparkling glance. "'Pon my word, you are in the right of it, sir," he admitted to the master. "Thank you."

And when eventually they emerged into the street, the Captain, still grinning, to continue his afternoon's undertakings and Dunphail and the boy to return home, they found over the walkway to be a canopy of raised umbrellas. For it had come on to rain.

Chapter XXX

1

Doused in a weakling fragile light, more dusk than dawn, the hall was still, and silent, but for the distant clatter of crockery which rose from the kitchen and the low voices of the servants. Half-awake, stuffing his arm into his coat sleeve and rubbing the sleep from his eye, Boy lolloped down the stairs on his way to meet More for their early morning ride. And yawning, he stopped. Someone was there. Below.

The russet hair, darker in the mauve grey shadows, the height, the shoulders, were Dunphail's. He was dressed for riding, his crop in hand.

Dunphail turned, looking up. And sensing the unspoken questions that would skitter across the planes of the boy's face even as he thought them, he said easily, "I've a mind to see you throw a knife. If indeed that is what you meant by being better with a knife…"

"What? Now?"

"Yes. Now," Dunphail said, unaffronted by the sudden surly lack of yessirs.

Boy stared at Dunphail through the dull and dim light of the unlit hall. His handsome Scots face, his dress as pristine as ever, his riding coat pressed, his cravat tall and starched and proper, his boots polished and clean. His overcoat lay across the chair. "You mean you want me to bring a knife? Now?" Boy said, his tone insolent.

"Aye," Dunphail nodded. "Fetch it down."

"What, now?" Boy demanded again, disguising neither his distrust nor his scorn.

"'Struth, you are a plaguey saucebox," Dunphail replied pleasantly. "Yes, now. And get your hat."

"Oh," Boy said at last. He shook his head, attempting to shift the vestiges of early morning doziness. "All right," he mumbled. And his shoulders dropping, he turned to trudge back up the way he'd come to his bedchamber, and returned a few minutes later, hatless.

He was muttering under his breath.

"Have you got it then?" Dunphail asked, still patient.

"What?" Boy directed an odd glance at him. "The knives? Yes…Yes," he repeated, coming to himself.

In the stable mews, More was waiting for them with three horses. His usual bay hack, the flea-bitten grey Boy rode and a great tall bay hunter for Dunphail. Mist hung still in the wet and heavy morning air and the only sounds were those of the animals, their breath as plumes of sudden fog as they snorted and stamped upon the wet cobbles.

Above, a pair of pigeons flapped noisily amid the first drifts of smoke from the kitchen fire which spilled from the chimney stack and vanished.

The Park was empty of few but themselves. Trotting, Dunphail led the way down along the side of the rutted tracks that lay beside the Serpentine. Then, the way ahead clear, he broke into a steady canter.

Gathering in his reins, Boy followed on, a length behind, with the watchful More bringing up the rear. The grey lengthened his stride. And then they were cantering, rushing into the cold embrace of early morning. Running. Without slackening, without checking, forgetting all but the moment, the feel of each horse's power, the strength and untamable desire to run. Running swift, cratering the earth with the steady rhythm of beating hooves, mud and turf flying to spatter all in their wake.

Exhilarated, breathless, the boy smiled. A handful of raindrops pecked at his cheeks.

Without warning, Dunphail veered off onto an unfrequented path. Staying close, Boy leaned a fraction this way, a fraction that, as the path zigzagged through the trees. And riding low upon the horses' necks, dodging the overhanging branches and brambles, their paces matching stride for stride, horse-hearts and lungs hard-thumping, speeding, slowing, their necks extended, they carried on until they reached a small clearing, where Dunphail pulled up. Patting the bay, he dismounted.

Flushed with pleasure, Boy came up alongside, and like him, dismounted and gave his reins into More's keeping.

Heavy dew lay upon the long grass. Putting their heads to earth, the horses rubbed their chins at their forelegs and then began to graze. In the trees, those birds too foolish to flee, twittered and clucked. Still, Boy stood and listened.

"I've never been here before," he remarked, looking about, recording it all, the trees and the distances between them, the sounds. His buckskin breeches were flecked with mudsplash.

Dunphail gave a careless smile. "Aye well, you should bear it in mind. 'Slife, it's a fine quiet spot for a kiss and a fumble." Idly, he pulled a sugar lump from his pocket and fed it to his horse, stroking his cheek.

Discomfited by the unexpected intimacy, Boy stared at his boot. Then, without reference to Dunphail, he raised his head to stand, alert, listening. And searching out a spot among the trunks of the oak and elm and ash, he drew a pair of wafers from his pocket and went to lodge them within the folds of an oak's bark. Overhead the sky was a mottled mass of lightening grey; it would not rain till later. His shoulders squaring, Boy walked away until he was halfway across the clearing.

He turned, easing his hand along his waistband to the lacing at the back of his breeches.

"On your word, my lord." There was nothing of the boy about him now.

Noting the sharpness about him and how the unspoken pleasure of even a moment ago had wholly dissipated, Dunphail waited, his eye fixed expectantly upon him. "Now."

He did not see the throw. Dunphail saw only a rapid movement, the brief disturbance in Boy's clothes, not the throw nor the arc of the knife as it flew. Only a bright rapid flash of something. He heard the thwack and looked. The knife was stuck hard into the tree trunk, the paper wafer sliced in two.

Boy remained where he was, his chin lowered and his eyes darkened, an unstalked wary elegance about him. Without Dunphail's even noticing, he reached for the second knife and threw. Like the first, it landed with a thunk, splicing the wafer in half.

Dunphail had seen nothing. Catching his breath, blinking and amazed, he studied the tree with the knife handles protruding, one atop the other. Boy appeared not to have moved.

"'Struth, you could kill someone like that," Dunphail said with a deceptive mildness.

"Yes," Boy agreed. And with that fluid, effortless gait, the athlete aware of his own skill and grace, he went to pull the knives from the tree and return them to his waist. "So I've been told."

And for the second time in as many days, Dunphail recalled their first meeting, and he narrowed his eyes with new respect. "Show me again," he said.

Boy threw twice more, while Dunphail stood, his whip in hand, watching, still and motionless, seeking to understand, to comprehend.

Boy withdrew the knives from the tree for the final time and came to stand beside him.

"My cousin, Hardy…he played his violin the way you throw the knife," Dunphail observed in a distant voice. "With a single-minded devotion to it. I always admired that in him."

Boy paused to glance up at the muddling sky. "You speak as though he's dead, sir," he said at last.

"Do I?" Dunphail gave a weak laugh, and sobered. "'Struth, he might as well be…no one has heard from him for six months. Not since he left." He frowned suddenly. Then gave another mirthless laugh. "Do you suppose, or would it be too much to ask, could you stop calling me 'sir' all the time. Upon my word, it makes me sound like a damned schoolmaster," he complained.

Boy slanted a glance at him.

"Dunphail," Dunphail enunciated, turning to stare him down. "'Struth, it can't be that difficult. Even the lowest crofter can manage it. Though usually with some mete epithet, I've no doubt."

"Dunphail…sir." He was tossing one of his knives up in the air and catching it by the handle, idly, much as any other boy would toss a ball.

"God's bawbles, I should cuff you hard!" Dunphail muttered, his genial smile beginning as he raised his hand as if to administer the mocked discipline. "…But you'd probably knife me, so I'll not risk it. Not today."

Boy caught the knife and held it. There was a glimmer of something, of humour or the appreciation of it, just for an instant in his steady gaze. He clamped shut his mouth. "I wouldn't," he protested.

"Aye, you would," Dunphail said, both unflinching and patient. "If Castlereagh told you to do it, you would. If you thought me the traitor, you would." He smiled, dispelling the tension. "Come, we'd best get back. Shuster's keen as mustard to administer a pinking to you today, and you won't want to be late for that…"

"I'll pink him," Boy scoffed.

With More still at the bay's head, Dunphail collected up his reins, slipped his foot in the stirrup and pulled himself back into the saddle. He grinned broadly. "Aye. See that you do, lad. I've put money on it."

Boy mounted and settled, then as More remounted behind them, said, with a rare earnestness, "Might you be willing to teach me to shoot…a rifle?" His expression was wary.

Dunphail smiled. "Aye. You'd stalk well," he approved. "But we'll want to go home for that…'Struth, there's a neat little fourteen-bore at Manton's. I've had my eye on it for several days now. We'll have a look later, see how it handles…To be sure, we can go up next month, if you like."

2

The salon at Angelo's was not so crowded when they arrived as when they had first visited. Coming up behind Dunphail, Boy stood in the doorway, regarding it all with silent eyes. A window had been thrown open to admit the rushing bouts of wind. Slipping from Dunphail's side, he went to the corner and there began to change into fencing jacket and shoes. Captain Shuster had not yet appeared. Dunphail drifted off to wander between the other bouts taking place near the centre of the room, watching each with unequal measures of interest and idle curiosity.

Eventually, damp from a burst of clouting rain, Shuster came in, laughing, his younger brother in attendance. And with them, a collection of Harry's friends, bloods all of them, all laughing and not a little drunk. Someone's tongue had been very busy.

"'Struth, so where's this promising youngster of yours, Dunphail?" said a tall, blond man. His hat was tipped back on his head like a schoolboy's. "His blood's up, is it? For I've laid a pony on him to pink…"

Dunphail turned, amusement etched in the smile lines about his eyes. "Pem." He nodded in the boy's direction. "He's there. And I've laid on rather more…"

"I know. That's why I did it." Pemberton said, eyeing the slim figure flexing the fingers of his black glove, checking the straps on his leather wrist guard. "You're bamming me, Dunphail. 'Slife, he's going to take on Georgie Shuster?" he demanded.

Dunphail nodded. It had seemed as nothing when Georgie proposed it. "Yes."

Pemberton looked the young man over a second time, straining to see what could have so impressed Dunphail. "But taking on Georgie…?"

Dunphail shrugged.

Making his apologies for his tardiness to Sr. Angelo, Shuster too went to button himself into his padded practice jacket and to change his boots for shoes. He joined Boy in his corner. "All right, bantling?" he said by way of a greeting.

"Captain Shuster." Boy bowed politely.

Georgie looked him over. "'Struth, you're looking well, you know," he observed casually. "What's Dunphail been doing to you? Feeding you?" He ignored Boy's sudden bristling. "He'll have to put a stop to that though. You'll be needing another trip to the tailor if he don't."

Sr. Angelo brought forward an armful of weapons—all light sabres, they were. Offering the choice first to Boy, he waited while he held and weighed first one and then another and finally chose a third. Turning to Captain Shuster, he said, "And now you, my good Captain…."

Together they went to the centre of the floor.

"I trust you both know the rules of engagement here. You will adhere strictly to the Lessons, in order, step by step, and any drawing of blood will signal the end of the bout. Are you in agreement? Gentlemen…"

They stood as they had two days since, the one tall and dark, the other slight, hardly more than a boy, paly dressed both among the milling sea of sombre-coloured coats. Raising their blades, they held them before their faces to present, then placed them upon their shoulders. There was an instant of hush.

Boy stilled. Though none but Dunphail saw it. Saw in that brief minim, the blankness encroaching, replacing all else in him. Leaving only the fierce wisdom. The savage duty.

His feet planted, Boy tucked his arm behind his back and raised his sword arm, pointing the tip of his blade at Georgie's foot. Shuster did the same. And their swords held and crossed for that brief instant, it began.

The First Lesson.

As before, Boy cut at Georgie's head and fell back to guard his own. Sliced at Georgie's leg, then stepped back to guard his head. And again. Through the Lessons, just as they had two days previous. And then again. Only now, now, it was no more a lesson nor a sequence of steps, but a whole, and all performed faster and faster, the sabre blades slashing, cutting, guarding, defending.

From the outset it was clear the boy lacked the strength and polish of Captain Shuster. Which was not unexpected. Shuster was a professional soldier of honour, distinction and reputation, a captain and A.D.C. to their Commander in the Peninsula. Shuster had the advantage of at least half a head in height too. But what the boy lacked of those, he possessed in agility and deftness of wrist, and a lionine passion such as Dunphail had not before witnessed.

It was no practice bout. The crowd of onlookers had swelled.

And their footsteps thudding across the floorboards, their sabres crossing and cutting, the blades clanging, slashing at such a rate, none but Angelo or the finer swordsmen among them might have discerned much of the movements.

Behind Dunphail, two hatted gentlemen were wagering on the

outcome. "I'll give you odds on the younger one...the bantling…a little fire-eater, ain't he…?"

Across the distance of the room, Dunphail saw Jesuadon stroll in from the street, drinking. And with him another. Wilmot, it was.

"Your cousin, ain't he, Dunphail? The lad?" someone said.

"Yes…yes, he is…" Dunphail agreed, unable to look away, his insides clenching with an intensity of will, as if by sheer force of mind he might drive the boy forward, strengthen his purpose.

"Ought to buy him a pair of colours is what you ought to do. Rides as well as he fights, does he?"

"What? Oh, yes, so he does," Dunphail said absently. "Like a centaur…"

Boy was playing, parrying with quick turns of his wrist. His face set in rigid concentration, he sought to press home his advantage of speed and intellect and Shuster's long convalescence, with slashes to the head, first from the right, then with a quick twist from the left, his blade flashing in a sudden stream of sunlight. And again.

Shuster, with his greater strength, guarded his head. Slashed and turned, parried, defended, cutting at the ribs. The Boy slashed again, the blade passing just inches from Shuster's face, nose to chin.

About them, gentlemen were cheering each cut, each deflect, stamping their feet, shouting wagers to each other, encouragement to the boy and to Georgie.

"Well, that's it then…A cavalry regiment! He'll be a credit to you, my lord…"

Dunphail nodded, paying no heed. "Yes, yes, I'll think about it…"

Georgie, roused, determined, his expression hardening, counter-attacked on the outside with fierce leg cut, beating the boy back and back. Cut, cut, parry, twist, and feint.

Moving like windswept wheat, away then toward, the crowd gave place as Shuster and the boy progressed and fell back.

Shuster was beginning to tire. They both were. And still they fought, still the brash tocsin of clanging, grating metal continued.

But Boy was back on the attack, and with a display of lightning speed and skill, he drove Shuster hard onto his back foot.

Sweat stained the grip of their gloves, had wetted their hair, shone glistening upon their faces, and soaked their stockings so that they clung tight to their muscled calves.

Rapt, the crowd were silent.

Driving, slashing, their blades ringing, Boy feinted, parried, side stepped and with a riposte slashed his sabre across Georgie's shoulder. The fabric of his jacket gaped open.

"A hit, dammit!" shouted Harry. "A pink!"

"A hit! A hit!" The cry went up like a baying of hounds.

Dunphail brightened, delighted and laughing at the sheer daring of it.

Astonished, Georgie glared at the boy.

This should have been finished minutes ago.

But Shuster had spent all those long weeks with the army in winter quarters in Portugal, where they'd nothing to do but hunt and fight each other. His breathing harsh in his throat, he surged forward again to beat the boy back as he defended. Still Georgie pushed on in an unrelenting drive, keeping his arm tight and neat, counter-attacking on the outside. Then, with a sudden off-hand parry, he slashed upward, snicking the boy's jaw.

The crowd gasped.

Angelo inserted his stick, driving their blades upward and apart.

Breathing hard, they stood back.

It was over.

Boy reached up to feel his chin, swiping at the stripe of blood there. Still panting, he bowed. "Captain." Blood was slipping down to form a red edging upon his collar. Boy raised his blade to present once more.

Georgie saluted, then bowed as well, first to Boy and then to Sr. Angelo.

The courtesies observed, a roar of approval went up.

Then the crowd were surrounding Boy and Shuster, clapping them enthusiastically on their shoulders and backs, shaking their hands, congratulating them. Jostling them, drinking, laughing. There was no need for introductions. Tirrell was known to them all now.

Amidst the press, Jesuadon passed close by to say softly, "That was well done, runt. You've captured his attention…" He raised his bottle and drank.

Dunphail came up, and draping his arm over Boy's shoulder, handed him first his handkerchief, then a flask of brandy. Harry approached, laughing, and swearing he too would have a bout. Though not today, for he was too drunk.

Finally, accompanying Boy out into the driving rain, his arm as ever about him, Dunphail felt the exhausted drain and droop of the shoulders beneath his hand. Glancing at the sky, he hailed a hackney carriage to convey them home.

Settling into the stinking cab, the handkerchief held to his chin, Boy drank from the flask again. He closed his eyes briefly.

Dunphail leaned back against the squabs and groped in his pocket for his snuffbox.

"On my word, that was, ah, a very pretty piece of swordplay back there," he commented and sniffed hard on the grains of snuff. "Where did you learn that?"

Boy held the handkerchief away to inspect it. "In Prussia, mostly," he said. "A bit in France. But not so much." He refolded the handkerchief and daubed at his chin again, then rechecked it for a sign that his bleeding was lessening. "Was it enough?"

Dunphail beamed his satisfaction. And contemplating the perennial vacillation of pleasure and suspicion writ at the backs of the boy's eyes, as if he had no knowledge of the former and dared not trust it, Dunphail said, "Oh, aye. Aye. 'Struth, you did me proud. You did me damned proud."

A spectre of a smile appeared, pulling at the corners of his boy's mouth. With a wry screwing up of his face, almost like the lad he was, he admitted, "To be fair, I'd never have got that near if the Captain'd had two swords, as he likes…"

"Ah…" Dunphail took the flask back and drained the contents. "Would you not?"

Boy shook his head. "No. No," he admitted. "Shuster don't do much fighting any more, I don't think. Not now."

"Oh," Dunphail said, uncertain what to make of this newfound loquacity. "Why's that, then?" he enquired.

Boy shrugged, his face paling with the onset of fatigue. "Well, he was wounded, wasn't he? And now, he's Wellington's interrogator, ain't he? Doesn't get much chance, I shouldn't have thought…" He turned to peer through the new fall of rain.

Dunphail waited. Then: "I'll set Frazer to heat the water for you when we get home," he said. "And after a bath, you should go to bed."

3

It was gone midnight when Dunphail emerged, unsatisfied, from the house on Bury Street. The rain had eased to a heavy mist which glutted the sky. Just coming up the walk, within the dispersing light of the torches on either side of the door, were Jesuadon and his companion of the afternoon, that prinking fellow, Wilmot.

"Dunphail," Jesuadon slurred. "Well met. Left any diddling for Wilmot here, have ye?" He steadied himself with his hand upon the iron railing of the house next door.

Wilmot giggled foolishly, his feet weaving beneath him.

"A few, a few…" Dunphail said, not liking himself.

"That bantam cockie of yours, Dunphail…whatshisname?" Jesuadon began. He took a deep drink from his bottle. He smelled foul, like he bathed in stale claret. "Does he do anythin' besides fight, eh?"

Wilmot straightened. "Yes, yes…" he belched. "What else does the dear young fellow do?"

Dunphail affected to smile. "He, ah, plays piquet rather well…"

"Well, God's balls, man," exclaimed Wilmot, forgetting himself. "Damn and blast, why d'you not bring him out gaming then, eh?"

"A bit young for the hells, ain't he, Wilmot?" Jesuadon declared. The bottle dangled from his fingers, then dropped, chinking onto the front step. He turned and flicking back the fronts of his coat, bent over to vomit in the road.

"Oh! Oh, is he?" Wilmot questioned. "Well then…well then…I tell you what I shall do. I shall hold a private card party. Invite Byron and Waley and all the fellows. And I shall send you and your boy an invite too, Dunphail, that is what I shall do…"

"A private party? 'Struth, I can see no objection to that," said Dunphail, the skin tightening across his cheekbones. His stomach tightened to match. "No indeed. No harm at all. Excellent. Aye, that would be well..." He inclined his head. "I shall bid you good night, then, gentlemen. Wilmot. Jesuadon."

Chapter XXXI

1

More did not come early to wake the boy in the morning. But let him sleep.

And as autumn deepened into winter and none or few of the yellow leaves remained clinging to the trees like orphans to that one place they know, Boy's days took on this new pattern. As the sun rose later and later, so did he. Then, in the privacy of his locked chamber, he bathed and dressed.

Then to breakfast with Dunphail, and with him to spend the remainder of the morning shooting wafers at Manton's, being guided and affably chided.

"'Struth, there are books in the library…can you not read?"

"Yes, I can read, sir. German and French. As well as English. Sir."

"So whom have you read then?"

"Goethe. Laclos. Voltaire. Mme de Staël." Boy shook his head.

Dunphail rolled his eyes. "Christ's baby ballocks, child, 'tis no wonder you don't like books, if that's the pap you've been reading. Lord love you. Have a look at *Joseph Andrews*. You'll enjoy it. And when you've finished that, there's Smollett. And Scott…" He affected to look ill. "De Staël? Grief, you'd do better with Monk Lewis."

And having seen that he might be taken to the Park and displayed with pride, most afternoons he rode with Dunphail, together racing over the thickening ground on oft-ignored paths through the trees. Or occasionally, faced him for an amicable bout of sword-play at Sr. Angelo's when the burdened clouds unloosed their wretched wares or, like a basting of wheat paste, the fog lay thick over the city turning the day to waking night. All as if he were a gentry boy and had never felt the defacing cold upon his cheeks and hands as he ran the breadth of Europe, or as those boys who now stood, alone and watchful, outside Dunphail's house to guard him in his duty.

The invitation to the proposed—the designed—card party, hosted by Wilmot, did not arrive for several days.

When finally it did arrive, Boy held it, turning the ivory board over and over in his hand. That evening, instead of making his way to the fortepiano once Dunphail had left for the theatre and his club, he drank himself to sleep, readying himself for that which could not be avoided.

New clothes for him to wear had arrived only a day earlier. The evening clothes of a young gentleman, they were. Pantaloons of black, knitted of silk, a fine twill waistcoat, and a dark blue coat with gold buttons, well-cut, and with hidden pockets, easier to reach, in the back panels, just above the waist.

2

Carved out of the depths of Sparrowhawk's cellars, lying far beneath the street, windowless and dank, it was a room within a room. Reached only by a passage within a passage. A place of unbroken murk with only the distant lapping of a nearby underground stream to intrude upon the steeping cold silence. A place known only to Sparrowhawk and his Molly and to one other. A strong room for the strong spirits which had not nor never would see the stamp of an Exciseman upon them.

Holding a lantern aloft, peering beyond it into a blackness as thick as slurry, his other hand upon the stone wall, Barnet edged his way down the roughened plank steps. "Thos?"

"Bolt the door behind you."

At the centre of the room, surrounded by the walls against which the kegs of Hollands, Porter and French brandy were stacked upon broken cobblestones and from thence to the ceiling, was a small table with an open ledger upon it. Beside it, his red-gold hair haloed by the light of three thick candles, as undrunk as a person could be, sat Jesuadon, the image of a sullen, festering rage.

"You've been long enough getting here," he muttered. "Is everything in place?"

Groping his way toward the table, Barnet placed his hand into the deep funnel of an ancient cobweb and hastily withdrew it, wiping it back and forth on his leg. He grimaced, then sat down heavily upon the remaining three-legged stool to regard Jesuadon without concern. "I don't know why you're so bothered, for there's no cause as I see it. The boy's done this a hundred times before," he said dismissing the whole.

Jesuadon threw down the quill with which he had been totting up the lines of figures in the ledger. "No. No, he has not," he snapped. "That boy is a master of breaking into empty buildings in places that have been emptied of their menfolk by that crab-faced little Corsican turd. Houses with few servants, in countries where no one knows him or has ever seen his plaguey slipgibbet face before. He has never—never—broken into someone's desk when there is a party of a dozen or more in the next room, all in plain sight, all of whom know his name and where he lives. By God, it is the most damnably bubble-headed plan ever conceived! Any one thing could happen and it will be a infernal catastrophe. And then there will be Hell and all its angels to pay."

Having listened, Barnet rubbed his hand over his mouth, then blew out a breath. "But his lordship…"

Jesuadon swore. "Red hell and bloody death, Barnet! The Guvnor in his infernal folly thinks that brat is some kind of Circus conjurer who can magick up the contents of a ledger with a snap of his fingers. Like playing cards from the air. And that ain't how it happens! The Guvnor knows nothing! Absolutely nothing."

Barnet paused, waiting to see if there was more. He scratched his head. "So…what do you want me to do?" He disliked the muffling, enclosing silence of the cellar room.

Jesuadon pulled a bottle from his pocket, set it hard on the table, uncorked it, and drank. "I want you there. Outside. With a couple of bands of cutthroats, one front and one back."

Regarding him steadily through the gloom, unblinking, Barnet saw that Jesuadon's expression had grown still uglier.

"I want you ready to storm the house. On my signal. At my nod, I want you to throw a brick through the window. And if that don't cause a rumpus, bung another. And another after that. And the instant any of them sets a foot outside the house, I want an almighty set-to. And leave me to get the boy out. D'you understand?" Jesuadon's jaw was flexing with anger.

Barnet shifted his weight uneasily on the stool. "This is in Chesterfield Street, Thos," he protested softly. The still air made his words fall like damp leaves. "Chesterfield Street. It ain't the Rookery… How am I meant to…"

His jaw still working, Jesuadon said, "I'll see to it that Flint keeps the militia as far away as possible. As for the Watch, they don't matter. That piss-insolent brat is all that matters." He took a long swig, swallowed, then glared at a possible rat rustling in the corner. "That sodomitical little monkey's turd, Wilmot, has been messing us for months and I want to know what every fecking piece of paper in his house says. If there's a list of our names there, then God knows what else he's got—the boy's name, perhaps? Od's death, we've worked too ruddy hard for this. And I want to know. Every sneaking traitorous bit of it."

Barnet swiped a hand under his nose. "But…well, what about Dunphail? Ain't he…"

Jesuadon stopped and shook his head, his anger curiously somewhat dispelling. "Dunphail is in up over his collarpoints and near drowning in it—and he don't even know it, the poor sod." He drank again, then scowling, regarded the bottle in his hand. "'Struth, for all that I don't like him," he admitted, "and as unlikely as it may seem, I reckon he's the only friend that pestilential scrub has in the world. But don't ask me how…."

"Well, then," Barnet began reasonably. "Surely, it'll be up to him to get the boy…"

Jesuadon brought his fist down hard on the table. "No, you cretinous clod pate! What in the blazes do not you understand? What if it's a double-cross to get the boy?"

Barnet put up his hands. "All right! All right…"

Jesuadon, shifting tack, rested his chin in his hand, allowing his eye to run over the open ledger page. "Tell me about Ladyman," he said softly.

Barnet, disliking the question, the shift, shrugged his shoulders. "He's improving. Still can't remember much of what happened."

"And Waley?"

Warily, Barnet shook his head. "He's not taken his boat out though. That I do know."

"So that devil, John Brown, is still here then, is he, the sodomising bastard?" Jesuadon said, his mood souring once again.

Barnet nodded, seeing suddenly beyond his own small part to understanding something of Jesuadon's larger concerns. "He can't be down Sussex way though," he said quickly. "For I've put them on the alert. The Warne gang too. They're on the watch for him as well." Then: "You reckon he's here, don't you?"

"I do, yes. Yes, I do! I think the frigging Frenchie bangster's here," Jesuadon said threateningly. "And I want him. I want him. And Wilmot. Together. Before they top another of us."

"So…when will you take Wilmot, then?" Barnet questioned, running his tongue over his lip, readying to weigh the answer. To begin the planning.

"When I'm ready."

Barnet regarded him severely. It was not the answer he'd wanted. "All right, then. I'll call in the lads…we'll be there. Chesterfield Street. On your word, it'll be." He rose, and picking up his lantern, he turned to make his way back through the passages, back and up, to the light and noise of the living.

3

They met in the hall, on the upstairs landing, Dunphail and Boy. Just outside Dunphail's bedchamber with its adjoining dressing room.

Dunphail closed his door firmly behind him. Looking Boy over with a critical eye, he paced about him to study him, front and back, the lay of his lapel, the cut of his collar, the understated sheen of his waistcoat, the fit of his pantaloons. His mouth set in a thin line, his grey eyes determined, he twitched at Boy's cravat, pressing lightly at the Gordian knot that it would lie flatter and squarer. "Aye, I dare say that'll do," he allowed, all unsmiling.

They were dressed nearly identically. Though Dunphail's waistcoat was of silk dobby, and the tie pin which held the ends of his cravat in place was a marquis-cut diamond.

"Thank you, sir." Boy took a look at Dunphail's face, flushed with annoyance, his mouth set into a frown. "You don't wish to go, do you?" he observed with equal emphasis.

Dunphail drew a long breath and felt in his pocket for his watch. He frowned hard. "No. No, I do not," he admitted, as side by side they headed for the stairs. "You may take my word for it, Wilmot is a scrambler. The wine is likely to be inferior, the soup tepid, and the roast pigeon overdone." And proceeding down the stairs together, Dunphail went on: "The company will be insignificant, the conversation wearisome or worse, their wit lewd, and the play mediocre. Though I dare say the stakes will be such as few of them can afford. 'Struth, my one consolation in all of this is that that pestilential braggadocio, Byron…" he pronounced it with a decided sneer. "…Having been given the ding by the Millbank chit, has now taken up with Lady Oxford and will therefore, I trust, be passing his evening docking with her, with his face stuffed in her ample dairy, and not boring tonight's company to distraction with his interminable stories of riding through the wilds of Albania on horseback, dining off rancid mutton grease…or whatever sack of rum cods he's touting about now…" He paused on the bottom step to adjust his cuffs.

"But you said…" Boy began.

"That I admire his poetry? Aye, so I do. Very much indeed." Dunphail sniffed hard. "It's him I can't stomach."

They had reached the front hall, where the servants stood waiting to hand them into their hats and cloaks. The candles in the wall sconces had all been lit as had those in the great hall lantern which was suspended from above.

"Of course," Boy agreed cordially. "Anything else?"

"'Sblood, yes." Not without amusement, Dunphail gazed upon Boy's smooth, still face and narrowed his eyes, a quirk of sudden pleasure gleaming in his grey eyes. "'Struth, had I wished to spend the evening playing an inferior hand of piquet with a trifling, feckless hobbledehoy, I might have stayed in with you." He checked his quizzing glass for specks of dust. "Then at least I should have avoided the underdone…"

"Do not you mean overdone?" Boy interrupted with an almost wry expression.

"Aye, that too…dinner," Dunphail finished.

"Yes, sir."

"But as Jesuadon chose the precise moment of Wilmot's invitation to turn and shoot the cat in the road," Dunphail continued dryly, "I inferred that he wished for us to attend this party and that it was of his designing…"

"Yes, sir…"

"Though upon mine honour, why in Christ's name, he should have chosen a card party hosted by that twiddlepoop, Wilmot, for your first evening outing, I cannot think. Wilmot is a…"

"Scrambler?" Boy supplied.

Dunphail slanted him a mock-withering glance. "Aye, he is exactly that. To be sure, Wilmot is no fit companion for a boy of your age. Hell and confound it, he is no fit companion for a gentleman of my age." Dunphail sniffed, then shook his head at the folly of it all. "We'll take the carriage," he concluded.

Again, he subjected Boy to a full scrutiny, first of his evening clothes, and then searching in his face for a hint of the emotion he imagined must be lodging in his limpid eyes. But it was absent. Or buried. Certainly, he could not see it.

"God's balls, I should have taught you to take snuff," he exclaimed with an annoyed jerk of his head and slipped his hand into his pocket to pull out his snuffbox. "For it will surely be sent 'round with the port, this evening."

"Teach me now," Boy said solemnly. And he stood, patiently observing Dunphail's practised opening of the box and inhaling of no more than a few grains from off his thumbnail. "Will I like it?"

"Probably not," Dunphail admitted. "That pestilential cakey, Wilmot, is more than likely to prefer some highly perfumed odious mixture and just as unlikely to store it as he ought. Therefore it will be dry and wholly disgusting." He slipped the box back into his pocket. "Pass it along when it comes to you and have none of it," he said with finality. "Shall we go?"

Within the damask-sided space of the town carriage, as it shook and rattled over the uneven surfaces of road, stalled in traffic outside those houses where the torches burned bright, lit by linkboys walking, not running ahead, Dunphail regarding the subdued figure beside him, sought some words which would convey his backing, his assistance if it were required, and knew of none. For the boy, his hair freshly barbered, and his face above his starched cravat as still and as blank as a wall, had turned from him.

Eventually, the carriage halting in Chesterfield Street, Dunphail, holding his hat in his hand and regarding the brim, said in a low voice, "I trust you do know that I shall do whatever it is you need…"

Boy shook his head. "No. Thank you. But I know what to do," he said plainly. He opened the carriage door and climbed down. He stood for a long instant gazing about him as he ever did. Calculating. Measuring. He affected not to notice the sweepers on each corner who were there at Jesuadon's bidding.

Like the others on the short stretch that was Chesterfield Street, Wilmot's was a narrow house of painted white stone for the ground floor, with dark brick above. Jesuadon had described it all to him. Two windows wide only, and three floors, two rooms on each. A ground floor of a front hall and dining room, a first floor with library and drawing room, and on the second, the bedroom and dressing room. All connected by a central staircase. Though Jesuadon said there was a hidden staircase in the rear corner for the two servants Wilmot kept.

Wilmot had chosen the house for its proximity to Mr. Brummell's residence, in the vain conceit that this would confer *bon ton* upon him. Ahead, two others had just arrived on foot, arm-in-arm, and were admitted by the manservant—a wide-mouthed man with a peevish expression.

Dunphail stepped down to join the young man on the pavement. He placed a protective arm about Boy's shoulders, squared and straight beneath his hand. "For heaven's sake, avoid Wilmot, if you can…" he said determinedly. "He is a…"

"Scrambler?" Boy said, looking up to exchange glances. His left shoe pinched. But they were fine evening pumps and allowed him to feel the floor through their soles.

"No." Dunphail sniffed hard. "'Struth, I was about to say a ranging cod's head," he returned coolly. "Shall we go in?"

They were admitted by the vexed-faced manservant into a small front hall, well-lit and tastefully littered with Buhl side tables—an expensive taste for a gentleman of limited means—and with the staircase rising up from the rear wall, beneath which was the door to the dining room, and from there, shown up to the drawing room.

Wilmot, his dark hair frizzing and arranged in corkscrew ringlets over his forehead, turned to greet them, his boyish face open with delight.

"Sir Robert." Dunphail inclined only his head. Beside him, Boy performed his deeper bow. Then they were welcomed into the room and Boy introduced to those whom he had not yet met—a dozen other gentlemen of varying degrees of insignificance, one a tubster, gamesters all, and no Byron. Boy saw, amidst further evidence of their host's taste in expensive trifles and Buhl marquetry, that Jesuadon was already there, for once dressed as a polished gentleman, though one smelling of champagne, and already glittering with that dangerous anticipation of violence. Or triumph.

The dinner proved to be exactly as Dunphail had predicted. Wilmot, in fine form at the table's head, was at his voluble best, alternately playful and waggish or smirking with top-lofty arrogance as the meal progressed through removes of overdone breast of wood pigeon, pheasant pudding and dry roast beef. All punctuated with frequent ribald toasts to the manifold graces and attributes of various ladies of the company's acquaintance.

Boy, seated between two strangers, said little and watched all. His youth required that he contribute nothing beyond attentive silence and an apparent pleasure in the indelicate conversation which prevailed. His explanation that things were not quite settled at home, so when Dunphail had offered to have him, they thought it a good notion, served to answer the one question posed to him.

At length, their faces flushed with unhealthy excess, their stock of tired witticisms and bad puns exhausted, the dregs of the second-rate port finished and every whore on King Street's health drunk, tripping, laughing and loud, the party scrambled back up the stairs to the drawing room.

"'Wilmot," Jesuadon called. "I say, Wilmot. What d'you say we take on Dunphail here and his young relation? For a hand of whist, what?" He gave an unlikely, friendly smile, showing his very white teeth. His eyes were glittering without mercy.

"What's that? Oh, yes, to be sure!" Wilmot said, turning on slightly unsteady feet. "Indeed! Dassett. Dassett, where are you, man?" he called. "Bring up more wine, will you? Jesuadon will be in want of claret. As shall we all. Ha ha."

About them, the gentlemen settled at the various small tables. And within moments as the decks were shuffled and dealt, the intent hush of fierce engagement with the cards, of determined money-squandering and steady drinking permeated the salon.

Boy sat opposite Dunphail, and with Jesuadon and Wilmot played two hands of whist, checking himself always against perfection, ensuring that Dunphail won steadily. And refused to catch his eye.

Then Jesuadon proposed a change of partners—Tirrell to partner him and Dunphail to partner Wilmot. Now, Jesuadon and Boy could not help but pull ahead, their combined mastery of numbers, of memory and of each other proving too hard to contain or counter until at last, Dunphail complained that he must stand aside and give his poor brains a rest.

But for Wilmot, though the candles were already half-burnt in their silver sockets, the evening's pleasure was just beginning. "Well, if you must," he agreed, when Dunphail rose from the table where the cards lay among a scattering of counters and untarnished guineas.

Boy had risen as well.

Wilmot craned his neck slightly over the starched points of his collar. "Your guardian tells me you prefer piquet, young Tirrell. I'd fancy a Partie or two, if you like…" he drawled. The manservant called Dassett replaced the bottle of burgundy at his elbow. The other gamesters were all still engaged.

Boy bowed properly. "Thank you, sir. I should welcome it," he said and sat again.

Dassett brought forward a fresh pack of cards which Wilmot deftly sorted, removing the twos, threes, fours, fives and sixes before he handed it to Boy to shuffle.

They had been playing piquet for nearly an hour, Boy, wary and alert, balancing his knowledge of the game with the odd miscall of a greenhead, to allow Wilmot the satisfaction of a condescending titter and a patronising look or comment.

"'Struth!" Wilmot exclaimed as Boy totted up the points for the last three games. They had just completed a Partie and Wilmot moved quickly to refill the glass at his elbow.

Boy had done well, scoring an extra hundred points in the last hand. It should have been more.

"Is that the score?" Wilmot demanded, peering at the tablet across the small table. "Good lord! You'll ruin me," he declared in mock horror, laughing heartily.

Boy did not like his laugh. He drank down the whole of the glass and set it back on the table. Then as he paused to look about the room at the other tables, the other gentlemen there, the wine hit. He wobbled in his chair. He shook his head to clear it. Blinked. And shook his head again. He stared hard at the cards upon the table before him which Wilmot was now gathering toward himself.

Boy belched softly and passed his hand over his left eye to rub it clear. He sat silent for a moment, gathering his breath. Glancing about surreptitiously, he leant forward and said in an exaggerated whisper: "Sir Robert?" He hiccoughed. "Sir, I fear…I fear I may have…that is to say, I regret to say that I may have overindulged, sir, and may be in danger of being…a little cut over the head."

He tried to focus, blinking several times and saw the smirk on

Wilmot's soft mouth. "Have you an antechamber nearby where I might retire for a little while I…gather my wits…sir?"

Like warm cream slipping from a cold basin, sleek, Wilmot's smile grew. "But yes…yes, of course, m'dear Tirrell." He rose and he too leant forward conspiratorially. "But not a word to your fierce relation, Dunphail. For I should not wish to be accused of corrupting a youth, ha ha…" His dark eyes were full of some joke.

Helpfully, he came round to assist Boy to his feet.

Across the room, Dunphail made to rise, but Wilmot shook his head and said loudly enough that all might hear, "'Struth, a turn in the library will be just the ticket, I do believe. Damme, I'm feelin' the fatigue m'self, after losing so heavily to you. Makin' me feel my age, ain't you? Ha ha."

Wilmot tucked his arm genially through Boy's. "Shall I show you those drawings I mentioned, Tirrell? 'Struth, I am convinced you will like them…they are just across the hall…"

Straightening, and alert with a sudden prickling fear he could not explain, Dunphail darted a concerned look across the room, but Jesuadon was paying no attention. He was lolling back in his chair, his glass dangling precariously from his long fingers as he swirled his wine round and round. He belched, drank and belched again. And the play continued.

Chapter XXXII

1

Above the fading embers of the untended fire, upon a carved mantel of mottled grey marble, the four candles in a pair of candelabra, with blackened bronze putti supporting the sinuous arms, gave off a soft, gentling glow, a warm haze of yellow light fading into draped semi-darkness. Ahead, its back to the windows, was a sabre leg sofa upholstered in striped silk. Across from the fireplace, a desk.

Wilmot shut the doors behind them, revealing on either side of the doorframe a pair of matched bookcases. The library.

"Here we are," he pronounced, leading the boy toward the long sofa. He had lowered his voice to suit the privacy of the surroundings. "Upon my word, you do play a neat hand of piquet, don't you?" he admired. "'Struth, I must confess your cleverness quite surprised me back there…Now, just you sit down there and I shall fetch you something to look at…while your head clears."

Obediently, Boy sat. And looked about. Desk, fireplace, one wall of books. Over the mantel, a half-length portrait of Wilmot himself, recently painted. One arm chair. And the sofa. In the dim light, there would be no shadows thrown. The curtains were drawn in any event. Not quite a library in the true sense of the word. To be sure, he preferred Dunphail's book-lined room.

Strolling back and forth before the shelves of books, looking high and low, Wilmot halted before a shelf of tall leather-bound volumes, his hand poised over one slim folio. He stroked his finger down one of his luxuriant sideburns, then drew the volume forth. "Yes," he murmured, smoothing his hand over the embossed leather cover. "Yes, I do believe you shall enjoy this one…" he said, his head tilted slightly to one side. "'Struth, yes. This will do well."

He came and sat down close beside Boy. An odd look, a waxing compound of anticipation and languor, of pleasure and kindling hope, played over his delicate features and darkened his eyes.

Just such a look had Boy often seen on the faces of French soldiers. Though it had not been for him.

Wilmot laid the folio in Boy's lap and pulled open the pale blue ribbon fastening. He lifted open the cover, spreading the folio open across Boy's knees. A smile pulled at the corners of his beautifully curved mouth. "There. Now tell me true, what do you think of that?" he said, leaning closer. The buttons of his coat were of gold, spun and plaited gold rounds, they were; it was the same coat as he wore in his portrait.

"Wilmot! Wil-mo-ot!"

It was Jesuadon. Bellowing. He could be heard clearly, even from the street.

"Oh!" Wilmot started. "Good lord…" he blustered and shook his head. "Jesuadon," he whispered with exasperation, rolling his eyes.

"Wilmot! Where the devil are you, dammit!"

Wilmot pursed up his mouth. And with great reluctance, rose from the sofa. "'Upon my word, I do believe I shall have to leave you to look at these on your own, dear boy. But never fear, I shall return to see how you get on…and…you need not concern yourself about us…" He smiled. "You shall be completely private"—he laid great stress upon the word—"in here."

He crossed to the door, then stopped at the door to add, languorous and enticing still, "There are some very delightful pictures toward the back…I trust you will enjoy those most especially…"

"Thank you," Boy said quietly. "…sir."

"Wilmot!" Jesuadon yelled.

With a last lingering smile, Wilmot went out, closing the door upon him.

Boy watched him go. Watched and waited. Still. Unmoving. Patiently waited and listened to the sound of Wilmot returning across the landing and Jesuadon's gabbled greeting. The book lay open, uncontemplated, in his lap.

The servants' door, cut in the wall, was in the far rear corner. There was no key in the lock. Not in either of the doors. And still he waited. Measuring the sounds from the street and from the drawing room beyond the landing.

Returning to the drawing room, his cheeks flushed, Wilmot smiled seraphically.

Jesuadon regarded him wisely and rocked his chair precariously far back on its spindly mahogany legs. He brightened. "Od's bodkin, there you are, Wilmot!" Two more bottles lay on the floor beside his feet. "I am desirous of a hand of piquet…What d'you say?"

Wilmot made a moué. "Are you now, Thos?" he teased.

Jesuadon righted his chair. "I am." He gave a seated half-bow. "I do." He stifled a belch and cast an eye about him. "Wilmot, this is a damned tame party. 'Sblood, what say you we make it a trifle more interesting?" He stifled a second belch. "What say we make it ten pound points and a monkey to win…"

Wilmot laughed. "Dear one," he drawled. "'S'truth, is that not a touch steep? Even for you?"

Observing Wilmot's look of mild surprise, his lips puckering—an expression he had come to know well—Jesuadon exclaimed, "No, no. No, no!" He let out an extended burp. "I need to pay my tailor, don't you know?"

There was much general laughter. "Have you ever paid your tailor, Jesuadon?" enquired the finely dressed tubster at the near table to Jesuadon's left.

Jesuadon hiccoughed. "Not to my knowledge, no," he declared. "'Struth, the poor fellow wouldn't know what to do with such wealth, now would he?" he exclaimed airily. "It'd be the ruination of him. He'd squander it…grow soft…and in all justice, I cannot permit that to happen. Far better for him to continue dinin' off cucumbers…" He lifted his latest bottle to his lips and drained the contents, then dropped it to the floor. He slouched back in his seat. "Now where was we? Oh, yes, Wilmot was callin' for a fresh pack…" he mumbled, turning to his host.

Wilmot's eyes were further glittering with suppressed excitement. "Dassett! Dassett, where are ye? Oh, there you are. Mr. Jesuadon and I need a fresh pack. Ha ha. Probably we need fresh packs all around, don't you think? And another few bottles…and get rid of these on the floor, will you? Build up the fire, too, before Jesuadon here catches his death…I can feel m'luck turning already, you know…"

And still Boy waited, counting out the commotion in the next room, listening to Jesuadon's incoherent ramblings and Wilmot's measured responses. To the bursts of random laughter. Then laying the book on the empty seat beside him, he rose. Paused. Listened. Then walked over to and around the two-sided desk, to examine it from all sides, measuring. Most particularly, the depth of the drawers. He bent to test the handle on the right hand drawer. Locked.

"Stupid cock…" he murmured on an exhalation of breath. And untroubled, he withdrew the wire pick from his cuff.

Hardly needing to look, standing close to the desk, Boy poked the bent end of wire into small keyhole and rotated it until the lock produced that modest satisfying click. He stopped again to listen as a one-horse carriage—a hackney—drove past in the street. Then replaced the pick in his sleeve, and silently slid the drawer open. "Fool," he added softly.

Rocking his chair back and forth, each time farther back on its legs, Jesuadon rubbed his face, while across from him Wilmot shuffled the deck. His eyes were drooping from a lack of sleep and an excess of claret. "'Struth, fancy payin' m'tailor," he mumbled. "It'd be the ruination of 'im," he repeated.

Wilmot slid the shuffled deck across the table. "Cut."

A few of the other gentlemen had dragged their seats forward to follow the game, flipping their chairs round to drape themselves over them backwards. Dassett had brought another trayful of burgundy up from the kitchen.

"Dassett, I shall need more light," Jesuadon complained. He wasn't laughing, but sat sprawled, his legs ungainly and awkwardly spread.

"Fetch some fresh candles, there's a good fellow…or I shall fall asleep…" he explained

Sneaking frequent glances at Jesuadon across the small table from under his lashes, Wilmot dealt the hand.

Letters. That was all the drawer contained. Letters. Gingerly, Boy lifted the first, unfolded it, read it. About a sightseeing trip up the east coast, it was. Signed G.W. Lying underneath, there was another similar, this about a proposed house party in January. In Sussex. There were a dozen or so of the things. All crammed together into the one drawer, all in a disorder. None of them of any obvious significance neither. And each of them signed the same.

Boy read them all, scanning them, allowing the words to register and remain as they did in his brain. He slid a hand along the inside lid of the desk to ensure that nothing remained. Nothing.

Meticulously then, Boy returned them, replacing them just as he had found them. He closed the drawer and relocked it. Then turned his attention to the left hand drawer. Which was also locked. "Nupson," he grumbled out of habit.

Dunphail, engaged in a dismal hand of whist, and hardly able to keep his attention fixed on the discards or calls, observed Jesuadon from out of the corner of his eye. He checked his watch. Jesuadon was calling for a morsel of gammon or a sandwich of tongue or cold beef; he was losing by several hundred pounds. Wilmot had piqued him in the last hand.

Stopping, turning his head to listen, Boy heard all he needed to hear. It was all still, as it must be. He rose from the desk chair and went to the servants' door, to cautiously edge it open. He peered into the darkness of the stairwell. Nothing. Not even the distant voices of the servants' gossip in the kitchen.

He returned to the desk. The central drawer held nothing but accounts and bills. From Wilmot's several tailors. His glover. Lock's, the hatter. From his bootmaker. And a bill for snuffboxes and snuff. Boy read them all. And then the account book—running his eye over the pages before him. The odd and irregular accounts of a gamester whose income depended on his luck and skill at the tables, they were. Still, he read them.

And trailing his fingers over the columns of figures, feeling the indentations of the nib on the pages, the pattern of the dried ink as it varied, he found…a regular listing of fifty guineas. He turned over the previous two pages…Every month it came in. Sometimes twice. There it was again. Fifty guineas was a great deal of money. A very great deal. And an exact sum of money. Nothing like a gambling debt. But it wasn't enough to hang him.

Boy read the final page, then returned it, just as it had been, to the drawer. And with it, the bills, unordered as they were. Silently sliding the drawer closed, he relocked it.

Thoughtful and silent, he looked about the room again, reading its shadows, studying them, the leather bound volumes that lined the bookshelves, the ornaments and fitments, the mantel clock, ticking inexorably. Where was it?

A sheen of febrile excitement had spread itself across Wilmot's features. Jesuadon was going down heavily. The score had climbed into the thousands. And Wilmot knew that his luck was in at last. "Another hand, Jesuadon?" A couple of gentlemen cheered them on, then hushed.

Jesuadon bestowed a lazy smile which grew slowing into a chuckle deep in his chest, grating and suggestive. "Od's sugar stick, how much do I owe you now, Wilmot?"

"I make it just over three thousand…" the tubster declared loudly.

Jesuadon cast him a sodden glance. "Where would I be without you, Nyp?" he muttered. Then as the fubsy gentleman recoiled, blushing, and fumbled himself into the background, Jesuadon rebalanced himself on his chair. "Wilmot…deal. Dassett, I shall need another bottle of claret. And a pitcher of boiled water."

"You cannot mean to continue all night, Jesuadon…your luck's turned…" another from the crowd exclaimed.

Jesuadon smiled patiently and serenely, and toying with the cork from his last bottle, spun it hard. It whirled and rolled, then dropped to the floor. "Can I not? 'Struth, Wilmot is ready to win twice as much off me again…Nor would he be so ungracious as to refuse me the chance to even things up a bit. Would you, m'dear fellow?"

Wilmot shook his head, his eyes glittering in the candlelight. "No, indeed!" he protested, blithely laughing. "Jesuadon still has to pay his tailor, don't he?" He shuffled the cards again and smiled, more smirk than an expression of joy it was.

Boy surveyed the carved marble mantel. They were all the same, these mantels, whatever country you were in. He ran a tentative exploratory finger along the upper edge, then along the dentil band below the mantel proper, experimentally pressing against each small block. Nothing. They all held. Until he reached the third from the right…He pressed it again. Hard. The scored marble lozenge below sprung open. Boy smiled.

"Cod's head," he murmured, liking Dunphail's term.

And peering into the cavity to see what it contained, he reached in to withdraw the heavy roll of papers, bound together with a pale blue ribbon.

Jesuadon's play had been erratic all evening as he paid little attention to his discards and less to Wilmot's. He downed several glasses of water. "Fuck me, I need a piss," he said suddenly, tumbling from his chair. Nearly upending the neighbouring table, he struggled to his feet. Then fumbling already with the buttons at his waist, he ambled over to the screen in the corner behind which were several chamber pots, only eventually returning to his seat.

Flexing his shoulders, he downed another glassful of water. "'Struth, Wilmot, after all that, I fancy I shall need to capot you at the very least, what? My deal is it?" His eyes had gone cold and clear.

Tenderly Boy held the page in his hand. And his bottom lip between his teeth, he read down it twice. Here it was. The list of names. They were all here. Semple. Flint. Wyndham. Fiske. Ladyman. Taylor. Bretherton. Barnet. Hillier. Wilson. St. George. Norman. Planta. A boy operating out of Rye—brown hair. Myddelton. Gransby.

Seventeen names and the description of himself. Beside several of the names, a cross. Beside the names of Bretherton, Semple, Gransby and Hillier, a double cross. Beside Ladyman a question mark. All here. All listed. Four of them dead.

And resistless in that pooling of imperfect silence, for a long moment Boy sat, reading and rereading the list of names—all listed and four of them dead—able to do nothing beyond sit and taste the familiar flavour of harsh anger in his mouth.

He closed his eyes. To still himself. To steel himself against the fragments of weakening sentiment or care. And forcing himself to perform as he must, to think and not to think, he glanced toward the servants' door and considered whether he should search Wilmot's dressing room too. He lifted the page of names to read over the pages of correspondence underneath. And beneath that, several more pages written in cipher. Dutifully he let his gaze travel over the lines of code, page after page of it, weaving the mixture of letters, numbers and symbols into the fabric of his mind.

The candles were burning low in their stands, the flames guttering against the unevenly pooling wax.

At last, Boy retied the pale blue ribbon around the sheaf of papers and returned them to their niche, turning them half on their side just as he'd found them. He pressed the spring door into place as it had been. And stretching his chin above the height of his stiff cravat, he squared his shoulders, then went to close the servants' door. He glanced over at the book which lay upon the sofa, open still to its initial engraving of a young flogging cully with the scripted caption:

Plunge and caper! Roar and cry!
I have you now within my power!
No kind protector now is nigh,
Thro' life I'll make you bless this hour,

Keep down your legs, let go my hand
Let, let your breeches remain down.
This efficacious reprimand
Shall make you the best boy in town.

He looked it over the room for a final moment. Ensuring that it was now as it had been, once again, almost as if he had never been there. And banishing the burden of his thoughts, noiseless, a melting shadow, he quitted the room and returned to the drawing room.

No one looked up as he re-entered the room. For all their attentions were focused, rapt upon Jesuadon and Wilmot. Jesuadon bore a look of patient malevolence. Wilmot's eyes were darting between his cards, the discards laid out on the table and Jesuadon's fair face—a kind a desperation it was, as he watched his luck slipping from him and his winnings dissipating. All that he had won in the last hour had now been lost.

For an instant, Boy stood hesitant on the threshold. Then, silently, he came to stand behind Dunphail and bending close beside his ear, smelled the unperfumed, unsweet scent of him, of country-washed fine linen and of nothing else—so unlike that of Wilmot. "May we go now, sir?"

Dunphail glanced up, an inarticulate question forming in his eyes. Unconsciously, he drew a deep breath. He did not require an answer.

Jesuadon was declaring his final hand, a Quatorze. As one, the onlookers gasped.

Dunphail looked hard at the boy. Without a word, he stood and gave a nod.

As one, they approached the gaming table where Wilmot sat, poring over his hand, the buttons of his coat polished like his treachery, the object of his fleeting desire forgot. His winnings were slipping away as the pile of guineas before Jesuadon increased.

"Gentlemen, I give you good night," Dunphail said and together he and the boy bowed.

"I make that just over three thousand..." Jesuadon said smoothly, never raising his eyes.

Dunphail and Boy were hardly settled in the hackney carriage when Boy said, "I shall have to go on to the Foreign Office after this."

"What, now?" Dunphail scowled.

Boy nodded.

Dunphail paused. "What did Wilmot want with you in there? As if I can't guess..."

"To show me pictures of some female flaybottomist," Boy said, shrugging his shoulders as though it were not unusual. "I expect he meant to have a feel of my cock too," he said dismissively.

Dunphail raised an eyebrow. "Aye, and give you a taste of his by the back door, I shouldn't wonder," he said coldly. "'Steeth, fellows like him should be whupped…"

"Yes," Boy agreed. "I dare say." Then, bored by the whole improbable business, he added, "As if he'd get that far…"

Reassured, Dunphail looked away. Then, idly: "So if you wasn't looking at his bumbrushing pictures, what was you doing in there?"

Boy closed his eyes and leaned his head back against the corner squab. "Going through his drawers," he said, matching Dunphail's tone for prosaicness.

Dunphail turned to stare at him, at his still, impassive face which sat so odd with his youth. Then he smiled. "God's whirlygigs, next you'll tell me that you've been through the drawers in my house."

Boy opened his eyes to regard Dunphail openly and not without a measure of surprise at his surprise. "Yes."

Dunphail blinked, then gave a mellow chuckle. "Oh, aye. Find anything of interest, did you?" he said doubtfully.

"Only that Bonaparte toy with his pop-up cock." Boy pulled a wry face. "'Struth, I've seen better in Berlin though."

Dunphail eyed him with a measure of scepticism. "Oh aye?"

"Oh, aye," Boy mocked. A smile imped briefly about the corners of his eyes. "There was this one…where the Empress was facing away from him, not toward as yours is," he described. "So when you pull the lever, her skirts fly up and she sits down atop him, doesn't she?"

Dunphail exploded with sudden laughter. And as the idea formed and took perfect hold, he found he could not stop.

"Do you want one?" Boy offered. "I'll bring you one back, next time I'm there…if you like."

Chapter XXXIII

1

Seated at the table, his head bent over his work like any colleger, Boy was still writing when Lord Castlereagh arrived early. The burnt out sockets in the nearby candlestands, dried pools of wax with only a blackened stump of wick end remaining, were a testament to the hours he had spent there, and in the grate nothing but ashes. Before him, pages of foolscap were spread across the wooden surface like a collapsing pile of ensigns on a deck. Pages and pages, covered in his angular scrawl, his night's work, all that he had read of Wilmot's effects now drained from the receptacle that was his mind, the words and symbols commuted onto paper for others to read and interpret. His eyes were bleary and his fingers ink-stained and aching.

Gazing upon the scene, upon the boy, in the daylight his hair nutbrown against the olive of his coat, Lord Castlereagh stood in the doorway to the inner office and leaned forward, his hands folded together on his cane handle. "Last evening went well then, did it, Boy?"

Boy stirred and straightened. Then blinking with a sudden realisation of exhaustion and of where he was, he laid the quill to one side and struggled to his feet. His legs were stiff from sitting. He bowed. "My lord. Yes. Yes, thank you." There was a wanness about him this morning. "Yes."

Lord Castlereagh came further into the room and gave a nod. He could not, despite the high cost, the loss of his men, of Bretherton especially, conceal his keen pleasure in the success of the moment. Eagerly, his gout forgot, he hobbled to the table, looking upon Boy's still face and upon the fruits of his mind. "Good! Good. I could think on nothing else last evening, I can tell you. But first, was there any risk? Any risk to you? Any suspicions? You must tell me all," he demanded.

Boy thought. "No. No, I do not believe so. No, my lord, no risk," he lied. He brightened. "Jesuadon put on a fine show, sir," he said, reverting to the truth. "'Struth, I defy anyone to have suspected a thing of that performance." He managed a half-smile. "He was on best form when we left, and Wilmot was badly dipped, so I should think the party went on till dawn and no one the wiser."

Nodding his approval, Castlereagh removed his greatcoat to toss it onto a near chair. "Oh, excellent. This is very good news, Boy. Very good news, indeed?" Approbation was apparent in every line of his face. "Yes, yes, upon my word, this is very good news. I am very glad to hear it! And Dunphail?"

Boy did not respond instantly. But paused, for once not knowing how to answer, before saying carefully, "Lord Dunphail…is well, sir."

"Good, good!" the Foreign Secretary approved, hurrying himself to the table, his expression like a terrier which has nosed its prey. "Now, tell me, what did you find? All of this?" His eyes narrowing, he peered intelligently and knowledgeably over the pages nearest him, reaching out to shift one so that he might peruse the page underneath.

"Yes, my lord. It is all here. There were bills. A ledger of Wilmot's incoming funds, not unusual in itself. But with regular payments of fifty guineas. I've copied them all out. And there were several pages in code." He gestured toward the table. "I've just finished writing those down, now…"

"Code, you say? Code?" Castlereagh repeated with a glint of a smile in his dark eyes. "Ciphers, you mean? Not the Chiffre?" he asked in with growing enthusiasm. "Not the Grand Chiffre?"

"No, my lord. Just code, I think…." With his fatigue nagging at him, Boy felt no answering measure of excitement.

"Oh, that is excellent. Aha! We shall have him! We shall have the traitor now…" Castlereagh exclaimed. "Planta!" he called. "Planta, where are you?" He raised his voice and yelled. "Planta!"

The Office's outer door slammed shut. Out of breath, still in his greatcoat, Planta ran into the office, the keys still clutched in his hand. "Sir?" He was late.

"Planta, get me Myddelton!" Lord Castlereagh bellowed. "Now!"

Nodding emphatically, Planta glanced quickly at the boy, at the table, then at his lordship, and back at Boy. "Yes, my lord. Right away. I'll go myself…Anything else?"

"No. Just get me Myddelton." Castlereagh did not turn to see him rush away, but remained standing, surveying the table of pages. "Well done, Boy," he said quietly. "Very well done, indeed. And was there…a list? Of my men? Did you find a list?" he enquired in an urgent undertone.

"Yes, sir," Boy said, sobering. "Yes, my lord, I found it. It is here…"

Lord Castlereagh drew a deep breath, contemplating again the page-strewn table. "Good," he said softly. He searched the boy's face for some emotion, some trace of aftermath, but found only the shuttered patience of that unearthly pallor. Then: "Was you on it?"

"Yes, my lord. Semple, Flint, Wyndham, Fiske, Ladyman, Taylor, Bretherton, Barnet, Hillier, Wilson, St. George, Norman, Planta." He disregarded Castlereagh's sharp intake of breath. "A boy operating out of Rye—brown hair, Myddelton and Gransby."

The Foreign Secretary sobered. "What, all of them? All my men? I see…" Thoughtfully, he contemplated the pages of Boy's night's work, then looked up to say with some kindness, "But now, if I am not much mistaken, you need to return home to your bed. At least for a few hours.

"Shuster will want to question you later, I make no doubt of that. As will I after I have read all this. But for now, you must away home to your bed, Boy."

Uncertain, Boy remained as he was. "Yes, my lord. Thank you, my lord. But, sir, there's one more thing."

"Yes?"

"The list. It was not writ by the same person who wrote everything else I read. It was in a different hand. Writ by someone else—with a

French script. Not at all the same."

Castlereagh stared at him. "What are you saying, Boy? That it was writ in Paris? Does this business go all the way to the top? To Savary? Was it writ by Savary?"

"I don't know that, sir. I can tell you that it was not writ by Fouché. But you'll want Sir Charles Flint or the Foreign Letter Office to look it over...they are better placed than I to know the writer." He reached to close the standish, then began to tidy the pages. His eyes appeared to have drained of colour. "Shall I make up the fire before I go, sir?"

"No, leave it," Castlereagh commanded. "Planta shall see to it all."

Boy made his obedience. "My lord." And his shoes as ever making no sound on the carpet, he exited. Down the darkened stairwell he knew so intimately and out into the deceiving unwarm sunlight of the early December morning. Into the small garden, the beds of which were now emptied and raked over and only the clipped box hedge still shone green. To walk the few streets' distance to Dunphail's house, past those still slumbering households where the roofs were crusted over with hoar frost, where he was no longer a stranger, no longer one boy among a city of plain-faced boys. Alive to the cold as it nipped and grazed, ruddying his cheeks, and to the brightness of the day, though it made his tired eyes sting. And he would have run had he not been a gentleman. So he walked, his hands thrust in his pockets, thinking of his breakfast, of nothing and of horses, watched by all those others put in place to guard him through the day and night, looking on from their street corners and from behind their brooms. Walked safe, protected, and unapproachable. Walked.

And when later he awoke to find much of the day gone, Dunphail was still from home and the house about him quiet. So without further ado, he washed and dressed and went to the music room.

2

Returning from his solitary ride in the eking light of late afternoon, Dunphail came home to music, to a front hall filled with it. To the singular music of someone playing the fortepiano just upstairs and playing it well. Playing it beautifully. Brilliantly even.

And wholly arrested by the sound, for a long instant Dunphail stood under the bright halo of the overhead lantern, listening. Just listening. He looked up in the direction of the music as though he might see through the ceiling and floor to its source, his attention rapt. For such music could mean one thing only: Ned was home. His cousin, Ned was home. His breath caught in his throat; he smiled.

The music stopped.

And started again. The same music, driven and delicate, with the unrelieved urgency of a fast-cantering horse. Played from the beginning.

It was Ned, practising.

Carefully, so as to make no distracting noise, Dunphail removed his hat to lay it with his gloves and his whip on the side table. And just stood, listening. For until that moment, he had been unconscious of how keenly he had felt his cousin's absence all these months. How he had missed the unsilent hours of Ned's daily practice and perfection. For they had been always closer than brothers. But now listening, reflecting, his aching assuaged, a contented smile grew from inside him, played about the corners of his mouth, and grew wider as exultant delight fair knocked the air from his lungs. Great God in heaven, Ned was home. Not dead, not drowned, not lost, but home again.

And he paused to listen for just one moment more while the smile pulled at him and he recovered some measure of control over himself.

The music stumbled and stopped. And again resumed. Again from the beginning. But this time a fraction slower, with greater clarity and control. Yet still, there it was, that rocking, cantering, haunting melody.

And suddenly, more pleased than he could say, happier than he could recall, Dunphail raced up the wide staircase, the words of greeting tumbling about in his mouth. Ned was home, the rum bastard! Gone for six months, but now returned. Dunphail hurried down the hall, his smile broadening. And nearly laughing with untempered joy, threw open the door to the music room.

And saw.

It was not Ned.

It was the boy.

Playing like a virtuoso. Wholly absorbed, impassioned and with a technical mastery Ned had never possessed.

Stunned speechless, Dunphail stared, and did not move as the joy drained from him. There was no Ned. It was the boy, the sullen-faced scrub of a boy. Dismay, loss, betrayal locked in Dunphail's throat. It was the boy. Playing Ned's fortepiano, his instrument, his companion in music. And as Dunphail's face contorted with instant outrage, the brimstone words came from nowhere: "What in the devil do you think you're doing, you insufferable scut? Who gave you…" he broke off. "Who gave *you* permission to come in here?"

At the sound of the door opening, Boy raised his head to glance up from the keyboard, from that place of solace and salvation—all that he had left of a time so long ago it had no name, that time before his father had died. And he froze. And for one brief instant, torn from the delight of his mind and his talent, from the musical presence of the Maestro, like some trapped creature, he gazed at Dunphail—imprinted on his face, the sudden wise fear of one captured by a ravening army, certain that only death could follow.

He rose. And he would have bowed too but Dunphail was before him—pleasure turned and replaced with irrational, implacable anger—dragging him from the piano stool, hauling him halfway across the room.

"What in Christ's name do you think you're doing in here?" Dunphail said roughly. "That's Ned's fortepiano. No one touches that! No one, do you hear?"

Staggering backwards, Boy said nothing, though his expression had blanked as his nimble mind calculated and measured.

"What do you mean by coming in here? Who said you could touch his fortepiano, you hell-born snatchgallows? Who?" Dunphail shouted, stalking forward, the smouldering resentment over his multiple injuries—the deceit and lies, betrayal and now crushing loss—ripping through him, consuming him with a seething, blinding fury.

Boy squared his shoulders, his limpid eyes ablaze with a staunch, fierce calm. "'Struth, you're a fine one to talk," he said, lifting his chin. "Who are you but a coward Jacobite and a traitor to the king?"

Blinking against the bolting, shuddering rage, maddened with it,

Dunphail loomed over the boy. "Od's death, do you dare to speak to me so?" he ground out. He cuffed the Boy hard across the face. "Do you dare? 'Struth, I am no traitor." he said, and loosed a second blow across his cheek.

His pale skin burning bright with the imprint of Dunphail's hand and his cheekbone flaming red where Dunphail's signet had hit, Boy offered nothing but insolence. "Fool."

"What?" Viciously, Dunphail threw a punch to the side of Boy's face, to his eye.

Boy's head jerked backward, recoiling. But still, he straightened. "That's right, sir," he said, turning the word into an insult of such disgrace. "Go on," he goaded. "Just like they all do. Fool. Why do you not go back to Louseland and stay there? Where you belong." There were no tears.

"Out!" Dunphail muttered, laying hold of Boy's collar, pushing him backwards toward the door. "Out. I want you out of this house now. Get out of my house."

"What?" Boy taunted with a savage expression. "So that when your precious Ned comes home his fine instrument will show no sign of me? Is that it? What is he, then—this precious cousin of yours—your molly pratt? Your lover?"

It was too much. Dunphail hit him hard on the side of the head. His wrath exploding, uncontainable, he hit him again. Above his lip with a full fist.

Boy staggered backwards, blood spurting from his nose.

His mouth tightening, Boy threw one arm up to smash Dunphail's grip. And there was a flash of steel in his hand.

Dunphail saw it and pulled back. Lowered his fist and stepped quickly away.

Blood streamed from the boy's nose. His lip was swelling and bloodied. About his eye, the skin was mottled and stained scarlet to speckled crimson. "Keep your bloody hands off of me, Jacobite," he breathed. "D'you hear?" he said. He jutted his chin forward, his knife poised. "Cock."

His breath uneven and uncatchable, Dunphail stared at the broken and bleeding face, stared at the knife, and felt a trickle of sweat slip from his temple and the strangling hold of his cravat tight about his neck. And could not believe what he saw, what he had done.

Boy returned a cold glare, then turned, and proud, slipped from the room. Down the stairs, his footsteps a rapid descending tattoo. Wrenching open the front door, he slammed it shut behind him. And then he was running. Running through the puddles that splashed and stained his pale trousers. Darting down the alleyway to the stable mews where the grey did not lift its head from its feed, nor the stableboys from their spreading of fresh hay. Running. Pushing past the hawkers and horses, through the byways of Mayfair onto the streets of St. James's toward Charing Cross. Losing himself, swallowed up once more into the twilight city of boys.

Dunphail heard his steps and the sound of the front door slamming. And still he stood, sickening and silent, aghast. At himself. At the boy. At the deceit. The weeks and weeks of deceit and betrayal and dishonesty—and no answers. He stood, still staring after him long after he had gone, until at last, drained of all strength, he sank down into one of the gilt music room chairs.

As if suspended in water or a kind of haze, he looked down at his fist and saw the skin grazed and bleeding over his knuckles. His mind echoed with the unwelcome knowledge of his own infamy. He had beat the boy. Just as he had seen that bully rogue doing all those months ago. He had proved no better. No better than the rest of them.

Chapter XXXIV

1

"Ow."

It was a disgruntled exhalation of breath, no more, barely heard amidst the clanking of dishes and tankards, the shouting and bustle of the serving wenches, red-faced and sweating in the heat and steam of Sparrowhawk's vast kitchen.

Molly pursed her pudgy lips. "Hush, my lamb."

"Ow…"

"Sit still, my lamb…sit still, will you, Boy?" she chided. She glanced up and about at the coordinated chaos. "There are more pies in the larder, Annie, so stop making such a potheration…" she called above the din. "Jenny, fetch more pies…"

Boy was seated between the table and the great hearth, where a rack of skewered chickens were slow roasting above the fire, the fat spitting and popping, while Molly dabbed efficiently at his face—washing away the smears of blood and dirt, testing the swelling beneath his eye with one gentle finger. About them, the maids and menservants continued the business of feeding their customers, gathering up the supper plates filled with pies and joints and sausages, and paid them no heed. On the scrubbed table, beside a stack of dirty plates, the basin of cool water was turned pink; beside his stool a pile of damp reddened cloths lay on the flags. Boy held a fresh wad of linen to his bloody nose which was still truculently refusing to be stoppered.

Molly peered at his cheekbone and blew out a puff of air. Spiralling tendrils of her wiry hair curled tightly against her temples. "It's bad, my lamb. It's not cut, but it's bad." She shook her head over it. "Tis just your face, though, ain't it?"

"What happened?" Sparrowhawk demanded, bursting through the door, followed by Captain Shuster, dressed like a commoner, a well-bred commoner. Together they shouldered their way through the maze of huffing, scrambling wenches.

Molly looked up. Shuster did not belong in the kitchen, though she was saying nothing.

"Dunphail…" Boy mumbled. He tossed the bloodied cloth onto the table.

"Let me see," Georgie said, standing over him, then dropping down on one knee beside him. With his forefinger, he lifted Boy's chin higher to examine both sides of his face, his eye, his broken lip. "'Struth, t'ain't the worst I've seen. Though it'll take a few days to heal. Dunphail did this? What happened?" he asked.

Shrugging, Boy did not respond.

"Boy!" Shuster warned.

"It was nothing." His words sounded like blubbing mush through his split, swollen lip.

Georgie stood up. "Nothing, eh? Just like the last time. What, didn't you put any effort into it?

"Stay here," he commanded. "Sparrowhawk, see that he stays here." And then he was gone.

2

He heard them first. Pounding on the front door with full fists, the sound echoing throughout the house. Then, downstairs, in the front hall. Their voices, loud, raised in anger, the voices of authority, demanding to see him. Then their heavy and determined footsteps on the stairs and thudding down the hall. How many there were, Dunphail couldn't tell. Nor did it matter. 'Struth, it didn't even matter who they were.

Dispassionately he regarded the drying blood, the neat row of fresh scabbing across his knuckles.

Dunphail had been sitting in the music room since it happened. For how long, he could not have said. Sitting, while the candles in the mirrored wall sconces burnt down in unheeded increments, never noticed, until that moment when they guttered fitfully and faded—golden light into sinking gloom. Sitting, while the rest of his world went about their preparations for the evening. Sitting, while in the hearth the fire the servants lit each afternoon had long since died to embers and outside a shower had passed over with a hard burst of evening rain, darkening the sky to an impenetrable, smoky pitch, soaking the sweeping boys, then to move on. And he was no wiser for it.

What had happened? He couldn't say. Why had he turned on Boy? For that he had no answer certainly. What had made his temper snap? Christ only knew. For until this afternoon, he would have said they rubbed along well together. Indeed, since that splendid bout with Shuster, he'd grown quite fond of the boy.

He gazed about the music room, at the fine fitments and especially at the fortepiano—and acknowledged his folly. Ned would not have begrudged Boy the use of it. On the contrary.

And at some point too he had realised that the boy had been playing without music—something to do with his memory, Jesuadon would doubtless tell him, though he hardly knew what that meant.

But he could make no sense of it. Except to recognise that in attacking the boy he had become what he deplored—in so doing, he had violated his every principle, dishonoured and degraded his title and himself. And he wondered what they would now demand he do? That he put a pistol to his head? For what did this make him? What was he now? A traitor?

He heard the rolling crunch of carriage wheels and the even clop clop clop of horses trotting in the street below.

He heard them throw open the door. But still he remained where he was and did not look up. Not until their hands were grabbing hold of his cravat, laying hold of his lapels, and yanking him to his feet did he raise his eyes. It was Georgie and Jesuadon.

Inch for inch, either of them was his match. And one alone, he could have taken. The pair of them, acting together, not a whore's chance in heaven.

And back of them, another. A bear of a balding man, built like Tom Cribb with his neck as wide as his head and pale lashless eyes—a likely ribroaster. He was in for a bruising then.

So be it. It was no less than he deserved, despite his title.

"What the blazes do you think you're playing at, Dunphail?" Jesuadon barked. He was dressed still in his clothes of the previous evening and smelled like he been drinking steadily since Dunphail had last seen him.

Together, Jesuadon and Georgie hauled him up and shoved him against the near wall, pinning him there.

"'Struth, Dunphail, do you have any idea what you've done? What the devil are you about?" Georgie demanded.

Dunphail looked from the one to the other, their faces charged with anger, and braced himself.

"I should fecking kill you for this!"

"Have you taken leave of your senses?"

"Do you know how many lives you've put at risk?"

"Castlereagh is going to demand your bawbles for this…"

"…A whole mission snabbled and for what?"

"Do you know how long we've been working on this, just to get this close?" Jesuadon slammed his fist into Dunphail's ribs. Dunphail gasped, caught a breath, recovered.

"And now you…"

"Who are you working for, just tell me that?" Jesuadon ground out the words, pressing his fist hard to Dunphail's chin.

"What in the blazes happened here?" Georgie repeated. "What? Tell me!"

"I give you my word, I don't know," Dunphail said at last.

"What the devil do you mean, you don't know?" Jesuadon snapped. His temper was dangerously fraying.

"'Struth, I don't. Upon my life. I don't know. 'Sblood, I came home and I heard him playing the fortepiano. Od's teeth, I didn't even know he could play the damned thing. So I thought it was Ned, come home. And I came up expecting to find him, only it wasn't. It was Boy. And I lost my head. That's all."

"That's all, is it? Well, that don't explain the state of his pretty face," Jesuadon said sourly.

"No. No," Dunphail agreed as reasonably as he could. "I was angry that it wasn't Ned and I told him to stop…I meant only to give him a wee dunt. Then before I knew it, he was abusing me, so I hit him again. Then he pulled a knife on me."

Georgie eyed him warily. "That at least sounds likely…" he agreed in an undertone. "But why'd you hit him in the first place? Why?"

Dunphail felt a trickle of sweat sliding down over his chin. He tried to frame a sentence, tried to imagine how he might explain and could think of nothing, nothing but that one instant of fear he saw in the boy's face. "I don't know…" he said.

Jesuadon cuffed him hard, just as he had cuffed the boy, hard on the side of the head. "Think harder."

Dunphail looked from one face to another and saw what he had not seen before, professional soldiers whose job was to kill and be killed. And he knew they neither would nor could shew him any mercy. Jesuadon's hold on his cravat had not loosened, but had rather tightened.

"'Struth, I told you, I don't know!"

Rage, murderous and cold had hardened his amber eyes, and his control snapping, Jesuadon grabbed a handful of Dunphail's hair, jerking his head back.

"Jesuadon!" Georgie barked. It was the voice of a commander used to being obeyed. "Don't." And there was a look in his eye that his men would have recognised.

Jesuadon darted Dunphail a skewering glare, then released his head.

"Tell me again what happened, Dunphail?" Georgie barked. "Tell me again," he said, needing to hear, driven to find whatever it was that had set the boy off. He could already hear the Foreign Secretary's tirade.

"I came in," Dunphail whispered, swallowing tightly. "I heard the fortepiano and came up expecting it to be Ned, come home. But it wasnae. It was the boy. And I lost my head…"

"You lost your head?" Jesuadon mocked, banging Dunphail back against the wall. "Well, ain't that fine? A whole six months of tracking down Frenchie bastards who kill our men, all brought to nothing, because you lost your head. Do you know what you have done, you overfed dunderer? How many months I've been working on this?" he breathed, and punched him hard, this time in his stomach.

Dunphail gasped, his breath spurting out of him, and buckled, then struggled to right himself.

"Jesuadon, enough!" Georgie warned.

Dunphail's head held immobile by Jesuadon's hand twisted tight in his cravat, he looked at Georgie. "I lost my head…because I thought it was Ned come home. Upon my life. That's all there is to it."

Behind them, the lashless man was leaning into him, his considerable strength adding to theirs and barring all escape, all movement.

"You expect me to believe that you beat him for touching a fortepiano?" Jesuadon demanded. "Have you lost your poxy head? You gave the boy a basting because he was playing a damned musical instrument?"

"Aye…yes, I…'struth, it was stupid…"

Jesuadon drew back his fist. "Not good enough!" he snapped. "Who are you working for?"

"Guvnor, no! The Captain says 'no.'" the big man grumbled, catching hold of Jesuadon's arm in one hand. "Leave it!" he said, dragging him back.

"Get off, Barnet! And shut your bone box," Jesuadon muttered. "Dunphail gets what's coming to him."

Georgie glanced at Jesuadon, saw the murder in his face and pushed his way in between the pair of them. "No, Jesuadon, stop it…"

"Who are you working for?" Jesuadon raged with renewed ferocity.

"What?" Dunphail muttered. "God's truth, I don't even know what you're talking about…" he said and closed his eyes, bracing himself for the explosion of pain.

"Please, sir?" a small piping voice, a child's voice, broke in.

As one, Shuster, Jesuadon and Barnet looked toward the doorway where a small boy in soiled breeches and without stockings stood, staring open-mouthed at them, even as he darted the occasional glance about the ornate room.

"Please, sir." He looked directly at Shuster. "Capting Shuster? Mr. Sparrowhawk says I'm to tell you, sir, 'He's gone. Mr. Tirrell is gone.'"

"What?" Georgie demanded.

The boy darted a look at Georgie and back at Jesuadon.

"'e's gone,'" he repeated apologetically, as if he were somehow to blame. Then catching sight of the expression in Jesuadon's face, he took to his heels.

"We're all dead men," the lashless man said.

Jesuadon rounded on Dunphail. "This is your doing, Dunphail. He'd still be here right and tight if it wasn't for you. I tell you, if anything happens to him, anything at all, I shall holding you responsible. D'you hear me?"

"We're all dead men," Barnet repeated under his breath.

"Shut up, Barnet."

Jesuadon took a final opportunity to ram Dunphail hard against the wall, then he turned to stalk away, Georgie beside him.

Georgie stopped, and swivelled about. "If you're wise, Dunphail, you'll stay away from Castlereagh. And me. Stay away from me too, and keep away from Ailie. Because of you, that boy has walked straight into a trap. So you'd better start praying that his luck holds and he evades them as he always has. Because I tell you this, I can't answer for what will happen if he don't. D'you understand?"

His breath shallow still and harsh in his bruised and contracting throat, Dunphail nodded. "Aye. Yes."

Jesuadon looked at him again, his expression mean. "Stay out of my way, you fuckster…" he muttered. "Or upon my word, I'll have you…By God, I will have you."

3

In the enclosed darkness, Lord Castlereagh did not see Captain Shuster at first, standing in the distant corner of the inner office, as far from the window as possible. He set the candlestick down upon his desk and thoughtfully regarded the pages of Boy's scrawled transcription. And the list.

"My lord," the Captain said, stepping forth to bow.

"Shuster?" Castlereagh said, spinning around. "What are you doing here at this time of night? Is there news?"

"Yes, my lord."

"And it could not wait until the morning?"

"No, my lord."

Lord Castlereagh raked the corner with a glance, unable to detect more than a darker shadow among shadows, onyx against coal, soot among soil. "Well?"

"The boy, my lord. He's gone."

His reaction was all that Georgie had anticipated. Unseeing, he turned to face him though he was still no more than a voice hidden in the gloom. "What? What has happened?"

Georgie straightened, deliberating, as he had been for the past hour, over his choice of words. "It would appear that he and Dunphail had a bit of…an altercation, my lord."

"An altercation over what?" Lord Castlereagh spoke the words as if they were physical. The irascibility was not far from the surface.

"Dunphail *says* that he came home and found Boy playing Ned Hardy's fortepiano. This, he claims, set him off. And they had words."

Georgie noted that Castlereagh had reacted sharply to the word fortepiano with an almost silent intake of breath. "Should that mean something, sir?" he asked quietly, watching the subtle changing of the Foreign Secretary's expressions in the uncertain light of the single candle-flame, wondering if he imagined the sudden caginess amidst the distorted shadows thrown upon the rear wall.

"No, no," Castlereagh said instantly. "So Dunphail took snuff at that, did he? And then what?"

"Yes…" Georgie hesitated, again for a fraction of an instant. "They had words, which ended with Boy leaving the house, his face looking like a fricassee of beet root." He could not explain his sudden conviction that Castlereagh knew something.

"What? 'Struth, I don't understand," the Foreign Secretary said.

"Dunphail whipped the boy for playing Mr. Hardy's fortepiano?"

"So it would seem, my lord."

"What then?"

"Tirrell made his way to Sparrowhawk's which is where I saw him, having his face seen to. But while I was out…he…disappeared."

Castlereagh narrowed his gaze, peering angrily into the dark. There could be no mistaking his mood. "Do you tell me that he's gone missing? And that no one, not one of Jesuadon's army of sweeping boys, or Barnet's heavies, or any of you have the least idea what has happened to him? You do realise, do you, what this means?"

"Yes…"

Castlereagh carried on as if he had not spoken. "It means, Captain, that the entirety of the case against Wilmot is thrown into the balance. If we need to go in there again, we cannot. It also means that wherever he is, the boy is no longer safe—that is if he's still alive. What the devil were you thinking? How could you let this happen?" Castlereagh picked up a book from his desk and slammed it down hard. "Before God, I am surrounded by fools and miscreants!"

"Yes, my lord."

"You lost him." Again the words were as a hard slap.

Georgie squared his shoulders, though in the dark there was no one to see. "Yes, sir."

Lord Castlereagh's eyes gleamed as he warred with himself. "I should have you court martialled for this." It was quietly said.

"Yes, sir. I deserve no less, sir." Georgie lowered his chin while he assessed the Foreign Secretary. "But if I may, sir, I cannot find him for you if I'm in irons awaiting a court martial."

The Foreign Secretary looked away and did not reply. "Do you believe that Dunphail is working for the French?"

"No, sir."

"No, nor do I."

"Sir," Georgie began. "Is there any reason that I should know of why Tirrell would have fled after being discovered playing a fortepiano?"

Lord Castlereagh hesitated, his eagle's beak of nose hideously large in the sputtering light of the candle.

Georgie watched, then said: "To be sure, I had no idea he was musical. But then, I barely know him, only his reputation…and the few times I've worked alongside him, well…"

Lord Castlereagh groped his way into his desk chair, and sat, cradling his chin in his hand, pondering the list before him. "Who knows anything about Boy?" he said softly.

"Have Jesuadon search the docks and send men down into Kent. Having seen his name upon that list, I must assume he will have avoided the place, but one can never tell. Sometimes he likes to…cant with death," Castlereagh said, his mouth twisting into a pensive line. "Tell Jesuadon too to set a watch on everyone on the list." He gave a snort of bitter laughter. "Those still alive, that is. And tell him to press on as he thinks best. We must proceed with what we have…"

Georgie stepped into the small light. "Yes, my lord. Thank you, sir." And making his obedience, he made his way from the room into the blackened shell of the outer office and from thence into the street, striding now, through the grinding whirr of the darkened city to Charing Cross.

Chapter XXXV

1

There was no dawn, just a slow thinning of night into the obscuring mist which lay sagging and inert over the city like a slattern in her bed. Jesuadon gazed out of one clouded window to the dockside and drank down his tankard of flip. Fistfuls of fog swirled and eddied before fading about the forest of masts—all he could see of the multitude of boats, skiffs and barges, all confined to port, becalmed beneath the stagnant sky, the bustle and rush of St. Katharine's Docks brought to a muffled, deadening halt.

Barnet stumped in, a scarf wound high about his neck, small comfort against the insidious damp, and slamming the inn door behind him, peered at the barometer of Jesuadon's fair face. Finding it calm, placid even, he instantly distrusted it. He came over and squeezed his bulk into the space between table and settle. "So…did you find out where the lad's gone?" he asked, noting that at last Jesuadon had changed from his soiled evening clothes into a green coat and a buckskin waistcoat, both of which had seen better days.

"No." Jesuadon appeared untroubled. "I fancy I know how though…"

"Oh yes?"

About them was the daily grind and hubbub of sailors in their torn jerseys—Jack Nasty Faces to a man with their knuckles and hands tattooed—river plunderers, lumpers and threepenny uprights, all drinking and grumbling and coughing their phlegm as the publican ran up their scores in chalk on the walls nearest the bar.

"Not that this excuses the sweeps in any way, but I would imagine the unlicked cub did nothing more ingenious than slip through the streets as he always does, and when he got down here, met up with someone he knew who was about to up-sails. No more to it than that."

"The Guvnor ain't going to like it."

"No, I dare say he's not," Jesuadon observed, his attention still focused on the inactivity beyond the window: the dull clap and slap of the waves against the docks and sea wall and the ropes against the masts. "And that being the case, I feel I shall in this instance leave his mind unburdened with the unpalatable truth." He drank down the final swill of flip and then signalled to the publican for another. "Besides, he's already blaming Shuster, so I can see no reason to apportion any of the blame…Now, what did you want to tell me?"

Barnet eyed him warily, distrusting the passivity, the supine good humour. "And no idea where he's gone?"

"No, none. With the fog, no one recalls much of anything…" Jesuadon shrugged, as if to dismiss the whole. "But I feel sure you have something to tell me, do you not?" he coaxed.

Barnet slanted him a speculative glance. "It's about Wilmot, Guv. The thing is…he's gone." He braced himself for the sudden, inevitable damning.

"Yes, I thought he might do that," Jesuadon said as the the second tankard was brought to the table. "And another for my friend here," he said to the publican.

"…For you see, I rather cleaned him out the other night. So I fancy he has gone off on a repairing lease. Though he will no doubt have put it about that he's gone home to Hampshire for the holidays. Which serves us with a bit of extra time." He smiled amiably as if he were very drunk and knew no better.

"I thought you said you wasn't going to ruin him at cards…"

"I did. But I changed my mind. I didn't like him."

Barnet gave a rumble of unpleasant laughter, displaying his browning and broken teeth.

"I also fancy," Jesuadon continued evenly. "That he has gone down to see what Waley's been up to. Or perhaps to touch him for a bit of rhino."

Barnet chuckled. "He'll not get much joy there..."

"Will he not?" Jesuadon said, as if he had no care in the matter.

"Not unless he grows fins like a merman..." Barnet smile grew, repellent, confident.

Jesuadon's eyes widened expectantly.

And still the smile grew. "A very sad business, it were...Waley took his boat out—where he was headed I cannot say—but it weren't but a league away from shore when it began to sink. The Gentlemen managed to save all the crew, but Waley, well, whatever the cause, he went down with his boat..."

"Did he?" Jesuadon contrived to appear saddened. "Did he, indeed? 'Struth, that is a tragic tale, Barnet. Most tragic. '*Halb zog sie ihn, halb sank er hin, Und ward nicht mehr gesehen...*'" he mocked. "Ah, you don't speak German, do you? Never mind. Still, it is a wonder that you can tell such a tale without weeping." He downed the second tankard full. "But speaking of tragic tales...I am in need of a corpse," he said softly.

And suddenly Barnet saw that Jesuadon was no longer smiling and that his eyes had begun to glitter dangerously, and he paled. "A corpse? What d'you want with a corpse?" he dared.

"Not just any corpse. A new corpse. A woman. About five and twenty years of age, no taller than my chin, of slight build, dark-haired and dark-eyed."

"What do you want with a corpse?" Barnet repeated.

"Just do it."

Covertly, Barnet eyed him. "And when I've found you this corpse, what then?"

"We'll bring in Wilmot."

"But the Guvnor said to wait," Barnet protested, his voice rising. Then he hushed: "That he wants to bring in all of them..."

"I don't give a damn what the Guvnor said. You have a fortnight." And sniffing hard, Jesuadon stood and without a backward glance, strode from the squalid taproom and out into the choking mist.

2

Boy arrived to a city in uproar. A dull, fearful uproar of confusion and loss and dismay. A city quaking with disbelief amidst a riot of grief.

Winter in Paris. And walking, listening, he moved through the chaotic shoving crowds of pedestrians, past the jostling, creaking carriages, upon streets coated with stinking mud—the tainting effluvium of uncollected stable sweepings and refuse, ground into a glaucous black mass that coated the boots and shoes of all who ventured forth. Past the tradesmen—the tinsmiths soldering the pots and pans and basins, working shoulder to shoulder with the caners reweaving the buckling chair seats—who set up shop in the midst of it all. Past the water-carriers with their wooden pails and their constant cries of 'À l'eau!' Past the wounded veterans, who having outlived their usefulness to the Emperor now stood daily, begging, impassive, under the fine arches in the Rue de Rivoli, silently saluting the officials who passed on their way to and from the Palais du Louvre. Down alleys barely wide enough for two to pass. Beneath the high brick and stone walls of the abandoned monasteries and convents and churches—the homes from which their inhabitants had been torn by the Revolution only to perish—that bordered the maze of narrow streets of the Latin Quarter and the Île St. Louis. Along the cold banks of the Seine, where the slow barges drifted that carried the wood and wheat and wine that fuelled the city. All the while listening to the snatches of conversation which he could neither explain nor understand. Listening.

And everywhere it was the same, the same hiccoughing silences, the same trembling fear as handkerchiefs were held up to shield the grieving, gasping mouths. In maze upon maze, enclave upon enclave, district upon district. All the same.

Snow had fallen earlier in the week only to be washed away by days of freezing rain that fell like iron filings from the sky. And amidst it all, the misery and confusion, like some airborne thing, spread, contagious as cholera.

About him, and on every street, women young and old had put on their blacks and shuttered their windows. For anyone who had had a son or husband or father or lover gone with Emperor Napoleon to Russia now knew to lose all hope. For they would not be returning. Not covered in glory nor bearing home the treasures of the East. They were all widows now. Their men were dead. All dead.

And so he walked, purposeful, watchful and alert through the knotted, shadowed streets, one more stony-faced boy in this golden city of walled gardens and courtyards, grand Baroque hotels and Renaissance palaces, this city numbed by misfortune. Until eventually he fetched up amidst the bookshops near the ancient buttressed church of St. Séverin, with its flamboyant towers and spires like chateau-turrets, determined to find a copy of the 29th Bulletin of which they all whispered. And was eventually rewarded for his patience and tenacity.

Tucking the cheap pages inside his coat, Boy made his way to a large, barely lit room full of tables and benches which served soup and the chicory they called coffee, run by a man known only as Flicoteaux. And there in the gargote, among the poor students and workmen, the tilers and masons and water-carriers, cradling a too hot mug of coffee in one hand, he removed the pages, spreading them out on the table before him to read.

"Monsieur. Jeune Monsieur…"

Boy looked up. She was young, dressed in ragged blacks, pale beneath a tatty bonnet and with dirty hands. She gestured toward the papers on the table. "It is the Bulletin, yes? The one they published yesterday?"

Boy nodded. "Oui."

"You will read it to me, please? For the price of a coffee? Here…" She counted out five centîmes on the table.

Boy gathered the coins up and replaced them in her hand. "But yes, I will read it to you, Mademoiselle. There is no charge."

Tentatively she lowered herself onto the bench beside him, to perch as if she might flee at any moment.

"Vingt-neuvième bulletin de la Grande Armée, le 3 décembre 1812.

"Until the 6th November, the weather was perfect and the army accomplished all

its manoeuvres with the greatest success. The cold began on the 7th. From that moment, each night we lost several hundred horses in the bivouacs. Upon arriving at Smolensk, we had already lost most of the cavalry and artillery horses...."

"Tous les chevaux? C'est impossible," she whispered. "My fiancé, he was a blacksmith..." she explained, blinking against her tears, biting hard on her bottom lip. "There were more horses than you have ever seen..."

"The cold that had begun on the 7th, suddenly increased and from the 14th to the 15th and the 16th, the thermometer showed 16 and 18 degrees below freezing. The roads were covered with ice. The horses of the cavalry, artillery and baggage train perished during the nights, not by hundreds but by thousands—above all the horses of France and Germany. More than thirty thousand horses died in a few days. Our cavalry found themselves all on foot; our artillery and our transports found themselves without teams. It was necessary to abandon and destroy a good part of our guns, our munitions and victuals. This army, which was so beautiful on the 6th, was so different by the 14th—without cavalry, without artillery, without conveyance."

Boy paused to drink the bitter chicory, and remembering Poland, knew this to be untrue.

"Without cavalry, we could not reconnoitre more than a quarter of a mile; equally, without artillery, we could not risk battle and so we waited unflinchingly. It was necessary to march to avoid being forced into battle for the lack of munitions...without cavalry who could reconnoitre and liaise between columns. This difficulty, added to the excessive cold, rendered our situation painful. Men whom Nature had not tempered strongly enough to rise above these kinds of hazards and bad luck seemed shaken, lost their cheerfulness, their good humour, and dreamed of nothing but misfortunes and catastrophes; those who were created superior to all kept their cheerfulness and their customary manners and experienced a new glory in overcoming these different difficulties..."

"What is he saying? Who could withstand such things, eh?"

The young woman was pressing her hand to her mouth. "Les hommes...les soldats...ils sont morts, n'est-ce pas? If the horses, they could not survive the cold, then how could the men?" she protested against her fingers.

Across from Boy, three masons had squeezed close together on their bench, leaning forward to hear, the plaster from their fingernails and the ridges of their knuckles crumbling onto the table top.

"The enemy who saw on the roads the evidence of the frightful calamity which struck the French army, sought to profit from it. They enveloped all our columns with their Cossacks, surrounding us like Arabs in the desert, the train and the vehicles which carried us. This despicable cavalry, which is nothing but noise and is not capable of penetrating a company of voltigeurs, was made formidable by the favourable circumstances. However the enemy were to regret all these serious endeavours that they tried to undertake; they were knocked down by the viceroy...and lost all their men...

"The Duke of Elchingen (Ney) who with three thousand men formed the rear-guard… was surrounded and found himself in a critical position..."

"Le Maréchale Ney?" the eldest of the masons exclaimed. "Bah! Then all is lost." He folded his arms across his chest.

Boy could feel the presence of others, crowding close behind him, the warmth of their bodies packed together as they leaned toward him, desperate to hear someone read what they could not.

"However, the enemy occupied all the of the Berezina: this river is more than 260 feet wide; it was full of ice and its banks are marshy for over 600 yards which makes it a difficult obstacle to clear. The enemy General had placed his four divisions in different fords where he presumed the French army would want to cross."

From behind, there was a sudden intake of breath.

"On the 26th, at daybreak, the Emperor, after having outwitted the enemy by various manoeuvres during the day of the 25th, came to the village of Stoudienka, and despite the presence of an enemy division, constructed two pontoon bridges across the river. The Duke of Reggio crossed, attacking the enemy and after two hours' engagement, the enemy retired to the head of the bridge at Borisof. General Legrand, an officer of great merit, was grievously but not dangerously wounded. All day of the 26th and the 27th, the army crossed...

"The Partouneaux left Borisof at night. One brigade of that division which formed the rear-guard and which was charged with burning the bridges, left at seven in the evening. It arrived between ten and eleven o'clock. They searched for their first brigade and their division general who had left two hours earlier for they hadn't encountered them en route. Their search was vain and they were consumed with anxiety. All that we have been able to learn is that the first brigade, leaving at five o'clock, had got lost by six—had taken the right instead of taking the left, and had gone two or three leagues in that direction—that in the night and the numbing cold, they were rallied by enemy fire who took them for the French army, surrounded there,

they were wiped out. This cruel misunderstanding lost us two thousand infantry, three hundred horses and three cannon. Rumours were flying that the General of division was not with his column but had marched separately…"

"Nom d'un nom! No news for months except that the Emperor's health has never been better, and then this. Then this!"

Boy glanced over his shoulder, scanning the faces of those now pressing close, for informers, for anyone he knew, for Savary's men.

"The next day, the 29th, we remained on the field of battle. We had to choose between two routes, that of Minsk and that of Vilna. The route to Minsk went through the middle of a swampy, uncultivated forest and it would have been impossible for the army to feed itself. The route to Vilna, on the contrary, passed through very good country. The army, without cavalry, low on ammunition, horribly exhausted after fifty days on the march, bringing in its wake the sick and battle-wounded, needed to reach their depots…

"All the officers and wounded soldiers and all those with stomach troubles, baggage, etc. made for Vilna.

"To say that the army needed to reestablish discipline, recover its strength, restore its cavalry, its artillery and its equipment, that is the result of what has now been done. Rest was the first need. Equipment and horses are arriving. General Bourcier already has more than twenty thousand horses for remounting at different depots. The artillery has already repaired its losses. The generals, the officers and the soldiers have suffered much from exhaustion and want. Many lost their kit following the loss of their horses, some by the Cossack ambushes.

"The Cossacks took numerous isolated men, geographical engineers who were surveying the areas and wounded officers who marched without caution, preferring to run foolish risks rather than to march calmly and in convoys..."

Behind him, he could hear the murmurs of dismay. "Always the Emperor, he tells us of victories and glory, even when they are no victories, like in Spain. If he is now telling us of these terrible losses, what can this mean but that they are all dead?"

"Or taken prisoner by the Cossacks!"

"We shall never see them again."

Boy read on: *"In all these marches, the Emperor always walked in the middle of his Guard, the cavalry commanded by the Duke of Istria, and the infantry commanded by the Duke of Danzig. His Majesty was satisfied with the good spirits of his Guard has shown: it is always ready to go wherever circumstances necessitate; but the circumstances have always been such that his mere presence has sufficed and they have never needed to be to be asked...*

"Our cavalry was dismantled so we had to unite the officers who still had a horse into the forming of four companies of 150 men each. The Generals took on the functions of captains, and the colonels those of NCOs. This sacred squadron, commanded by General Grouchy and under the overall command of the King of Naples, never lost sight of the Emperor in all his marches.

"The health of His Majesty has never been better."

Boy looked up upon them all, noting their faces, the pallor, the disconsolate grief, the disbelief. "And…that's it."

Again there were murmurings from before and behind him, mumbled thank yous and terrible silences, gentle claps on the shoulder and soft 'bon soirs'. His chicory had grown cold. The three masons, pooling their money, brought him a fresh mug of chicory and a bowl of hot soup, with their nodded thanks. Boy turned the bulletin over and began to read it again—to read now all that was not being said.

And knew that he must return to England. And not to Vienna.

Chapter XXXVI

1

Boy had been walking for hours, still walking—listening to the silence of a city where women wept into their pillows and were not comforted. Walking from the Étoile on the hill, where the great stone base of the Arc meant to celebrate Napoleon's victories was half-built, now deserted—a suitable replacement for the monstrous painted plaster elephant which the Emperor had caused to be erected there, before it decayed to become home to thousands of rats. Avoiding the Bois de Boulogne where the bands of thieves and deserters made their wretched camps and the narrow streets where pickpockets clung like barnacles to the shadows, away from the meagre light of the oil lamps strung on ropes between the buildings, tottering in the feeble breeze.

And walking down the Champs Elysées where no light was, only the clean scent of Paris by night, the stars crowded out by clouds from which fell some first indolent flakes of snow, to waft, heavy and floating, in the hushing darkness. Avoiding too the Palais-Royal and the gambling dens there where one might encounter that diamond-studded peacock of power, Cambacères, and where still the rich and foolish sought sanctuary from the desperation of their lives in the rolling of dice or of prostitutes. Walking amongst the shimmering dazzle of falling snow, which spun and rested on the bare-branched trees only to melt—the silence and pristine clarity of the air, so different from London. And even the numbers of whores who nightly strolled under the arches of the Rue de Rivoli were reduced, their ranks thinned by cold and grief.

Not far beyond stood the Palais des Tuileries, surrounded by its maze of formal gardens and a spiked iron railing of a fence. Looking up upon all those darkened, sightless windows and slumbering chambers, secure in his conviction of Castlereagh's fullest disapproval, Boy paused. And heard, not far behind him, the pounding, thundering rush of galloping horses and an unaccompanied coach.

And then he was running. As swinging and lurching, a travelling carriage swept past the corner of the Champs Elysées and onto the Rue de Rivoli, from there to career around the corner of the Palais des Tuileries, still at a full gallop. And running, determined, Boy followed it. For it must be news from the front.

The coach sped under the central archway of the Arc du Carrousel without the sentry guards stopping it. Tired and cold, country boys without a hearth, they came together in its wake to murmur and to shake their heads at the recklessness of the driver—such speed on such a night and in the snow.

With an ear to their mumblings, Boy slipped behind and past them into the expanse of the deserted parade ground that was the palatial courtyard. Crouching down, bent low to the ground, he ran along the stone base of the iron fence. Over the gravel surface as soundless as he might, a moving shadow swallowed up in the darkness and scattering snowfall.

Ahead at the vast entrance, two men were alighting from the carriage, both swathed in heavy cloaks and fur hats.

Edging along the wide stone frontage, from pilaster to window, pilaster to window, a wraithy figure in the unlit gloom, Boy listened, straining to hear. Flattening himself against the darkest side of a column. For it was not just news. He knew the roughened peasant Corsican pronunciation, the coarse oaths and imprecations, of the one who waited, while the other tapped imperiously and continually at the heavy glass of the locked door.

Slowly Boy allowed his hand to creep along his waist to the hilt of his knife. He closed his fingers around the smooth horn handle. Ready to draw. Readier to throw.

The door swung open.

A fat porter in his nightshirt held a single candle in a nightstand aloft.

"Oui?"

And then it was too late.

"Cock." It was an exhalation of breath, no more, into his cupped fist.

And so he waited, there in the unbroken darkness, as the snow flurried and waned to leave no trace on the hard ground. Listening to the blustering explanations which the porter did not believe from the men he did not recognise. Until at last, the porter's waddling pigeon of a wife, herself swathed in a woollen dressing gown, came to investigate, exclaiming in surprise and confoundment, "It is He, Himself. It is the Emperor."

Squeezed between a pillar and the stone wall, hidden within the blackened courtyard, Boy waited. Within minutes, the palace windows shone with yellow light which spilled onto the courtyard gravel as servants scurried to perform His bidding; as the Emperor's totty-headed Austrian wife was roused and fell upon his neck with shouts and screams of joy which were heard even by the sentries; as messengers, dragging themselves into their coats, their nightshirts hastily tucked into their ill-buttoned breeches, tumbled from the doors, sent by the Emperor, demanding the presence of his officials. Now. At midnight on the eighteenth December 1812.

Waiting, Boy huddled against the cold as his feet and legs cramped and grew numb. Waiting, he blew into his cupped hands so that there would be no cloud of breath to betray his presence. And eventually was rewarded for it, heard it confirmed by two different messengers: tomorrow there would be a normal levée. In the morning. And all Bonaparte's officials, from the Arch-Chancellor, Cambacères, downward, were to be there.

Each day then Boy returned, once even to work within the palace, carrying wood for the Emperor's fires into the rooms they had not used for months, each day a different room for dining, each evening a different salle for Imperial entertainment. Each day and night, gathering news, listening, as about the city rumours abounded, echoing in the thick air of the gargotes and in the shops of the bourgeoisie and as widows sat over their sewing.

For each day, the Emperor refused to say what had happened in Russia. He said there had been a battle during which he had crushed the coward Russians whom he called the lowest, meanest troops on earth. He said they had occupied Moscow. And then he said nothing. Nothing of the troops he had left behind, or were they dead? Nothing of the wives and children who had accompanied the soldiers. Nothing of the hundreds of thousands of horses. Nothing. Not of artillery or cavalry. All he said was France needed to raise a new Grande Armée to take on the new enemies of the Empire. He said they must begin at once. And if all the fields of the Empire must be cultivated by spade so that there might be horses for the cavalry, then so be it.

And with each denial of loss, each tirade, the terrified whispered criticisms multiplied to wend spectre-like through the streets, along the quays and through the charcoal-tinctured air that hung clear beneath the brilliant winter skies. While in their wake came Savary's dust-coloured army of informers and secret police, one day sitting in corners of restaurants, the next lurking in the gargotes of the Left Bank or wandering leery-eyed and predatory amongst the putains. And the price of bread soared still higher.

And now Boy did run.

Always with an eye over his shoulder. First through the chessboard of mazes of the Left Bank, where alleys led to blind closes as enclave abutted onto enclave, there to clamber over the crumbling walls of those abandoned gardens and courtyards—bloodstained still from the September Massacres. And waiting until there were no more footsteps, friendly or otherwise, silently to lower himself into the street on the other side. In a crush of drunken medical students he crossed the Pont Neuf past Notre Dame to the Right Bank; then made his way through the noisiest, most crowded and chaotic streets, swallowed up in the swells of pedestrians and beggars and jostling carriages to the ruins of a convent near the Porte St. Denis. And from there, through a cellar door deep in the old vault of the refectory, into the stone-clad tunnel that led under the city's walls and customs' gate, a passage known only to smugglers. Smugglers, or intelligence men.

2

Barnet had been searching for Jesuadon all evening. Searching the doss houses to which he escaped when he wasn't luring Wilmot to his doom by degrees. Walking among the street arabs who gathered information for him as they stood beneath the street lamps, arms wrapped about themselves and their brooms, hugging the chilling freezing fog to themselves. Stopping in Sparrowhawk's kitchen for news of him. And did not find him.

And finally gave up and went to stand at the bar of the King's Head where at least he could be certain he would be left to drink in peace.

"What?" Jesuadon said dangerously, coming up from behind. Like all Londoners, he was wearing a heavy greatcoat and muffler up about his jaw. Like them too, he now scanned the heavy skies each time he stepped out for signs of snow, and finding nothing but scavengers, crows and pigeons upon the frost-laden rooftops, wondered if the fog would lift or just freeze and freeze the Thames solid with it.

Barnet regarded his tankard with fondness, the thin foam across the top, the edging of golden liquid peering out from beneath it. He slipped one hand into his pocket, drew out a letter and dropped it on the floor. Bending to retrieve it, he belched, then handed the missive to Jesuadon. "Yours, sir, if I am not much mistook." He did not look him directly in the face, but returned his attention directly to his tankard. And raising it, smiled into his ale as he took a long swill.

Beside him, ignoring the boisterous crowd about them—merry with liquor and the holiday spirits which inspired them to sing a bawdy version of 'Wassail, Wassail'—Jesuadon broke open the green wax seal and spread open the single page. "Come at once," was all it said. But he knew the hand. It was his aunt's.

"Ballocks," he murmured to be heard by none but Barnet. He signalled to the publican for a bottle of Hollands to be brought. And downing his first glass, he blinked against the sting in his eyes and his throat. "I have to go." He stared glassy-eyed at the rear wall and saw none of it.

Barnet took the letter and peered speculatively at the neat copperplate he could not read. "Where?"

"North," he said, his expression still as his mind racing through the catalogue of calamities which might have overtaken Lady Wilmot and his aunt. It had to be Wilmot. But how?

"Riding there, are you?"

"What?" Jesuadon looked about distractedly. Or worse…John Brown. Sweet holy Christ, they'd been caught out again. His mouth twisted with fury. "Yes."

"Is she all right?"

There was no need for a name. Jesuadon tightened his jaw. "I don't know."

"When do you leave?"

"Tomorrow, first light." He was breathless with anxiety, and baring his teeth, clamped them together.

Barnet gave a simple nod. "I'll have a horse ready for you. Take the Great North Road—it'll be safer if there's snow. Stop every three or four hours at the sign of the White Horse to change horses."

Jesuadon poured himself another glass of sky blue and drank it down, his eyes narrowing. "Wilmot's still away. You're certain he's in Hampshire? Right. That shabbaroon of his—with the bad teeth? Find him. And get rid of him. Keep an eye out for Brown too. If you need anything, Shuster will see to it." And setting the glass back on the bar, he turned and stalked away, through the singing, drunken crowd into the night.

3

An early seeping of light was slipping under the eastern horizon. Jesuadon, wrapped still in his greatcoat, a pistol strapped to his thigh and another pair in the saddle holsters, stood on the jossing block of Sparrowhawk's innyard while Barnet brought up the barrel-chested bay.

Barnet regarded him plainly. "He's a bit fresh, but he'll settle…You'll want to change just before Alconbury. Mebbe in Baldock," was his only farewell.

Jesuadon mounted, adjusted his stirrups and turning the bay, disappeared into the foglit dawn. To weave via the back streets his way to Smithfield and from thence, as the dawn hawkers—the purveyors of milk and coal—began to clog the streets calling out their wares, up St. John Street and out of the city. Following in the wake of the stage coaches, through Highgate and Barnet and Hatfield, where like them, he lengthened his stride into a long loping canter. And leaving the traffic and murking skies of London behind, he rode into the deep countryside of Hertfordshire, racing between borders of bare hedge and chittering small birds and fields of stubble laying fallow beneath a covering of hoar frost, shimmering white and eerie in the wintry sunlight.

Through the day, he rode. Stopping only to change horses. And while grooms saddled and refastened his pistol holsters to a fresh horse, to drink down a pint of ale and eat a bite of cheese or cold pie. And remounting, he would ride on, making the most of each fresh horse. Riding. Keeping to the softer ground of the verges, across the flat lands of East Anglia, past Peterborough and Grantham, through the counties of Leicestershire and Lincolnshire, home of the Melton men, and on, up the length of the land. Beneath skyfuls of birds and mountainous, blowing clouds that threatened to soak him, then billowing, shuffling, mounting, raced away. Riding, running against time, against Wilmot, and the early sunset of winter's night. Never slackening nor easing. As hard as his body would allow, staying light in the saddle until his legs and back ached and beyond. Pressing on into the freshening wind of the north, blowing cold and fierce over the moors from the North Sea, buffeting him, flattening the bay's mane against his neck. On. Leaving the neat cultivated fields of the south far behind, and now only the rolling hills of browning bracken and bleaching green and a wide scattering of grazing sheep, shewed in the waning afternoon light.

Riding into the night, as the wind dropped and a biting cold descended. Until at last, stopping to change horses, he walked stiff and slow into the deserted taproom, and easing himself onto a long settle beside the dying fire, gave orders to the innkeeper to rouse him in two hours.

Waking, with the moon high, he remounted to ride on. Over the frosting hardening ground. Still north, where the high ground of the endless moorland was steeped in snow, the road a strip of blue grey between rising black on either side, and there was none but him and the owls abroad.

Dawn was breaking over the eastern horizon of moors, paling the unharrowed land beneath the light, when he passed York. And stopping to breathe deeply, to renew his strength, Jesuadon nudged the bay forward once more. And without stopping or slowing, he cantered on steadily on the winding moorland roads until he came to the top of the rise before the descent into the parkland of Roseberry Lodge.

He halted to survey the scene below, searching out any sign of recent distress or attack or armed men. Anything at all. And could see none. Not in the approach to the house, nor the parkland. Not in the stable block, nor the adjacent farm buildings. Upon the rear hill, the herd of milkers was grazing as they ever had. Which did nothing to calm him. But even the chickens scrabbling in the dust by the stable block seemed as normal.

Alert and wary, he came to the house via the back lane and through the cobbled yard, where the washed linen was hung to dry in the early light of the glaring Yorkshire sun, bright of itself, brighter still reflecting off the surrounding snow-speckled hills. Dismounting, he gave his reins to one of his aunt's cowmen. And stopped at the pump to wash his hands and face. A robin was drinking at the near trough. Dripping, blenching against the stinging cold of the water, Jesuadon came into the kitchen through the open door. Still no intruders, no sign of distress nor dun-clothed watchers.

"A towel, Matcham, if you please," he said, surprising the flustering housekeeper.

He dried his face, then made straight for the keg of ale which stood in the far corner. Drawing himself a tankard full, he drank it down. His eyes and shoulders ached. And his greatcoat flapping about his boots, his pistol in plain sight, fatigue creasing his bleary eyes, he went up into the house to find his aunt.

"I came as soon as I had your letter. What is it?" he said, walking in on Mrs. Richards in her estate room. He bowed. "Ma'am."

The dogs set up a noise, the small terrier dancing and leaping about his feet.

"Dogs!" The voice of absolute authority.

The barking and prancing subsided.

Removing her spectacles, Mrs. Richards looked up upon her nephew, his face grey with exhaustion, his dirt still upon him, coating him with the mud and splash of a day and a night in the saddle, and her face did not warm.

"You gave me your word she was not your mistress, Thomas."

Jesuadon put a hand to his eyes and forehead, rubbing gently at them. Looking up at her again, he saw no sign of affection in her kindly old face, not in the peachlike soft mouth, not in the sparkling blackcurrant eyes. Silently, he blew out a breath of air, then looked away for moment, his mind working to find ramifications even as fatigue gnawed at every muscle. But could find none. And was too tired to care. "What exactly would you wish me to say, Aunt?" he said sourly.

Mrs. Richards made a sweeping motion with her hand. "Is the child yours?" Her mien was as harsh as his own.

Jesuadon stilled. For an instant did not move, not even the muscles of his face. "What?" he sputtered, even as his knees made to buckle. Suddenly lightheaded, he reached for the door handle to steady himself.

"Is the child yours?" she demanded in rising decibels.

Stunned, winded, dumbfoundered, Jesuadon blinked, and could not think. "What?" His eyelids flickered several times more. He shook his head, unable to grasp what he knew his aunt was telling him, even as his mind raced back through the months to measure out the time Lady Wilmot had been at Sparrowhawk's, then rested upon their nights and days together at sea and his possession of her there. Closing his eyes briefly, picturing her in his bed, he shook his head to himself as all remaining colour drained from his already pale features. "Undoubtedly."

And his mind stalling and stumbling over the knowledge that she carried his child, he cast about him for the first time since entering the room, and seeing a wing chair near the fire, crossed to it and sank down.

And just sat while his mind fumbled and the warmth returned to his numbed hands and feet.

Finally, he looked up, his face a still taut blank. "But, has she said…how do you know?"

His aunt looked at him strangely. "She is sick every morning and has no monthly cycle…"

And when he only nodded, still with utter confoundment, she added, "She doesn't know, Thomas. She believes it all to be a bit of fish that didn't agree with her during her journey up here…"

When he did nothing but nod vaguely, she continued, "You must marry her, you know."

Looking up, Jesuadon dismissed it. "I can't. I cannot," he murmured. Then he looked away, out of the window onto the winter lawn and the trimmed box hedge frosted with snow and hoar. "She is married."

And the skin stretching tight and pale over his cheekbones, his eyes emptied of expression, he said, "I shall…ehm…make arrangements to remove her today." He shook his head again, his mind still joltering over the news. He straightened. "This was all my fault. She is blameless in this."

Mrs. Richards rose, her tiny round figure shrouded in the much muslin of her grey wool gown, and came to stand before him. To frown over his folly. "Heavens, do not be silly, Thomas. This child is as close to a grandchild as I shall ever have. But you cannot expect me to protect her, if you will not tell me whom I am protecting her from. Who is she?"

He looked up from his hands and saw that her affection for him had not altered. She rested her gnarled farmer's hand on his cheek for an instant. Then bustled back to her desk, surprised perhaps at her own show of emotion.

"I cannot tell you," he said soberly. "…She fell into my care because of something she knew…" he began.

"About her husband?" she asked, her gaze intelligent and shrewd.

He hushed her with a glance. "And when London became too dangerous, I could think of no one better to care for her," Jesuadon shook his head yet again. "It is all my doing. 'Struth, I should never have brought her here."

"Don't be foolish, Thomas." Mrs. Richards sat for a moment, her hands crossed over her ample girth, pondering her next words. "I have thought very hard about this over the past sennight, you know. Under other circumstances I would have welcomed this young woman into my home—for she is a dear child. Upon my word, I cannot think how I contrived to go on without her here. And it is evident in every word she speaks that she loves you…

"You look surprised. Well, I have never believed all that nonsense about your behaviour, so I do not find her sentiment so very wonderful—you know I believe your father to have been the greatest fool to ever have walked the earth so we needn't revisit that episode."

Jesuadon opened his mouth, but she forestalled him. "No, listen to me. It is decided—I am changing my will and shall leave everything to her and the child. You don't need my money, you have your own. But you should put your house in order now that you have a child on the way. I don't mean for her to live there. She shall live here with me, of course. She cannot be expected to raise the child on her own."

Undone and breathless with the news of this unborn child, his child, now doubly lost in the presence of his aunt's abiding affection, shuddering almost with exhaustion, Jesuadon nodded in agreement. "Yes. Yes, to be sure. I shall leave that to you and to her. She must…do with it as she wishes." He glanced up to see her look of triumph and gave a tired laugh. "Which was no doubt your plan in any event…" And in that moment, she glimpsed, for one brief instant, the young Thomas as he had been all those years ago, before his father wiped the joy from his fair face.

"Where…is she now?"

"Upstairs, lying down. It helps with her morning sickness…"

Her smile was so kindly, and so bright, that he knew nothing could please her more than the knowledge of his child being born in her house. And this too made him lightheaded. Jesuadon closed his eyes upon the grit that stung and burned his eyelids. "May I take her up some tea?"

She looked him over dispassionately. "Take off your coat first. And wash your hands…I must go into town and shall be back later this afternoon…And this time, you *will* spend the night." None of this was as she would have arranged matters, but it was what it was. Mrs. Richards looked at him wisely and he knew she would brook no argument. "It is a pity you were not here for Christmas. The goose was very fine this year…"

A cup of fine China tea in his hand, Jesuadon stood in the doorway watching Lady Wilmot as she slept and was gripped by a new fierce possessiveness, a desire to protect her—she, so beautiful in her trusting sleep, the most precious sight in the world—wrapped in her dressing gown, covered by a quilt, her dark hair spread and curling on the white linen of her pillow. Silently, he closed the door behind him, and setting the cup down upon a near table, came to lower himself onto the bed, to sit beside her. He brushed a curl from her forehead, feeling again the soft texture of her dark hair, breathing in the scent of her and her chamber—lavender and pinks.

Her eyelids fluttered open. "Oh!" she exclaimed. She smiled in her half-sleep, struggling at the the sight of him to sit upright, dozy and alight with instant happiness.

"Oh! Oh, Mr. Jesuadon!" she almost laughed, dizzy with amazement, pleasure and embarrassment. "What are you doing here?"

Jesuadon looked down upon her, upon her pretty face, her dark eyes so filled with happiness, and she saw his rare smile. "My aunt wrote to me that you had been ill," he said, taking her hand. "So I came at once."

Lady Wilmot drew back and shook her head. "Surely not. It's nothing, I do assure you." She pulled herself almost upright and looked down to check that she was properly covered. Then shook her head again at her own frailty. "She needn't have brought you here. I am certain it is nothing serious. Some bit of fish I ate on the boat…that is all. And it passes, you know. Indeed, today, I am quite well."

Jesuadon sat for a moment, just holding her hand, quiet as was his wont. He searched her face. "It is…nothing you ate."

"I beg your pardon? How can you know?"

Jesuadon hesitated. "Because you…" Unusually, he stammered over the choice of words. "…you are with child. My child," he explained.

"No! No, that is impossible!" she stammered, her eyes widening with shock, and fear, at this proof of her infidelity and wickedness. "It cannot be. No! All those years. And…And Sir Robert said…he said…I was barren. And that it was my fault." She looked wildly about her as her mind hastily assembled the facts and conclusions. "No. Oh, no!"

"It would seem that none of that is true."

"Oh Mr. Jesuadon, what have I done?" she cried. For she was, and there was no escaping it, ruined. Wholly ruined. Everyone knew what happened to cast-off mistresses and their bastard children. They died in the gutter. "Oh no!" she said, pressing her hand to her mouth, crumpling into weeping. "Oh, no!" And the tears streaming down her face, she fell back onto the pillow, gulping and hiccoughing as sobs of black terror began to wrack her.

"Marianne, no. None of that is true," Jesuadon said, pulling her into his arms, bending to kiss her, to smooth her hair from her forehead. "No." And wiping her tears, he whispered, "Marianne, no."

Her face and eyes reddening, she struggled to push away from him, to free herself. "Mrs. Richards will demand I leave as soon as she knows. I must rise. No, I must. I must rise and pack."

"Marianne, no!" he said softly. And meant it.

Hearing the command in his voice, she stilled, fluttering and afraid.

He regarded her, half-smiling. He brushed away her tears, gentling her. "No. You are not about to be thrown into the street. Whatever put that into your head? Aunt Richards has merely gone to town. She…she means to make over her will in your favour. And…even if she were not. I would always look after you. Always. You must know that."

She blinked through new tears, hazy and soft. "Oh." Her hand crept to her stomach and she looked down upon it, surprised and now, marvelling, pleased, and tentative with incipient delight. "Oh. I…I did not know…Oh. Forgive me…"

Twining his hand in her soft hair, cradling her yielding against him, Jesuadon bent to kiss her. And kissing her as always he longed to do, tasting her, the softness of her mouth, the smell of her skin, forgetting his past in her, he found her as perfect as he ever had. Even from that first moment at Sparrowhawk's. More perfect now that she carried his child.

He twisted round to sit up and remove his boots and then his coat. Then, turning back to her, he lay down beside her, kissing and kissing her, stroking the hair away from her face, smoothing his hand over her breasts which were firmer and fuller than they had been, and reaching down to rest his hand against her stomach where his child nestled and grew.

"Mr. Jesuadon…" she began.

"Thomas," he said. "My name is Thomas." More perfect.

Chapter XXXVII

1

Jesuadon did not leave his aunt's until after New Year, but stayed, setting his affairs in order, and sleeping late into the morning in the blue chintz-hung bedroom. And only as new snow was beginning to cover the ochre-coloured hills and the winds swept still colder from the North Sea, did he make his dawn-goodbyes, leaving Marianne within the embrace of Mrs. Richards' generous arms, to begin his journey south.

And as the snow turned to sleet and then to freezing rain, as his hands stiffened on the reins and his feet lost all sensation, as his successive mounts slipped in the muddying roads so that he could not often canter, Jesuadon rode on, planning how he might best destroy Wilmot. One more night of deep play would ruin the jemmy devil. And that was easy enough to accomplish. One evening's visit to the Macao Club would suffice for that. But then? Treason was a slippery business, hellish and elusive. Without Brown in custody, without even knowledge of his whereabouts, what could they prove against Wilmot? And if he swung for treason, what might happen to Marianne?

Decided, Jesuadon arrived back in London late on the afternoon of the second day, tired and weary, while overhead, the sky had ceased to issue forth its fury and the wind had dropped, and high above all a pair of black kite hovered, stalking their next meal. Striding through Sparrowhawk's innyard, he sent for Barnet. And was there in his private chamber, stripped to his smallclothes and shaving his chin, golden in a rectangle of spilled candlelight, when, as ordered, Barnet finally appeared—looking and smelling as though he had been trawling the tidal pools with mudlarks.

Barnet remained standing just within the door of the darkened parlour.

Jesuadon did not turn, but viewed him in the oblique reflection of the angled mirror. He drew the razor up the length of his throat, scraping through the lather. "Have you found me a body yet?"

Barnet, holding his hat in his hands, twisted the brim round. The parlour was cold though a small fire had been lit in the grate. A listless cloud of steam was rising from Jesuadon's waiting bath to hang, wilting the air, before drifting out through the dressing room doorway like cloud of summer haze.

"I think I have. A woman, young, with dark hair, you said. No taller than your chin, neat figure. That is what you said, right?"

Jesuadon scraped another bladeful of lather from off his jaw and wiped it on a rough dobby cloth. "Where is she now?"

"A cold cellar down the Mint."

With short strokes Jesuadon shaved his cheek. "Wait there. I shall give you the clothes I want you to dress her in…"

"What?" Barnet ogled.

"'Sdeath, just do as you're told this once, Barnet. And when I give you the word, I shall want the body dumped in the river. Anchor it, so that it can be found a couple of days later, yes?" He ignored Barnet's reaction. Contorting his face, Jesuadon shaved his other cheek. Then finished, he wiped the remaining lather from his face with the cloth and turned.

His eyes were as cold as Barnet had ever seen them, shining hard like stones.

"I shall want you to beat the face about a bit...break her nose, that sort of thing...before she goes in the water," Jesuadon continued deliberately.

"What?" Barnet rebelled.

"'Struth, she'll not feel it, you mush pate. She's dead." His glance was unpleasant. "Or if you dislike the business so much, have one of your shit-sack cutthroats see to it."

But Barnet's glare was an unyielding match for his own. "There's no need," he grumbled. "Whoever she was fell to her death and broke her neck and nose and all sorts on the way down." He shrugged and his lashless eyes flickered. "Reckon she had a bashing with her bawd before she fell."

"Ah…Then as you say, there is no need. Better and better."

Barnet regarded him, studying him openly. Then ventured, "So…all was right and tight, up North, was it? You got there? The horses went all right?"

Jesuadon's face cleared and briefly softened. "Yes…yes."

2

The 29th Bulletin sewn into his coat-tail and all that he had seen and heard imprinted upon his mind, Boy came ashore in Kent and began to run. Landed not far from Rye—Rye, where he should never have been. *Semple. Flint. Wyndham. Fiske. Ladyman. Taylor. Bretherton. Barnet. Hillier. Wilson. St. George. Norman. Planta. A boy operating out of Rye—brown hair. Myddelton. Gransby.*

And London-bound, he ran. Across a seamless, now unfamiliar landscape, blanketed as far as the eye could see, steeped in snow, the landscape reversed, the colours paled and dimmed by the cold, all drained to dull, to a muted grey and white beneath skies that loured and gave no light.

Running.

Upon the pristine byways, deserted in the dawn. Slowing, he listened to the peculiar creak and crunch of the snow beneath his boots. Walking. Along lanes and paths near the coach road but never on it, lanes pockmarked with the footfalls of hares among the cart-rutted snow, scratched with the three-pronged prints of small birds. Paths dappled and swept with the scattered random crossings of dog prints or those of lone fox, or a trail of badgers.

In the distance, he heard the dull pop of a fowling piece—a hunter out for his dinner. And in village after village, where the vague, acrid scent of coal-fires—the scent of warmth—flavoured the cold air, as the sun rose across the fields, there were gangs of boys, laughing, and lobbing balls of snow that broke and feathered in the air, and the barking tocsins of dogs, their noise clashing with the stillness. But between, nothing. Nothing but the silence of the country in winter, of birdsong echoing strangely from the muting surface of clean white, underscored by the sounds of rippling streams as yet unfrozen.

He had not come to stay. He had had to come—come as a spectre merely, to be seen by no one. And he would not remain. He would leave the Bulletin on the Foreign Secretary's desk with a full report of Bonaparte's intentions and commands, and then be away again. Before Castlereagh returned and could order him otherwise. Perhaps going to Hohenkirchen, perhaps never to return, but to find service elsewhere. In Vienna perhaps.

And walking, unpursued and solitary, he stopped at Goudhurst by the old Hope Mill, timber-framed and bright against the bleakening sky, on the bridge over the sluice gates, to look out over the river and up. To rest his chin upon his folded arms and there to listen to the rushing of the Teise, unnaturally loud. To watch it churning and rippling grey and chill. An uncompanioned moorhen scudded out from the roots of a willow planted downstream at the river's edge, out across the slatey surface of the water, her cry rasping and harsh.

The wind, cruel and unforgiving, was now dying, and a new falling, of snow upon snow, beginning. And snow falling on his face and his ears, pinpricks of cold above his muffled chin, Boy curled his fingers within the woollen peasant's mitts against the chapping cold, to walk on.

Thick like lambswool, the winter fog lay over the city of London to be seen for miles. Lying upon the roofs during the day, with nightfall it descended to the streets, to the cobblestones and doorsteps, to freeze. London, where there had been little snow, and what there had been had been mashed into a thickening mud-spackled slush, lumpen and grey in the afternoon dusk.

Numbing cold and gutfoundered, Boy sidled his way into the city through the thinning lock at Westminster Bridge. Invisible among the costermongers and cowmen, between the horses and carriages and carts, he stayed to the centre of a group of masons returning to town after a few days in the country with their families. And with them, silent, had his dinner in the reeking confines of a mutton pie shop off Haymarket. Then unobserved, he slipped from their midst to make his way though the darkened streets, the many street lamps as yet unlit and unlightable, to the Foreign Office. This one last time. Huddling within his coat, amongst the ranks of holiday drinkers, rowdy in their laughter and song, passing alongside the pairs of cackling, coughing doxies, the foysts and natty lads, along empty passages, heading for the unsampled but bright pleasures of Covent Garden, he slid into a side alley to avoid one of Jesuadon's sweepers.

His collar drawn high against the creeping cold, he hurried down the deserted wall-lined passage and through a mews where rats squealed amongst the refuse. And head down, turning toward Long Acre, he collided against a hulking giant of a man, a bangster by the size of him.

"I beg your pardon, sir." Pushed aside against the brick wall, Boy looked up.

John Brown.

"'Eh, what do you think you're about, petit scélérat..." Brown snarled, towering over him.

John Brown, drunk. The same beetle-brows with dark eyes and low forehead, pox-scarred cheeks...the matted hair.

He grabbed at a handful of Boy's coat collar and shoved him hard against the wall.

There was no time to think. Boy rammed his knee into the Frenchman's balls. "Fuckster."

Brown doubled over with a roar.

Backhanded Boy slammed at his jaw.

Brown straightened. Fast. Too fast. And shaking his head like a stupid roused bull, his breath had shortened to snorting. A love of pain ignited in his eyes. Whetted for violence, fuelled by a week's drinking, he unfurled his fists with a satisfied roar, lashing out with all his strength against the boy—the chitty-faced shrimp who had once eluded him, the one he'd followed for weeks. With a pair of punches he drove him back into the alley.

Grazing his face against the bricks, Boy twisted. And ducked. And swerved. And felt the vicious splintering of shuddering pain as Brown's fists collided with his face and chest and shoulders.

Boy could not hope to win. Only to survive.

Boy ducked another punch, a glancing blow. Brown's fist slammed into the brick wall and he cursed. Backhanded, Boy hit him as hard as he could. With both fists knotted, knocking his head to one side.

Brown shambled and turned. A black trickle slid down his temple. Shoving him, Brown sent him back, then swinging from both directions, he caught Boy between his bundled fists. Left and right and left again and sent him reeling.

Survival.

Every inch now torn with hurt, everything—ribs, face, hands—bruised and bruising, Boy kicked and dodged, ran and swerved, hitting out at Brown with doubled fists, with random blundering punches that made no difference. And with each of Brown's driving blows, Boy's hope faded. The pain numbed his brain. He shook his head. How much longer?

Still Brown kept on. Thump, pain, twist, dodge, run.

Boy heard the scratch of a knife against the brickwork and saw the silvery glint of steel. In Brown's hand now, a cold-iron. A long-bladed hunter's knife. And he was thrusting and slashing like a blinded man gone mad.

This wasn't just a basting.

Dodge and swerve. Duck, *fool*, duck. Run. Turn. Defend with an arm thrown up over his head. Launching himself, throwing his full weight against Brown, Boy tipped him off-balance. And pulled his own knife. Held it tight.

Catching sight of the blade there in the dark, a snarl of pleasure contorted Brown's shadowed face and he roared forward, his mouth gaping like a black maw, still thrusting and slashing against the darkness. He lunged, catching at Boy's coat.

Boy twisted. This way. That. And this. Jabbing with his elbows, scrabbling and kicking.

Laughing greedily, Brown dragged him forward into the street so that he might see his dying face. Jubilant, he thrust the knife into the folds of Boy's coat and slashed outward.

Pain sliced through him, paralysing, searing. Boy stilled, froze. Gasped. Then, shot through with sudden fury, he clenched his teeth and lifting his arm, struck upwards. In a savage slashing arc across Brown's face, across his eyes.

Brown shrieked. Dropped his knife and covered his face.

Boy twisted a final time. Brown lumbered backwards, crumbled to his knees, screaming now, clutching at his face.

Boy could see the blood. "Froggie shit-eater!" And doubling over, he staggered a few steps, gathered the side of his coat against him, clamped it hard against his pierced side. Limping, his breath shortened and shortening, he stumbled and scrambled away. Brown was moaning, keening.

Tripping, Boy shuffled on, one foot in front of the other. Beads of sweat and fear crawled down his face, down his back, down through his breeches. On, until he could no longer hear the Frenchman's bawling.

Through the emptying night streets, his coat pressed hard into his burning side, his mind shrieking against the strident pain, he lurched and staggered, heedless and swaying like a drunkard. House to house, street to street. Blood was soaking into his breeches and shirt, warm and wet in the cold. He could feel it. His breath laboured and shallow, his side afire, he stopped, bent like a cripple against the agony. Supporting himself against a lamp post, shadowless in the murk and fog, he tried to think. Held his coat in place against him, not daring to inspect the damage, and stared blankly about him.

A constant stream of hackney carriages passed him, the horses trotting briskly in the deepening night, the steam rising like clouds from their flanks.

Help. He needed help.

He lifted the fabric if his coat away from his side to peer down upon his waistcoat and saw even in the darkness that it was soaked dark with blood, the fabric gaping. He glanced up. Help. He needed help. Christ, who was there?

Faint, his knees buckled and he nearly fell. Sparrowhawk?

Coming toward him, a trio of tall bevor-hatted gentlemen, bundled deep in their fur-collared greatcoats, their canes tapping against the pavement, saw him—a boy reeling with drunkenness beneath the unequal blur of a street lamp, a boy like so many others in this city of gin-soaked lads, probably a cutpurse—and crossed the road to avoid him.

Steadying himself against the iron railing of a darkened house, Boy looked up and about on the shuttered buildings surrounding him, craning his ear for the sound of a lone hackney. One he might hail. And heard none. Where were they all? Gone for the winter.

He squinted into the fog-smothering darkness, at the neat knockerless houses. Where was he? It had grown colder. Mayfair. He was in Mayfair. Sparrowhawk's was too far. Castlereagh was closest. But he'd be away. In Kent still. Who then?

Only one hope. Pray God he'd be there. Boy wiped his hand, sticky with his own blood, across his mouth. His chin ached with bruising.

Pray God…For there was none else.

A party of fellows, a half dozen or so of them, ambled across the street at the corner, laughing and singing together, badly out of tune, and did not see him.

Straightening, Boy gathered his scattering thoughts, and bundled the front of his coat against his side, to staunch the bleeding. And slowly, his side throbbing and screaming, tearing against every step, every step a triumph of resolution, he walked on. Dragging himself, step by bleeding step, through the night to the house in Mount Street. His only hope.

He'd vowed he'd not go there again. But there was nowhere else. Nowhere else he'd be safe. Safe with all his secrets. Not dead and stripped by eriffs. There were too many people at Sparrowhawk's. At least there he'd be discovered and the Guvnor told. And he still had the key.

Racked and tortured, near to weeping, he set his face to walk on. Still he bled. It was the one place he could think of. The one place he knew he'd be found. Dead or alive, it didn't matter. Someone might be home. And Georgie would be given his coat.

His only hope. Wadding the folds of fabric against the wound he knew was seeping still, a spreading pool of warmth that stiffened the wool as it dried, Boy paused to rest against a wall, his breath coming in short gasps. And still crushing his clothes against his side, he walked, staggering unevenly, in the direction of Dunphail's.

More would be there. More would help him. He could trust More. He had to. And there'd be none to see. More could go for Shuster.

Get to More. But sweet Christ, it hurt so much. Clenching his jaw, clutching his side still harder, he looked about and crossed the final street.

It was late. Well past midnight. Dazed and clumsy, he let himself into the darkened house. A lamp had been left burning on a side table, an unlit taper beside it. There was no noise coming from below stairs, and not even the porter or a footman sitting in the hooded porter's chair. Drowning in pain, he stopped, drooping, and hung onto the newel post while he caught his breath, and willed himself the strength to climb the stairs.

Then, packing the folds of his coat once more against his side, he made his way up, stopping, starting, stumbling along. At the top, he faltered. Then, knowing he was nearly there, nearly, so nearly, he made for Dunphail's bedchamber. Here…here, he told himself, someone would find him. Someone. For Dunphail always slept in his own bed, and someone would come.

He leaned against the wall, out of breath, out of strength, out of courage, doused in a morass of raging pain and weakness. Gasping, he rolled himself toward the door, opened it, fell inside.

A fire was burning in the grate, a newly lit fire, casting a warm orange glow over the darkened and deserted chamber. The candles in stands were lit too. Ahead was Dunphail's bed—large, canopied and hung with heavy dark curtains. Near the fireplace, a Moroccan covered wing chair with a table beside it for Dunphail's wine. Boy clung to the doorframe, closing his eyes against the dizzying lethargy of blood loss.

Then pushing himself forward, with his little remaining strength, he left the door, and staggered forward, fell to his knees before the sofa at the foot of the bed. Inched himself onto it. And silent with relief, he lay there, his arms crossed over his stomach, hugging himself against the pain, keeping the folds of fabric pressed to his side.

Pray God Dunphail returned soon. Please heaven, let him come soon.

Chapter XXXVIII

1

At the sound of the rustle and click of the door-latch, puncturing the silence, Boy opened his eyes.

Taper first, Dunphail entered the room and closed the door. He paused. Though not unsober, he hesitated, uncertain, regarding the lumpen shape huddled upon the sofa.

Boy raised his eyes from Dunphail's boots to his face. "Forgive me." The voice was less than a rasping whisper. "Dunphail," he swallowed.

Dunphail frowned. "Boy? 'Struth, what are you doing here?"

There was a trail of…blood, it looked to be…across the carpet. Aghast, Dunphail looked from the floor to the boy's whitened face.

"Please. Will you get More for me?" It took all his effort just to speak. "He'll know what to do." His breath coming in short, laboured gasps, as Dunphail came to stand over him, alarmed, shocked at the sight of him. "Please…get More," he said so softly.

It was the voice of the desperate, the dying. "Boy, what's happened? You're hurt?" Dunphail knelt to hold his face. "Boy, what has happened?"

"Please," Boy rasped again, his eyelids flittering uncertainly. "Get More."

There was something in the voice. Suffused with sudden fear, with dread, Dunphail looked hard at him. "Aye. Yes. Of course." And then he was gone, nearly running.

Closing his eyes, conserving his strength, consumed with pain, Boy willed himself to wait and to continue breathing. Silent, holding himself still against the raging heat in his side, he waited. Then, at last hearing them outside the door, he opened his eyes once more.

More pushed past Dunphail and came to bend over him, searching the pallid face, seeing the reddening flushes of new bruises and grazes. "What is it, lad? What's toward?"

Boy reached out to take his hand, gripping it hard. "They got me, More. They got me. John Brown. He got me." He swallowed convulsively. "So I need you…to stitch me. Stitch me up. A'right?" His hand was wet, covered in blood.

More looked, and seeing the dried trickles of blood on the long fingers, said urgently, "Where are ye hurt, lad? Show me."

"My side," Boy whispered. He wetted his parching lip. "You must sew me up, More…" His eyes were grown hazy with pain.

More lifted away the coat and looked. Blood had soaked through the dark wool waistcoat, turning the colour to an unseemly black. A pool of it, all up and down his side, soaked into his grubby breeches. He was everywhere blood. "You need a surgeon, lad," More declared.

"No," Boy mouthed. "No surgeon. No doctor." He was emphatic, pleading. "You do it. I've seen you…stitch the horses. Just think of me…as one of your prize lads. I'll be good," he insisted, though his voice shook.

More searched his child's face, divided. Tears had gathered at the corners of his eyes. "Right then."

"And More, there's papers," he mumbled. "In my coat. Get them to the Guvnor. They're sewn in. Get them to Shuster, will you?" He tried to nod.

"A'right, lad. I'll see to it. Now, I want ye to hold fast. D'ye ken? I'm goin' tae move ye to the bed."

The boy gave a jerky little nod, and tears still collecting at the corners of his eyes, he clamped shut his teeth, preparing to be moved and jarred and not to scream.

"Milor'! Pull back the coverlet, will ye?"

For the past weeks, Dunphail had been stricken by a sense of shame which dogged his every waking moment, soured his every pleasure, and all emphasised by the subtle distrust with which he was now treated, and the even subtler ostracisation he had experienced at the hands of Shuster and Castlereagh and Jesuadon. And all of it now swept away, now, by the return of the boy, wounded, perhaps to die. As if in a dream, hovering silent, too stunned to think, staring, Dunphail did as he was bid.

"This'll hurt. But I've got ye," More grunted, and scooping up the small weight of the boy, he brought him round to lay him, white-faced and in a new sweat, on the bed. Cautious as if he were handling a frightened mare, More began to peel away the blood-soaked garments to reveal the wound. He glanced up at Dunphail. "We'll need a razor. You cut away his boots and breeches while I go tae fetch ma things." He gave Boy's hand a squeeze. "I'll no be a minute, lad."

A moment later, stripped of his coat, Dunphail returned from the next room with his razor. Boy was still conscious, though his eyes were already showing signs of fever. He groped for Dunphail's hand.

"Please…forgive me." His voice was fading. "Dunphail? Forgive me…"

Solemnly, Dunphail regarded the anxious, whitening face, then shook his head. "There's nothing to forgive. Not anything. Now stay still…" he said, bending over him, turning his legs so that he could slit his boots away at the seams. First the one and then the other—the worn thread shredding and coming away easily. He peeled them off, then dropped the pieces on the floor.

"Dunphail," Boy pleaded. "Please…"

Any residual anger long since dissipated, gone, Dunphail looked down upon him. "Shh…Hush Boy, don't waste your strength. I need to roll you onto your side so I can cut your coat away…"

And as gently as he could, certain of the courage that kept the boy from screaming, he rolled him onto his side and bent to slice up through his overcoat. Then, his coat. Along the side so as not to damage whatever he'd sewn into the back. A courier. Why had he never even suspected? How could he have been so blind? Then, the waistcoat.

He eased the boy onto his back.

"Tell Jesuadon," Boy insisted. "You must tell him what happened. Tell him I marked Brown for him. Across the eyes. I blinded him. They'll find him easy now."

Dunphail stopped and stared. It was all too much, too brutal, like some form of savage madness. But catching the urgency in the Boy's demand, he gave a nod. "I promise," he declared. He would have promised anything.

He rolled down one of Boy's stockings, then the other, pulling them away from his icy pale feet and threw them on the floor. He came and stood at his head.

The boy was watching. He reached out with one hand. "I'm sorry," he whispered.

Dunphail shook his head. "Hush. 'Struth, there's nought to forgive. You're Castlereagh's boy, remember." He lifted Boy's arm up to remove one side of both his coats together. Then did the same with the other side. Then, he started on the waistcoat buttons.

Boy stretched up, grabbing his hand. "No. Please…" he cried, tears of anguish sliding down, washing his temples of grime as they seeped into his hair. "You don't understand. I never meant…never…to deceive you…" he finished.

Dunphail shook his head again. "I know." Then: "…I need to get your breeches off you…this will hurt."

His eyes brightening, blurring, wandering with fever and pain, Boy kept hold of Dunphail's hand. "No. No, listen." He rolled his head from side to side on the pillow. "Non. Non. M'écoutez, m'écoutez. Il faut que vous le dites qu'on mentait…" He shook his head as if to clear it and began again.

"Nein. Hören Sie mir zu! Sagen Sie…" He nodded.

Dunphail looked to More, seeking guidance, but he was not yet returned. He leaned close. "English, Boy. What is it? Tell me in English…"

Boy tried to focus. "Il faut que vous le dites. Il doit. M'écoutez. Il n'y a rien des chevaux ni des soldats non plus…" And when that elicited no response, he squinted at Dunphail, and tried again, trying to fix his mind, lost between countries, languages.

"Nein? Sagen Sie ihm…das sind alles…Lügen. Tous les soldats, ils sont tout à fait morts…"

"No, Boy!" Dunphail exclaimed. "In English. For God's sake, tell me in English! It's all right. You're safe. Tell me again."

The boy stared upward, unseeing, gripping, crushing Dunphail's hand in his own, blinking at his own uncertain vision. "Le dites…" He gave a small shake of his head. "No…Nein." He drew a panting breath. "Sagen Sie ihm…No. English. Speak English," he scolded himself. His eyelids flickered as he dragged the words from his memory. "Le…" He shook his head and swallowed. "Tell him…tell him it's not what happened. And they're all dead. The horses. The men. Only he and Caulaincourt…it was only him and Caulaincourt who returned that night. And tell him, he's called for a Nouvelle Grande Armée. To be ready by the spring. You must tell him."

"I give you my word, I shall tell him. Upon my honour," he vowed and saw that the boy's eyes had closed.

"Tell him…" Boy mumbled.

Dunphail let go his hand and bent to unbutton his breeches, first on the one side and then on the other, and saw the bloodied stomach and the wound laid bare, a slice deep and clean across his side, just above the hipbone and below his ribs. With the razor he cut open each leg and peeled back the buckskin and the linen smallclothes beneath. And saw something else. And stopped, staring, his mind struck wordless, reeling and unable to comprehend.

Dazed and disarmed, stunned, his mouth falling open, Dunphail looked up, his eyes blank.

More was standing in the doorway, his sack of horse instruments in one arm, a jug of steaming water in his other hand. "Aye," he concurred gently, nodding. "Yon's a lass."

He had no words. He could only blink and stare ahead. He shook his head to clear it and looked down again upon the bloodied stomach and feminine flatness. "Sweet Christ," he murmured. "Sweetest Christ…" he said again, looking down upon her as she bled. "Oh my dear Saviour…" And now, at last, he understood.

More came to stand beside him to survey the wound, still open and sluggishly weeping. "Right, cut the rest away. I'll get ma things ready."

Awkward with knowledge now, Dunphail unknotted and unloosed the neckerchief about her throat, and took the razor to her shirt. Below it, like a tightly fitted waistcoat, a short stained corset of kidskin laced over a thin chemise held her flat and shapeless as any young lad.

Beside him, More had poured the water into a basin and begun to sponge away the dried and drying blood from about her wound.

She cried out when first More poked the needle into her tortured flesh. He stopped, glanced worriedly at Dunphail. "Get some brandy down him…her!"

Dunphail rushed to snatch up the bottle and glass from off the table by the fire. Pouring out a glass, he slid his arm beneath her shoulders to raise her head off the pillow and tip down as much of the liquid as he could. She drank slowly, like a child, obedient in her sleep, until her mouth overflowing, the liquid dribbled down her chin.

More squeezed his eyes shut and wiped the sweat from his forehead and eyes with his forearm. And observing the deepening pallor of her wax-white face, drew the thread through.

Briefly her eyes flickered open, and unfocused and bleary, she sought out More's homely and familiar face as she mouthed the words on a whisper of breath: "Thank you."

And for the next hour, as if in a gin-soaked trance, stern and watchful, Dunphail looked on and did as More bid him in the candle-lit room, in silence, adding new logs to the fire, mopping away the oozing blood or holding the candelabrum closer so that More might take the many tiny stitches required to mend the gash in her side.

At last, More knotted the black thread, and straightened, surveying his work. It was not, perhaps, the neatest of needlework. But it would do. "She wants washing…" he said.

Dunphail looked at him oddly, stupid with exhaustion and strain. "What?" he croaked.

"Aye, and we need to do it the noo while she's still in a faint. It'll pain her less. I'll gae doon tae the kitchen an' heat the water."

Dunphail shook his head, preparing to protest.

"It's no less than I'd do for your horses," growled More.

"I don't even know who she is," Dunphail murmured.

"It doesnae matter who she is," More said patiently. "She's yours. An' she wants bathing."

Dunphail drew himself up, preparing to dispute, to assert his mastery and his position.

"Ye're playin' wi' fire, laddie," More said wisely. "Ye've seen the state o' her. They're no' amateurs, these bully-boys she's up agin. An' I've no wish tae come doon one fine mornin' tae find ma stable laddies wi' their throats slit frae end tae end, d'ye ken? Sae we'll bathe the lass."

Dunphail gazed upon her, this pale child of a girl, stabbed and in a faint on his bed. Sweet Christ, how had it all come to this? Was this war?

"Yes." And still in that haze of a life that had become beyond understanding, he nodded, and went to the dressing room to lay out the towels and to light the candles himself.

And was waiting there for More when the water had been heated and he had carried it up in large canisters. Together, they filled the bottom of the bath and stretched a linen sheet out over the copper tub.

"I'll do it," Dunphail said, going to the side of the bed. Then as tenderly as if she were a new-dropped foal, he bent to gather her up in his arms, lifting her from the bloodied bedclothes. He carried her through to the bath. And there in the irresolute light of a pair of guttering candles, gently he lowered her into its shallow warmth. Her eyes remained closed, her breathing feeble and unsteady.

More soaked the sponge in water, then dampened her cropped hair, rinsing away the sweat of so many weeks of running. He handed the sponge to Dunphail. "I mun go change the bed for her. Be soft, lad. Try not to wake her."

Dunphail took up the sponge. And there in the begrudging grey light of waning night, he began by soaking it first in the warm water. Holding her hands, one and then the other, gently and tentatively he smoothed and washed, rinsing away the grime of who she was not. With awkward tenderness, he soaped the fragile arc of her bruised ribcage, her arms, her legs. And then as he had with her hands, gently he sponged them clean. Then her throat and her face, daubing at the bruises on her cheekbones and temples. Her shoulders and her breast, all of her, as if he were bathing the lifeless form of a beloved child, deriving a comforting numbness from this final and basic act of reverence for the dying.

Finally, his task done, Dunphail scooped her up from the bath and went to sit on the near chair, and there in the silence to cradle her, naked, pale and beautiful in his lap, her limbs hanging heavy and still in the diffusing moonlight that poured suddenly through the tall arched window, broke on the transom bar, pooled on the carpet. Sat, flooded with wave upon wave of loss, surge and reflux, while More dried her. Then, in silence still, he rose and carried her back to the bedchamber, to lay her upon the newly made bed.

More leaned forward to smear a stripe of liniment, pungent and heady, the scents of myrrh and basil and lavender combined, over her stitched side.

"What are you doing, More?" Dunphail exclaimed, sputtering with a sudden noseful.

"'Tis good enough for your horses," More bristled. "Or is she of less value than them?" He pressed a folded linen square against the final trickling from her wound.

Dunphail wiped his nose. "No. Of course not," he said quietly.

More placed yet another pad over the first, then with Dunphail's help, he wrapped her in strips of clean linen, binding the pads in place across her side. Finally, he gathered one of Dunphail's nightshirts over her head and drew it down to cover her as best he might. He pulled the sheets and blankets and coverlet about her, tucking them against her sides.

Standing for a moment, looking down upon her, sleeping and unstirring, her breath settling to a patient shallowness, More let out a sigh. "Right then. Ye'll need to get those papers tae his lordship," he said, bending down to retrieve her slashed coat and feeling it for some sign of stiffness. "Aye, here they are. An' there's Captain Shuster tae inform, like she said."

Still, disconsolate with loss, inchoate with regret, Dunphail gazed upon her. Who was she? What was she? Sweet Christ, how had a young lass come to be involved in this, this young lass, this girl he himself had come to strike? Wearily, he shook his head. Dear God, what game was this? "Aye. Aye, I'll go now." He looked up. "You stay with her."

2

Dunphail stood in the not so much dawn as a lessening of night and banged on the rear door of Shuster's house in Curzon Street. Where the blazes were they? His breath made clouds in the bitter air. He beat harder on the door. Harder, relentlessly.

South Audley Street had been treacherous beneath a layer of black ice, frozen fog, invisible at that early hour.

Dunphail banged again.

From within, he heard the locks being drawn and the bar lifted. The door swung open, revealing Shuster's batman, home from the Peninsula to tend to his master.

"Fetch the Captain, if you please, " Dunphail ordered, stepping into the unwarmed kitchen. Beneath his arm, he carried her coat and waistcoat, rolled together like a saddle pack. Ailie's Angus rose from his bed before the stove and came to be greeted.

The batman returned and began poking at the embers of the previous evening's fire.

Minutes later, his hair tousled, his face flushed still from the warmth of the marriage bed, Georgie stamped into the kitchen, his dressing gown and breeches hastily thrown on for decency's sake. "What?"

"In private," Dunphail ordered and followed Georgie into the cold darkened hall. "The boy…" Dunphail did not know what Shuster knew of her identity.

"What have you done to him this time, Dunphail?" Georgie barked.

He did not know then. And after such a night, Dunphail was not prepared to suffer insolence. "Nothing," he said scornfully. "Or rather, More has passed the whole of the night sewing him back together."

"What?" Georgie murmured, shocked and now fully awake.

But Dunphail did not halt at Georgie's expression of surprise. "Here are his clothes. He said he had papers sewn into his coat, but I've brought his waistcoast as well." He thrust the bundle into Georgie's hands. "He was set upon, I don't know where, but he said I was to tell you it was

John Brown. And that he marked him for you. Apparently he knifed him across the eyes. And blinded him. More than that, he didn't say. He also said to tell you that…" He stopped, then carefully recalled: "It's not what occurred. They're all dead, horses and men both. Only he and Caulaincourt returned that night. And that there's to be a Nouvelle Grande Armée. To be ready by spring…

"I trust you will know what he means…" Dunphail finished.

Slowly, barely able to grasp it all, Georgie nodded. "Yes. Caulaincourt is Bonaparte's secretary." He looked from the coat, which he had begun turning over in his hands to Dunphail and back to the coat again, the whole side of it stained and stiffened with Boy's dried blood. "How bad is he?"

"Bad," Dunphail admitted. "Very bad. More stitched him up…but I don't know how much blood he'd lost. He's not waked from his faint yet." He sighed heavily as a sudden weight of fatigue hit him.

Georgie nodded.

"I'll see m'self out. He wanted Jesuadon told about Brown…"

Georgie gave a nod. "I'll tell him. And when he wakes…tell him, well done."

But Dunphail had already gone. And lifting the coat to inspect it a second time, Georgie added soberly and to no one, "If he wakes…"

Chapter XXXIX

1

All through the day, as the sun laboured to lift the weight of fog which hung grey as a pigeon's breast over the housetops, shrouding the great dome of St. Paul's and all church towers, Jesuadon, himself dull as a mouse's back among them, half-walked, half-ran. Ran with all his boys, their ceaseless footfalls swallowed up in the clanging, grinding noise of the city, through the labyrinths of the squalor and refuse of men, from Cat's Hole to Pillory Lane, among the clapped-out, clapboard houses of St. Katharine's Dock where the dwellings were as the nests of human rats. Running, their faces a blur as they ran. Running, their hundreds of eyes alert all, stalking, hunting, the man who had struck down the Guvnor's Boy. Slashed him open so that somewhere he now lay dying.

From the gin houses of the Rookery to the shadowed passages of moral decay in Devil's Acre to the dank cellars of the Mint, where the leaning houses blotted out the sky and the streets eked with night soil. Through them all, running. Looking, searching. Listening to the whispers and the unsaid, unspoken answers. Marching through puddles of freezing slurry to prowl the narrow passages that led off Dark Entry and Pye Street, combing the pushing, jumbling crowds in the markets of Petticoat Lane and Whitechapel with their pinched or ruddy faces, looking for the sliced man. And haunting every corner, awake amidst the shuddering clamour of the city, the sweeps, huddling numb amidst the harshening temperatures, stood sentry. They'd all know him now, so they would. John Brown. For he'd been marked, hadn't he—sliced across the eyes—now to be flushed out like the vermin he was.

Running. Down to the Docks at Wapping and Blackwall Point, Jesuadon and his army of irregulars, seeking word of him among the lumpers as they shifted the cargoes of spices and silks. Searching. Among the ragged, vicious children of St. Giles where all decency had been abandoned—the nips and and coveys of young whores, among the bulkers and fraters, wasting out their brief days in the acedia of crime. Buying Brown's life in shillings, with the glint and slip of silver changing hands. For Jesuadon wanted him taken, taken alive.

Along the riverside, where the wind blew fiercest and the shore was crusted with aging blackened mounds of snow. Among the barges and flotsam the iron-grey water was speckled with ice floes, floating down-stream from the Wey Bridge where the river had frozen over, only to break, sending this flotilla of ice, crashing and bungling to build and break against the piles of Westminster Bridge. And only the eelhaulers and river police were out, their ragged scarves woven high to their noses. While above, the gulls cried and dipped and soared.

All day Jesuadon half-ran, half-walked and did not rest. Asking the same questions of the jarkmen and traders and bulkers, the clustering poor with their gin-flushed faces. What had they seen? What did they know? In the dark public houses where the publicans doubled as fences. Searching the desolate shanty towns that spread beyond the city limits, asking of the upright men with their cudgels in hand, surrounded by their leery-eyed, lawless crews.

Running. On through the night. Through the cold and bitter hours, as Barnet's heavies came out to join in the hunt, their torches held alight, their coshes in hand. Hunting among the Covent Garden bawds, out with their ware, among beggars and building sites and half-wrecked ruins. And could find no word, nor any sign.

Brown had vanished. Slipped through their net. Again.

Until towards dawn, the night a spent force of fruitlessness, of folly and gin and sullen-eyed apathy, Barnet met up with Jesuadon, wearing the splash and soil of the streets, in the pie shop off Porridge Island, as he stopped to eat and to wash the night grit from his throat.

For once he was pleased to see Jesuadon's handsome, angry face. Barnet liked a good hunt. "No word yet?"

Jesuadon, warming himself with a steaming toddy, slowly shook his head.

Barnet eyes gleamed, pale and lashless in the eking light. "We'll have him yet, Thos. He's not gone anywhere. You mark my words, he'll come out when he's hungry and then we'll have him. You'll see."

"You had better be right, Barnet. You had better be right," Jesuadon warned, threatening, dangerously close to eruption.

Barnet gave a smile, repellent and confident, showing his browning teeth, then without another word, rose to rejoin the search.

2

"I seen 'im." It was a whisper. No more.

Jesuadon, waking bleary-eyed, lifted his head from the rear table in Mrs. Meadows' Chop Shop. The shopfront was empty, but warmed now by the ovens in the lower kitchen where the day's pies were baking.

"You going to pay me?" the boy said, stretching forth his filthy hand, opened upward, the creases of his palm blackened. It was doubtful he'd ever seen a cake of soap.

Jesuadon shook his head, shaking off the softening remnants of hot toddy drowsiness. He clamped his hand round the child's bony wrist. "Who've you seen?" he asked, his mouth twisting.

"John Brown," the child mumbled. "It's what you call 'im, ain't it?"

Jesuadon's eyes lit. "Where?"

The boy, aged seven or eight, underfed, and dwarfed by poverty and gin, dressed in mismatched rags with a shawl tied over his waistcoat, grey all, shrugged. "How much?" His hair hung in lank strings over his eyes. Recent bruises shewed purple beneath the grime.

Jesuadon slid two fingers into his waistcoat pocket and drew forth a shilling. He laid it on the table. "Where?" he repeated.

The boy looked at the shilling, looked at Jesuadon taut and fair in the lamplight, and licked his lips. "Down the Devil's Acre he was. But he ain't there now."

"Where is he?"

The boy darted a worried glance toward the door.

"Where is he?" Jesuadon growled. "Who is he with?"

"Dunno." It was said too quickly. "He's goin' down to the river, 'e is. Means to head out on the tide. An' there's three of 'em, ya see? An' two slags what keep 'em."

Jesuadon scrutinised the boy's filth-caked face, the dark shifting eyes. "Who are the other two?" He held on hard to the boy's wrist.

The boy gave an insolent shrug. "It were jus' the four o' them, till he come. Now he rules 'em, don't 'e?"

Jesuadon eyed him over, taking in the ragged breeches held together with a bit of rope, the bare legs, the holed overlarge shoes, the lank hair. "How much?"

The boy darted a second glance at the shilling. "If you give me siller, they'll take it, won't they? Beat me for it, won't they?"

"What then?"

The boy hesitated, eyed Jesuadon, weighing him up, shifted from one foot to the other and made up his mind. "I can bring 'im out for you."

"How much?" he said it even softer this time.

The boy lowered his chin. "She's a slag, ain't she, my ma? Allus beatin' me. They beat me too. But she's a whore, ain't she."

Jesuadon examined the wizened face—there was a crusting of blood under his nose—and did not lie. "Yes, she is."

"I don' like it. It's cos o' her, he stops there. Beats 'er, rapes 'er, like they all do, but she allus 'as 'im back, stupid trull, dunshe?"

"How much?" Jesuadon ground out.

The boy swallowed and lowered his chin still further. "A place…" he whispered boldly. "Wif Mr. Barnet. As one o' 'is lads." His eyes dared Jesuadon to deny him.

Jesuadon eyed the boy over with a marked dislike. And waited. "Yes. All right," he agreed. "When?"

"Tonight. I 'eard 'em talkin'. They mean to move 'im tonight. Send someone down to follow me. Not you. Not Mr. Barnet. They'd know 'im. I'll bring 'im along to Blackfriars Bridge…an' then I don't know nothin'."

"You're sure it's John Brown?" Jesuadon demanded.

"Sliced acorse the peepers, ain't he? Big 'n ugly 'n sliced right acorse th' ogles," he said brazenly, a thread of enjoyment lacing his gruff little voice.

"I shall be there." Jesuadon gave a nod. The boy pocketed the shilling and slipped away.

3

Jesuadon wanted John Brown taken quiet. No fanfare, no fuss, quiet. Snatched from Blackfriars Bridge and disappeared. Like a Hindoo conjuror's trick. And not a word to the Bow Street boys nor Flint's lads at the Alien Office. He wanted not one of them told.

For he wanted Brown, to himself and Shuster. Shuster was looking forward to it, said it was for that woman in Dunbar, though Jesuadon knew there was more to it than that—there often was, after all he'd seen. And after they'd finished with the fuckster, the rest of them could do with him as they liked. But first, he wanted Brown emptied, like a cask with its bung pulled, bled of all his secrets. For however long it took.

Along every route to Blackfriars Bridge, he placed his lads, his sweeps and runners and horsemen. Spreading them finely along Holborn, which way he thought they'd probably avoid, and across the lanes and byways, from the Temple with its soot-stained stone buildings and from Newgate, along the river front itself, down among the shoremen, mixing them in amongst those who worked the riverfront and the wooden docks there. And all beneath a patchwork sky pieced of cloud and darkening clear, fading with the day, their ways unlit by torches or dark lanterns, all of them waiting. For however long it would take.

Waiting as the evening hours crept by and inside their boots their limbs turned clay cold. Waiting, their chins buried deep in their soiled neckerchiefs and cravats, their scarves wound high about their faces, their hats pulled down low, and their breaths like the belching of chimneys into the cold night air, and the fog settled in thickening clumps on the black water.

And then he heard, heard the shuffle and thump of one who no longer knew his way. Jesuadon peered into the fog and saw little, saw nothing. A set of shadows creeping and fumbling in and out of the weak lamplight along the stone bridge approach.

Across from him at the bridge entry, Shuster noticed his shifting stance and straightened, now to peer himself into the waste of shifting shadows, now there, now gone.

Jesuadon waited, holding his hand raised against the readied attack. Waited for a glimpse of the face, the bound eyes, and the great shoulders. And drew a soft, gaping breath, for Tirrell had not lied, though he'd doubted him at the time—it was a hulk of a man and would be hell to take.

Brown let out a sudden cry.

For the boy had ducked from beneath his hand to scramble away, caught up and stowed by a pair of sweeps on the near corner. And the cutthroat at his side had been got from behind, got and dragged away, his cries muffled and strangled by two of Barnet's heavies.

And then, Jesuadon was on him, coshing him hard on the side of the head.

But blindness had not lessened Brown's taste for violence. It had freed him, releasing him from the hated shackles of caution or wisdom. Seeing nothing, he lashed out at everything. His flailing fist caught Georgie square across the jaw, and sent him reeling. And delighted at the contact, he threw a punch at his attacker on the right, hitting him in the gut. He could tell it was the gut by the softness of the landing and the whoosh of air it elicited.

And blind, he fought them all, fought them both, taking pleasure in the bursts of roaring pain, pummelling whatever he could sense, hear, and smell, more often than not, hitting one or the other of them. Whoever they were. Driving them off, shattering their faces with brutal punches. For even blind he was more than a match for the weakling English goddams.

Chapter XL

1

Dunphail awoke to the sound of his bath being poured out in the room next door. Awoke unrefreshed, cold, and grit-eyed, his neck and shoulders stiff from sleeping in a chair. Awoke disconsolate and discomfited, grieved by an inexplicable loss. Across from him, in his bed, quiescent and quiet, with only the steady and shallow rise and fall of her breast to shew that still she lived, the nameless girl did not stir.

He rose and went to gaze down upon her, her face paled to an unnatural white and marked with the redding of bruising, the fine veins beneath her eyelids showing blue against rose pink, her brown hair ruffled against the linen pillowcase. She had not moved all night.

In his dressing room, Frazer had cleared away all the mess from the previous night—the water remaining in the bath, the sodden towels, the discarded bloody linens—when he went through. He stood, as ever a curious figure with his swarthy Scots face at odds with his precise appearance, waiting for the laird to appear, the blood-soaked rags in his hands. He did not wait to speak. "I apprehend that Mr. Tirrell has returned, my lord."

Dunphail nodded wearily. He sat to pull off his boots. "Yes, Frazer. Yes, he has."

He held out the soiled linen. "If I may, my lord, offer my services in nursing the young gentleman. I…"

"No, Frazer," Dunphail cut him off. "But thank you. More and I shall attend to him."

"Very good, my lord." He bowed.

"But if anyone calls, I am not home," Dunphail said, stripping off his waistcoat—also bloodstained, he now noticed—and dropping it on the floor, to be followed by his breeches.

"A slight indisposition, my lord?"

"Aye, that'll do."

"Very good, my lord. And if you need me, I am here…" he said, earnest in his longing to be of service.

And throughout the day, Dunphail remained at her bedside, having dragged his chair over the heavy carpet so that he might see always her pale face. Dozing sometimes, and again waking stiff and awkward, watching, snared by remorse and tugged by a thousand regrets for all that he should have seen and known and said, questions he might have asked, observations he should have made, kindness he should have extended, things left undone that he ought to have done and did not. Yet still she did not wake, and still he watched, as the candles on the mantel were lighted and spent and more brought. Or rising, to stretch his legs and his back, he would take a turn about the room, to stand at the window and gaze out into the fog, to be nagged by that litany of missed opportunities, of all that he had left badly done.

Several times, More appeared with trays of food for him. And each time Dunphail asked for news from Castlereagh, from Shuster, from any of them.

But the answer was always the same, "No, milor', no news."

Until Dunphail thought he might shout with unstoppable rage. Then, his anger subsiding in a recognition of its futility, he said finally, "How did you know?"

More stood beside the bed, looking down upon her. He turned. "What? That yon's a lass? I told you." He shrugged, dismissing it. "She couldnae rise in her trot those first days, but she had as deep a seat as ony."

Dunphail shook his head, still not seeing.

"Sidesaddle. She'd learned tae ride a sidesaddle," More explained.

Dunphail gave a silent laugh. "Of course. How stupid of me." And added that one more thing to his list of abject failures.

"You're no' to blame yourself, milor'. But did you not see the roll of fabric sewn into her smallclothes in place of a willy when you stripped 'em off her?"

Dunphail rubbed his forehead. "No. I confess, I wasn't paying much attention to her smallclothes at that particular moment, More."

More grinned patiently. "No, so you weren't…Has she stirred at all?"

"No," Dunphail said.

"I don't like that," More confessed.

"No more do I," Dunphail agreed.

"Do they know?" More asked, nodding his head in the direction of the street.

Dunphail shook his head. "No, I shouldn't think so. Captain Shuster certainly gave no indication of it when I spoke to him this morning…"

More gave a nod, then left the bedside to return to the stables where he might brush the horses till they shone.

Through the night too, as outside the fog lifted and swirled and settled once more, Dunphail remained beside her, watching her silent form, going to build up the fire as it died down and danced again, then coming to stand, gazing down upon her, or to sit, to keep watch over her, listless and lethargic, till sleep overcame him.

Late on the second afternoon, as Dunphail sat staring out over the top of his copy of *Marmion*, More came in with his tray.

Roused, Dunphail looked up. "Any news?" And at More's shake of the head, he added, "Not from any of them? Nothing from Shuster or Jesuadon? 'Struth, what are they doing? Why have they not caught the...madman who did this? 'Fore God, it's insupportable!" he raged in a hushed voice.

More ignored his fury. "Has she stirred?"

"No!" Dunphail snapped.

More stood, his jaw working as he looked upon her, and left. And did not return for another two hours, when he came hurrying down the corridor and threw open the door.

"News?" Dunphail demanded. It was written there in his gillie's face, an urgency.

"Aye," More nodded. "The lad—the sweep they've had on the corner since Boy first stopped with us—he says they're to take him tonight. Down at Blackfriars Bridge."

Instantly, Dunphail was on his feet, heading for his wardrobe. "You stay with her, More. Anyone but me comes nigh her, shoot them."

"What are ye doin'?" More bristled. But already Dunphail had pulled on his boots, taken his greatcoat and hat and gone. More came to stand at the bedroom doorway and heard him below, in the library, throwing open his gun cases. And heard the front door slamming shut behind him.

And then Dunphail was walking and running. Through the fine streets of the West End, past the elegant brick houses, their frontages dark or lit by lamps, running like the huntsman he was, his eyes sharpening in the skirring whirls of fog, seeking out and noting all movement exactly as if stalking the Highland glens near his home—the sweeps on the corner, the trios of gentlemen, the echoing and distended sounds of laughter or loud conversation muffled and magnified by the eddying mist.

There was no hackney carriage to be hailed any closer than Bond Street.

"Temple Bar," he ordered, piling into the smelly interior of the first to stop. "Quick as you can..." He shut the doors upon himself as the horses lurched into a trot.

Through the half-empty wintering streets, down the wide length of the Strand, unstopping, the jarvey drove, while Dunphail gazed out, watching, searching, scouring the mist for every figure he could make out. Then before the jarvey had come to a halt at the Temple, he was out, jumping into the street and tossing a half-crown up to the man. "Keep the change."

The fog was denser down here, so close to the river, hanging heavy like wet canvas. Dunphail turned up his collar. And every sense alert, alive to every danger, he strode down the street. She was his now, his to avenge.

He ducked through the gated archway into the Inner Temple, where on all sides the ancient Tudor and Jacobean buildings rose tall, half-timbered and brick side by side and unevenly distended in the mist, their many coloured brickwork turned to black with the night. Past the great silent stone edifice of the Temple itself, once home of the Knights Templar, and across the crusting grass, frosted over with hoar, then out through a side passage into Dorset Street. Listening. Craving some sound, some indication, some notice of his quarry—footsteps, a cough or sneeze or heavy breath—his eyes seeking out any small movement. But there was none.

Then as he rounded the corner onto New Bridge Street, he heard. Heard the indistinct shuffling of a fight, of the footwork of men, engaging at close quarters, struggling. That and the muffled thuds and grunts of well-aimed punches and their inarticulate replies. Reaching for his pistol, he did not speed, but slowed. Watchful, edging forward into the mist, step by step, unafraid.

There were three of them, grappling together in the open space of Chatham Square.

The tallest he recognised—John Brown, his eyes bandaged over with a strip, and as yet unbowed, striking out in every direction. The others… Georgie and…Jesuadon, both reduced to insignificance by Brown's vast height and shoulders.

Across the way, against the wall, another heavy stood over a fallen man—dead or unconscious—and looping his arms under those of the other, had begun to drag him away.

Ahead, Brown landed a face-breaker which sent Georgie back. He jabbed and rammed with his other arm, struggling to shake Jesuadon off his shoulder. Jesuadon reached up from behind throwing a strangling headlock about Brown's neck.

Maddened, Brown roared and leaned forward, lifting Jesuadon off his feet. Throwing his weight this way and that, he tried to toss Jesuadon off.

Jesuadon held fast.

From behind, a small boy, a street urchin, inched forward, his mouth covered with one hand as he watched.

Dunphail adjusted his hand on his pistol grip.

Georgie leaned in and slammed his fist into Brown's stomach. Then, as Brown bent forward with a whoosh of breath, he knocked Brown's head with his own.

Unfazed, for this was what he lived for, Brown threw a backhanded fist up against his attacker which sent Georgie spinning. He jabbed his elbow hard into Jesuadon's ribcage. Jesuadon dropped to the ground, recovered, and thunked his cosh down hard on the side of Brown's wild head.

Brown staggered and spun, then righted himself. Spittle flew from his mouth.

Georgie came at him once more.

Jesuadon locked his arm about Brown's, twisting it back. Brown grunted, and shoving his weight against Jesuadon, almost dislodged him.

Georgie, clearly weakening, drove home a left hook.

Watching, Dunphail knew one thing of a certainty. They'd never take him. They'd die trying. Raising his left arm, Dunphail lowered his pistol to rest the barrel on it. Cocked the weapon. Took aim. Down the barrel, straight to the heart. And waited for a clear shot.

Jesuadon rammed an elbow into Brown's side. Brown hurled a wild jab at Georgie, clipping him under the chin. Georgie reeled back and fell, striking his head on the wall. He did not move.

Dunphail steadied. Narrowed his gaze. Fired.

Brown's head flew back. He guggled, his mouth open in shock, then slumped, buckling at the knees.

Jesuadon staggered beneath the sudden dead weight of him. And looked out into the mist, scanning it. "Red hell! What the devil have you done, you infernal cod's head?" he cried, his breath coming in short bursts. He dropped Brown, who collapsed onto the cobblestones, a patch of dark spreading from his throat.

And his rage so great he nearly wept with the force of it, Jesuadon cried again, "What have you done?"

Lying still at the base of the wall, Georgie had not moved.

Tucking the pistol into his coat pocket, Dunphail strode forward, his features hardening to a severity. "The boy lies near death in my house and my kinsman lies there bleeding on the cobbles," he said roughly. "God's balls, you would hae been next, laddie. I think I had the right."

With his boot, Dunphail pushed Brown onto his back to regard the evil face, his matted hair spread coiling dark on black like some vile Medusa on the ground. Then, without another word, he went and stood over Georgie. His eyes were closed, his face battered and bruised. But he was still breathing.

Taking hold of his outflung arm, Dunphail hauled Shuster up and straight onto his shoulder. He stopped for a minute to adjust the weight of him, then turned and walked back down New Bridge Street, back into the mist from whence he had come.

More was standing as he had been, when Dunphail finally returned home. Dunphail came in and stood beside him, silent too in his contemplation the sleeping girl and of her stillness.

"I'll look after her. You're needed 'round at Captain Shuster's. Shuster's had the wits knocked out of him and Ailie's in need of your ken," was all he said.

More searched the proud Scots face, the flushed cheeks, the patient grey eyes. "John Brown?"

"Is dead," Dunphail said carelessly. "Go. See to Ailie and her sodger laddie."

Chapter XLI

1

Jesuadon had not slept, of that Barnet was certain. For he had been to all of his rooms, dotted about the city, and not one of them shewed signs of his having been there. Not at Sparrowhawk's, not in the Rookery, not in Stephen's Hotel, nor in any of the others. No one had seen him. And neither was he in the deepest corner of the Blue Boar, the fug-filled public house on the parish boundary of the Clare Market, waiting for Barnet as arranged.

Barnet stood at the bar and listened disinterestedly to the exchange of news between the publican's buxom wife and her brother-in-law, news which included the sorry tale of a fracas not far removed from the premises—something about an old whore from a bawdy house and a rogue and a child gone missing—a girl-child. As if it were a mystery. Barnet kept his suspicions to himself. Finally, the barmaid turned from her gossip and filled Barnet's tankard.

"Thank 'ee kindly, ma'am. Much obliged…" he said and came to sit across from where Jesuadon was meant to be. He set the tankard on the table and applied himself to the appreciation of it, swilling the ale pleasantly in his cheeks. Then finishing it, he headed out to begin the search again and hoped it would not take all day. Not like the last time.

He ambled down Portugal Street and from thence to the Strand, through the press of pedestrians and horsemen, and saw no one he knew.

Shrugging, he turned down to make his lumbering way to the riverfront, to walk among the mud and herring gulls and river debris of the shore, for the fog had lifted beneath a weak show of sunlight. Ahead in the distance, his hair bright as pale new copper, Jesuadon stood among the foot traffic of Chatham Square at the entrance to Blackfriars Bridge.

Barnet climbed up from the shore and through a narrow brick passage, eventually coming up beside him. He looked out upon the hoddy-doddies and pedlars pushing their way onto the bridge. "Brown's body was taken…" he said quietly. "With orders to dump it near Gravesend." He smiled, liking the irony of his own wit. "The tide'll carry it on from there."

Jesuadon's jaw had begun working. He stared in stony silence at the wall where Shuster had broke his head open. He did not turn. "You know it means we have nothing. Nothing at all to pin on Wilmot."

Barnet looked away. He gazed out upon the Thames, a chopping mixture of liquid grey. A pair of barges, piled high with coal and firewood, emerged from under the bridge to float down river. "The boy gave us all we need to pin it on Wilmot," he said mildly.

"I wanted more," Jesuadon said.

"Understood," Barnet said. Then: "You still sore about Dunphail dropping your man, are you?" he asked, risking the inevitable drubbing.

"I wanted him," Jesuadon said.

Unimpressed, Barnet watched the scows and barges and eelhaulers.

"And yes." Jesuadon covered his face with his hands and rubbed it hard. "If I disliked Dunphail before, I find that today I dislike him intensely," he admitted.

Barnet frowned. "For all that he saved your neck?"

"All the more so because of it," Jesuadon said bitterly. In the freshening wind, cold against his face, the hem of his greatcoat flapped about his ankles, just as below, the sails of several fishing boats snapped taut in the breeze.

"But…without him, Captain Shuster'd be dead."

"God's whirlygigs, save your reproachful glances and your sermons, Barnet. They're a waste of time. I have no finer feelings. I thought you knew that."

And there in the shadowless clarity of day, without the tempering kindness of candlelight, Barnet saw that Jesuadon was both angry and resigned. And tired too.

Overhead two herring gulls were screeching, fighting over a scrap of fish.

"Have we got a witness ready to testify against Wilmot?" Jesuadon said at last, gazing off in the other direction.

Barnet gave a nod.

Turning, Jesuadon saw it. "Well, all right, then. Have your lads find the woman's body this afternoon. Inform the Runners. And have them make the arrest this evening, late. And I want to see it."

"I don't see why we need to do it this way…" Barnet complained. "The boy got all we need on Wilmot, and you know it."

"'Struth, it don't matter what we've got or not got. The Guvnor won't want the noise. He won't want the press and the mob getting hold of it and turning Wilmot into some kind of damned folk hero and romping through the streets, turning the city into a figger's paradise."

Barnet shrugged. All this he knew. "Where will you be?"

"The Macao Club."

"With Wilmot?"

"Oh yes," Jesuadon said silkily.

Barnet gave a comprehending nod, but Jesuadon had already gone.

2

A muscle ticking in his cheek, Dunphail stood in the outer office of the Foreign Office, eying the place over without discernible curiosity. Little better than a too-small dressing room with a desk and chair replacing the wardrobe and mirror, it looked to him.

Planta, a man of whom he knew little except that he was the son of that Swiss fellow over at the British Library, had put his head through the double doors to announce him. Then, stepping back, he said, "This way, my lord."

Dunphail went through. He would give it a quarter of an hour.

The Foreign Secretary rose as he entered the room. Behind him,

Planta shut the doors.

Dunphail bowed politely. "I was given to understand you wanted a word," he said evenly.

Castlereagh subjected him to a shrewd, intelligent study. Encountering him, his measured ease and affability, his courtesy and good-humour, one too easily forgot he was a Scottish nobleman of ancient title, who regularly took his seat in the Lords, as well as a laird in his own country (whatever that meant)—Dunphail of Abriachan. Until moments like these. Perhaps he had made a mistake in his first approach?

Castlereagh gestured for him to be seated. He hardly knew him. "Jesuadon tells me that it was your shot that killed Brown," he began.

Dunphail lifted the tails of his coat and sat himself down. "Aye," he said coolly. "It was."

Castlereagh pinched his mouth together in disapproval, but his tone did not alter in amiability. "That was…unfortunate. We had wanted to question him, do you see?"

Dunphail raised an eyebrow. "So I infer," he said, matching the Foreign Secretary for ease and condescension. He drew out his snuffbox and did not offer to share. He waited.

Castlereagh narrowed his gaze. "There will be, you may be relieved to know, no investigation by Bow Street…"

Still, Dunphail waited, saying nothing.

"But I feel I must tell you, you have put an operation at risk, one with the most dreadful consequences. Men have been killed. My men," Castlereagh said, raising his voice.

"Oh, aye?" Dunphail drawled, still unmoved. "And my kinsman was nearly killed last evening. Or did you not consider him one of yours?" The calculated smoothness of Dunphail's tone was at odds with the fiery expression in his eyes. "Had I not shot Brown when I did—the same Brown who nearly killed your boy not once, but twice—Captain Shuster would now be among their number."

Surprised, Castlereagh recoiled. "I beg your pardon?" He had not been prepared for Dunphail's ire. Nor his lack of deference. Nor had he been given all the facts.

"Ah…did your informant not tell you of that?" Dunphail's level gaze meeting that of the Foreign Secretary, silenced him.

Castlereagh shook his head a little. "Captain Shuster?" he repeated, bemused and wrong-footed.

"Aye, Captain Shuster, my kinsman. And Jesuadon would have been next," Dunphail continued deliberately. "Make no doubt of that."

"Good heavens," Castlereagh exclaimed, much dismayed. He had heard none of this. "No, nothing was said to me. I trust…I do trust that Captain Shuster will mend?"

"He had his wits knocked out of him!" snapped Dunphail. "And would be being measured for a pine box had I not brought him home when I did." He stopped, willing his anger to dispel. "My gillie tells me he has woken now, though, and seems to be no more than badly bruised with a rib or two broken."

Castlereagh blinked, his mind struggling to piece together what he had been told with this new information. "That is good news. Very good news, indeed. Not the ribs, of course," he hastened to add. "Forgive me, my lord." He tried to smile. "This has been a most trying business, you know. But…well," he said, attempting an adroit recovery. "But now, thanks to your care, the boy is on the mend too, I make no doubt." His expression matched the brightening in his voice.

"No," Dunphail said, dispelling his hope. "No, the *boy* is not on the mend," he said distinctly, and shook his head, the rage now filtering through the aristocratic polish. He stood and paced to the fireplace, then turned. "He is on the wane. He has not moved once, nor stirred. And even now, he is lying there, dying in my bed. Neither More nor I can know how much blood he lost, nor if he is like to recover. Nor is there any sign that he will improve."

Castlereagh's face whitened and fell still further. He looked away, overcome with sudden despair, then back at Dunphail. "I see…I had not been informed."

"Had you not? For Christ's sake, what in the devil were you thinking sending that child out there to be beaten and stabbed like a snatch gallows?" Suddenly, he could hardly bear the close room and wanted to be out of it, out on the hills with his dogs, walking to clear his head. He had been too long in the South.

"I had little choice." Castlereagh chose his next words carefully. "Her memory, you see, is so very remarkable…"

Dunphail was hardly placated. "'Struth, I was given to understand you had a care for the lass. That being so, how could you keep sending her out like that? She's a wee slip of a thing, and a lass!"

But Castlereagh too had had enough. "I do have a care for her. Upon my life, I have always had a care for her." He looked down on his desk, spread with reports and maps and dispatches, translated ciphers, and the 29th Bulletin. "But I also have a care for this country, my lord. And for the King. And all else must serve that end—regardless of the cost to myself." He paused, briefly, covering his eyes with his hand. Then, with solemn earnestness, he added, "And I am more grateful than I can say for your care of her…"

With a nod, Dunphail acknowledged the Foreign Secretary's admission. Then, leaning against the mantel, considered the room—the many chairs and the two library tables loaded down with maps, both rolled and spread flat—he said, "Tell me at least that you have the ring leader of this infernal business. Or was Brown it?"

"No. No, no," Castlereagh lamented. "He was the muscle. Not the brains. For that, I fear, we must look to Paris and the minister of police." Then he hastened to add, "Jesuadon is…a good man. A very good man. But he takes on too much. And this business has been more tortuous than any we had before encountered. 'Struth, none but you had ever seen Brown before—though he has left a trail of destruction from here to Dunbar. And from beginning to end, we have encountered little but incompetence…" He shook his head as if to dispel, at least momentarily, the strain of office. "So they could not have known…"

"'Fore God, you should have asked me," Dunphail ground out, his eyes darkening with a fierce new anger. "You should have trusted me instead of playing off your schemes."

Bristling, Castlereagh turned the fullness of his shrewd intelligence upon the younger man. "And had I come to you, my lord, and laid the whole situation before you, without dissimulation, would you have said yes?" he snapped.

Dunphail glared, but was honest enough to own the unflattering truth. "No. On no account," he admitted with a measure of chagrin.

"Well, then?...I say again, I am more grateful than I can tell you that you did take her in. And for your care of her," said the Foreign Secretary.

The silence stalled uneasy between them.

"I have been too long away," Dunphail said abruptly. "Sir." Then with nothing more to say, he bowed, turned and left the room.

3

It had been three days and still she had not moved. Still she did not stir. And still Dunphail remained, locked in his chamber, at her bedside, now joined by Comfit—the spaniel having been sent south with a hamper of pheasant and venison, to stop her crying and pining for her master.

They had washed her, and renewed the dressings on her side that morning, and as before More had changed the bedding while Dunphail bathed her. They had found too that her side was closing well. Yet still she did not wake.

After his visit to the Foreign Office, Dunphail returned to the bedchamber, to sit, watching for any sign of fever, any change. Sitting without knowledge. And there he stayed, sitting as morning melted into afternoon and the daylight faded into gloom, and Comfit rose, turned circles on the hearth rug, and settled again. Staring without seeing at the blue green walls of the room, the architraves, overmantel and reeded frames of the fielded panels picked out in white, the ornately moulded ceiling rose overhead.

And as he dozed over Scott once more and the book fell open in his lap, with a sly look at her master, Comfit went and hopped onto the bed. Then wriggled and burrowed her head until it rested beneath the girl's motionless hand, and with a contented sigh, went to sleep.

More, entering with Dunphail's dinner tray, saw the animal at once upon the pale quilt; she cocked one innocent eye. "What did I tell ye…" he started in, the grumbling reproach intended for both the dog and her master.

Dunphail shook his head, shook off his sleep and stood. His book fell unheeded to the floor. And saw. He laid his hand on More's arm, halting the tirade. "No, More. Look."

Tentative, Boy laid a finger upon the soft silken head of the dog as if exploring a thing never before encountered. Touched with uncertainty the surface of the fine fur. Smoothed it. And was nudged in return. And again, prompted by Comfit's insistent, prodding nose, hesitantly, with one finger, she caressed the fine head, felt it, dwelt upon it. Then was still.

Drawing a great breath, she filled her lungs and exhaled. And slept on.

More's middle-aged face, so lately drawn with worry, broke open with a wide smile. He gave a satisfied nod. "She lives, my lord. Aye, she lives. She'll do."

Chapter XLII

1

His eyes glittering with menace, with satisfaction, his bright hair tarnished in the linklight, Jesuadon tumbled down the steps of the Macao Club into the half-deserted street and straight into a puddle. He let out a stream of obscenities, each more colourful than the last.

Behind him, Wilmot laughed as Jesuadon inspected the streaks of wet filth on his ankle and continued to curse. "What'd I tell ye, Jesuadon, eh? Ha ha. What'd I tell ye? M'luck's turning a'ready!" he crowed with a gamester's delusion. "You may have had me tonight…what was the final tally? Ten thousand? Ha ha. Never mind that. For you see, t'morrow, I shall have you. You shall see. I can assure you, m'dear boy, m'luck's turned and there's the proof," he declared, pointing at Jesuadon's muddy shoes, still laughing heartily. He followed Jesuadon down the steps, missed the final one and nearly fell.

They were both drunk as emperors.

His soft mouth pursed and petulant, Wilmot looked Jesuadon over knowingly. He fingered his sideburn. "'Struth, you are a mess, ain't you?" he chortled. "Still…I know a little place, just along from here…" he continued. "Verr' discreet they are, and won't be particular about your damned stockin's, so long as your sugar stick's working." He winked and giggled. "Come along now…" He plucked at Jesuadon's sleeve.

"'Struth, what's that?" Wilmot exclaimed, now peering into the darkness where further down the street a crowd of men were surging toward them, greatcoated and hatted against the cold, their puttering, blazing torches casting them into a single force as they moved and merged, shifting in shape down the quiet street.

Wilmot sniggered. He did not see Jesuadon's steady gaze darkening, nor the slight smile which he, for all his practised stillness, could not prevent nor contain.

From somewhere nearby erupted the mournful howling of two tomcats preparing for war, followed by the scrabbling cries and shrieks of their skirmish, then the chink of a bottle on the cobbles.

"'Struth, not a mob of peep o' day boys, is it?" Wilmot complained. "Ha ha ha. Where's Byron when you need the fellow, eh?"

The crowd of men, all led by one tall, balding, round-bellied man, were striding along at quite a pace and with purpose. "There he is!" one of their number exclaimed.

Wobbling, his hand still on Jesuadon's arm, Wilmot turned to ogle him. "What have you done now, dear boy?" he murmured, his mouth stretching into a stage sneer. "Debauched some Cit's daughter?"

The balding man laid hold of Wilmot's shoulder. "Robert Wilmot? Sir Robert Wilmot?" The remainder of the men crowded round, their faces sinister in the uneven flame and shadow of their torches which poisoned the night air with the acrid scent of burning pitch.

"What d'you want? Take your hands off me this instant!" Wilmot demanded.

"Robert Wilmot, in the name of the Law, I arrest you for the murder of Marianne Wilmot."

Wilmot choked, struggling to free himself from the tightening grip on his shoulder. "What? My wife? That bitch? Leave go of me! I didn't kill her. I don't know where she is. Take your hands off me, you poxy bangster!" he demanded, striking out and missing, squirming, trying to prise himself free. "What the devil is this? I didn't kill her!" he insisted. "She ran away. Who in the blazes d'you think you are?"

Two others, burlier than the first, stepped up to loop their arms beneath Wilmot's.

A lone hackney clattered past, the jarvey stern-faced and unheeding.

The balding man stepped back to consult his notebook in the wavering light of a torch. He subjected Wilmot to a pitiless, disinterested scrutiny. "Yes, that's him," he confirmed to himself. "Bring him along, lads."

"Jesuadon. Jesuadon! Where are you?" Wilmot screamed, turning this way and that, trying to catch sight of his friend. "Tell 'em, I've not killed the bitch! 'Struth, I don't know where she is. She ran away! Take your filthy hands off me…"

The porter from the Macao Club had opened the door to investigate the noise and commotion. He watched in eager silence. Behind him, a bevy of gentlemen were craning for a better look.

"Come along now…" the Runner said, tucking his notebook back inside his coat pocket. "This don't need to take all night. I've my bed to get to."

Another man, also tall, also balding, detached himself from the crowd of armed men to blend into the shadows. He gave a nod.

Beside him, Jesuadon gave his rare smile. "Where are they taking him?" he murmured.

"First to the Magistrate. Then to the cells."

"Delightful…" His eyes bright, unblurred, Jesuadon paused to savour the moment, this moment of Wilmot's fall, the which he had been crafting all these months. "Now get yourself over to Chesterfield Street before the bailiffs arrive. I want that list of agents. And anything else you can find. Boy said there was a cache in the study—in the mantelpiece. I want his account books too."

The porter shut the door firmly. The owner didn't like trouble or the law on his doorstep.

Pushing, hauling, half-lifting, the Bow Street men carried Wilmot down the street.

"Jesuadon!" he yelled again. "I didn't do it. Jesuadon!"

But there was no reply.

2

As the drifting progress of a drop of rain upon a window, unhurried and incurious, slowly Boy came awake to a dull throbbing in her side, to an ache rather than a searing pain. Came awake warm, cocooned within the contenting layers of bedclothes upon and about her. Came awake and sensed the bed linen soft against her fingertips, and her limbs, her shins, her feet, heavy with sleep, but well, unhurt and unharmed. And slowly, opening her eyes to a high canopy of pale pleated silk gathered into a central rosette which she did not recognise, she emerged into sentience. Slowly still, searching, her gaze travelled over the bed draperies, down the carved and gilded bedposts—she recognised none of it. Could grasp nothing beyond a pellucid distillation of knowledge that she was, somehow, safe and no longer in danger, alive and not dead.

Against her skin, she felt the linen strips bound about her waist, the bandaging of her side, the lumps and folds of a large nightshirt tucked about and between her legs—undressed by someone, sometime. Known. Cared for.

The curtains were drawn and a pair of candles lit upon the mantel. Night, it must be. The bedsheets smelled soft—of lavender and of ointment, hinting of herbs. A fire burned in the hearth, hissing and popping, scoring the comfortable silence with the sound of warmth, of home. Beside it, his long legs stretched out before him, Dunphail sat reading.

Glancing up as had become his habit, he saw that her eyes were opened.

Immediately he laid aside his book and came to stand beside her, his smile sombre, tender with kindness and with relief, and without condemnation. "You're awake." His smile broadened with unfeigned pleasure. He took her hand to hold it, warm, in his own.

"I shall get More," he murmured. Then he hesitated, stalling, just to gaze upon her for a moment longer, quietly delighting in the happiness of her survival. "I'll get More," he repeated. "Are…are you thirsty?"

Speech was still too far beyond her—a journey which neither her mind nor her emotions had yet the strength to make, one she could not yet comprehend nor entertain. Considering his question, bereft of words, she nodded.

Dunphail gave her another smile. Gently he released her hand, laying it on the quilt. "More has insisted that what you will want is barley water," he said lightly. There was a wry twist to his mouth. "I suspect you'd rather have brandy. That, I admit, would be my preference…"

She watched him pour out a glass of the barley water from a jug. Then he came, and sitting down beside her, he slid his arm about her shoulders to raise her up, holding the glass while she drank. When she had had enough, he set the glass on the table beside the bed, but himself continued to sit, with his arm warm and close about her. And when More arrived with his fresh ointment and linen strips and warm broth in the spouted invalid's cup, she was again asleep, her soft brown hair, clean from all More's washing, tousled against Dunphail's shirt sleeve.

Chapter XLIII

1

Barnet slipped into Bow Street Magistrates' Court by way of the yard, into the lime-washed back passage begrimed with the years and the passing soil of so many felons who'd walked, stumbled or been dragged through its narrow precincts. A liberal scattering of lime-wash flakes, peeled back and fallen from the patches of rising damp, dappled the filthy paviors. Barnet paid no heed. But, making his way along the dank corridor where the cellar-cold seeped into the bones even in midsummer, sniffing hard at the river must that permeated the place, he emerged into the bare room where the duty officer sat with nothing to mind but a charcoal brazier.

"Vickers," he said, greeting the burly man who sat at the table, his feet propped up beside his ring of keys, paring his nails with his knife.

Vickery looked up at the sound of Barnet's boots echoing in the murky hall, a smile spreading across his homely face. "Ah, Mr. Barnet, good morning to you, sir. What brings you down here to this friendly little pit of Satan?" Tired and bored, he welcomed the company and was ready to chat.

Barnet drew out a folded paper and dropped it onto the table beside Vickery's overlarge shoes and the ring of cell keys. "Sir Charles Flint has a few questions he'd like put to Wilmot."

Jesuadon had said to let Wilmot languish in the cells for a few days. He said it would aid his powers of recollection.

"Sir Charles Flint of the Irish Office, eh?" Vickery picked up the paper and tossed it back at Barnet, without having even glanced at it. He waved him in. "If Flint had wanted the bothersome little pego why'd he have us bring him in? Take him, and good luck to you," he grumbled.

"What's he done, then?" Barnet exclaimed, much surprised. Usually Vickery was a deuced stickler for the rule book.

"Farthest cell down the passageway," Vickery added. He went back to paring his thumb nail.

"You have him in a private cell?" Barnet wondered. And prepared to listen.

Vickery tossed the knife onto the table. "The others would have throttled the nigmenog if'n I hadn't...What's he not done, the simpering frigpig?" Vickery scowled as he thought back on the last two nights. "Hasn't shut his stupid gob neither day or night, has he? Kept on about how it was all a mistake, how he'd not done anything, crying, shouting, moaning, pissing himself..." he said, rolling his eyes. "Finally Jenkins went and give him a chafing which shut his gob...and not before time, the other sad dogs down there was complaining so."

"You have my sympathies, Mr. Vickery," Barnet murmured with a conspirator's smile.

"Save 'em, Barnet," Vickery muttered. "You'll be having mine after ten minutes in his pestiferous company."

Barnet winked. "Right then. I take it you don't want him back talking?"

Vickery gave a jeering laugh. "Do me a favour and knock his damned teeth out."

Barnet grinned with silent laughter. "Has he confessed yet?"

Vickery rolled his eyes again. "He swears he's not seen her for months."

Barnet smiled serenely, giving an approving twist of his head. Vickery had seen it all a hundred times before. "Do you believe him?"

"No," Vickery stated, dismissing it. "It's what they all say." He shook his head over it. "His servants say he mistreated her, beat her and such, and that he was set to pimp her favours to his friends, deuced cod's head. I reckon she said no. So he got nasty, then dumped the body."

Barnet nodded. "Aye," he agreed. "Sounds likely enough. You have proof?"

"Not all of it." Vickery rubbed his ugly face. He'd been there all night while Wilmot had rabbited on. Should have stuffed his ears with cotton wool, is what he should have done. "There's a sweep who swears he saw her arrive in the autumn but can't be certain as to when. And I'm off to his place in Hampshire in the morning to question his servants down there. See what they know about the business."

Still curious, Barnet asked, "Has he identified the body?"

"He refused, the little scrote." Vickery curled his lips. "Guilty conscience, no doubt. And that's what the judge will think too. So his manservant did it. It was her all right. He recognised her ring, her clothes..."

Barnet took up the clanging handful of keys and presented a genial smile. "Mind if I take him for a little stroll down by the river?"

"Do what you like," Vickery said. He shrugged. "Only don't bring 'un back blubbing, will you? I can't abide any more o' that...And neither can Tolly, I tell you..."

"I shall bear that in mind, Mr. Vickery," Barnet said. He let himself into the cells. "You may depend upon it."

He walked past the other cells and their inmates without interest, stopping only when he came to the the cell farthest from the main grille, just as Vickery had said. He studied Wilmot through the cell bars—de-swaggered and undandified, the little fuckster—taking in his linen hanging dirty and slack about his neck, his soiled waistcoat, his grimy and bewrayed breeches, his uncrimped hair now frizzing and stringy. His swollen, purpling jaw. Prinking diddle-boy.

Barnet inserted the key and jangled it in the lock, turning it. Wilmot sat up straight. He folded his arms, sulking, as Barnet pushed the door open.

"You there. On your feet," Barnet ordered, all affability vanished.

Wilmot glared at him.

"Now," Barnet said, soft as soft.

Wilmot shuffled to his feet. "I don't want any of your evil slop, so you can…"

In a single step Barnet was before him, hoicking him to his feet. He took hold of his jaw in one large hand. "Don't," he threatened.

Wilmot looked into the face of the man with the pale lashless eyes, opened his mouth, then shut it. There was something, some quality in those eyes, which silenced him. A prickling of sweat, cold and stinging, broke out beneath his armpits, in his groin.

Barnet pulled a length of cord from his pocket and wrapped it round Wilmot's wrists, binding them together, then knotted it. "Come on," he said, pulling on the long end he'd left as lead.

Barnet dropped the keys on Vickery's table as they passed him. Vickery acknowledged them with a nod, but barely looked up.

Outside, Barnet had the black coach waiting. Wilmot tried to fluster, but found himself shoved into the vehicle and onto a seat. The far side shade was pulled down over the window. Barnet favoured Wilmot with a single look. "Don't," was all he said again.

He needed to say no more.

Wilmot sniffed. He smelled of night soil and vomit. And suddenly, inexplicably afraid, he retreated into a corner of the coach. "Who are you? Where are you taking me?" he demanded.

Barnet looked him over. Wilmot clamped shut his petulant mouth.

Barnet turned away to ignore Wilmot, regarding with an equal lack of interest the noising traffic, the bustle of the city, the shouting of drivers and tradesmen, as they drove down through Covent Garden and through the narrowing streets of the riverfront to a stretch of empty shore.

As soon as the carriage halted, Barnet opened the door and stepped down, tugging on the cord so that it bit into Wilmot's wrists. Wilmot golloped out of the coach, slipping in the slime underfoot. "I am a baronet," he began, struggling to his feet, his arrogant tone at odds with his filth.

"Shut it," Barnet ground out. "You speak when I say so. Do you understand?"

Wilmot looked up upon Barnet, upon the breadth of his shoulders and chest, his great arms, thick as hams in a butcher's shop, the cold patience of his pale eyes. His parody of courage deserted him. He nodded fearfully.

Barnet jerked upon the cord and they began to walk, the wind buffeting Wilmot so that he shivered in his evening clothes as he trudged behind. Upon the river, vessels of every description, scows and barges, rowing-boats, wherries and cockleshells were travelling in every direction it seemed, their multi-coloured sails caught in the freshening winds.

Barnet stopped and looked out upon the waterway, then up and down the shore where the cold, bubbling water lapped at the sandy mud which was peopled with mudlarks and shoremen, fishermen and eelhauler, and the ranks of boatmen, ready to row anyone across to Surrey for a few pennies. He looked up at the clearing sky, the odd snippet of blue showing amidst the billows of churning, scudding grey. "Wind's from the west. There'll be rain tomorrow…" he remarked. "Tell me about George Waley?"

"George?" Wilmot exclaimed, his eyes widening. "George? What do you want to know about Waley?" he temporised.

Barnet was not diverted. Ahead, pacing through the mud, a clutch of godwits were feeding, spearing the ground with their long, narrow beaks, wheezing and squeaking amongst themselves. "How often did he go to France and who did he see there?"

"George went to France? Really?" Wilmot exclaimed.

Barnet took the cord in his other hand and reached up and squeezed Wilmot's jaw until his eyes watered. "Don't," he repeated, his mouth hardening into a frown.

Wilmot began to shake. He swallowed. "He was going over long before I met up with him. He had friends there. That's all I know."

"What friends?"

Wilmot shook his head quickly. "I don't know. I never met them. I know that in Paris he used to frequent the Palais-Royal. He always liked a bit of an orgy, George did…and he always managed to find his way to one there…But…"

"But?"

"I never knew more than that," Wilmot said in a rush. He tripped in the mud that sucked at his evening pumps. Out over the river a curlew cried, the haunting sound carried on the wind.

"He's dead," Barnet said, biting off the words, enjoying the shock they caused.

"What?" Wilmot cried. He glanced up and saw there was neither pity nor regret in Barnet's full moon of a face.

"So was it he who gave you the list of London agents?"

"What?" Wilmot cried again, but the word was drowned out by the racket of the herring gulls. He shook his head in disbelief. His whole world had caved in three days since. At least he thought it had. But this, he realised, scrambling for coherent thought, was worse. Despite the cold wind, sweat broke out on his forehead. "Yes, yes! That was Waley's doing!"

"And John Brown? Was he Waley's doing as well?"

Still, he resisted. "I don't know what you're talking about." Wilmot glanced down, then up, his breath shortening. "I give you my word, I never heard of any such person."

"Oh, I think you have," Barnet disagreed softly. "In fact, I know you have, because he's been living in your house. Just off the kitchen. Though your cook don't like him much, does he now?" Barnet's pale eyes glowed with triumph.

Wilmot swallowed, and opened his mouth wide to protest. "I never heard of such a fellow."

And his tone unchanged, Barnet said, "When do you want me to start slicing off your ballocks, Wilmot? Just tell me now. I like to do the job inch by inch. But the other fellows, they prefer 'em whole so they can hang 'em as trophies."

Wilmot paled. His mouth went dry. He stared at Barnet. There was a stillness about his interrogator's face, a quiet detachment. A dark stain spread over the front and thigh of his soiled silk breeches.

"It was arranged in Paris," Wilmot spluttered. "I needed the money." He began to cry. "And George said if I'd keep that Brown person, I'd be paid. They'd already got him captured and sent up to Edinburgh Castle. All I had to do was sent a parcel up there when George said. My address was written into the book for him. And then, when he was here, I just gave him the names on this list they'd sent me…He was horrible. Always smelled. Rude. But I needed the money…" he repeated, as if that were justification. To him, it was.

Barnet looked hard at him, disliking him more than ever, more even than John Brown. "You needed the money," he repeated. A look of patient disbelief crossed his face, at odds with his rosy cheeks. "And the abigail?" he said softly. "What happened to her?"

"What?" Wilmot croaked. Then tried to recover. "What abigail?" he replied.

"Your wife's abigail. Fat ugly creature," Barnet enunciated. "With a temper like a scalded cat."

"She was a disappointment to me," Wilmot explained, quite reasonably as he thought. His nose was dripping, running into his mouth.

"So you had her killed." It was a statement and no question.

"No! Yes. I needed the money," Wilmot restated passionately, now angry. "And she hadn't done what she'd been hired for, had she? She was meant to kill the bitch."

"Was she now?" Barnet said, turning to face him. They had walked down a length and then back, and were nearly returned to the carriage. His pale eyes glinting, he laid a weighty hand on Wilmot's shoulder and throat—half a strangling hand. "Now that…I can't abide," he murmured.

Wilmot began to shrug, his mouth slack with insolence. "Well, I don…"

There was a snap. Wilmot's mouth stopped, half open. His eyes stilled. He went limp.

Barnet caught him as he buckled forward. "There now…"

"What the devil are you doing?" Jesuadon came running, had launched himself out of the shadow of the black coach, and was running toward them.

Barnet looked up and patiently shook his head. "How was I to know his bones was made of paper?" He widened his eyes with innocent surprise.

Jesuadon stared. Then glanced quickly about. No one appeared to have noticed the sudden death in their midst. "For God's sake, get him in the coach, Barnet," he said, struggling with his rage. "Now!"

Easily, Barnet slipped his arms about Wilmot's sagging body—as if he were drunk—and hauled him the few steps to the coach and bundled him inside. He climbed in beside him, followed by Jesuadon.

"What in the blazes were you doing?" Jesuadon rapped on the roof to drive on. "Have you gone mad? Wilmot was our only link, our only chance to close this business with the Frenchies for once and for all. What am I meant to tell Castlereagh? What?" He gripped his head in his hand. "When he asks me, what am I meant to say, you rollicking pillock?" he yelled.

Barnet eyed the crumpled body of Wilmot and exhaled a deep breath. He looked at Jesuadon and shrugged. "Would have been bad luck if you'd done it, wouldn't it? Marrying her after you'd snabbled him. Wouldn't have been right." He folded his arms across his chest comfortably.

"What?" Jesuadon nearly screeched.

"Reckon you should get one of those funny licenses, though," Barnet continued conversationally. "Because you won't want to sort out the business of what happened to Wilmot until after the squeaker's born. If you ever do, that is…"

"What?" Jesuadon repeated. He shook his head. He tried to catch his breath. Looking up, he suddenly caught the momentary kindly expression in Barnet's lashless eyes, and quieted. He placed a hand on his forehead, Wilmot entirely forgot. "I can't," he insisted. "I can't. She can't want me. She can't…Christ, you know what I am."

Barnet waited. He drew a flask from his pocket, and took a long drink, then handed it to Jesuadon. "It don't matter what you think you are, Thos," he said patiently. "It's you she wants. There's a squeaker, and you're the father. It's you she wants."

Jesuadon was silent. Then: "Tell me at least where the list came from. Tell me the leak wasn't here."

"He said it came from Paris, that he'd been sent it."

Jesuadon caught his breath, calmed, somewhat mollified. He rubbed his face. At last: "That's all right then. It'll be up to Bayard to track it at that end."

Barnet nodded toward the carriage door. "Now go. I'll see to this one." He eyed the glassy-eyed corpse slumped in the corner, as unattractive a cur in death as he had been in life. "Now get on with you…"

Chapter XLIV

1

Boy had not spoken since that first night. It had been three days too since she had first waked.

And during that time as she drifted from sleep into waking and back to sleep again, as her side healed and More tipped as much broth as he could into her, Dunphail found his days reordering themselves so that he might be there with her in the lingering quiet of that place, that world contracted to within those four walls. To watch over her. For heaven knew she needed someone to.

It was nearly February. He stood at the window where the curtains were open to admit the rarely seen sun, looking out onto a street awash in light where a pair of jarveys were arguing over a fare and there were ladies, bundled up against the wind, out to enjoy what they could of the fine weather before it lapsed back into another week of cold rain, where the sweep on the corner, as ever lounging over his broom, kept watch. There were sparrows too, hopping and pecking amongst the dust.

She lay against the pillows, fed, washed, her bandages changed, her hand as ever on Comfit's head, regarding him outlined against the diffuse morning light. Summoning her courage, her memory. "What happened…" she whispered, tentative. The words felt odd in her mouth, her tongue clumsy.

Barely hearing, Dunphail turned.

Tears bit at her eyelids. She looked up at him, desperate for his care. "John Brown?" she murmured. It was a soft, breathy sound. "Did they…"

Dunphail crossed to her and sat down. "Dead," he said, nodding. He looked down at the floor while his face creased with indecision. "I bungled it." He said it without equivocation.

She gave him a quizzical look.

"I shot him," he said, admitting the whole.

She swallowed and expelled a quick breath. His answer was not what she'd expected. "He should thank you for it," she said softly.

Dunphail darted her a doubtful glance. "Oh? Why's that?"

She swallowed again. "They…" She paused, garnering more of her courage, the formation of words still an oddity. "They would have tortured him," she explained. "…Until he told them everything."

"Who would have tortured him?" Dunphail asked, almost forgetting in his sudden curiosity that she was speaking. And perhaps how much he had missed her.

"Georgie," she said. "Or Barnet…or both." A sadness had crept into her solemn gaze. "Where did you hit him?"

Dunphail puffed out his cheeks. "In the throat."

Her eyes, pale still, glowed with admiration—a difficult shot, the throat—and her shoulders shook slightly, as if she almost laughed. "Nice shot."

"No," Dunphail disagreed. "I was aiming for his heart."

She gave a sudden short laugh—a hollow, painful sound, more an eruption of air, than amusement.

Dunphail regarded her with approval. "You're talking again," he observed and his familiar smile appeared. "That's excellent." And as he sometimes now did when he sat beside her, he took her hand. He looked down upon it, pondering. He hesitated a long moment, weighing in his mind what he should say, if he should speak and what might be her reaction.

"What is your name?" he said at last.

She turned her head away from him. It had had to come. She knew that. A tear slid down into her hair, followed by a second and then a third, all silent, all unannounced, without weeping or sobs, unacknowledged. She did not look at him. "Anne-Elouisa," she said finally. "Anne-Elouisa Tirrell."

Dunphail sat, holding her hand, cradling it in his own, but did not reach to brush away her tears.

"...My father called me Lulie." Then adding, as if it were of equal matter, "The Maestro calls me Schätzlein."

Patiently, Dunphail waited, piecing together what little he knew with what she had just told and not told him. "Is it true, what Castlereagh told me?" he ventured.

She sighed. And her answer was long in coming. "That I watched?" She nodded. "Yes. I was twelve when he died. It was just after war had been declared again. We had been there, in France, performing." She was silent for a moment, remembering, thinking back on that which she always avoided. She shook her head as if to send off an unhappy ghost. "But of course, he was spying too, though I did not know it." She turned to look at Dunphail. "What year is it now?"

"1813."

She nodded. "So many years. I didn't know," she admitted, though it sounded foolish, even to her. "Not really. I stopped counting. They were all the same."

Dunphail sat, still, contemplating all that she had just revealed. Her name, her age, her life story in so few words. She was nothing of what those others thought her.

His eyes narrowed suddenly with the remembered pleasure. "I saw you perform, you know," he said, smiling. "With your father. He gave lessons to my cousin, Hardy, for a time. And Ned insisted that I accompany him to a concert. It must have been—oh—twelve years ago now."

"I don't remember," she admitted.

"I shouldn't expect you to. But I remember you. You were very charming. And your father...It was hearing you play that convinced Ned that while he might play the violin well, he would never be more than adequate on the fortepiano."

She grimaced. "That doesn't sound very charming..."

"No." Dunphail shook his head. "But Ned was quite sanguine about it as I recall." He paused. "May I use your name?"

Her tears had returned. "I don't know…"

And so he called her nothing at all. Nor did he need to, for there was none but her in the large bedchamber with him. Or More, come to fuss each day, to hector her into eating, to tell her as he removed the stitches and she did not cry out that she'd healed as well as Dunphail's prize stallion and he'd be pleased to stitch her any day.

And each day then she grew better and stronger. And all with Dunphail, who condensed his estate business and solitary rides in the park to those few hours each afternoon when still she slept. Day upon day, of learning her life through the odd remark ("What did you do when there was no food?…Went hungry…"), playing piquet late into the night, sleeping on the bed More had made up for him in the dressing room. And every day, he became more certain that they could not continue on as they were but was unwilling to change, deferring the discussion until another day—another day, when she was better.

"I have been thinking," Dunphail began and narrowed his eyes, focusing on the cards in his hand. She was already three hands up in the Partie and like to win the whole. "I should very much like to hear you play…"

She held her cards against the ruffles of her nightshirt. "I didn't come out very well the last time that happened," she observed mildly.

Dunphail smiled, a wry twist to his lips. "Though you think to spare my feelings and to deny me the opportunity to revisit my mortification, which in the main I must appreciate, what you mean is I basted you soundly." He reordered the cards in his hand. "I could, should you prefer it, remain on the other side of the door. Or even locked in another room…But I should still like to hear you play…er, without threat of violence this time, of course."

"Of course." Her expression was deceptively meek.

"And I am convinced that Ned would wish it most heartily."

She appeared to consider it as she studied the cards in her hand once more. Then laid down her discard. She was set to beat him again.

Dunphail eyed her discard and smiled. "I have also been thinking that you are nearly well enough to travel. So…" He could not anticipate her reaction, but still, he was determined to suggest it. "What do you say we go home, up to Scotland. Perhaps in a day or so…and when you are truly recovered and fit, I shall teach you to shoot?"

"I don't own a rifle," she said casually. "…I've nearly finished *Joseph Andrews*."

His expression was prim. "Have you now? And who provided you with that smut, eh? You should be reading sermons…"

She gave a whisper of a laugh. "You did, sir."

Dunphail offered her a severe frown. "So I did. Ah, me. So what do you say? Shall we go?"

"I'm tired." She looked up at him. "Can we stop now?"

Dunphail glanced at the mantel clock, ticking away. It was gone one. He laid down the cards on the board which rested on her lap. "You won't have beaten me. For once. But yes, of course." He lifted the tray away and she watched him as he carried it to its stand.

"Don't make me sleep alone."

He heard the apprehension in her voice and came to sit beside her on the bed, holding her there within the safety of his arm. And only when her eyes were closed and her breath came deep and steady, only then, as he had so often these past weeks, did he sleep himself.

In the morning, she was gone.

2

Lord Castlereagh sat at his desk, a dozen or more letters spread before him. One letter he still held in his hand. This from Paris. Confirmation of all that the boy had told him. The few dregs of the Grande Armée had finally dragged themselves home—crawled really, poor beggars. It seemed there were fewer than forty thousand remaining, and none of them fit for service. The Army of Italy was utterly destroyed. The Bavarians all lost too. On paper Napoleon had claimed to have six hundred thousand troops last June, and this was all that was left—not forty thousand men. And about five hundred horses. Truly it was unthinkable. Unpardonable.

The Russians meanwhile were in fighting spirit, with Alexander determined to negotiate a new pact with Prussia—the beginning of a new Coalition against Bonaparte. To be sure, they would need money. And muskets. And Russia would need wool for uniforms. Never mind that Austria was nearly bankrupt, that could be averted…And then there was Metternich to be dealt with.

Still…it was just possible, just possible, that this time, they'd have the Corsican devil for good.

Resting his chin in his hand, Lord Castlereagh scanned the letters displayed before him, once again, and permitted himself a satisfied smile, a private surge of excitement. He must get Myddelton in…

He heard the commotion in the outer office and looked up.

Dunphail, looking like fury, threw open the door. Planta, rushing to bar the way, was a stride too late.

Dunphail stood, framed within the doorcase. "Where's my lass? Where is she?" His Englishness had all but deserted him.

Castlereagh laid down his letter. "Planta, my dear fellow, were you not in want of some nuncheon? It is all right. Lord Dunphail and I shall do very well together."

Planta cast a wary eye at his employer, then with a slight bow, turned, collected his hat and coat and left the office.

Dunphail remained standing, his cheeks flushed with anger, his eyes blazing. "Where is she?"

Lord Castlereagh rose from behind his desk. He shook his head. "Who can say?" he said mildly. "Vienna, Paris…she might be on her way to any number of places. Berlin…I did not send her, if that is what you're asking. And even if I had, I am very much afraid she does exactly as she chooses. That, in any event, has been my experience."

He wandered over to stand within the reveal of the window, looking out upon the street, imagining for a moment her running in all those places he had never been, running in those countries he did not know, places he only knew through what she had told him.

"Berlin?" Dunphail echoed. He stopped, bereft, and closed his eyes to reassemble his thoughts. "She once said she would bring me back…"

"What?"

Dunphail shook his head dismissively. It was a bagatelle, it would mean nothing to Castlereagh. And it had been a joke between them, a moment of intimacy he did not wish exposed. "A toy—nothing really."

"A toy?" Castlereagh asked, intrigued by the unlikeliness of it.

"Yes," Dunphail said. "Yes." He paused, feeling a momentary embarrassment. This was after all the Foreign Secretary to whom he was speaking. "Bonaparte in flagrante with the Empress," he explained at last. "She said she had seen better in Berlin and would bring me one back...if I liked."

Lord Castlereagh turned from the window to regard the younger man with a new interest, a light kindling in his dark eyes. She had told him everything in those few words. "Then you may depend upon it, my lord. She will return. She will come back."